The Space Between
"Filled with vivid images, mystery, and a strong sense of danger . . . Sokoloff interlaces psychological elements, quantum physics, and the idea of multiple dimensions and parallel universes into her story; this definitely adds something different and original from other teen novels on the market today."
—*Seattle Post Intelligencer*

"Alexandra Sokoloff has created an intricate tapestry, a dark Young Adult novel with threads of horror and science fiction that make it a true original. Loaded with graphic, vivid images that place the reader in the midst of the mystery and danger, *The Space Between* takes psychological elements, quantum physics and multiple dimensions with parallel universes and creates a storyline that has no equal. A must-read."
—*Suspense Magazine*

T0072255

cold moon

Books By Alexandra Sokoloff

The Huntress/FBI Thrillers
Huntress Moon: Book I
Blood Moon: Book II
Cold Moon: Book III

The Haunted Thrillers
The Harrowing
The Price
The Unseen
Book of Shadows
The Space Between

Paranormal
D-Girl on Doomsday (from *Apocalypse: Year Zero*)
The Shifters (from *The Keepers* trilogy)
Keeper of the Shadows (from *The Keepers: L.A.*)

Nonfiction
Screenwriting Tricks for Authors
Writing Love: Screenwriting Tricks for Authors II

Short Fiction
The Edge of Seventeen (in *Rage Against the Night*)
In Atlantis (in *Love is Murder*)

cold moon

Book III of the Huntress/FBI Thrillers

by
alexandra sokoloff

• • • • •

THOMAS & MERCER

Published by Thomas & Mercer, Seattle

www.apub.com

Amazon, the Amazon logo, and Thomas & Mercer are trademarks of Amazon.com, Inc., or its affiliates.

ISBN-13: 9781477821626
ISBN-10: 1477821627

Cover design by inkd

Printed in the United States of America

This book is dedicated to Children of the Night, MISSEY, and all the organizations that are tirelessly working to stop the trafficking of women and children and helping the exploited to new lives.

"Until we are all free, we are none of us free." —Emma Lazarus

Prologue

The moon is high, spilling icy light through the pine branches.

Roarke is in the forest again, in the clearing outside the dark house. His breathing is labored . . . his heart pounding out of control. And the night is alive . . . with a presence other than his own.

He reaches into his jacket for the Glock—but his shoulder holster is empty.

He stares into the night and scans what there is of the yard: dead rosebushes in a rock garden, the wooden trash enclosure, the empty spaces beneath trees, the swing set off to the side of the house . . .

One of the swings is swaying.

The wind? Or did someone touch it? Someone . . .

"FBI!" he shouts into the night. "Drop your weapon and come out with your hands on top of your head!"

The darkness swallows his words.

He hears a *whuuff* . . . the deep snuffle of a horse . . . but he knows with a sudden gut-twisting certainty that it is not a horse that has made the sound. He spins toward the trees. An eerie, high-pitched giggling comes from the bushes. He shouts toward the sound, "Come out *now* or I'll shoot."

He eases sideways, looking for a better vantage point between tree trunks, but the snaking mist and the dead underbrush obscure his view. He tenses at a rustle . . . stares through the dark . . .

There is a sudden, animal-like snuffling, then a scrabbling that is nothing like human. He twists toward it, sees flying hair, wild eyes rolling back like a horse's in the night, and a shadow. Bigger than he is. Bigger than a man.

Not a man. A monster.

Talons slash across his chest. Pain explodes in his rib cage, and he is falling, hitting the ground.

The beast is on him, a dead, stinking, intolerable weight. The horse smell surrounds him as his own blood gushes from the deep scratch of claws; he feels it, hot and thick and pumping from his chest. He chokes through blood, the copper stink of it in his nostrils and throat. Above him, jagged teeth in crocodile jaws yawn open—

There is a thunderous boom . . .

And the monster disappears. The weight disappears. There is no blood, no pain, only Roarke's own gasping breath.

And now he sees her, standing over him, a lithe shadow against the light of the moon.

Cara.

She moves forward, and the light glints off her pale gold hair, and her eyes are locked on his as she raises the gun—

Roarke sat straight up in the dark, knowing he had shouted aloud. Panic surged through his veins. For a moment he saw trees looming above him in the icy moonlight . . .

Then he focused and recognized his own bedroom around him, the night lights of the San Francisco skyline outside the triple windows.

He lay back and inhaled slowly as the adrenaline buzzed through his body. His heart was pounding out of control.

Dream. Just a dream. The Reaper is dead.

There were pills on his nightstand, an unopened bottle that the Bureau shrink had prescribed him. For post-traumatic stress disorder.

Instead of reaching for it, he reached for her in his head.

Fair as the moon and cold as ice.

Cara.

He held her until he slept.

• • • • •

The walls breathe.

She lies listening to the thick concrete slabs around her inhaling and exhaling, a rasping breath. From the cells on either side of hers come the muffled cries of others *It* has swallowed. The stench of blood and offal. The belly of the Beast.

And outside in the maze of halls, there is the shrieking scratch of talons on metal bars, coming closer . . .

Trapped. Trapped . . .

Her eyes fly open. Her breath comes quick and hard in her chest as she orients herself. Lying flat. Thin jailhouse mattress beneath her. Stained concrete walls around her. And a presence . . .

Her eyes scan the space, searching the dark.

Through the metal bars, she sees the glow of rabid eyes. Jagged teeth in jaws dripping with foam. A man. A beast. *It.*

Watching her. Waiting.

She is trapped in this cage with the monster, and they both know it. *It* will toy with her until she is spent, and then *It* will sink *Its* teeth in. She stares back through the dark and knows that she will use her nails, her jaws, every muscle in her body, whatever it takes to fight. Or she will use her teeth on her own wrists, die in blood, before she will let *It* take her.

Its lips curl back from *Its* teeth, a feral promise . . . and the guard turns away from her cell.

For now.

DAY ONE

DAY ONE

Chapter 1

"It all comes down to one," said Singh.

The team sat in the conference room of the San Francisco Bureau, four of them at the long mahogany table. Special Agent Damien Epps: tall, fierce, and black as midnight; Special Agent Antara Singh: luminously calm and strikingly exotic, with her gold wristbands and shimmering fall of hair; Special Agent Ryan Jones: young, blond, buff, and as laid-back as a surfer. And Assistant Special Agent in Charge Matthew Roarke. Their leader. Though more and more lately, he doubted he'd continue in that role much longer. Or in his job, for that matter.

Roarke said nothing in response to Singh's pronouncement. But Epps looked like he had plenty to say.

"*One*? One fucking case?" He was a study in outrage, and you really didn't want to have Special Agent Damien Epps pissed.

Singh looked back at Epps calmly. "In terms of legally actionable evidence, yes. There is only one case among these that can be prosecuted."

All of the agents looked automatically toward the whiteboards surrounding the conference table: three eight-foot-long panels filled with dates, crime scene photos, news articles, and photos of dead men. A detailed chronology of mass murder.

Thirteen men slain that the team had documented. Many more that they knew were out there. A years-long rampage by the woman pictured in the center of the middle board: blond and slim, with fine features and high, carved cheekbones. As beautiful and feral as an animal. And far more deadly.

Cara Lindstrom.

The timeline was a concrete representation of a vortex of a case. A case Roarke knew he was far too personally involved with to approach with anything near rationality. And he knew that it would all come down on him soon enough.

"No way that's right," Epps said. "*One?*"

Roarke cut in before the other agent could continue. "Take us through it," he told Singh.

Singh rose from her chair with the elegance of a dancer and stepped to the first board. "The cold cases: Edwin Wann, in Salt Lake City. John 'Preacherman' Milvia in Portland."

They were the first of Cara Lindstrom's murders that Roarke had discovered. Wann, a Salt Lake City construction engineer who had mysteriously fallen to his death from the twentieth floor of his own unfinished building, and Preacherman, a homegrown Portland anarchist whose throat had been cut while he was sleeping off a drunk in a culvert.

Local law enforcement agencies had been stumped by the deaths. It was Roarke who'd made the connection to Cara Lindstrom, who'd discovered that Wann was the molester of his own fourteen-year-old daughter, that days before his murder, Preacherman had been planning the bombing of a downtown street fair.

Roarke hadn't expected any charges to come out of the cold cases. He'd discovered only the most slender thread of connection between Cara and the deaths.

"That was never going to happen," he said aloud. "There's no evidence in those cases." Other than the slightest possibility that a mentally ill, homeless person could identify Cara as being in the same city on the day Preacherman died. It was vapor. It was only in his own soul that Roarke was certain.

Epps looked to the second whiteboard. "The trucker in Atascadero," he said. "Hartley."

"They cannot prosecute that case," Singh said, and Roarke was surprised to hear an edge under her characteristic serenity.

Epps countered. "She slashed the man's throat—"

"He came after her in the women's bathroom of a rest stop," Singh said without raising her voice, but Roarke thought he saw a flash in the dark depths of her eyes. She did not add what the team knew. Hartley had had a record for aggravated sexual assault.

Epps took a breath, visibly containing himself, not an unremarkable thing in a man who stood six feet three. "I'm talkin' 'bout evidence. There was print evidence on that Honda she stole that got picked up in Pismo Beach. We got her on tape stealing the fu—" He stopped. "Stealing the thing. It proves she was there."

"It proves she was in contact with the car," Singh said with murderous calm. "And not even conclusively. Also, there is no evidence to connect Hartley to the car. Unless you are suggesting that we prosecute Lindstrom for auto theft."

"What about Greer?" Jones asked, deflecting the standoff between the other two agents. *Probably unconsciously*, Roarke thought. Jones didn't have Singh's depth perception.

None of the rest of the team even bothered to answer. The death of Special Agent Greer was a complete nonstarter as far as evidence was concerned, though Roarke had witnessed the agent's demise himself. His own undercover man had been killed in front of his eyes, on a business-district street, mowed down by a commercial truck while Cara stood on the sidewalk behind him.

She'd spoken to Greer before he stepped out into the street but had not touched him. No one could possibly prove his death was a murder.

And it was only because of Greer's death that Roarke had learned the agent had been sexually assaulting women held hostage by the trafficking ring he was supposed to be gathering evidence against. Another bad guy felled by Cara Lindstrom's fury.

"And the killings at the concrete plant . . ." Singh moved to the third whiteboard but paused to glance at Roarke. "Also problematic." The largest number of Cara's victims they knew of had been killed all in one night, a little over a month ago at a concrete batch plant in the Southern California desert. A total of seven human traffickers dead: five by Cara's hands and two by Roarke himself. Another situation too fraught with complications to prosecute, given Roarke's involvement, the number of trafficking victims who had been killed by their captors, and Cara's rescue of an eleven-year-old girl from imminent rape.

"But the Reaper . . ." Epps said. And even as he said it, his voice trailed off.

"Never," Singh said flatly.

"No," Roarke said, and for a moment he was back in the moonlit forest, lying in a bed of pine needles and snow. Blood on his face, on his clothes, the copper stink of it in his nostrils and mouth . . . and the gaunt shadow of the Reaper looming over him.

A man. Not a monster. Just a man.

He wrenched himself out of the memory.

Prosecuting Cara for that particular murder was impossible. Completely impossible, though Cara had cut Nathaniel Hughes' throat and Roarke was a material witness to the killing.

But the whiteboards around them told only part of the story.

Cara herself was a legendary victim of a horrific and borderline mythic crime. Twenty-five years had passed since a psychotic killer known only as the Reaper had slaughtered three California families, then disappeared without a trace. Five-year-old Cara Lindstrom had survived the massacre of her family with her throat slashed and her mental state shattered into a million pieces. The case had gripped everyone in the state, including nine-year-old Matt Roarke, and had started him on his lifelong quest for justice through a law enforcement career.

Then just two months ago, either randomly or by some strange confluence of fate, Roarke's own path had collided with the adult Cara Lindstrom's.

He had hunted her. And then the Reaper had resurfaced.

Two more families slaughtered, a third targeted. A total of twenty-five people dead, fifteen of them children.

Roarke looked up at the photo of the man who still attacked him every night in his dreams . . . until Cara killed him yet again.

She'd saved Roarke's life—and he'd ended hers. Maybe not literally . . . but he had serious doubts she would survive captivity.

The thought was a black hole of dread, and he had to press his hands flat against the table to stop the sudden tremor.

Singh glanced at Roarke as if to assess his state of mind before she continued. "Special Agent Snyder is in Montana on an active case, but we have been compiling a family and criminal history on Nathaniel Marcus Hughes, aka the Reaper. We will continue after Agent Snyder's return. But that will not help us with the prosecution of Cara Lindstrom. Rather more the opposite."

No. No district attorney in his right mind would try Cara for the Reaper's death.

The team sat with this.

Epps finally spoke. "So it's all down to San Francisco."

"One case," Singh agreed. "It is the Ramirez killing or nothing." She looked back to the middle whiteboard, where the image of a wolf-ish man with a rock-star flair stared insolently out of a mug shot. Danny Ramirez. A pimp who'd been running a stable of six underage girls . . . until Cara had slashed his throat in a tunnel in Golden Gate Park, just a few miles away. As far as Roarke was concerned, Ramirez was the lowest form of humanity. Cara had freed three of his teenage victims from the street life when she cut him down. But no matter how deserving Ramirez had been of his fate, it was an out-and-out vigilante killing, and the courts did not look kindly on the practice.

Jones was the first to say it. "Which means it's all down to Jade."

Singh clicked her mouse and a mug shot came up on the conference screen.

Far-too-mature eyes smudged with kohl stared boldly out of the photo. The flesh exposed by her sequined halter top was smooth and rounded with baby fat and covered with intricate body art. Her hair was a wild mass of blond curls.

Their entire case against Cara Lindstrom rested on the word of a sixteen-year-old girl.

Chapter 2

Singh aligned a stack of color-coded folders in front of her and began her summation. "Cara Lindstrom is being held at County Women's #8 on the charge of the first-degree murder of Daniel Alfonso Ramirez two weeks ago. Assistant District Attorney Stanton is handling the prosecution. The key evidence in this case is the eyewitness testimony of 'Jade Lauren,' real name unknown, age approximately sixteen years, real age unknown, who claims to have seen Lindstrom cut Ramirez's throat inside the tunnel on the night in question. Lindstrom's attorney of record is Julia Molina. Molina has invoked the ten-day rule; thus the preliminary hearing has been set for three days from today."

Epps and Jones shifted in their seats in surprise. Roarke took in the news with shock and unease. California law required a preliminary hearing for a judge to review the prosecution's evidence and decide whether the evidence was sufficient to warrant a trial. The hearings were generally brief, lasting as little as a few hours or even less; they usually involved the presentation of just the prosecution's evidence and the defense's examination of the prosecution's witnesses. Since Jade was the key witness, she would need to testify. The team knew all that already.

However, also under California law, preliminary hearings were required to be held within ten court days of a defendant's "not guilty" plea, unless the defendant waived that right. Singh was saying that Cara and her lawyer had not waived and had instead demanded an immediate hearing. It was an unexpected turn of events, given that more time typically helped the defendant. Although it was quite possible that Cara had pressed for the hearing. Roarke wasn't entirely sure how she'd survived jail for a week.

Epps spoke up. "Can we ask for a court-ordered detention? To make sure Jade doesn't do a runner?" The tension was clear in his voice, and Roarke understood where his agent was coming from. Jade Lauren was a prostitute. Or, to use the FBI's new consciousness-raised and more accurate term, a "commercially sexually exploited youth." Roarke didn't want to speculate on the horrors the girl had experienced, but those experiences had turned her into a loose cannon: clever, narcissistic, a meth addict—and sixteen years old. The height of instability.

Singh turned to Epps to answer. "She has been living at the Belvedere House under Rachel Elliott's care, with no such restraint. In the two weeks she has been at the House she has not disappeared. There is no basis on which to convince a judge that detention is necessary. Also, Rachel Elliott is serving as her court-appointed special advocate, and I believe that Elliott would fight such a detention very convincingly." Singh gave Roarke an oblique glance, and he felt a twinge of unease. She couldn't know about his ill-considered one-night stand with Rachel. Unless his agent had somehow picked up on his ongoing discomfort at any mention of the social worker. Of course Singh was more than perceptive enough to have done just that. The thought that she might actually have sussed him out caused him a fresh wave of guilt.

He forced himself into professional mode. "I think if anyone can keep Jade in town, Elliott can. The girl is bonded with her."

"The girl is also a stone liar," Epps pointed out. "We can't trust her as far as I could throw a church."

Epps had seen Jade only through the two-way mirror of an interrogation room, but it didn't take a road map. She was a piece of work.

"No, we can't," Roarke admitted. "I'll call Mills. We'll head over there this morning to prep her for the prelim." *And check on her state of mind*, he thought. "All we can do is keep tabs on her . . . and hope."

As Roarke walked down the corridor, he was so deep in thought that he almost ran into Epps, who was waiting for him in front of the elevator. The two men looked at each other for a long, tense moment.

Two months ago, Roarke would have said he had never worked so well with another human being—with the possible exception of Snyder, who was on such a different plane that he didn't really count.

And then came Cara.

The relationship between the agents had deteriorated since Cara, because of Cara. Epps' disapproval had been instant and militant. Not without reason, Roarke had to admit.

Epps finally spoke. "You aren't thinking of doing anything insane, are you?"

Roarke turned to face him straight on. "Insane like what?"

Epps looked at him impassively. "Now, there's the trouble. It could be just about anything." And they both knew what he meant. Roarke wasn't sure how detailed Epps' fears were, but he was willing to bet they extended to Roarke's somehow breaking Cara Lindstrom out of County #8. Which was entirely insane. And impossible.

He answered equally impassively. "I wasn't thinking of anything too insane, no. Not at the moment."

"A'ight then. Good to know." Epps gave him a last, hard look before he turned to walk down the hall.

Roarke stood in the ringing silence and wondered how many more lies he would tell today. Until the elevator door pinged, releasing him.

Chapter 3

Inside the detention facility known as County #8, the prisoners are walked down the dingy halls past the cells, two guards monitoring the single line of women in loose khaki uniforms. There is a listlessness, a defeatedness to their movements, a vacant quality to their eyes.

Cara moves with them in the center of the line and breathes slowly to calm her panic. She has not been confined since she was fourteen years old. It is worse than she remembered.

Every instinct in her wants to fight the vacuum of her surroundings, but she is too aware of how she stands out already. So she takes on the aura of the hopeless women around her, makes her body go slack and shuffling, lets her face assume a mask of blank uncaring.

She knows the rules. It has been sixteen years but it never leaves you. *Don't look at the guards unless they tell you to look at them. When they walk you in the hall, stay in line and keep your eyes straight in front of you and don't speak to anyone. Go where you're told to go. Stand where you're told to stand. Stop where you're told to stop.*

And never, ever be alone where a guard can find you.

The line moves through the doorway of the "common room" of the jail: an open space between two tiers of cells, smelling of ammonia and sweat. It is sparse: a few table-and-chair sets, a few rows of bright-blue chairs below a high-mounted TV, everything bolted down, and all supervised by a corrections officer behind a raised desk accessible only through a gate. The CO is a woman today, which makes Cara relax slightly. Seventy percent of the guards are men. Foxes guarding the henhouse. Like the one with the feral eyes and slathering jaws, the one who watches her with *Its* eyes. The one outside her cell last night.

He will not wait for long. She will have to be ready.

She breathes in and looks around the room, memorizing the details. There is a hierarchy to this place, to the chairs and tables, and she is new: low woman on the totem pole. So she waits until the alphas are seated and chooses one of the remaining chairs, farthest away from the drone of the television hanging in a frame in the corner, which is her own preference anyway.

She slumps in her chair as if half-asleep and looks without seeming to look. She remains still, as she has been since her arrival. Very watchful, very still. She is listening for signs. Even in this place, the night talks to her. She can hear it under the sounds of crying and screaming, under the chaos of nightmares of the women who share this cage.

There are two dozen of them in this "recreational" shift, and every one of them is profoundly damaged, each in her own way. She can see the deep scratches that *It* has left on them, the long histories of abuse, homelessness, prostitution, addiction. They are sick, broken, marked by a presence she knows only too well. Driven insane by years of looking into the depths of a beast that hides behind the masks of ordinary faces: fathers, brothers, uncles, husbands, random men on the street . . . and the mothers and grandmothers who turned a blind eye to the abuse.

She can feel their pain radiating from them like heat. And there is one flare hotter than the others.

Her gaze stops on a frail, hunched woman at one of the tables. This one does not look at the TV or at the other women. Her face is blank and she rocks back and forth, loosely hugging herself.

This is the one who screams in the night, Cara is certain. Few of the others have the same raw anguish. The scars are deep in this woman, both psychic and real; Cara can see the streaks of dried blood on the woman's khakis. She cuts, this creature, slicing herself probably with her own ragged nails, to distract herself from some immense pain.

Looking at her, Cara feels herself slipping back to that long-ago room in the group home, the night that resulted in her sentence, at twelve years old, to a maximum-security facility where girls, much less girls of twelve, are rarely sent.

She had nearly killed the boy, it was true, but it was the group home counselor who was responsible for the Youth Authority sentence, the harshest penalty for a juvenile offender. The counselor had insisted. Payback for her fighting him, for his humiliation at being bested by the twelve-year-old girl he had intended to rape.

In her mind she is there again, that night in the tiny locked room, the metallic scratching on the door announcing *Its* presence, the four-legged, four-armed creature slipping stealthily in, in the form of the counselor and the fifteen-year-old bully he has brought with him, for company or for camouflage or maybe for both.

She has that few moments' advantage because she knows *Its* sound, *Its* smell: the hoarse and grating breath, the stink of sweat and malevolence. She knows what has come for her because she has been in a room with *It* before. She is only twelve now, but she is bigger and stronger and deadlier than she was at five. And she has something else. This time she is angry. This thing, this excrescence, has stolen her family, has left her alone and scorned and shunned. This time she will fight, and fight to kill.

It is caught unawares, and she is a spitfire, punching and scratching and kicking. It happens in moments: the boy's nose broken, his eye bleeding, the man's testicles crushed. And as the boy howls and the counselor lies moaning and clutching himself on the floor, she breathes through the fire in her chest and picks up the man's foot in both hands and holds the leg straight and brings her foot as hard as she can down on his knee to snap the joint—

She is pulled from the past by the feeling of eyes on her in the present.

She scans the room to find the gaze.

An inmate seated under the television is watching her with a laser stare. A large woman—not physically large, though she has the doughiness of long confinement. But large in aura, in anger, in sheer domineering energy.

Cara has noticed her before, as someone to be respected and avoided at all cost. But she has drawn attention regardless.

The woman's eyes are fixed on her from across the room and she can feel the other's anger building. Senseless anger, nothing to do with her. But unmistakable, and dangerous.

The woman rises suddenly and walks the concrete floor toward her. A walk meant to be casual so as not to alert the guard behind the desk to trouble. But trouble is what it is.

The inmate sits heavily across from Cara. She is bulldog muscular under the layer of fat, her hair spiky in a butch cut. Cara knows the other women call her Kaz. She gives Cara a blistering glare, which no doubt has reduced any number of other prisoners to tears. Cara looks back at her without nodding, without posturing. Just looking.

"So, Blondie." The woman's drawl makes the word an insult. "What's your story?"

She doesn't answer right away. When she does, it is in the most neutral tone she can muster. "It's all the same story, isn't it?"

She can feel the anger sparking off the other woman. "You being smart with me?"

"No," Cara says, and nothing more. Kaz waits. Cara waits with her.

"You in for murder, or izzat some story you think is gonna keep you safe from all the scary people in here?" She makes a "boo" gesture, a mock lunge.

Cara doesn't flinch. "I didn't do it," she says evenly. Not just the standard answer to the question, but the only rational thing to say in a world where snitching is often the only ticket out of hell.

"Riiight," Kaz says.

"I'm not looking for trouble."

"It just somehow found *you*," the other woman sneers. She does not know how accurate she has just been.

"I'm not looking for trouble with you," Cara answers.

The large woman gives her a cold smile. "That ain't your call, Blondie." She pushes back from the table and rises. "I'll be seeing ya." She turns to stroll back to the row of chairs from where she came. All the other women watch, without seeming to watch. And Cara knows this is not the end of the encounter, but only the start.

Chapter 4

Roarke signed out a fleet car from the underground lot in the Civic Center and drove the mile through the downtown corridor of Hyde Street to 850 Bryant, the Hall of Justice, known to the lawyers and law enforcement professionals who frequented it as "the Hall of Whispers." It was attached to San Francisco County Jail #8 where Cara was being held.

He felt his body tighten as he glimpsed the curve of concrete ahead, knowing she was just behind that wall. But he drove past and made the turn at the corner and slowed beside the curb in front of the wide granite steps of the courthouse.

San Francisco Police Homicide Inspector Clifton Mills slouched against a stone urn by the side of the tall wooden doors, chewing on a toothpick as he scrolled through his phone. He looked every bit as disreputable as any of the other shady characters loitering on the steps, and not just because of his hangdog, silent-comedian face. His pants were threadbare khakis, his shirt a garish vintage Hawaiian, and in deference to the season he'd wrapped a red velour reindeer scarf around his neck.

He looked up before Roarke could honk the car horn and ambled down the steps past a collection of San Francisco's criminal flotsam, his large feet slapping the granite in open-toed Birkenstocks despite the winter fog. He pulled open the passenger-side door, and the car rocked as he dropped his comfortable bulk onto the seat.

"Always a treat to see your pretty face," he greeted Roarke.

"Wish I could say the same about yours," Roarke responded, and pulled out into holiday traffic.

Mills waved his phone at Roarke, his rubbery features as morose as a bulldog's. "Another email from Stanton," meaning the ADA who was prosecuting Cara's case. "He wants to see Jade again before the hearing."

Roarke tensed. "Is he coming today?"

"Hell, no. Not letting him near her. Pompous little prick."

"No argument there," Roarke agreed.

"You believe this clusterfuck?" Mills muttered, and lowered the window to spit out of it. "The DA assigns Stanton, for Christ's cunting sake. They couldn'ta used Bryce? Delgado? Hell, *anyone* in a skirt?"

Roarke knew what Mills meant. Strategically it would have made worlds more sense to assign a woman ADA to Cara's case, both to deal with Jade and in terms of the delicate gender dynamics of the situation. Cara was a female crime victim who killed male criminals. A female prosecutor would have an implicit right to condemn her in a way that a male prosecutor would not. But it was a huge case, and the San Francisco DA's office was as political as any, and Stanton was the district attorney's golden boy. He was also so abrasive that his assignment tipped the case very slightly in Cara's favor.

Roarke turned his mind away from the thought. "So what's the game plan here?" he asked Mills.

"This girl *is* our case. Lock, stock, and smoking barrel. I want the little bitch to like us," Mills said. Roarke rolled his eyes and waited for the real response. Mills shook his head. "We need to get her to tell us who she is. We need a *name*."

Jade had refused to say where she was from, how old she was, or anything else about herself. *Like Cara, in her way,* Roarke had to reflect. While many parents these days had their children fingerprinted so they could be ID'd in case of emergency, Jade's prints were not in the system. And running photos of her highly unusual tattoos through the Bureau's Next Generation Identification system had resulted in zero matches: she'd never been arrested before.

He'd known all that but hadn't considered the legal implications.

"Is that a crime?" he asked aloud. "Not to give a real name?"

"It is, actually. Supremes said so in 2004. Obviously we're not going to arrest her for it, being that she's our own fucking witness. But if she refuses to answer these questions in court? Judge'll cite her for contempt. Not helpful for our side. And y'know Lindstrom has engaged Julia Molina."

In fact, Roarke had not been able to stop thinking about it. Molina was a feminist lawyer who specialized in controversial cases. She was nowhere near as famous as Gloria Allred, though several attorneys of that caliber had also approached Cara, wanting to take on her case. Privately Roarke worried that Molina didn't have the clout to do what Cara needed her to do. But that was another thought he wasn't supposed to be having. He focused back on Mills' gloomy summation.

"We can't introduce any of Lindstrom's past murders because she hasn't been convicted for a damn thing. She has no motive for killing Ramirez or for being in that tunnel to begin with. Her story is that she *wasn't* there. Which would be my story if I was there. So it's her word against Jade's."

Roarke felt a fluttering of what he knew was traitorous hope. He looked out the window, impassive, as he made a turn past the Panhandle strip of Golden Gate Park, with its towering eucalyptus trees. Mills rattled on.

"Oh yeah, Molina is going to be all out to destroy Jade, credibility-wise. Key witness is a drug addict and a pathological liar. Molina can prove the kid is a user. She was drug-tested the night we brought her in to juvie."

Roarke kept his voice even. "Are you thinking it could be dismissed in prelim?"

Mills looked grim. "My guess is it's going to take Molina all of two seconds to establish reasonable doubt. The deceased had a violent criminal history. The area in which he met his demise was well trafficked by other violent criminals. The deceased had no money or drugs on him, for probably the first time in his miserable shitbag life, suggesting robbery as a motive. The area was poorly lit—make that not fucking lit at all: Jade claims she saw Lindstrom by the flame of a lighter. And let's not forget that Jade admits to being there, her prints were on the lipstick case we found at the scene, and she had more motive to kill the asswipe than Lindstrom does."

Roarke tightened his hands on the steering wheel, feeling lightheaded. For a moment, he could almost believe that Cara might go free. He felt it as a rush of blood in his head at Mills' next words.

"Put it this way: if I had to bet today, I wouldn't be betting on us. So work your wonder, Wonder Boy. We need a name."

The Belvedere House was located in the heart of the Haight, San Francisco's legendary hippie mecca. Roarke drove the fleet car past Victorians painted in rainbow colors, bottom floors largely taken up by cafés and grunge boutiques. The shop windows they passed were lavishly decorated for Christmas. Many of the displays showed more than a touch of a black humor: steampunk-dressed mannequins trimming a tree with grotesqueries, a skeleton in a Santa costume driving a team of skeletal reindeer. That was the Haight: flaunting convention, finding beauty in the outcast, the outré, the unacceptable.

Beside Roarke, Mills tunelessly hummed "Chestnuts Roasting on an Open Fire" as he looked out the passenger window at the street.

As usual, a clutch of ragged, homeless teenagers hung out, seated cross-legged, on the sidewalk below the stopped clock on the corner of Haight and Ashbury. There were similar groups congregated up and down the street. And as always, Roarke cringed inside at the number of obvious minors. Throwaway kids, following some hopeful dream of a more colorful, more liberated, even slightly magical lifestyle . . . and finding instead drugs, despair, and the most vile abuse by sexual predators.

It was here that Cara had encountered Jade and apparently had taken enough interest in the girl to stalk and kill her pimp. She had also interrupted a john soliciting a prostitute even younger than Jade and had beaten the john nearly to death in an alley just a block away. It was what Cara did.

Roarke made the turn on Belvedere toward the shelter, an old Victorian painted a garish shade of purplish pink. It was a rare and vitally important haven, a nonprofit halfway house providing shelter and services for the Bay Area's rapidly growing population of exploited teenagers. Trafficking was a vast and virulent problem, far exceeding the capacity of law enforcement to control. Nonprofit organizations like the Belvedere House were left scrambling to take up the slack.

Roarke realized that Mills had spoken and was now looking at him, perplexed.

"Sorry, what?" Roarke asked blankly.

"At least the media's been distracted by the election. The Lindstrom story is out there, but they haven't sunk their teeth into the particulars yet."

They will, though. Roarke could feel that storm coming.

He parked the fleet car illegally in front of the historic old Belvedere building and put his "Official FBI Business" placard on the dash. He found his palms were sweating as he and Mills mounted the steps of the shelter. He had not seen Rachel since they'd fallen into bed together one night two weeks ago, after a long, ambiguous interview with Jade in juvenile detention. Roarke had been moved by Rachel's fierce protectiveness of the troubled girl.

The hookup had been a disastrous misjudgment on his part. Not that judgment had been any part of the equation.

Now, at the same time that his stomach was roiling, he could feel his groin muscles tightening, and he had to turn his mind toward business. He forced himself to look at Mills. One glance at the scruffy detective was enough to put a damper on any illicit thoughts.

The porch was gated and the lawmen were buzzed in after announcing themselves into a speaker on the wall. The rope of Nepalese bells on the doorknob jingled as the door closed behind them.

In the front hall, crystal light catchers strung in tall bay windows cast rainbows on the walls. A lounge to the left was filled with battered and overstuffed furniture, some mismatched tables and chairs, a massive old television. A set of stairs in the hall led up, and another set led down. Roarke could hear the chatter of young, feminine voices on the lower floor and the ever-present thump of street music. There was a sweet, clean scent to the air—a faint layering of perfumes and bath and hair products.

He glanced at the wall of photos hung in the hall: teenage girls captured in snapshots, printed-out candids from camera phones. Not just dozens but hundreds, rows of them, a photo gallery of lost girls that Rachel was doing her best to save every day.

Just as Cara was, in her own merciless way.

Roarke led the way down the hall toward Rachel's office and pushed through the door into a round room with built-in bookcases and a worn love seat. Behind a battered antique desk, Rachel waited for them.

He didn't know her well enough to know her age; he thought mid-thirties, about what he was. Her hair was a natural red-brown and curly, past her shoulders; her body was slim and curvy and toned. But it was her anger that had drawn him. She simmered with a crusading rage. The same rage that set Cara on fire.

He couldn't help but glance at the inner door behind her, cracked open to a small side room with a single bed. The bed that they'd shared just weeks before.

He saw from Rachel's face that she'd caught his glance toward the inner room. She didn't spare him by looking away. Her eyes locked with his for an electrifying moment, crackling with sexual tension.

Then she shifted her glance to Mills, taking in his outfit. "Mills, you're a fashion plate as always."

"Born this way," Mills answered, unflappable. "The kid still here?"

Rachel rolled her eyes. "I *would* actually let you know if that changed." She stood. "Let's do this."

"It's the light of my life." Jade greeted Mills sardonically as Rachel pushed open the door of the front lounge to let the men enter. The teenager slouched in one of the worn lounge chairs—a beautiful girl, with a wild blond mane and a blistering energy that rolled off her despite her posture of supreme uncaring. Roarke was surprised at how good she looked after just two weeks off the street. The meth sores had cleared up and her skin was back to the soft, glowing plumpness of her age.

Her gaze flickered over him as he stepped in behind Mills. "Whoa, you brought the Fed this time. You don't watch out, you're gonna make me feel important."

"It's your sunny disposition," Mills deadpanned. "Draws us like flies. Mind if we sit down?"

She waved a languid hand. "Any position you like."

Roarke flinched inside at the blatant sexuality of the reference, but he didn't show it. Rachel crossed the room to sit at the far corner of the table. Mills lowered his bulk to sit on the edge of the battered couch opposite Jade.

"So how you feeling, Danger Girl?" the detective asked.

"I'd be better with a smoke," she challenged him.

"Now, you know that shit's bad for you."

Jade widened her eyes disingenuously. "Right, and I'm a brand new me. Livin' in the pink cloud."

Roarke moved to the recessed window and leaned against the sill so he could study her. Rachel, the expert, put her age at sixteen. To Roarke's eyes she sometimes looked more like twenty-five. Other times she looked twelve. And any thoughts he had about a sane universe dissolved in the face of what this girl had been subjected to in her short life.

And yet, Jade had fought back, in her way. The girl lounging in the chair was not crushed, not broken. She was covered with body art, her own defiant statement. Her back was especially startling: an intricate design of trees dropping fiery blossoms, a girl dancing in flames.

A girl on fire.

"So what's shaking?" she challenged Mills.

"We just wanted to stop by, see how you're doing."

Jade gave them a knowing and infuriating smile. "Sweet. But we've been through this. I was meetin' up with Danny in the tunnel. When I get to the arch I can hear him talking with someone. He lights up and I see that crazy woman with him. He says, 'Want something, bitch?' and she grabs his hair and slices his neck open with a razor. And I haul ass out of there. Fast as my fuckin' feet can carry me."

Roarke had an uncomfortably clear picture of the scene. He'd stood in that stone tunnel, looking down at the pimp's body lying in its own blood. When he closed his eyes at night he could see how it had been, Cara and Jade in the cold darkness, their eyes locking above the corpse . . .

"See, I know what to say," Jade finished loftily.

Roarke and Mills exchanged a glance. The detective cleared his throat. "Well now, it's not about knowing what to say. We want you to tell the truth."

Jade rolled her eyes. "*Sure* you do. You can chill, I get it. She slashed the living shit out of Danny. Gone baby gone. Can't have someone like that running around loose, can we?"

Roarke was paying special attention to the words she used, her inflections. He had the strong sense of a California background: her breezy confidence, the hint of Valley in her vowels, the casual use of hippie expressions that were ancient history to a girl her age, and yet she dropped them naturally, as if she'd been hearing them all her life.

Jade narrowed her gaze as if she knew he was analyzing her, but she didn't look his way. She arched her back against the couch. "You charging her with other murders? Besides Danny?"

Roarke and Mills barely refrained from looking at each other.

"Do you know of any?" Mills asked her.

"That's *your* job, isn't it?" she retorted.

"Doesn't mean I can't use some help."

"Like all you can get," she agreed, and her eyes slid toward Roarke. "I heard there might be a whole lot more. Charges."

"Oh yeah?" Mills countered with exaggerated surprise. "Where'd you hear that?"

She widened her eyes. "I do read the papers."

"Newspapers, huh? I thought those had folded."

"L-O-L," she drawled. "You're a riot, Mills."

"You're very interested in Cara Lindstrom," Roarke said, speaking for the first time.

Jade finally turned her eyes on him, though he knew she had been quite aware of him since he'd walked into the room.

"Someone kills someone in front of you, it makes an impression." She watched him for a reaction. Roarke didn't give her one. "So *has* she killed other people?"

It was not a question they could answer, officially. Roarke settled for "That's under investigation."

"Were they all like Danny?"

Roarke paused. Now that was a question. "Like Danny," meaning pimps, abusers, bad to the bone? The fact was, they were. Some arguably worse.

She was still watching him closely, and he repeated, as neutrally as he could manage, "It's under investigation."

"How many?" she demanded. Both men looked at her. "How many people has she killed?"

Mills spread his hands. "She's in jail, held without bail. You don't have to worry about that."

"You mean *you* guys aren't worried about it?"

Roarke studied her. "What is it that's bothering you, Jade? You think Cara Lindstrom will come after you?"

Jade raised her eyebrows. "Shouldn't it bother me? I *saw* what she can do." Her eyes turned shrewd. "Unless you're sayin' she wouldn't do it to me."

"It's not an issue, Jade," Mills said with something approximating patience. "Lindstrom is in jail. If you're telling the truth, she'll stay there."

"Because the bad guys always stay in jail, right?" She glanced at Roarke again, her eyes mocking him. Roarke chose the truth.

"No, you're right, they don't. But you're in a safe place, with people who want to help you. As long as you let them."

"Let them help me," she repeated flatly. "Why wouldn't I do that?"

Roarke sensed some undercurrent in the question, but before he could figure it out, Mills was answering.

"So why not tell Rachel where you're from?"

Roarke saw a protective wall crash down in the girl's face, shuttering her expression. What came up a second later was exaggerated boredom.

"Get with the program, Mills." She lifted her hands. "The past is *over*. All there is, is the *now*."

Roarke knew they were losing her, and it didn't take a crystal ball to guess what she was escaping from in the past. Rachel had told him, "Runaway *is a literal word. They run* away." He began, "We're not going to send you back to—"

Her response was a flash of anger, cutting him off. "Fuckin' right you're not. Because you can't. Nothing to send me back to." She stood. "Sorry, guys, but three-ways always wear me out."

She strolled, loose-hipped, toward the door and turned in the doorway to deliver a last line. "Been real."

Roarke stepped to the door and glanced down the hall to make sure she was gone before he turned toward Mills. He was about to ask a question, but he realized Rachel was still in the room, seated at the table. She'd been so still he'd forgotten she was there.

She caught his look and stood. "I'll be in the office." She walked to the door and out.

Now Roarke faced Mills. "So is it like that every time?"

"Every time," Mills answered. "The kid's doing the interviewing."

"She wants something."

"Yep. Not sure what. Good news is she seems up for testifying."

Seems was the operative word in that sentence. At moments Roarke had gotten the feeling that Jade wanted to testify against Cara to avenge Danny's death. Other times he sensed a calculation underneath that willingness that concerned him. Maybe even a plan.

She was unfathomable, and that was worrisome.

Rachel closed the office door behind Mills and Roarke. Mills sat heavily in a chair. "There must be some fucking way we can get traction on where she's lived."

"Mills, I've told you. I've tried. I don't have a clue—"

Roarke felt the rise in Rachel's temperature and stepped in verbally. "Anything unusual about her, then?"

She looked toward him. "She is unusual, obviously. Lots of issues there, but she's smart."

Roarke thought on that, tried to work with it. "You hold classes here . . ."

"Tutoring. GED stuff."

"So Jade's taking those?"

Rachel half-smiled in spite of herself. "Sort of. She does schoolwork. Sometimes." Her gaze turned inward. "I think she's good at math."

Mills pounced on that. "You *think*? My hazy recollection of math is that you know it or you don't."

Rachel shook her head. "The teacher we have here does a multi-level math class. The other girls are at a very basic level. Jade makes a big show of being bored out of her mind, of course. Drawing instead of listening. But I watch from the door sometimes. One day I saw she was working in the back of the book, doing what looked like algebra equations. But when she saw I was watching she crumpled up the paper."

"Why would she do that?"

Rachel gave him a tired grimace. "Girls hide math skills more often than you think. Six million years of evolution, but brains still aren't sexy." She looked toward the window.

Roarke wanted to tell her that wasn't the problem between her and him. Not for him. But of course he couldn't. Not with Mills there. Not even if he hadn't been.

Rachel spoke again, looking out the window. "But I think it's a different thing with Jade. She's hiding *everything*. You're looking for indicators of where she's lived, and I think she's being just as careful to hide anything like that. Everything is an act."

"You've asked her about it, though?" Roarke asked.

"Of course, but I keep thinking I'll get more if I just keep watching."

He was sure she was right. "You think we could find where she's from by following up on this math thing?"

Rachel shrugged. "Well, put that together with what she looks like, there are teachers who might recognize a talented girl."

Mills arched a bushy brow and nodded, impressed. "How would we follow up on that?"

Rachel looked at him stonily. "Start calling schools, I guess."

"Thanks, Elliott, you're a real help."

"Anything for you, Mills."

Mills looked from her to Roarke. "No one has to tell me where I'm not wanted. I'll be in the car." He shuffled out the door, leaving Roarke and Rachel alone. The silence was instant and awkward.

This is why they have rules about getting involved with people you work with, he chided himself.

Although it was a strange kind of "working with." In ordinary circumstances this would be the way to do it: connect with someone with common interests, a shared mission, while on that shared mission. But none of the circumstances were ordinary. They had never been ordinary. Even now the specter of Cara hovered in the room between them.

Rachel finally broke the standoff. "It's not like I haven't been trying. She absolutely will not talk about that part of her life. She may even have blocked it mentally. But it's always the same story. The ones who aren't actually, physically abducted . . . they run away from abuse at home and run straight into it on the street."

"I know," Roarke said. "I know." There was a pimp saying that he'd learned from Rachel: *The best kids to have are the ones that have been had by their daddies.*"

But how Jade actually felt about her pimp, or ex-pimp, or dead pimp, was maddeningly unclear to him.

He knew that Ramirez had been a "Romeo," a variety of sex trafficker who romanced and groomed vulnerable girls, playing on their desperate need for love and acceptance. Rachel was right, outright abduction of children and teens was more and more common, ever since gangs had caught on to the fact that selling kids was more lucrative than selling drugs and carried lighter criminal penalties. But the gradual seduction of a child was a tried-and-true method. The pimp started out playing the boyfriend, buying the teenager clothes, jewelry, meals, making promises of a house or marriage, then coaxing the girl into having sex with a "friend" to prove her love . . .

"Does she talk about Ramirez?" he asked aloud. "Do you think she . . . had feelings for him?"

Rachel shook her head. "I don't have a clue what she feels. She's clearly better educated, and seems less naive, than most of the girls we get here. But she's still just a kid. And obviously not perfectly mentally stable. I'm pretty sure she's bipolar, for one thing."

Roarke nodded. That blazing charisma, the brazen confidence Jade exhibited was a typical sign of the disorder.

"And the pimps do such a number on these kids. They are fucking experts at breaking them down, mentally and physically. Sometimes I think my whole job is nothing but deprogramming."

She looked away from him now, at the window. "So . . . Jade is pretty much the key to this trial, right?"

He kept his tone even as he answered. "Yes."

"I've been reading about it." She half-laughed, without humor. "It's hard to miss." She glanced at him. "And *she* saved your life, didn't she?"

Roarke knew she meant Cara now. For a moment he was back in the forest, in freezing, pitch-black night, his head throbbing from a vicious blow, pine needles digging into his flesh, and the weight of a

Monster

madman on top of him . . .

He pulled himself out of the memory and answered with effort. "Yes. She saved my life."

Rachel looked toward the window. "What can anyone say to that?"

She was right, in her way. There was nothing Roarke could say.

Chapter 5

Roarke dropped Mills off at the steps in front of the Hall of Justice. As the detective reached to open the passenger door, he turned to look back at Roarke.

"How many kids do you figure in the California school system?"

Roarke took an educated guess. "Ten million. But only half of them are girls."

Mills grimaced. "Who says Feebs don't have a sense of humor? Piece a' cake, right?" He shut the car door and ambled up the steps.

Roarke watched him go.

The interview with Jade had left him unsettled. He had the distinct feeling the girl had something in mind, some plan.

Or paranoia's taken over entirely. Get a grip.

But once Mills had disappeared through the doors of the Hall, Roarke felt an entirely new agitation, disturbingly similar to the rush of an addict. He knew before he did it what he was going to do.

He drove down the street as if he were leaving. Instead he parked off the street a bit and furtively backtracked to the jail.

County Jail #8 was a pretrial holding facility on the sixth floor of the curved building next door to the Hall of Justice, a relatively new building with none of the Deco panache of the Hall. Roarke walked past a big black sculpture of tubes and platforms, vaguely mechanical, that twisted out of the grass beside the front entrance of the jail building.

Inside he signed in at the desk, turned over his weapon and cell phone, and went through security. As he had each time he'd visited, he had a moment of holding his breath, not entirely sure that he would be allowed in, that instead he would be caught, thrown out, disgraced.

But no alarms went off. The guards let him pass, returned his shoes. He turned away and rode the elevator up to the women's wing, feeling his own pulse elevating at the ascent.

There was no way he could justify seeing her. If he were caught— and it was only a matter of time before he was caught—he had only the ghost of an excuse to offer: that he thought he could get her to tell him what had happened to Special Agent Greer, and that the only way he could get her to do that was to see her alone.

Epps would never buy it. Epps would know. On some level he already knew. But the boss, Special Agent in Charge Reynolds, might buy it. Barely. Enough for Roarke to keep his job, if he still wanted it. He was no longer sure what he wanted, except that he must see her. His nightmares were constant and layered: that she would kill herself, that the confinement would kill her . . . or that her special way of seeing the world would put her in the middle of something irrevocable.

He became aware that the elevator had stopped; the doors were standing open. He stepped out into the garish fluorescence of the corridor, and walked down to check in with visiting. He signed the log and looked down at his name. Proof of his sins, there for anyone to find.

He turned away.

The visitation booth was a narrow cubicle with an equivalent cubicle on the other side of a metal-threaded Plexiglas partition. A small stool was set under a shelf on each side. Roarke faced the glass and for a second saw himself inside the booth, a glimpse of his reflection in the smooth surface: thick black hair, black eyes, tensely muscled frame.

As always, his heart began to race as he sat on the low seat in the claustrophobic room. He cleared his throat, put his hands on the shelf to steady them, and waited for the opposite door to open.

In his days as a profiler, he had spent many hours in booths like this one, interviewing some of the worst mass killers of a generation. Cara exceeded some of them in numbers of victims. But he knew too much about the psychology of serial killers to call her that.

Behavioral profiling was based on statistics. The statistics said it was rare for a woman to kill at all, let alone numbers of people, and the patterns and motives of female killers were completely different from the psychology of what profilers called "sexual homicide." Women killed for money, and they killed unwanted children. A few in medical professions killed out of some twisted sense of euthanasia or power.

But even Aileen Wuornos, the truck-stop prostitute so often cited as "America's only female serial killer," did not fit the pattern of homicidal sexual predators. Wuornos had shot and killed seven men in a very constricted time frame, just over a year, with none of the cooling-off period and slow build to the next kill that characterized serial killers. She had snapped, most likely from the trauma of a rape, and had gone on a killing spree. Most notably, there was a strong element of revenge to the murders, and no evidence whatsoever that she was getting sexual gratification from the kills. In Roarke's book she had been acting out rage built up over a lifetime of sexual abuse.

Cara was different, one of a kind: a ruthless, calculating female vigilante who had operated under the radar for over a decade.

Even Roarke's mentor, the legendary profiler Chuck Snyder, was fascinated by her, eager to learn the workings of her mind. Roarke knew that had Snyder not been consulting on an active case in Montana, he would be right here interviewing Cara himself, hoping to learn what drove her to kill in a way that no one had ever seen from a woman before.

But Roarke was far beyond pretending to himself that professional interest was what drove him to see her.

The door opened on the other side of the Plexiglas, and blood rushed to his face and other places that it had no business rushing as the corrections officer let her into the cubicle. She wore an olive uniform; her feet were shackled, her hands cuffed in front of her. But she moved with grace, with the complex musculature of a cat, as she lowered herself to balance on the stool. Roarke saw that underneath the prison jumpsuit she wore a cotton jersey back-to-front, so that the neckline hid the scar on her neck.

He had memorized her face: the curve of cheekbones, the watchful green eyes, the stillness. She still took his breath away, every single time.

He picked up the phone. The cord was too short, forcing him to lean forward toward the partition. On the other side, Cara picked up her phone and bent her head to the glass. It was always this way, bowing to each other, foreheads inches away . . . and the clear wall between them.

Time stopped as it always did, and they did not speak for a minute, minutes, he didn't know.

"Are you all right?" he asked finally.

She nodded.

"Would you tell me if you weren't?" he said.

She half-smiled at him and his heart leaped. But she didn't answer. After a moment he tried another tack.

"So Molina used the ten-day rule. Are you comfortable with that?"

Her eyes were veiled. "I wanted it."

"Why?" he asked, before he remembered that she couldn't answer, shouldn't answer. She said nothing.

"What about Molina? Are you okay with her?"

She tilted her head, lifted her shoulders. "She sees."

"She sees . . ."

For a moment he thought she wouldn't answer.

"The way things are."

"*It*, you mean." His voice was low. *It* was what he always wanted to talk about. He was not fooling himself: he came to see her. But the draw to understand how she saw the world was its own, separate vortex.

She looked at him, speculative green eyes under long dark lashes. His throat constricted.

"He's dead now, Cara." She had stood over them in the moonlight and slashed Nathaniel Hughes' throat. Roarke could still feel the weight of him, the gushing of his blood . . .

Not a monster. Just a man.

But on the other side of the glass, Cara's head jerked up.

"No."

"You killed him."

She stared directly into his eyes. "*It* doesn't die."

It.

She was unshakable.

For two and a half months that already felt like a lifetime, Roarke had chased her over three states, interviewing witnesses, picking up clues to a vast mystery—a mystery that in some part of him he believed might explain his life, his work, his purpose. She *knew*. She chose her victims with a precision that baffled him, and slew them without compunction.

He couldn't get it out of his head. He knew *why* she killed. Because anyone with a human feeling would want to kill the men she killed. Because the killing she did prevented the further agony of innocent victims. Because someone had to do it.

What he didn't know was *how* she knew.

This much he thought he understood: The night the killer known as the Reaper had slaughtered five-year-old Cara's entire family, had cut the child's throat and left her for dead, she had seen him not as a man but as a monster, like the rabid thing Roarke saw in his dreams. Snyder called it "magical thinking." It was the way most five-year-old children saw the world. But Cara still saw what she called *It*—as an adult. For her, it was no dream. It was how she recognized the criminal intent of the men she killed. Over the years she had been diagnosed as schizophrenic, delusional—suffering from post-traumatic stress disorder, borderline personality disorder, dissociative disorder, and various assorted psychoses. But whatever anyone called it, she seemed to be unerringly right.

"But how do you know?" He could hear the raw agitation in his voice. "What do you see, Cara? Tell me."

"You know," she said. "*You* see."

For a surreal second he thought she knew his dreams.

"I don't—" he started, then stopped, because it would be a lie. He hadn't seen in Greer, his own agent, what she had seen. But sometimes, it was true, bad intentions were not so difficult to spot. "Cops' eyes," they called it. The ability to walk into a bar, or along a crowded street, and pick out the bad actors.

"Not like you," he finished. She looked at him. The expression on her face was patience, and pity. Almost as if she knew he was lying.

"But why—" he started, then paused. He meant, *Why you? Why do you feel responsible? Why is it your job? Why do you need to be the one?*

Her eyes met his. "Why *you*?" she answered.

And as he stared at her, lost in her, the metal door behind her opened, and it was as if Cara slammed shut, her face instantly becoming a neutral mask. Roarke tensed in frustration at the interruption.

Behind her a corrections officer stepped in, different from the one who had delivered her, a white male in his forties, coarse-featured, with black hair in a comb-over. A new anger overtook Roarke as he saw the instant stiffening of Cara's body, the way she drew back, shrinking herself so she was physically as far from the CO as she could make herself.

Roarke felt his own body tensing protectively at the sight. He rapped on the Plexiglas. "Give us a minute, officer," he said, full-voiced.

The CO twisted toward him. Roarke already had his credentials wallet out and pressed against the Plexiglas. "A minute."

The CO gave him a hard stare, then stepped out through the door. Roarke could feel the fury trailing in his wake.

"Are you all right?" he asked Cara again. "Tell me." He looked at the door where the CO had just exited.

"Don't," she said. "Don't." And she turned to knock sharply on the door, summoning the guard.

Roarke strode through the halls, his stomach churning at what he had seen. He was too aware of the statistics: sexual abuse of women prisoners by male guards was endemic. Other countries prohibited the overseeing of female prisoners by male guards, but US laws put its incarcerated women in constant physical jeopardy in the name of equal opportunity employment. And of course Cara stood out from the crowd of her desperate sisters. She was beautiful, she was healthy, there were no meth sores, no broken teeth, her body was slim and elegant. She might as well have had a spotlight on her.

Roarke made an abrupt turn and walked back, heading toward the guard station. At the booth he slapped his credentials wallet up against the bulletproof glass.

The guards in the glass cube looked up at him. Roarke pointed at the coarse-faced one.

The guard's face turned stormy. He moved with deliberate slowness to the door and took his time opening the locks.

"Yeah?"

Roarke stared him down. "Just wanted to introduce myself. Assistant Special Agent in Charge Roarke, San Francisco Bureau." He glanced deliberately down at the nameplate pinned to the guard's chest. "And you're Officer Driscoll. We'll be seeing a lot of each other, so I want to make sure you know me. And know that I know you."

The CO steamed sullenly under his gaze. Roarke nodded.

"I'm glad we had this little chat. I'm glad to have someone I can come to if anything seems off. And I will certainly be coming straight to you if anything seems off."

"Sure, *Agent* Roarke," the guard replied flatly.

As Roarke turned away from the guard he was shaking with adrenaline. He strode down the corridor toward the elevator, trying to regulate his breathing, and realized he had no idea if he had just made things better, or worse.

He rounded the corner . . . and his body stiffened. Cara was straight ahead of him, led by another guard, and coming right toward him.

He forced himself to walk forward at a normal pace as the guard steered her in a straight line.

As they passed, Roarke held his arm at his side . . . and felt her fingers brush his hand.

When he stepped into the elevator, he was still hard.

Chapter 6

Instead of exiting through the jail, he used the connecting corridor to the lobby of 850 Bryant so he could emerge from the Hall of Justice, as if he had been to see Mills rather than visiting the jail. He was still shaky as he pushed through the heavy and heavily decorated Art Deco doors of the Hall. Outside was a chilly fog, and the courthouse steps were crowded with a throng of reporters, cameramen, standing lights. Not an unusual situation; lawyers angling for publicity often used the entrance of the Hall for their press conferences.

Roarke started for the steps. Then he stopped, looking downward at the crowd. The focus of the press conference was a tiny Latina woman with upswept black hair, wearing a tailored suit and killer shoes.

Julia Molina. Cara's lawyer.

He circled the big, round stone urn by the side of the door and eased toward the edge of the steps. He caught a sound bite as he slipped past the stacked rows of reporters. " . . . this outrageous railroading of a victim of a tragic crime . . ."

But he'd hesitated just long enough. The lawyer had spotted him. Her dark eyes took him in, a quick calculation, before she went back to her statement.

"The DA's office should be protecting our most vulnerable. Instead the office is shamelessly looking to score political points . . ."

Roarke hurried down the sidewalk toward his fleet car, parked at the end of the block. He was reaching for the door handle when the voice stopped him. Latin, feminine, implacable.

"Agent Roarke."

He turned to face Molina. She was small and dark and trim in a lush, plum-colored suit. Her face was Aztec royalty and her eyes glowed with fire. A slow-burning fire.

"You've been seeing my client," she said to him, not a question. Roarke wanted to laugh; the word *seeing* was so absurd in the circumstances. It seemed almost that Molina had sensed what was inside him, which he knew couldn't be the case. But whatever was on his face, it made her gaze narrow. "It's egregiously unprofessional and a possible violation of my client's civil rights."

Roarke didn't know about civil rights, but he still felt Cara's touch on his skin, and he knew that the lawyer didn't even begin to comprehend how unprofessional things were. He cleared his throat and spoke tonelessly. "She put me on her approved visitor list herself."

"Have you ever considered that she may not feel free to say no?"

Something flared in him and he looked her straight in the eyes. "Not for a minute."

Molina appraised him. She took her time, and Roarke felt the heat of her gaze as a physical sensation: uncomfortable, intrusive, and sensual.

"What do you want from Cara, Agent Roarke?"

The question seemed to silence the street noise; for one moment it was just the two of them on the foggy sidewalk. "I want to understand her," he heard himself saying. The truth, but not the whole truth.

Now Molina's voice was cold. "She's not available for study. Especially not to you. You can destroy her."

The last was a twist in his gut. He moved to protest even as he knew she was right. "You know that nothing she says to me in private is admissible. You can get any of it excluded. It's a nonstarter."

"So what are you doing?"

"She's a very unusual case." Before Molina could say anything, he continued. "None of her other *alleged* killings are admissible in this trial. But it's my job to understand what she's done."

She looked at him almost with amusement. "Your *job*, Agent Roarke? Are you sure this is about your job?"

He didn't respond, and she tipped back on her heels to look up at him. "Is there something you would like to say to me about this case?"

Roarke felt an abyss open in him. He knew he was crossing a line. And yet he jumped.

"I wondered about the plea," he said. They had submitted a plea of not guilty.

"Do you?"

"I wondered why it wasn't an insanity plea."

"Irrelevant," Molina said instantly. "She is not guilty."

"But . . . have you had her evaluated at all?"

"Agent Roarke," she snapped. "What part of 'not guilty' do you not understand? I'm aware of her history—"

He didn't wait for her to finish. "It's more than a history. She believes in some . . . supernatural force. A living evil. Get her to talk about it."

She cocked her head and regarded him. "I appreciate your . . . *input*," she said, pausing as if to underscore the bizarre nature of the conversation. "But it's not necessary. The prosecution has such a ludicrously inadequate case that her mental state will never be an issue."

Roarke admired her certainty. He couldn't imagine having that kind of faith in the workings of fate.

She seemed to sense his skepticism. She took an iPad from her purse, slid a finger across the screen, and handed it over so he could read it. "Have you seen this, Agent Roarke?"

On the screen was a blog article. Roarke found himself looking down on an image he knew very well: a skeleton garbed in a long, white lace dress and a flowered veil, holding a globe and a long-handled scythe.

Santa Muerte. Holy Death. Lady Death.

And below it was another image, the photo of a little Mexican girl. He felt his stomach drop as he started to read.

Lady of Shadows

Meet Marisol. The eleven-year-old with the shy smile and liquid eyes grew up in the poverty of the state of Michoacán in Mexico, the third child in a family of eight. Her father is a field worker. Her mother is a cook. But her parents make sure Marisol and her brothers and sisters go to school every weekday. They want their children to have a better life.

Two months ago Marisol was kidnapped from her village. She and twenty-one other women and children became part of a human shipment, imprisoned in a concrete mixer truck and driven across the border into the California desert. Marisol's destination: a life of virtual sexual slavery in what are euphemistically known as residential brothels.

The thirty-two-billion-dollar-a-year sex trafficking trade ensnares two and a half million such victims worldwide, ten thousand women and children in Mexico City alone. These victims are lured, coerced, or kidnapped, some of them confined in Mexico, some of them transported to the United States. The brothels are located in homes, apartment buildings, warehouses, storage facilities, and trailers, where women and children are locked up twenty-four hours a day and forced to service an average of twenty men per day, often more. They are drugged, beaten, and threatened with their own death and the deaths of everyone they love if they attempt escape.

This could have been Marisol's fate.

One woman and two children had already died in that midnight border crossing, before the mixing truck dropped off its shipment at a defunct concrete batch plant used by the traffickers as a holding pen and meth lab. There Marisol and the two dozen other abductees were imprisoned in a concrete bunker. And that night Marisol was taken from that bunker by one of her abductors.

Most of the girls and women brought across the border are raped by their traffickers before they ever get to their final destination. Along the US/Mexico border, "rape trees" are a common sight: trees and shrubs on which coyotes have forced female clients to hang their underwear on the branches after they have assaulted them.

But Marisol was not raped. She never had to endure the living hell of the brothel. Instead, Marisol was freed from her captors, and is home in her village with her grateful family.

Local police attribute her rescue to the intervention of Cara Lindstrom. Cara Lindstrom, who now sits in San Francisco County Jail #8 awaiting trial for murder, on no bail, despite the flimsiest of evidence against her.

Marisol will not be testifying against Cara Lindstrom.

Marisol is quite sure of the identity of her rescuer. "Santa Muerte," she insists, fingering a medallion around her neck. The image pressed into the metal is of an unconsecrated saint known as Lady Death.

The Catholic Church has strongly condemned the worship of this icon, but that has had no effect on Lady Death's two million followers in Mexico, the United States, and parts of Central America. Many of her most ardent devotees are among the poorest citizens and those on the fringe of society: prostitutes, homosexuals, and transgender people, victims of the extreme violence of drug cartels. Some followers call her "the Eighth Archangel," others, "the Santa Muerte of the Seven Powers," "the Lady of the Shadows," "the Bony One," "the Skinny One," or "the Virgin of the Incarcerated."

Her worship is largely clandestine, performed in the homes of her devotees. Shrines can be found in the backs of small stores and gas stations. Many botanicas in both Mexico and the US are kept afloat by sales of Santa Muerte items. Numerous shops report half or more of their profits are earned from Santa Muerte paraphernalia.

Perhaps because of stories like Marisol's.

"Recé," *Marisol says.* "Le pedí a la Santa y me salvó."

"I prayed. I prayed to the saint and I was saved."

"Es un milagro," *she finishes. "A miracle."*

Roarke finally looked up from the tablet. Molina was watching him. "Powerful piece, isn't it?" she said. "Powerful ideas. Over six hundred thousand hits since yesterday."

"Did you plant this?" he demanded.

Molina smiled thinly. "I didn't have to. The word is out."

"So you're trying to make Lindstrom into a folk heroine."

"I don't need to *try*, Agent Roarke. The facts in this case speak for themselves."

Roarke felt a quick anger, the age-old resentment of law enforcement toward defense attorneys . . . and another emotion: acute discomfort, at seeing his own ambivalence projected wide.

"And *I* don't need anyone to tell me about Marisol. I was there." He felt again his own horror, seeing the child with her ripped shirt under the moonlight, her half-naked attacker lying dead in the bloody sand beside her. "I killed two of them myself," he said, unable to stop himself. Of course Molina jumped on that.

"And the difference between you and Cara is what?"

"A badge," he said automatically, and knew that his credentials did not cover him for everything he had done that night.

Molina's eyes bored into his. It was all he could do to keep his gaze steady.

"I'll tell you again," she said softly. "Stay away from my client. I can make your life very difficult if you don't."

He had no doubt that she could. But that, to use her word, was irrelevant.

Chapter 7

The lawyer is angry.

The woman is smaller than Cara is, even on four-inch heels, but she takes up most of the space in the jail's consult room with her furious pacing.

The smoldering is palpable. Distracting enough that Cara has trouble concentrating on the lawyer's words.

"What the hell were you thinking? You think he's on your side? You are here *because* of him. The man's job is to put you in prison for life."

She understands that the lawyer believes she has some control over the outcome. The woman must believe that, in order to play her role. But unlike the lawyer, Cara knows there are other forces far beyond them at work.

She shakes her head, which nearly sends the lawyer through the ceiling.

"What? What is that supposed to mean? He *won't* take anything and everything you just said to him to the prosecution?"

"He won't," Cara says. She can still feel the heat of Roarke's skin on the tips of her fingers.

The lawyer circles the minimal floor space, her eyes narrowed and watchful. "How many times?"

For a moment Cara does not quite believe the question. By the time she realizes what the lawyer is actually asking, the look on the other woman's face tells her she has given more away than she herself had even known to be true.

"How many times has he visited?" the lawyer says softly, an unnecessary clarification now.

"Twice," she answers. It has been four, but she is not accustomed to telling the truth and the habit of concealment is strong. There have been other visitors as well. She says nothing of them.

"Interesting," Molina says, and Cara sees the lawyer is no longer angry, but calculating. "All interesting. Has he told you that he would like to see an insanity defense?"

The word is like a glacial shock. "No," she says. She means, *No insanity defense.*

Molina understands. "That is what I told him." She stops her slow circling and sits across from Cara, leaning forward for emphasis. "You are to tell me if he comes again. This is not optional. Do you understand me?"

"I do," Cara says evenly.

Molina stares into her eyes. She is one of the few people Cara has ever known who can do so without looking away. This time it is Cara who has trouble maintaining the gaze. Finally the older woman nods. She gets up and goes to the door, raps to summon a guard. Then she turns back.

"This is your life we are dealing for. I will not help you throw it away."

When Cara has been escorted back to her cell and the cell door has locked shut behind her, she sits on the stained, flat mattress of her bed and feels the rough walls around her closing in again, feels the ache in her chest constricting her heart.

Insanity.

A word she has been hearing all her life, since *the night.*

An apt enough word. Insanity is *Its* special talent.

Until two months ago, she had never spoken with a living soul about *the night,* not since that long-ago year of police interviews and psychiatric probes. She learned quickly, even at five years old, that no one who asked wanted to hear the real story. Roarke is different. He wants to know. In some ways he knows already, however much he tries to reason it away.

He sees her. He believes her. He is not far from her, himself.

She feels the moment of their touch, like fire on her skin. She closes her eyes and breathes . . .

Then her eyes fly open at the sound of footsteps in the hall. Two sets of steps: the hard-soled shoes of a CO and the soft slap of jailhouse sandals. The steps slow as they near her cell, and she can feel the intent is for her, so when the steps stop in front of the bars, she is waiting. She looks out at a female guard holding the arm of an inmate.

"Your new cellie," the CO says without irony as she unlocks the barred door.

And the woman called Kaz steps inside.

Chapter 8

Roarke's apartment was half a Victorian in the San Francisco neighborhood known as Noe Valley, often called "Stroller Valley" by the locals, in reference to the influx of trendy young families that had made the relatively sunny and walkable district their home.

Darkness came early in the December days, and after business hours, curbside parking spaces were few and far between. Roarke's own car was already parked in the narrow garage of his building, and he circled the block in the fleet car three times, peering through the drifting fog with no luck. Cara's touch still burned on his skin, and thoughts he didn't want to have were dangerously close to the surface. The cryptic conversation with her. The brush with the lawyer who would happily see him kicked out of the Bureau. And then there was the blog article. It bothered him in some way he was finding hard to pinpoint, something far beyond the media shitstorm it could bring down on the team. It was Marisol's words that haunted him.

"I prayed. I prayed to the saint and I was saved."

Somehow, through the turmoil in his mind, he noticed the dark Prius on his first time around the block, parked a few cars down from his flat. Someone sat in the dark car, a shadow in the driver's seat. The second time he cruised the block, the figure was still seated behind the wheel of the parked vehicle, and Roarke's antennae went up. On his third time past, he slowed to look directly inside the car.

The driver was gone.

He was able to squeeze the fleet car into a space at the end of a parallel block, and something made him open his suit coat and unsnap his shoulder holster as he walked the block and a half through the chilly damp back to his street. When he rounded the corner of his own block his eyes went immediately to the dark Prius farther down the street. He approached the car warily and looked down inside to be sure. The car was still empty.

He let out his breath, turned away, and headed for home.

No lights were on upstairs; no pets awaited him behind the door.

He stood alone in the long hallway and went through the lawman's nightly ritual: removing his suit coat, then his shoulder holster, hanging the coat and holster in the closet, and storing the Glock in the top drawer of an end table.

He loosened his tie as he walked down the hall and through the archway into the living room with its views of city lights, and he felt the emptiness surround him. His ex-wife, Monica, had left over three years ago, and he had done little to fill the spaces left by her absence. There had been women, but none he had ever brought home with him. Lately his choices were running to the destructive, self- and otherwise . . . and the outright impossible. Epps had told him recently, "Your picker is broken." He hadn't been joking.

Roarke crossed to the triple windows and looked out over the city, then down at the street, searching . . .

The Prius was gone.

The empty space at the curb gave him a chill of unease that he knew made no sense. The Reaper was dead. Cara was imprisoned. There was no one who would be out there in the night, watching.

No one human . . .

He stepped back from the window abruptly, almost violently.

Now we're getting crazy.

He walked the room in a circle, but the thoughts remained. It was Cara's voice he heard now.

"You see It.*"*

It.

The way Cara saw the world was so far off his own personal radar that he couldn't process it, much less accept it.

But the fact was, she was right. He had once had an experience beyond the normal cop "blue sense"—the intuition that keeps cops on alert, that sometimes keeps them alive. He had been in a hospital room with a dying man, one some would call an evil man . . . and something else had been there that Roarke couldn't explain, that had disturbed him on such a fundamental level he'd transferred out of profiling.

Whether *It* was a separate, independent force or just a word for the evil that human beings do, Roarke didn't know. He only knew that evil was real.

It was evil.

He hadn't been able to handle it . . . and Cara had made it her life's work.

In the darkness, he could see eleven-year-old Marisol's pale, tear-stained face.

"I prayed to the saint and I was saved."

And then he saw Cara's face, the look in her eyes as they touched. And he heard his own question:

"Why you?"

And her response.

"Why you?*"*

He stood, abruptly, pushing the thought from his mind, and walked to the kitchen in search of food, or a drink.

Chapter 9

The evening passes without a word from Kaz.

Dinner is served in their cell, gluey macaroni and cheese, some form of overcooked vegetable, an equally gluey lump of chocolate cake. They eat as if the other weren't there.

The game is intimidation. Cara is aware that every move she makes is being watched, but she has no interest in playing. The other woman wants something from her, and she will reveal it when she is ready, so Cara waits in a silence punctuated only by bouts of a hacking chest cough from her cellie—whether from long-time smoking of various substances or some illness, it is not entirely clear.

After the dinner trays have been removed, Kaz finally speaks.

"I been studying up on you, Blondie."

Cara turns toward Kaz. Her next words are a surprise, and then not.

"You killed all those guys?"

Cara looks the other woman full in the face, holding nothing back. "I never killed anyone," she says. Her tone puts the lie to the words.

"Damn . . ." Kaz says softly.

She says no more, but Cara knows that her presence in the cell is no accident. There is something building. It will not be long.

She will wait.

• • • • •

She is in a maze, running, with hot, rasping breath coming from the walls. At the end of a corridor a shadow slithers from the adjoining one, falling in a black and loathsome pool on the cement floor . . .

The screaming wrenches her from the dream, and she sits straight up in the dark.

On her bunk, Kaz is awake, too, eyes wide and glistening, her arms wrapped around her knees. The screaming is elsewhere, at the other end of the cellblock.

"Lin," the other woman says hoarsely.

Cara is very still, listening. Screams are a language, too.

After a moment, she breathes out. There is no one with the woman who is screaming. Not this time. It is only her past that torments her. Whatever has wounded her is still with her every hour of her life.

Cara turns to her cellie. "What happened?" she asks.

"Driscoll," Kaz says, her voice full of loathing. And something new. Fear.

Of course. The CO with the feral face, the one who watches her. Watches them all.

"Lin's not the only one," Kaz says flatly. "He shows up at your cell, says he's takin' you to Health Services. But you never get to Health Services, right?"

Cara's body clenches all over. She tries to breathe through her fury and dread.

"Lin tried to fight it. She filed a report on him. So he comes to her cell one night. With two friends. Now she doesn't talk."

No. She screams.

The two women look at each other across the cell. There is no more anger in Kaz's face. Only fear.

And Cara knows. *It* will come for her, too. The only question is when.

The two women lie back on their bunks, and the screaming starts again. In the sound, Cara sees savage jaws, blood spurting as the beast rips into flesh.

Roarke, she thinks. *Roarke.*

DAY TWO

DAY TWO

Chapter 10

Roarke woke with his chest tight, his heart pounding. And an overwhelming feeling of anxiety, of danger.

He reached for the bed stand to check his phone for the time. Five a.m.

He lay back on his pillow, staring at the ceiling and fighting the urge to call the jail, to make someone check up on Cara. Absurd. Impossible.

You can't do that. You can't do any of this.

What happens will happen.

Take a day off. Let the prosecution handle this case. Stay away.

Instead he threw back the covers and stood to dress.

It was early, too early, and only the emergency lights were on in the office. But when Roarke stepped into the agents' bull pen, with its long maze of desk cubicles, he could feel a presence. There was someone else in the office, somewhere. With the lights out.

What is this?

He stood for a moment in the doorway, listening for sound, motion, anything to give him a clue. But there were no ordinary office sounds. Someone was being very still.

He moved forward slowly, easing his way into the first aisle between two rows of cubicle walls, his ears straining ahead.

Suddenly a dark shadow stood from a cubicle in the center of the room.

Roarke felt a jolt of adrenaline . . . then recognized the slim figure, the long black hair.

Singh.

He relaxed. He should have known by the quietness that it was her. Unlike other agents, who were always in restless motion, she seemed to create a pool of calm around her.

But as he moved toward her in the dim light, he realized she was tense. Nervous.

Of course. She's an agent, but she's still a woman alone in a dark office building.

"I'm sorry—" he began.

"My fault," she interrupted. "I was absorbed."

He was at her enclosed desk space now, and as he glanced down at her computer he could see a blog page on her screen. The same article Molina had shown him the previous day. *Lady of Shadows.*

"This blog—" she started.

"I know. Molina showed it to me yesterday."

His agent breathed out, something like a sigh. "It has been picked up by the papers. It is garnering quite an online following. It seems our luck on relative media silence has run out."

That was inevitable, but Roarke felt himself tense up again, thinking about the firestorm that might well hit.

Singh contemplated the screen. "Molina is clever. I do not see this often: Americans invoking an archetype."

Roarke stared at her. He had no idea what she was talking about.

She frowned, as if seeking words. "A divine energy," she explained.

"A living myth." She looked at Roarke and seemed compelled to be more precise. "A force beyond the simply human. The article suggests that there is something larger at work in Cara's actions, something cosmic. A female vengeance against outrages. In today's fundamentalist climate it is an alluring idea."

Though Singh never talked about it, Roarke had always assumed she had some sort of spiritual practice. But this was the first time he could remember her speaking in those terms. He hadn't read the article that way. He'd been focused on the telling of a criminal incident he himself had been involved with. But standing in the dark room with Singh, he wondered if he might have missed the point entirely—because it was not meant for him.

Singh glanced down at her memo pad. "Journalists have been calling. They want an interview about Cara Lindstrom. Media is asking if we are going to do a press conference."

Without thinking, Roarke snapped, "Obviously not."

He instantly regretted his tone. Singh looked at him in that thoughtful way again. He cleared his throat. "Do you think we should?"

She glanced at the article on the screen. "To be honest, I am more concerned about the viral potential."

Again, Roarke wasn't following her. He knew she meant viral as in online, but it wasn't until she turned the monitor toward him and pointed to the top of the blog that he understood what she was saying.

He had totally missed it the first time. The byline was not a full name, just the single word *Bitch*.

Immediately his mind was racing with the implications. What it meant on the surface was that the blog author was choosing to remain anonymous but simultaneously aligning herself with a political movement that called itself Bitch, a cyberfaction in the style of Anonymous. He'd heard them called everything from a vigilante lynch mob to cyberterrorists to modern-day Robin Hoods. And he knew that his complicated case had just gotten far more complicated.

He sat on the edge of the desk opposite Singh's. "Maybe you'd better tell me what you know about Bitch."

Singh nodded and leaned back in her chair. "The Bureau's Cyber Crimes Division has been tracking the group since its recent inception, insofar as that can be done. As you know, these groups are not conventionally organized. They are more like Internet flash mobs, often with a political focus. There is no 'place' to join. Anonymous is the obvious example. Anyone who takes the name of the group is accepted as part of the group. There are factions within factions, infinite splinters. After Steubenville, existing groups splintered even more radically."

Roarke knew that by Steubenville she meant the very publicized Internet outing of several members of an Ohio high school football team after the rape of a drunk and unconscious teenage girl. Members of the team had tweeted and posted photos of the prolonged molestation, which had brought the outrage of a splinter group of Anonymous down on the perpetrators and the whole town.

Singh continued. "Some people in some factions thought that the emphasis on pursuing sex offenders was too moral. They derided the crusading element as 'moralfags.' Other members of the collective felt they wanted to focus much more on cyberactivism in the vein of the Steubenville outings. While that debate was raging, a completely separate group surfaced, focusing on unequivocally feminist issues: rape, domestic violence, sexual harassment, discrimination." She glanced again at the computer screen. "So Bitch has not been around long, but it seems to have found a cause célèbre in Cara Lindstrom. The Internet is burning up with posts and memes."

She pushed her hair out of her face with a slender hand and looked across at Roarke.

"I have no doubt that Molina will not hesitate to use this group in whatever ways she can devise. It may well get ugly for us."

Roarke knew she was right. They sat in silence for a moment. Then Singh spoke again.

"I am not surprised they are making Lindstrom into a political cause. It is really quite radical, what she is doing."

"It's not political," Roarke answered automatically, before he realized how much he was giving away.

Singh looked at him quizzically. "Every act is political."

He answered back without thinking. "And is every act divine?"

"Of course," Singh said, without the slightest irony. And as they sat in the dim light of the computer screen, Roarke realized he didn't really know his agent at all.

Alone in his office, he sat behind his desk and considered seeing Molina, to try to suss out where she was going with this involvement with Bitch. Then he thought of calling Mills, to see if the detective had made progress on tracking Jade's real identity through the school system.

He did neither.

Instead he walked out through the office, stopping to give Singh a story about going in search of breakfast. She nodded without blinking and declined his offer to bring something back for her. He had little illusion that he was fooling her. What scared him was how little he cared.

Downstairs in the garage, he collected his fleet car and drove to the Hall of Justice.

The lobby was salmon-pink marble, lit by three huge and vaguely ominous Art Deco globes and still bustling in the week before the holiday. Roarke quickly scanned the space for anyone he might know, then turned toward the crossover to County #8. Even just entering the connecting hall, he felt his heart start to beat faster, a guilty, exhilarating hammering. His anticipation was so great he almost ran into a young woman as she stepped out of the elevator: slim, black-haired, olive-complected, and very, very distraught. And familiar, though for a moment her emotional state was so overwhelming he couldn't place her.

He reached automatically for her arms to steady her, and she flinched away from him. "Sorry—" he began, and then it hit him. "Erin," he said, looking into her face.

Cara's cousin, Erin McNally.

When Roarke had been hunting Cara, he'd gone to interview Erin at her medical school in San Diego. That had been just weeks ago, but the young woman who stood trembling before him bore only the slightest resemblance to the cool and direct med student he remembered. She was gaunt, shivering, a wreck.

Drugs? he wondered. Whatever it was, it was something.

When she didn't answer, he repeated, "Erin." He saw a hint of clarity in her eyes at the sound of her name, and in that moment of focus he could see a flicker of recognition of him as well.

"I'm Special Agent Roarke. We talked last month . . ."

Too late he realized that she might not feel friendly toward the agent who was directly responsible for her cousin's arrest. He hadn't spent much time with Erin, but his impression had been that she was quite attached to Cara. As people who spent any significant time with her seemed to become. If they didn't end up dead.

In fact Erin's last words to him had been a request: *"If you find her, tell her I'd really like to see her."*

Apparently she was there to do just that.

Erin's eyes suddenly filled with tears, and she was too pale for Roarke's liking.

"Here." He took her arm and gently steered her toward one of the wood benches lining the wall. She collapsed onto it, pressing her hands against her temples as if she were trying to squeeze her brain out of her skull. He crouched in front of her. "I'm going to get you a Coke." She took a deep, shaky breath and nodded.

"Stay here," he ordered, and as she didn't seem in any hurry to move, he stood and strode toward an inner hall where he knew there were vending machines.

He found the soft drink machine and fidgeted beside the wall while a young mother bought drinks for her brood of five unruly youngsters.

His thoughts were racing. Erin was several years younger than Cara. Her mother, Cara's aunt Joan, had taken Cara in for a few short months after Cara's family was slaughtered by the Reaper. Erin had been only an infant then, and still just a baby when her mother gave Cara up to foster care, citing overwhelming behavioral problems. From their interview Roarke knew Erin had seen Cara sporadically throughout their childhoods, but not recently, not for years. The fact that she had come up to San Francisco from San Diego told him the news coverage of Cara's arrest was spreading; it also hinted at how deep the blood tie ran between the two young women.

Other than that, Roarke had no idea what Erin could be thinking. To find out that a relative was a killer was enough of a shock. Add to that the circumstances . . . *Unique* didn't begin to cover them.

The harried mother finally turned away from the drink machine and herded her soda-laden children out of the snack room, leaving Roarke to make his purchase.

But when he came back out into the lobby with the Coke, Erin was gone.

"Damn," he said softly.

The guard who brought Cara to the visiting booth was not Driscoll. But as she seated herself on the low stool, Roarke could see Cara was even edgier than Erin had been. She was so tense that he could almost feel her vibrate.

His heart was pounding. He wanted to put his hands through the glass, to shatter it, to pull her against him. Instead he picked up the phone on his side of the wall, waited for her to reach for hers, then spoke into the mouthpiece.

"I saw Erin. She was just in to see you?"

Cara didn't look at him.

"She doesn't look good," he said softly, and waited.

She shuddered, from pain or anger, maybe both.

"What is it? Tell me."

She rocked on the stool, twisting her hands in the manacles. Suddenly she pounded her clenched hands on the table. Then she was up on her feet, thrashing like a wild, trapped animal, slamming her arms against the glass. Red drops burst out on her skin, blood welling at her wrists from the chafing of the cuffs.

Roarke was on his feet, alarmed. "Cara. *Cara.* Don't—" She had dropped the phone. It swung uselessly on its metal cord. He dropped his own receiver and hammered his hands flat against the glass. "Look at me. Look at me."

Somehow his words got through. She stopped still, looked through the Plexiglas at him. He could see the pulse pounding at her neck as she panted, gasping breaths.

He pressed his hands into the glass. Cara sagged forward. She put her forearms, then her head, on the clear wall. He leaned in, too, touching his forehead to the cold surface. They stood pressed against the wall, arms to arms, brow to brow, and he thought he could feel her racing heart through the glass.

Without changing position, he reached for his dangling phone with one hand and brought it to his face. "Tell me," he said into the phone, hoping she could hear.

He could see her chest rise and fall as she fought with something inside herself. When she finally spoke, her voice was low and hoarse. He could barely hear her through the dropped phone.

"Help her."

He felt his heart contract with longing . . . and dread. She had asked him for help once before. By the end of that night he had killed two men.

He felt himself nodding. "Where do I find her?"

"Stanyan Park Hotel."

He felt a touch of surprise, and something more concerning. The Victorian inn was in Haight Ashbury, just a few blocks from Rachel's shelter on Belvedere—and it looked out on the park where Cara had killed Danny Ramirez.

"I'll go. I'll see her."

She dropped her arms and now stepped back, standing with her head down, her hair hiding her face.

"Is there something else?" he asked, his mouth against the phone. "You have to tell me."

She looked up then. "Erin," she said.

So he nodded.

She held his eyes with hers. Then she put a hand flat on the glass barrier. Roarke reached out and put his hand on the cool, transparent wall, against the slim, small shape of hers.

• • • • •

Back at the office, between dodging phone calls from reporters and surfing the Internet and Bureau files for information on the group called Bitch, Roarke reached at least five times for the phone to call Rachel. Each time he stopped himself from dialing. By the sixth time he knew he had to see her in person.

Epps and Jones were buried in the mountains of paperwork Cara's case had generated, and Roarke was able to escape the office without notice. He texted Singh he was following up with Rachel on schools that might recognize Jade. He even told himself it was logical to check, as it was their best avenue so far to find out who the girl really was.

Lies. All lies.

Once out on Market Street he peered through the windshield of the fleet car, staring through the twilight fog. He felt a disquiet about heading back to the Haight. San Francisco was a small city, but the coincidence of locale gave him a twinge that he couldn't put a name to.

Erin was young, still a student . . . it was a natural enough choice for her to stay in the Haight. It couldn't have anything to do with Rachel, or with Jade, or with Danny Ramirez . . .

Could it?

He shook his head and focused on the traffic.

It was dark by the time he'd crossed town. Fog shrouded Belvedere Street, rolling like slow, gray ocean waves off the steep, green hill of Buena Vista Park. He parked and pulled his coat closed around him as he climbed the steps of the House. He buzzed the intercom by the door. Rachel's wary voice answered.

"It's Roarke," he said, and waited, his stomach in knots. There was only silence on the other side.

He was debating buzzing again, or using the phone to try to explain himself, when he saw a light go on inside. The front door opened and Rachel stood in the shadowed hall. She did not move to open the outer gate, but looked out at him through the metal bars.

"Forget something?" she asked, her voice dry and unwelcoming.

"I need a favor," he said.

Her eyes widened slightly. "You really are incredible."

He knew he deserved that, but it didn't stop him. "It's a girl in trouble, Rachel. A young woman. She's—I don't know. In danger, in distress. She needs someone to talk to. Not for me. For her. Please."

She glanced behind her. "Now?"

"She's just a few blocks away. I can take you over."

After a long moment she said, "Half an hour. That's all you get." She didn't look at him as she opened the gate between them.

Inside the House, she pointed him down the hall to her office. "Stay there. Don't move."

As she climbed the stairs, something perverse in him rebelled. Instead of stepping into the office, he moved down the hall past the photos, the watching wall of teenage girls, to the front lounge.

The room was dark. He felt along the wall for the light switch. A low voice spoke out of the blackness. "Special Agent Roarke."

His skin jumped, and his hand was automatically on his weapon. Then his eyes adjusted and he could see Jade, sitting in the shadows beside the window.

He breathed in to calm his racing pulse. And for a moment he wondered what the girl could be thinking about, sitting alone in the night. Her life was hard for him to conceive: an unending cycle of sexual and physical abuse. How could there ever again be such a thing as normal?

She reached to the lamp on the table beside her and flicked on the light. As she moved he caught the scent of perfume, some hippie, flowery kind of oil, jasmine, maybe. Then she tipped her head back on the headrest, her eyes on Roarke . . . on the hand resting on his holster.

"Nice reflexes," she said in that lazy, too-adult drawl. "What brings you here at this hour?"

"I'm waiting to see Rachel."

Her eyes slid toward the door. "Does that give us time for a quickie BBBJ? Maybe DATY?"

Sex worker terms. *Bareback blowjob. Dining at the Y.* He pushed down his anger and despair.

"What kind of guy would I be if I said yes?"

She smiled, and it was a hard thing to see. "Not much of one, I guess." She looked him up and down. "So can I ask you something, Special Agent Roarke? You like nailing bad guys?"

"Yeah. I do." He wanted to keep her talking, but also it was an easy question to answer. He didn't just like it. It was his life's purpose.

Her eyes were fixed on him, a startling gaze, a gray made up of changing colored flecks and lights. *Kaleidoscope eyes*, he thought. They didn't look anything alike, but he couldn't look at her without seeing Cara.

"It's like your destiny, yeah?" she prodded.

Roarke was struck by the word. That question was not so easy to answer. The idea of destiny made him hugely uncomfortable these days.

Before he could formulate a response, she nodded, as if he'd spoken. "So when did you know?"

He wasn't sure he was following. "Know what?"

"When did you know what your destiny was?"

Now he was not just uncomfortable but acutely disoriented. One way or another Jade had zeroed in on the exact question that had been haunting him since he'd first set eyes on Cara in the flesh, not even three months ago, the day when his destiny had derailed his life, or aligned it, or both—he couldn't tell the difference anymore.

Because if there was a destiny, his had started the day he learned of Cara's existence, when at nine years old he had seen the first news report of the massacre of her family and her miracle survival. The day he began obsessing over a career of catching criminals . . . not just criminals, but monsters.

The girl was watching him. "It's something you have to do, though, right? Once you know, you can't refuse the call."

He tried to get some grip on the conversation. "It's a job, Jade."

She looked at him and slowly smiled. "Sure, *Special Agent* Roarke. Right."

There was motion behind him and he turned. Rachel stepped into the doorway, now wearing a coat and twining a scarf around her neck. She stopped and looked from Roarke to Jade. At the same time Jade looked from Roarke to Rachel, a quick glance, like flame. And a look of understanding and amusement flickered on her face.

"Ohhh," she drawled, her voice dripping with innuendo. "Well, then. You have fun, kids. Catch you later."

As Roarke and Rachel walked down the steps outside the House, there was a tense silence between them. Roarke was still unsettled by the oddness of the—*conversation? encounter?*—he'd just had with Jade, but he knew he had to focus, to do something to break the tension.

"She's—"

"Yeah," Rachel said. "She is."

Roarke held the car door for her on the passenger side. She didn't look at him as she lowered herself into the seat.

He went around to the driver's side and got in, and he could feel her heat beside him. He started the engine and pulled away from the curb. Outside the car windows the shops on Haight were closed and gated; homeless were bedding down for the night in the doorways.

"What's the story?" Rachel finally asked.

Roarke knew she was talking about Erin now, not Jade. He concentrated on the misty street ahead and tried to refocus himself on the task at hand.

"Something's happened to her. An assault, maybe, I don't know. I met her . . ." He had to stop, calculate the time frame in his head. *A month. A lifetime.* "About a month ago. And when I saw her today . . ." He shook his head. "The change in her is extreme."

"And who is she?"

"A med student. Twenty-four years old." He knew he had to say it. "Cara's cousin."

Rachel twisted to look at him in the dark.

"She has nothing to do with—anything," he said, but knew it was a lie.

"Of course not." Her voice dripped bitterness. She sat rigidly in the passenger seat, staring straight ahead, shaking her head just slightly. Roarke couldn't think what to say but was spared from talking by the sight of the oriel windows of the hotel, a Victorian silhouette against the dark expanse of Golden Gate Park, which loomed forestlike just across the street.

He easily found a parking spot at the curb. Not many residents would risk leaving their cars overnight this close to the park. It was right here that Cara had stalked Jade's pimp, Danny Ramirez, had found him getting high in a nearby tunnel, had slashed his throat in front of Jade . . .

Why is Erin here, in this *hotel?* he wondered again.

Rachel was already out of the car and looking up at the inn, which seemed oddly out of a time warp: cozily lit, with thick, elegant drapes at the windows.

Roarke followed her, caught up with her. At the top of the steps he held the door for her, and she walked in without looking at him.

The front desk clerk was involved with a businessman. Roarke reached for Rachel's arm. She stiffened at his touch, but when he nodded slightly toward the staircase she played along and let him steer her forward without stopping at the desk. They walked up the stairs like a couple returning to their room.

Roarke had called earlier and knew what Erin's room number was on the second floor. Out of long habit, he stopped in front of her door without knocking and just listened for a moment. Rachel paused, too, watching him. There was no sound from a television, and he could hear movement in the room: muffled, sporadic footsteps on a hardwood floor, alternating with barely audible steps on some kind of rug or carpet.

He reached out and knocked. Behind the door, the movement stopped entirely.

"Erin, it's Agent Roarke."

Dead silence from within. Rachel looked at Roarke. He spoke again. "Cara asked me to come by. I'd like to talk to you, if that's okay."

Another long silence, then he heard the scrape of a chain lock. The door opened and Erin looked out.

If anything she looked worse than when he had seen her at the Hall: more pale, the circles under her eyes more pronounced. She was in a T-shirt and faded sweatpants, and they hung on her, as if she'd shrunk.

She met Roarke's startled look with hollow eyes; then her gaze went to Rachel.

"This is my friend, Rachel," Roarke said quickly. He hoped Rachel believed that he meant it. "Can we come in for a minute?"

Erin didn't respond one way or another, so he eased his way forward. Erin backed up in pace with his movement and he stepped through the door, pushing it open behind him for Rachel, who followed, equally carefully.

Erin moved farther back into the room and stood listlessly at the side of the oak wardrobe. "Did they kill her?" she asked in a dull voice, without looking at Roarke.

He knew she must be talking about Cara, but it was such a startling question it took him a moment to answer.

"No. No, of course not. She's . . ." he was about to say "fine," but that was such an obvious lie. "She's all right."

"They're going to kill her, aren't they? They're going to kill her for what she did."

It was Roarke's worst fear, too, but it wasn't on the table. Not yet. "The prosecutor isn't talking about the death penalty," he told Erin.

She ran her hand up and down the edge of the wardrobe, scraping her nails on the wood with a ferocity that reminded him of Cara's display in the visiting room that morning. "They will, though," Erin said softly. "They'll kill her."

"Erin, I think you need to—"

He felt Rachel's hand on his arm and stopped. He glanced at her. She locked her eyes with his, a significant look. Then she shifted her gaze to the desk beside the window. Roarke's pulse jumped as he saw the small, sharp knife on the blotter. There was blood on the blade.

"Erin?" he asked softly.

She saw them looking at the knife. Before she could move, he was across the room, blocking her. Simultaneously Rachel stepped toward Erin with her hands held out. Her eyes were focused on Erin's midriff. Roarke stood in front of the desk, in front of the knife, and followed Rachel's gaze . . . to the smear of crimson on Erin's shirt.

"It's okay," Rachel said quickly. "Let me see, Erin."

Erin backed away from her. Rachel dropped her voice lower. "I just want to check that you're all right."

She moved closer, as carefully as she would approach a wild animal, and reached slowly to lift Erin's T-shirt. Blood seeped from several precise cuts around her navel, forming a single word:

DIE

Roarke felt a jolt as he took in the letters. Rachel dropped the edge of the T-shirt and looked into Erin's face. Her voice was calm and firm. "Okay. We're going to get that fixed up." She put an arm around the younger woman and steered her gently toward the bathroom. Roarke automatically started to follow, but Rachel put an arm out, holding him back.

"Matt, I've got this."

He looked at her, startled that she'd used his first name.

"I mean it. Go home." Her voice was low and rough.

He knew she didn't hold him responsible for Erin's distress, but he felt a strange guilt nonetheless. He nodded and said softly, "Call me if you need—anything."

He watched them disappear into the bathroom. Left alone, he stood for a moment, taking in the room: the canted windows, the mussed bed, the open wardrobe door . . . and the bloody knife on the desk. He glanced around, pulled the liner from the trash can, and used it to wrap the knife. He put the package into his jacket pocket.

Then he moved quietly to the door and out.

Chapter 11

He is on the sidewalk on the hill . . . and she is there across the street. She stands in tight black pants and boots, with her past-the-shoulder blond hair and black sunglasses. She looks through the passing cars at Roarke. And he looks back at her, an endless moment, drinking her in. The sun on her hair. The black of her turtleneck and the taut muscles of her arms. The violent purple irises in the flower stand behind her. The smell of exhaust and coffee.

That moment. His destiny.

He knows what will happen, knows what is coming, the blood and the screaming and the death, but he is paralyzed, frozen on the street, helpless as the sound of a truck builds, an insistent rattling somewhere out of vision. And then there is the screeching of brakes straining against the downward plunge of the hill, the sickening thud . . . and the blood, crimson exploding over the truck's front grille and a man's body flying, and the screaming, one scream on top of another, and male shouting, a building wave of panic. The sidewalk is crowded with people turning away, shrieking in horror . . .

He looks across the street through the chaos and the screams ... and it is not Cara standing on the sidewalk, but someone smaller, with a wild mane of curly hair, and every exposed inch of skin covered in body art.

Jade.

Standing on the sidewalk in front of a river of blood.

DAY THREE

Chapter 12

The truck's rattling jerked him out of sleep. No, not the truck, but his phone vibrating, clattering on the bedside table. His room was dark, predawn, and his heart hammered in his chest.

The dream, the truck, the blood . . .

He lifted the phone with an overwhelming feeling of dread and heard Rachel's agitated voice. "She's gone."

For a moment he thought, *Cara. Hurt, killed . . . escaped?* He fumbled for words, any word. "What?"

"Jade. I just got back to Belvedere and she's gone. All her things are gone."

A dozen emotions spiraled through Roarke: disbelief, unreality, apprehension.

Our witness. The case. The trial.

Rachel was speaking, words tumbling out. "The other girls haven't seen her. I have no idea—"

"I'm on my way."

There was always a set of fresh suits and shirts lined up in his closet so that even if awakened in the dead of night he could dress to Bureau standard in minutes. He stripped clothes from hangers and pulled them on in a routine perfected over years, while alarming memories churned in his head. The weird conversation about destiny. The way Jade had seemed to be grilling him about something he couldn't get to . . .

Should I have known she would flee? Could I have prevented it?

And worse . . .

Did I say something to set her off?

And the dream . . .

The dream.

It came back to him in a rush of images, a feeling like falling from a great height, until he landed with all the force of gravity and just one vision in his head.

Jade standing on the sidewalk in front of that pool of blood.

Socks, shoes, a tie, his shoulder holster, and he was out the door, pounding down the stairs, through the front door and out into the fog, down the sidewalk toward the fleet car he'd left parked on the street.

As he strode on the sidewalk, he racked his brain, trying to remember everything he had said to Jade, everything she had said to him.

"When did you know?"

"Know what?"

"When did you know what your destiny was?"

His phone vibrated again just as he was reaching for the car door handle, spiking his adrenaline higher. It was Mills. Roarke punched ANSWER, was about to speak, when the detective's words stopped him in his tracks.

"We got another pimp dead. O'Farrell, between Polk and Van Ness."

"A pimp?" Roarke repeated through a suddenly constricted throat.

"Facedown in his own blood. Throat slashed with a thin blade. Any of this sounding familiar?"

Roarke felt a cold wave of apprehension, followed by a new rush of emotions that he didn't dare to sort. He stared out over the fog blanketing the hills. "When?" was all he could manage.

"After midnight is all the ME will say. You want to get down here and see, do it."

"I'm there."

He punched END and immediately called Epps. The other agent picked up saying, "Mills just called."

"Leaving now," Roarke said, and he pulled open the car door.

Chapter 13

The fog was icy, drifting sluggishly in the streets. The neon signs still blazed, lighting the entrances of the sex clubs with their theater-style displays: glassed-in posters of contorted female bodies in G-strings and spike heels, signs advertising "Massage," "Sauna," "Incall/Outcall."

The Tenderloin was San Francisco's infamous sex district, fifty square blocks on the southern slope of Nob Hill, sandwiched between the high-end shopping of Union Square and the scruffier Civic Center. Otherwise known as the Loin, the TL, the Trendyloin, and Little Saigon.

Madam Tessie Wall had opened her first brothel here in 1898, and no one ever looked back. By the 1920s the TL was infamous for its billiard halls, burlesque houses, theaters, and speakeasies. It was the birthplace of the porn movie industry in the 1960s; in the '70s it pushed the envelope even further with live sex acts on stage.

While the rest of San Francisco real estate had skyrocketed in value after the dot-com boom, the TL had resisted gentrification. Its streets teemed with junkies looking for a cheap fix, homeless looking for a cheap hotel, men looking for a cheap fuck.

The police barricade was set up at the entrance of an alley between two lurid sex clubs: Barely Legal and Wildcats. As Roarke parked, he saw Epps' tall silhouette striding up the sidewalk in the drifting fog. Roarke got out of the car to meet him.

"What the hell is this now?" Epps started.

"I don't know," Roarke answered. He was too tense to speak further.

The agents flashed credentials at the uniform guarding the yellow crime scene tape at the front of the long, narrow uphill alley and headed for the collection of cops, crime scene techs, and police photographers milling at the far end of the enclosed strip.

The sense of déjà vu was strong. The alley was narrow and dark in the fog, reminiscent of the tunnel where Jade's pimp had been murdered. Like Ramirez, this dead pimp was also collapsed in his own blood, at the foot of a short set of concrete steps leading down from a back door of the Wildcats club. Roarke could see the blood was thick and congealing around the edges of the spill, but still deep and liquid in places around the body. He hadn't been dead long.

Mills lumbered over to meet them. "Rear assault incised neck wound," he began without preamble. "No defensive wounds on hands or arms." He looked up toward the steps, the small landing outside the door. "I figure the doer was above him on the stairs. Grabbed his hair from behind, slashed his neck. Same kind of cut we got with Danny Ramirez. No hesitation marks, a clean slice left to right."

Exactly how Cara killed. Only Cara was locked away.

"Murder weapon was a straight razor," Mills added.

Roarke and Epps exchanged a sharp glance. Cara's weapon of choice, but it wasn't often that the type of weapon could be determined from an incised wound. The detective was watching their faces.

"How do we know, you're wondering? I'll tell you how we know. The perp left it. Right there." Mills nodded to the end of the railing, the concrete pillar of the steps, where a plastic evidence marker sat next to a dark smear of blood.

"So, friends and neighbors, I think you see why I've called you here this morning. Our case just got completely fucked up the ass."

"Wait a minute. Wait a minute . . ." Epps was already walking in a circle in outraged disbelief. Mills smiled grimly.

"Oh, I'm just getting started. It gets better. Mr. DeShawn dead-as-a-doornail Butler is a known associate of Danny Ramirez. They 'looked after' each other's stables. Took them on the road together when they went out on the circuit."

"So Jade knew him," Roarke said softly. There was a black pit of dread in his stomach.

Do you like nailing bad guys, Agent Roarke?"

"Jade?" Epps and Mills asked simultaneously, turning to him, but it was Epps who seemed to know what was coming. His face was a mirror of the dark foreboding Roarke was feeling himself.

"She's gone," Roarke answered. "She disappeared from the Belvedere House last night."

"What the hell?"

"*What?*"

Mills and Epps exploded at the same time. Epps' face was a study in consternation. "When?"

Roarke realized he hadn't yet talked to Rachel, so he had no idea when Jade had gone.

"Sometime last night. Rachel called me this morning, just before I got the call from you." He nodded toward Mills.

"Wait a minute. Wait just a goddamn fucking minute." Mills walked several steps, then stopped. "Are you trying to say . . ." He trailed off and they all looked toward the corpse, simultaneously realizing that they had a far bigger problem than losing their key witness. "Are we really saying a sixteen-year-old *girl* did this? A clean incised neck wound? No hesitation marks?"

"She saw Lindstrom do it," Epps said. He looked to Roarke and spread his hands slightly in a question.

Roarke's mind was racing. Jade was exceptional in many ways. Precocious, no doubt. But for a girl that age to coldly grasp a grown man's hair and cut through the tendons of his exposed throat . . . it was nearly unthinkable.

But if not Jade . . .

And suddenly he was thinking about Cara's first kill, or what he suspected was her first kill, a male counselor at one of the many group homes that had been Cara's childhood existence. She had been just fourteen years old. If Cara could do it, why not Jade at sixteen?

He looked around at the alley and the scenario spun out in his head. Jade *had* seen Cara kill Ramirez. But even if she'd grasped the mechanics of cutting someone's throat, what were the chances of her being able to duplicate the killing so perfectly? On the other hand, she would pose no apparent threat. If anyone could get close enough to a player like DeShawn Butler without arousing suspicion . . .

Roarke had seen Jade in action before. He looked at the short set of concrete stairs and pictured her bumming a cigarette, sitting on the step above the pimp to smoke it, fingering the razor in her pocket . . .

It was all too easy to visualize.

"You pick up any cigarette butts?" he asked Mills abruptly.

"Only about a hundred an' five," Mills said. "Interesting you should ask. Because the blood pattern looks to me like he was sitting on that step when he got slashed. Nice clean ass cheek prints in the middle of all that blood."

Sitting. It indicated DeShawn probably wasn't feeling any particular sense of threat.

"So yeah, we'll be looking at those stubs for lipstick prints," Mills said. "In fact, I'm having the razor and butts sent straight over to your guys, just on the assumption you're gonna be happy to use your extra-special speedy lab to get that testing done. We should be getting something for the privilege of involving you in this mess." He shook his head. "Lemme tell you. If it wasn't your fucked-up case we're talkin' about here, I'd be thinking pimp war. Some street retribution."

The thought stopped Roarke cold. He had always assumed Cara had killed Ramirez . . . but Jade was an expert liar . . .

Epps jumped in before he could voice a thought. "Oh yeah. Oh yeah." Roarke could hear his agent's righteous fury underneath the words. "Someone kills Ramirez with Cara Lindstrom's exact MO. 'Cause macks are favorin' straight razors for their killing these days."

Epps was right. It made no sense at all. It also suddenly occurred to Roarke that if the razor was the same type Cara used, Jade would have had to buy it. It spoke of a planning that completely unnerved him.

Did she have the razor on her when I saw her last night? he wondered. He felt a chill. *More to the point, did she deliberately leave the razor? Because if she did . . .*

"Hey, I said 'If,'" Mills told Epps, interrupting Roarke's thought. "Since it *is* your fucked-up case, I am certain there is some whole other shit going on here."

Roarke had a sinking feeling Mills was more than right. The detective continued.

"I've got my uniforms inside the club and canvassing the Loin. Not that we're likely to find anyone who'll talk. Your guys'll be printing the razor and DNA-testing the blood on it—we have Jade's prints from her last booking into juvie. Also it's a hella sharp blade so we might get lucky, get some of the killer's own blood off the razor."

Roarke had a sudden flash of the bloody knife he'd taken from Erin's hotel room and felt another wave of dread.

Mills paused and looked grim. "But we're racing the clock here. Prelim is day after tomorrow, and we just lost our key witness."

"The DA can ask for a continuance—" Epps started.

"Yeah. The disappearance of a key witness counts as good cause. But Molina invoked the ten-day rule. Delay the prelim and Lindstrom gets OR."

OR. Own recognizance.

California's ten-day rule not only stipulated a defendant had the right to a preliminary hearing within ten days, but also mandated that if a prelim was delayed beyond those ten days, an incarcerated defendant must be released, barring a very circumscribed set of circumstances.

Roarke realized Mills was saying that Cara could walk out of jail on bail. And if she walked, she was gone. She wouldn't just run; she'd vanish. She'd lived under the radar since she was eighteen years old.

He felt a whole new spate of emotions that he knew—if he stopped to analyze them—meant he shouldn't be anywhere near this case.

"So Stanton is going to have to go in with what he's got," Epps muttered, looking dazed.

"Or we're going to have to get Jade back to testify," Roarke said.

Jade . . . who was looking very much like the killer of the pimp in the alley behind them.

He forced himself from his own thoughts, struggled for a game plan. "Rachel's got two other girls from Ramirez's stable staying at the shelter. They're going to be our best bet for tying Jade to DeShawn. And tracking her down."

Mills shook his head. "Well, I'd be much obliged if you'd trot yourself over there and do some digging. We need to find that wildcat before the prelim, and we've got two days to do it."

Dawn was breaking, a knifelike gray, as Roarke and Epps walked out of the alley to the sidewalk. Without the neon lighting, now swirling with ocean fog, O'Farrell Street had lost any sleazy glamour it held in the nighttime. The street was as bleak and grimy as a hangover.

Roarke could feel his agent seething beside him. "What are the other good-cause reasons for a continuance?" Epps asked abruptly.

Roarke pushed his emotions to the side and tried to think like a lawman. "Defendant waives time, but that won't work. Molina would love to waive time. She'd waive time in exchange for bail. That's the usual gimme."

And Cara walking on bail was the same as walking free.

"So what else?" Epps asked tensely. "Illness of counsel, capital offense with preponderance of evidence . . ."

Roarke reached into his memory. "Counsel unexpectedly engaged in another trial, conflict of interest requires appointment of new counsel, a necessary witness becomes unavailable due to the actions of the defendant . . ."

He paused, and the two of them pondered that last for a moment.

"No evidence of that," Roarke said.

"That we know of," Epps countered.

Roarke had to admit there was something about the idea that felt strangely apropos. Cara couldn't have made Jade disappear herself, but he had wondered during the interview with Mills if perhaps Jade felt threatened.

"I'll ask Rachel— "

"Wait." Epps was tense with concentration. "The judge can't kick Lindstrom on OR if she's being held on other charges, right?"

"That sounds right," Roarke said, and felt a new stab of worry that he had no business feeling.

Epps looked triumphant. "One of the other agencies has to charge her, then. For one of the other killings. Singh will know which case we can push."

It was a plan. Whether Roarke liked it or not was a different story.

Chapter 14

They split up: Epps back to the office, Roarke to the Belvedere House. Rachel looked exhausted—pale and worn. And not at all happy to see Roarke. In her office, he took a seat in one of the armchairs and tried to relax his posture, make himself as neutral as possible, in the hope of lowering her obviously high agitation. He had not told her about DeShawn Butler's murder, although she would know soon enough. Instead he focused on the question at hand. "Did Jade show any signs that she was going to take off? Anything at all?"

Her anger flared up. "You think I wouldn't have told you—"

"I know," he said.

She pressed her fists to her forehead. When she spoke again it was more calmly.

"No one's confined here, but there's a curfew. Janet says that the girls were all here at ten p.m. There's a security alarm and she set it downstairs."

"So . . ."

"So Jade got the code somehow and used it."

Piece of cake for someone like Jade, Roarke knew. A quick mind could be turned to criminal pursuits just as easily as it could be to problem solving in a mainstream profession.

The question was about the timing. She'd been at the shelter for over two weeks, and according to Rachel she'd seemed content enough to stay. And as Rachel said, she wasn't being confined against her will. So why the sudden need to leave?

If not for the express purpose of killing DeShawn.

Roarke had never believed in coincidence, although this case was messing with his head about it.

"I need to talk to Ramirez's other girls," he said.

Rachel stiffened again, and the anger was back in her voice, more deadly this time. "They're not Ramirez's girls. They never were, even before that fuck was dead."

"You're right," he said, and he meant it. "I just don't know their names."

She softened slightly. "Shauna and Tyra. They don't know where Jade is, though. It's the first thing I asked them."

Roarke was sure she had. And he had no idea what he was going to ask a couple of street girls that could possibly get them to open up or say anything of use to him.

Rachel was watching him. "Are you here because . . . Do you think she killed DeShawn?" she asked softly.

Roarke felt the words like a hammer blow to the back of his head. He stared at her. "How do you know about DeShawn?"

Rachel gave him an oblique look. "The girls have been talking about it."

"*They* know?" He couldn't believe it. He himself had learned of the death only hours ago.

"People on the street . . ." She shrugged.

Roarke understood. The network. It was almost telepathic, the way word got around.

"Did you know him?" he asked.

"DeShawn Butler? Oh yeah. I knew him. Of him, anyway." Her voice was full of loathing. "He sold Shauna to Danny Ramirez. The way I heard it, she was better off with Danny. If you believe there's some kind of variation in the levels of hell."

Roarke didn't know what he believed. At a certain point it was all hell. "Can I see them?"

Rachel led him downstairs, to a room he had not been in before, a big basement hangout. Rumpus room, they used to call them. It was typical Bay Area retro: long, low, thrift store couches and overflowing bookshelves and a television surrounded by uncased DVDs. There was even a beanbag chair.

Two teenage girls were sunk into adjacent mismatched sofas. The older, whom Rachel called Tyra, was a mixed-race girl with caramel-colored skin, big pouty lips, big lashes, big silver hoop earrings. She moved with a sultry sulkiness, and when her midriff top shifted Roarke caught a glimpse of a tattooed cross over most of her stomach. She may have been seventeen.

The other, whom Rachel introduced as Shauna, was small and plump and dark, with wary brown eyes. The most striking thing about her was that she was clearly no more than thirteen. For the millionth time in his career, Roarke wondered what kind of man had so little conscience that he could use children like this for sex.

Rachel left him with the girls without leaving the room; she took a seat in front of a computer station on the opposite side of the basement space, unobtrusive but present.

Roarke settled himself on the wide arm of a chair facing the two teenagers.

"I understand you ladies know something about DeShawn Butler."

The girls were silent. Roarke looked pointedly to Tyra, the older of the two. She shrugged. "Heard he wuz *dead.*" And then for a moment her eyes were shrewd, assessing him. "That be right?"

Underneath the deliberate street drawl she had a slight Southern accent, maybe from living there, maybe just a legacy from some long-ago parent.

"He's dead, yes," he answered the girl. *And good fucking riddance*, he added in his head. "How did you find out about it?"

Tyra looked slightly smug. "Ev'rybody knows. Got hisself offed in an alley in the TL."

"That's right," Roarke said. "Do you know who did it?"

The girls looked at each other briefly.

"Guess you thinkin' it was Jade," Tyra said with an attempt at casual indifference.

"What do you think?"

Tyra cut her eyes Shauna's way. Shauna concentrated on the floor and gnawed at a fingernail. Roarke realized that the acne scarring on her cheeks was actually from old meth sores.

"Jade hated DeShawn, no doubt," Tyra finally drawled, and Roarke looked steadily back at her.

"Why was that?"

He had been watching both girls closely since he'd walked into the room. Now Shauna, who had been listless and passive throughout, stiffened and fidgeted.

"Shauna?" he asked gently.

The girl crossed her arms and kept her eyes on the floor.

"He broke her in," Tyra said from the other couch. Her voice was flat. "Danny took new girls to DeShawn."

Roarke felt his blood rising in anger. Typical pimp practice. Trauma bonding, psychologists called it. The pimps raped the girls themselves, or the more devious ones got friends and associates to rape a new girl so the pimp seemed like some comfort afterward, however perverse. An insidious kind of brainwashing.

"Shauna?"

Shauna wouldn't look at him. Tyra rolled her head back and looked at Roarke.

"Shauna too. She be walkin' home from school and DeShawn and some guys grabbed her, pulled her into his car."

Shauna's eyes were glazed. "I was walkin' and I hear them say, 'Get that girl.' *Get that girl*," she repeated softly.

Roarke sat still in his chair and tasted bile in his throat. "I'm sorry," he said to Shauna. His voice was thick and he had no other words. "I'm sorry."

The girl lifted her shoulders, barely. Her eyes never left the floor.

"He dead," Tyra said, with no particular inflection. "Nobody cryin' here. Whole hella lot of people coulda killed him."

At the moment, Roarke would have been more than happy to have done it himself. He forced down his fury and concentrated on Tyra's last words. "*A lot of people could have killed DeShawn.*" Not surprising, and it was a point that Molina was sure to make about Ramirez's murder as well. He tried to focus back on something, anything, that would move him closer to finding Jade.

"Do you have any idea where Jade is from?" he asked.

Shauna shook her head. Tyra shrugged.

"You think she's from around here?" he tried. "Or California in general?"

Tyra gave him a look that was as close to rolling her eyes as someone could get without actually doing it. "Could be you try lookin' her up on Facebook."

Roarke had to admit the girl had a sense of irony.

"We dint sit around jawing," she elaborated. "Not if we dint want to get beat. She dint talk about it."

"Okay," Roarke said, and took a moment to still his outrage. "But sometimes things just come out, right? You pick up things?"

He looked at Tyra and she stared back sullenly, then gave a ghost of a shrug. She was sunk into the couch and her crop top was riding up, and Roarke tried not to look at the tattoo emblazoned over her bare midriff.

He asked, "Can you tell me *anything* else about her? Things she did, things she liked . . ."

Tyra considered. "She was into that cosmic shit. Incense, candles, psychics. Third eye blind and all."

Another tick in the box for a California background, Roarke thought. He heard Jade's voice again. *"Do you believe in destiny, Agent Roarke?"*

He cleared his throat. "Did you get any sense of her family? Father, mother . . ."

"Stepdaddy," Shauna said suddenly. Roarke turned to her. Her brown eyes seemed liquid in the dim room.

"Really? She said that?"

"Once, maybe. I think. Somethin'." The younger girl faltered under Tyra's stare.

"Do you know where that might have been, where she lived?"

Shauna half-shrugged. "Uh-uh."

"Anything else—anyone else—she may have mentioned?"

Shauna shook her head. She seemed to have slipped back into a slightly dazed state.

"Did Jade own a straight razor?"

Shauna looked blank.

"It's a blade about this long. It folds up into the handle." Roarke gestured, making a V with his hands.

Shauna's eyes went a little wide, but she shook her head. Roarke looked to Tyra.

"Never saw it," the girl answered.

He nodded. "If you think of anything, I'd appreciate it if you'd let Rachel know. She'll get in touch with me. Or you can call or text me directly." He put two of his business cards on the table in front of them.

Shauna didn't move. After a moment Tyra leaned forward and picked up both cards. Then she stood, and Shauna stood with her.

As he watched the smaller girl start after Tyra, he remembered something Rachel had told him.

"Shauna, would you stay a minute? I'd like to talk to you a little more."

The girl looked alarmed. She shot a look toward Rachel, who nodded. After a moment, Shauna sat awkwardly back down. Tyra paused by the doorway and looked back, half-relieved, half-suspicious. Then reluctantly she sidled out the door.

Roarke leaned forward and addressed the younger girl. "I understand you saw someone beat up one of your tricks recently."

She looked at him, wide-eyed.

"Is that right, Shauna?"

She averted her eyes and nodded. He wondered what he was doing questioning her about it. She had seen Cara being violent; his lawman brain was calculating that she could act as a witness to that fact. Another part of him simply craved hearing what Cara had done.

"Can you tell me what happened?"

She looked down, away, anywhere but at him. She put her hand to her mouth, and for a moment Roarke thought she was going to suck her thumb. Instead she bit at the nail of her pinkie finger. "I had this guy in the alley . . ."

"Where was this?"

"Um . . . next to Karma Records." She moved on to the next fingernail. "I was, you know, startin' to go down on him, and this lady come up behind me and say she got it."

"She got it?"

"Like, 'I got this.' And she look at me funny, so I leave."

"What do you mean by 'funny'?"

The girl looked trapped. "I dunno."

"But you didn't really leave?"

She hesitated. "I was wonderin' what was up, so I stayed."

"You were hiding?"

"Kinda on the other side of the Dumpster . . ."

"And what did you see?"

The girl looked away.

"Anything you can remember would help," he told her gently.

"She step up and unbuckle him, pull his pants down 'roun' his knees." Her eyes were unfocused, as if she were seeing it. "And then she stand up and slam her fists 'gainst the side of his head, real hard . . . and grab his head and start beatin' it 'gainst the wall. Slammin' the shit out of him."

Roarke's mouth was dry, picturing it. The narrow alley. Cara approaching the man with that mesmerizing sensuality . . . and then the sudden explosion of her rage . . .

"He was big, too," the girl said, a bit in awe. "He was real big."

"And then what?" Roarke managed.

"He go all limp. And then she drop him. He lying there bare-ass and blood all over him . . ." Her eyes went dull; then she shook her head. "An' I take off."

"What did this woman look like, who attacked him?"

She bit deeper into her nail. Roarke saw crimson welling at the tip of her finger and winced.

"White. Blond. Thin . . . pretty."

"Dressed how?"

She frowned, concentrating. "Jeans. Hoodie."

"About how old was she?"

She shrugged. "Twenny?"

Cara was ten years older than that. Not that it was a surprising guess. Kids rarely could tell the age of anyone over twenty, but that kind of discrepancy never sounded good in court.

He had the sketch of Cara, though. He always had it. He'd reduced the official sketch to a size he could carry in a coat pocket, laminated. He told himself it was for situations like this, identification purposes that had come up fairly regularly since he had begun chasing her.

He stepped closer and showed Shauna the sketch: glistening laminate finish over that intense, focused image.

The girl went still. "Yeah. Her." She looked up, and the awe was back in her eyes. "She bashed the shit out of him."

Roarke nodded. He had no doubt. It was a slim connection, though, between beating up a john and murdering a pimp. Shauna's account could hardly replace Jade's eyewitness testimony.

He wondered, not for the first time, why Cara hadn't killed the john in that alley. It wasn't like her not to complete the act. Because she knew Shauna was watching? Because his crime was not as severe on her scale as the pimp Danny Ramirez's? He had no idea how she judged these things. Or if it was a conscious decision at all.

He slipped the sketch back into the inner pocket of his suit coat and felt it against his chest. "Thank you, Shauna. You've been a big help." He paused. "I hope you're liking it here."

The girl looked confused, then shrugged slightly. "S'all right. Rachel, she all right."

Rachel is all right, he agreed with her in his head. *She's more than all right.*

He watched as she stood, a short, slightly plump teenager who had already suffered more in her brief lifetime than he could bear thinking about.

She paused at the doorway and looked back at him. "DeShawn's for real dead? You saw him?"

"Yeah. I saw him."

"Jade killed him like that," she said. There was a dazed quality to her voice, and he was going to answer automatically that it was under investigation, but then he saw a flicker of something in her eyes, something more than ordinary. Something like triumph.

"I don't know," he answered, and was aware of how uneasy he sounded.

Shauna nodded, as if he weren't there. "She did it. She killed him."

And Roarke, who had spent six years of his life talking to serial killers, rapists, and the criminally insane, felt cold fingers at the back of his neck as the girl walked from the room.

When he turned, Rachel was still sitting at the computer station. He'd forgotten she was there.

She looked at him, then stood and walked out.

He climbed the stairs from the basement and stopped in the hall outside her office, found himself pausing to gather himself before he knocked on the half-open door.

She was sitting on the window seat, looking out the curved glass of the bay window at the park.

"They're looking good," he said to her. "Healthy."

"Sure," she said. "Just a couple of ordinary teenagers."

He was startled at the sarcasm in her voice. It wasn't like her. But under the circumstances, bitterness was hardly a surprise.

"Was it any help?" She turned from the window and looked at him.

"I don't know," he admitted. "Maybe."

"You do think Jade killed DeShawn." The way she spoke it, it wasn't a question, and technically Roarke had no business answering it, although he found it on the tip of his tongue to say everything. Jade knew how Cara had killed Danny Ramirez. She obviously had motive for killing the man Tyra said had "broken her in." And then there was the thing he had not been letting himself fully consider. The straight razor beside the corpse. Which the killer had left deliberately. The razor that could cast some serious reasonable doubt in the case against Cara.

Did Jade really do that consciously? Seriously? Not just kill a man, but plant evidence to exonerate Cara? A sixteen-year-old girl?

What are we dealing with here?

"What do you think?" he asked, deflecting Rachel's statement. "Could she have?"

"You heard Tyra," Rachel said. "A lot of people could have."

"Right." He sat on the armrest of the couch, suddenly bone-tired. "How is Erin?"

Rachel looked briefly surprised at the segue, then shrugged. "She wasn't cutting when I left."

"Were you there all night?"

She looked away. "Basically. The cutting's been happening on and off for a long time. She was sixteen, went to some party, she was drinking . . . she woke up to find herself in a bedroom, naked and bleeding. Someone raped her. She still doesn't know who. Or how many. Rohypnol, the jock's little helper."

Roarke flinched inside, feeling anger and despair. Not that he hadn't suspected.

"She went to a clinic by herself for pregnancy and STD testing instead of telling her mother or anyone else. I got the strong feeling she's buried it pretty effectively for years."

Roarke nodded. He'd had a real conversation with Erin only once, but he could see the quiet, independent young woman suppressing the attack and deciding that she would simply deal with it on her own. Of course buried trauma always came back eventually.

Rachel was speaking, and he tuned in again. "She says she hasn't done the cutting for years. Which may or may not be true."

"So learning about what Cara—about the killing she's doing, why she's doing it . . ."

"It triggered her," Rachel said. "Of course. On all kinds of levels."

He found Rachel's eyes, felt for a connection. "I feel like I've put you in the middle of all this. Jade, Erin . . ."

Something went blank in her face. "It's my job. I was involved with Jade before you ever came here about her."

Roarke realized it was true; Rachel had told him at their first meeting that she'd made numerous attempts to get Jade off the street and into the shelter.

"Fair enough. But Erin isn't your job."

"It's hard to tell where the job stops," she said.

"Yeah," he answered, looking at her. There was a sudden warmth in the room, the intimacy that had always been there between them, despite the walls.

She shook her head, breaking the moment. "We talked. I gave her the contact info for a good therapist I know, although of course she's only visiting here. But she has medical services through her university and she can go there. Cutting is a huge issue these days; every college has to deal with it. She can get help if she wants it."

"Does she want it?"

The shrug Rachel gave was like Tyra's. "She talked some. That's a release. Whether she chooses to pursue help . . ." She lifted a hand.

True, Erin was an adult. It was her choice. But Roarke was sure that Rachel was the best therapy Erin could have had at the time.

So he'd kept his promise to Cara for now.

Rachel was watching him. "Are you going after Jade, then?"

"We'll have to find her, yes."

Her lips were pressed tightly together as she shook her head. "You know what DeShawn was, don't you? A guerilla pimp. Shauna's a foster kid, no great student, but trying her best in a lousy system. She was walking home from school in Oakland and he grabbed her off the street. She's thirteen. Kidnapped, held hostage, and gang-raped by Butler's friends for a few days to take the will out of her. Then he drugs her, puts her out on International Boulevard with instructions to bring money back, beats her if she doesn't, beats her every time she looks toward a door or a window. When it's convenient to him, he sells her to Ramirez. That's the man who was killed last night."

Then she slammed her hands down on the desk and swept an arm across it, sending a pen jar, a binder, several books, a coffee cup flying. She pounded her hands flat against the suddenly bare surface. "Who cares? Who cares?"

For a split second Roarke was rooted to the floor in shock. Then he crossed to the desk.

"I know, Rachel." He reached across the desktop to put his hands on her shoulders, but she jerked back in her chair. She was pale and breathing hard.

"If *one* thing happened to me that happened to that child, I would drink bleach. I would cut up my wrists. I would kill myself any way I could."

"I know—"

"Someone should just take a blowtorch to all of them. Pimps, johns, the whole fucking lot of them."

She was shaking, halfway between fury and tears. Roarke knew the signals. In ordinary circumstances he would have stepped to her, held her, said with his body what he couldn't say with words. But the circumstances weren't ordinary and never had been. There was too much between them . . . and not enough.

"Rachel . . ."

Her eyes were closed now, and she rested her elbows on her desk and her head on her hands. "Just *go*."

And in the end, he did.

Chapter 15

The San Francisco Bureau had several crack Evidence Response Teams that handled crime scenes and lab work for the office. As far as Roarke was concerned, Lam and Stotlemyre were the best techs in the division: one a reed-thin, energetic, unflaggingly cheerful Vietnamese, the other a hulking, methodical German American. The two men had worked together so long that no one in the office ever referred to them separately: it was always "Lam and Stotlemyre." The Supreme Court had ended the ban on same-sex marriage in California in 2013, and in some part of his mind Roarke had been expecting a wedding invitation ever since. But San Francisco or not, the Bureau was still the Bureau. No one asked, and no one told.

The techs had been on Roarke's list to visit, but as he crossed the Federal Building's blue-veined marble lobby on the way toward the elevator, he got a text from Lam that sent him straight up to the lab:

Got something for you. Maybe.

The two techs were huddled at a lab table with a comparison microscope between them. They looked up in tandem as Roarke walked in.

"Got your message," he told them.

The techs nodded, and Lam stood.

"I was taking a blood sample from the razor to send in for rush DNA testing, but I typed it first. It's a mixed sample. Meaning there are two types of blood on it. One type is a match for DeShawn Butler—"

Roarke's pulse elevated. "So the other blood could be the killer's." *And if Jade's blood type is on record anywhere—*

The two techs exchanged a glance. "We're thinking maybe not," Stotlemyre said.

Roarke frowned. "Not the killer's blood?"

Lam jumped in to explain. "The second type is rare, AB negative. Less than one percent of the population has this type."

Roarke could feel a revelation coming from the prickling of his skin. "So who do we know who does?"

"Daniel Ramirez," the two answered simultaneously.

Roarke stared at the techs. "It's the *same* murder weapon Lindstrom used?"

"Let's not get ahead of ourselves," Stotlemyre warned.

"It's still just a blood type," Lam agreed. "We have to wait for DNA results to know for sure if it's Ramirez's blood. I pulled some favors to get a quickie analysis." And before Roarke could ask, he added, "Maybe tomorrow. *Maybe.*"

"But the odds . . ."

The techs exchanged a glance. It was Stotlemyre who answered. "The odds are . . . odd."

Roarke looked from one to the other. "You'll let me know—"

"As soon as we do," Stotlemyre promised.

As Roarke rode the elevator down to his own floor, his mind was already reeling with the implications. *Two pimps killed with the same weapon. Not just reasonable doubt. Exculpatory evidence.*

If Cara's odds of walking out of jail had improved with Jade's disappearance, they'd just shot up astronomically now.

And if the blood proved to be Ramirez's, the only explanation Roarke could think of was that the killer had deliberately left the razor with that blood evidence linking the two crimes.

He tried to slow his spinning thoughts so he could work it through.

The murder weapon in the Ramirez case had never been found. Jade had been on the scene; she could have picked up the razor.

And kept it for two weeks? But why? Surely she couldn't have been planning this kill all that time?

The idea was statistically so beyond the pale that he was already rethinking whether Jade was really DeShawn's killer, even though the timing made her the most likely suspect.

But is she? The most *likely?*

Who would be more likely to plant evidence to exonerate Cara?

He thought suddenly of the bloody knife he'd taken from Erin's hotel room. The hotel room that was just steps from the park where Ramirez had been killed.

Should I have that knife tested, too? Compare Erin's blood with the blood on the razor?

He almost turned back to the lab but realized that the point would be moot if the blood tested out as Danny Ramirez's. Which they would know soon enough.

Leave it, he decided. *We'll see what we see.*

He could hear voices in the conference room as he walked down the hall, but there was instant silence when he entered the room. Epps and Singh turned to him simultaneously from opposite sides of the long table.

The atmosphere was strained. It felt for a moment almost as if his agents had been fighting.

"I've just been up to the lab," Roarke began. "Lam and Stotlemyre—"

"We know," Epps said tautly. "Same murder weapon. At least that's what fucking Molina is going to say."

That explained Epps' level of agitation. "We don't know for sure yet," Roarke said. "Any progress on the other cases?" he asked, though he could guess the answer from the look on Epps' face. Singh's expression was harder to interpret.

"We are racing the clock," she said, echoing Mills. "If there had been a case close enough to file, I would have said so." Her tone didn't change, but Roarke sensed a rebuke to Epps in it, unusual for Singh. "But Agent Jones and I will be checking with every agency again to see if there is something that can be done to move any one of them forward." She sounded dubious, and Epps looked angry. And Roarke was a little tired of Epps being angry.

"Good," he said. "I'm going to check in with Mills."

As he moved out of the office, he heard steps after him and knew by the weight of them that it was Epps. More than that, he could feel his agent's eyes boring into his back. Roarke stopped in his tracks and turned on him. "What? What is it—?"

"Mills? You're going to see Mills? Or just that general direction?"

Roarke was momentarily struck into silence. So Epps knew about his visits to Cara. Or guessed. He could wait for the explosion, or he could just have it out. "Okay, let's hear it—"

"You were doing what with Rachel Elliott last night?" Epps demanded.

"I went by the House," Roarke admitted.

"You didn't *go by*. You *took* Elliott out of that house in the middle of the night. Just in time for that girl to disappear before the prelim."

Roarke stared at him. "You think I *planned* that?"

"Just before the prelim. Can't buy that kind of timing."

"Do you also think I somehow engineered the murder of that scumbag by a sixteen-year-old girl?"

His agent stared back, tall, dark, and murderously angry. "I think at this point you could've planted the razor yourself."

Roarke was staggered. "You are way out of line."

Now Epps was in full-tilt fury. "*I'm* out of line? *I* am?"

Roarke felt his own blood rising. They were close to blows now, and he summoned everything in him to stand down. "We'll talk about this tomorrow."

He turned to walk down the hall. Epps called out behind him. "Talk about what? Name it. Talk about *what*, goddamn it!" Roarke walked on, nearly blinded by his rage.

Chapter 16

He didn't go to the jail. Epps had made at least that much of an impression.

He got as far as the Civic Center garage, then called Mills and briefed him on the talk with the girls at the Belvedere House, which boiled down to a personal motive for Jade to kill DeShawn, but not a single clue to her whereabouts.

And then he drove home. The fog was so thick he had to hunch over the steering wheel, squinting out at the vague shapes illuminated by the hazy line of his headlights. His fight with Epps was still ringing in his mind.

Rage had dissipated, replaced by guilt. Guilt about lying to Epps, guilt about using Rachel. Above all he was taunted by the same questions he'd been struggling with since he'd learned of Jade's disappearance.

Were there signs? Should I have known?

Known what? That she was holding on to the razor that Cara killed Ramirez with? That she would kill DeShawn and plant the razor, knowing it would create reasonable doubt about Cara's guilt?

How could I have known? How could anyone?

Back in Noe Valley, he did the inevitable circling for parking and scored a space just a block and a half away from his apartment. By San Francisco standards, practically in his own front yard.

As he got out of the car and headed for his building, his head was still full of the scene from the alley and the rest of the day. The pimp sprawled in his own blood. The look in Shauna's eyes when she asked Roarke if Jade had killed him. Now that he was thinking about it, so eerily reminiscent of Jade asking about Cara's killings. . .

He was pulled from his thoughts by his own instincts, like an early warning system: an urgent flash of certainty that something needed his attention. He scanned the sidewalk, the pools of darkness beneath the trees. A cold breeze moved the shadows . . . but there was no one.

He relaxed, but not completely, and moved up the concrete steps to the gated stoop of his building, still on alert. As he pushed the key into the gate's lock, he heard a step, and he spun, his hand reaching for his weapon.

A figure stood at the bottom of the steps, looking up at him. A slim, slight shadow in dark pants and a hoodie. *A kid?* he had time to wonder. *Jade? Erin?*

He stared down into the dark. What he could see of the face was young and androgynously feminine: short dark hair, dark eyes, a sharp nose.

"Take your hands out of your pockets," he ordered.

She complied, slowly withdrawing hands from her hoodie. She held her empty fingers up ironically. "Feeling a little jumpy, Agent Roarke?"

The voice was slightly hoarse. An accent in the vicinity of New York.

"Who are you?" Roarke demanded.

The girl/woman smiled slightly and responded in that gravelly voice. "You can call me Bitch."

Instantly he knew. The blogger.

"I've been waiting for you," she continued.

"It's way past office hours," he told her. "And this isn't my office."

"I don't think you really care about that," she answered, and privately he had to admit she had a point.

"Did Molina send you?" he demanded.

"Molina?" she asked with exaggerated innocence. "I don't know what you mean."

"Then what do you want?"

"I thought I could buy you a drink and we could talk about DeShawn Butler."

Now everything in him was on alert. "What do you know about Butler?"

The young woman's voice went flat and hard like slate. "I know he was a predatory fuck, like Danny Ramirez. I know he sold teenage girls on the street because it's a safer gig for him than selling drugs. How much lower can a person be, Agent Roarke?"

Roarke moved down a few steps but kept his distance and watched her hands. "I don't disagree, but where are you getting your information?"

"The streets are talking. Lots of interested parties. Everyone wants to know about Cara."

Roarke felt himself tensing in spite of himself. "What about Lindstrom?"

"She's not the one who should be locked up, here. And I think you know it."

He said the only thing he could. "We have laws in this country."

"The laws aren't working."

He knew he had no counter to that. *But if there wasn't the law, what was there?*

"So that's the plan?" he asked sharply. "You're going to make her into a heroine?"

Her eyes drifted someplace far away. "There are lots of plans. Lots of them. And we don't have to *make* her into anything. She is what she is."

Roarke knew that for a fact. But before he could answer, the blogger added, with a slight, distant smile. "Maybe it's time."

For the second time that day, he felt spectral fingers on the back of his neck. "Time for what?"

"Time for a reckoning."

He looked down on her, and she up at him.

"So. DeShawn Butler," she said. "Any thoughts on that little bit of karma?" She waited expectantly.

He was about to speak, then realized that in the middle of a media blackout he'd ordered himself, he was talking to a journalist, and one whose reach he didn't even want to contemplate.

"No comment," he said. He turned back up the steps and unlocked the gate of his apartment, leaving the blogger outside in the dark.

Chapter 17

She wakes with *It* crouched outside the cell, watching her.

She sits up in the dim gray cube, her heart pounding in her chest, every instinct on alert. The barred door swings open, and Driscoll's long shadow slides into the cell.

It slowly smiles at her, and she sees jagged teeth. "They want you in Health Services," he tells her in a voice leering with anticipation.

In the other bunk, Kaz lies on her side. Her eyes are wide open. She does not move, does not make a sound. Her gaze meets Cara's, one sickened, terrified look, then she shuts her eyes and stays still. It is the only thing she can do.

Cara stands up from the cot. Every muscle in her body is tensed to fight. *It's time. Even possibly the final stand.*

She will need to kill . . . or kill herself. She has rehearsed it in her mind a hundred times, a thousand.

Not in the cell, though. He will not do anything in the cell.

She turns to be cuffed and waits passively, controlling her breath, while she holds her elbows subtly splayed. She learned to slip through cuffs when she was twelve. She has practiced ever since, folding her body as she drops into a crouch, stepping back over her wrists ... then standing in one fluid motion, bringing her cuffed arms up to use as a battering ram or slipping chained wrists over a neck. She can do it in seconds.

The guard's fingers close tightly around her arm, digging into the muscle. She feels the scaly grasp, smells the stinking breath of the Beast. She does not flinch. He pulls her out of the cell and shoves the door shut. The automatic lock clangs into place.

They walk down the dark, foul corridor, past the cells where some inmates lie sleeping and others lie still like Kaz, frozen in fear, willing themselves silent.

She breathes slowly, in rhythm with her steps. Balancing herself on her legs, feeling the strength in her thighs and hips, stilling her racing heart, focusing rage in her hands and fingers. And rehearsing the moves in her head. *Drop to a crouch, step through with right foot then left, unfold to standing.* Every muscle connected to another, connected to her bones, powered by will. And her nails carefully bitten to razor sharpness.

It will not have her.

The guard is behind her, pressing up against her now. "I know who you are," *It* croaks, the familiar rasping voice.

"I know what you are," she replies, too low for anyone but *It* to hear. She grounds her feet on the floor, her thighs over her knees, ready to drop.

There is a rattle down at the end of the corridor, and a second guard steps from the shadows at the end of the hall.

Two of them.

But Driscoll's grip has loosened.

Cara draws her breath deep inside her and drops.

DAY FOUR

Chapter 18

There is pounding. Some violent struggle. Cracking, splintering . . .

Roarke pulled himself out of a dazed sleep. Not to some epic battle going on around him. Someone was pounding on his front door.

He grabbed for a robe and stepped out into the long darkness of the hall.

As he approached the door he glanced at the side table, at the drawer where he kept his service weapon . . .

Then he heard a familiar voice. "Roarke, goddamn it. Open up."

Mills.

Roarke shot the bolt and pulled open the door. The detective stood in the dim hall outside, in a state of dishevelment and grim dismay.

"Your damn phone is off. Your guys got the DNA results back. It's Ramirez's blood on the razor that killed Butler." Before Roarke could even process the information, Mills continued, "Molina's going in to see the judge this morning."

The adrenaline jolt shook Roarke fully awake. "To move the prelim up? To ask for a dismissal?"

"All of the above, what the shit do I know? We need to get over there *now*."

Roarke backed up, then turned toward his bedroom. "Five minutes."

It was a zoo. The courthouse steps were entirely packed. Not just the steps; the sidewalks and the streets were jammed with people. Swarming reporters and news vans bristling with satellite dishes, illegally parked anywhere they could find a space. Protesters crowding the street, strategically placed at the intersection of Bryant and Seventh, so anyone driving by would get a full view of the commotion.

Patrol officers attempted to direct traffic at the clogged intersections, while mostly female demonstrators marched the sidewalks with hand-lettered signs: "Justice for Cara." "Free Cara Lindstrom." "Cara is my heroine." "War on rape culture NOW."

There were images on those signs, too, skeletal depictions of Santa Muerte, and a few actual masked skeleton figures. One was dressed in a long white gown, wearing a skull mask and flowered hat, carrying a globe in one hand and a scythe in the other.

Mills blinked at that one. "Jesus Christ," he muttered, and Roarke knew the detective was experiencing the same sick, surreal feeling he was.

Ahead in the crowd, Roarke caught sight of a tall hulk of a man, a dark, familiar face. Epps. The agent spotted him at the same time and shouldered his way through the crowd toward him and Mills. The three of them huddled, a tight knot in the surge of onlookers.

"What the holy fuck is going on here?" Epps looked around in disbelief.

Roarke recalled the blogger's words of the night before. *"Time for a reckoning."* The blogger, the people she worked with, Molina, maybe all of them, working in concert to make this case headline news.

He spoke it aloud. "Molina leaked it to Bitch that they were going in to see the judge. She must have."

Whether that would pressure the judge into dismissing the case was anyone's call. It could just as easily go the other way. Roarke was floored by the risk Molina was taking: an enormous, all-or-nothing roll of the dice.

"How did this happen so fast?" Epps demanded, shouting over the crowd.

Mills looked disgusted and resigned all at once. "Stanton disclosed the DNA results on the razor to Molina. She musta called the judge last night. I'm betting she's asking for a dismissal."

"Can that even happen?" Epps was in a fury. But they all knew the answer to that. A judge could do pretty much anything, and San Francisco judges leaned heavily on the side of protecting the rights of the accused.

"Lots of pressure from the media, too. This was the front page of the *Chronicle* today." Mills handed over a rolled-up newspaper that looked like he'd been using it for batting practice. Epps unfurled it to reveal the headline:

"*'Miracle Girl' held without bail, without evidence.*"

Mills summed it up. "Valiant survivor of unspeakable crime now unjustly accused, held without bail, exculpatory evidence, blah-dee-blah blah. There's a Twitterstorm, too, Facebook memes. All over the Internet. Looks like Molina called every reporter in the book."

With all kinds of help from Bitch, Roarke thought. He could see the young blogger on the sidewalk in front of his house, gazing up at him through the dark.

"*Maybe it's time.*"

"What does Stanton have to go in with?" he asked Mills.

"Without Jade? Fuck all. Our girl may be taking a walk."

Roarke's adrenaline surged. He tried to keep his voice neutral. "Is Lindstrom in there now?"

Epps was not fooled by his carefully bland tone. He shot Roarke a bitter look.

"I'm not clear on that," Mills answered. "Something weird is going on." Roarke felt an inexplicable shiver of worry.

The men shouldered their way up the steps, parting the masses before them. Even in a jacked-up crowd like this one, a phalanx of three law enforcement heavies was nothing anyone was willing to tangle with.

Inside the too-warm lobby of the Hall, the crowd was almost as thick: packed bodies massing in the marble halls, wrapped in winter coats. Roarke could see courtroom security guards communicating across the corridors with walkie-talkies. Expecting trouble.

Inside he was fixated on Mills' last remark. *"Something weird is going on."*

If Cara wasn't at the courthouse, what did that mean? Had something happened? What was Molina trying to do?

He looked over the sea of faces. And then he saw her. That explosion of hair, the mosaic eyes.

Jade.

It can't be. Roarke was dazed. *Would she really risk coming here?*

She hovered just inside the heavy front doors, dressed in a leather jacket and jeans. A hundred people between them. He stared through the throng, and, as if feeling him, she looked across the sea of faces, caught his eye . . . and she knew him. For one crackling moment she held his gaze, that intelligence blazing through the crowd. He was breathless with the life force of her.

Then in a flash she was slipping backward, pushing out through the front door.

Roarke felt someone grab his arm from behind. He spun and saw Epps staring into his face. "What?"

"I just saw her," he muttered. "Jade."

He pulled away from Epps and muscled through the milling people after her, shoved his way through one of the front doors.

Outside, the courthouse steps were even more packed than before. Protesters chanted on the sidewalk below, a swell of overlapping voices. "Free Cara! Free Cara! Free Cara!"

Roarke stood at the top of the steps, bracing himself against the ebb and flow of the crowd, and scanned the faces for the girl, focusing on anyone moving downward.

At first it seemed hopeless . . . but she was easy to spot: that wild hair. She was halfway down the steps, moving like water through the masses toward the street.

He lunged after her, maneuvering around bodies dressed in thick overcoats. *What had possessed her to come? Could she be thinking of testifying after all? Or she just couldn't stay away?*

He reached the protesters packing the sidewalk and scanned the crowd at street level, looking for Jade's hair. The chanting surrounded him. "Free Cara! Free Cara! Free Cara!"

There was no sign of Jade on the sidewalk. He turned slowly, in desperation . . . and lasered in on a young woman getting into a taxi at the curb.

Not Jade, he thought, staring at her. Short hair—wait, no, she was wearing a hat. And as she stooped to get into the car, he spotted the tattoo on the back of her neck, spiraling up into the curls at the nape. She'd scooped her hair up into a cap, taken off her jacket.

Roarke pushed forward against the crowd of protesters in front of him. He was jostled by startled and then angry onlookers, but he shoved back and burst through the last living wall of people . . . just as the taxi pulled away.

He started toward it, focused on the license plate. 4CND 542.

He was already reaching for his phone as he scanned the traffic for another cab. But San Francisco was not like New York, with its yellow cabs available every few seconds in a continuous stream. Here taxis were plentiful mainly around the bigger hotels and shopping strips like Market Street, and certain tourist havens, which the Hall of Justice decidedly was not.

He ran out in the middle of the street, at the same time auto-dialing Singh. He shouted into the phone, "I need the dispatch of the Yellow Cab company. Vehicle with plate 4CND 542. I just saw Jade get in. Track that cab."

"I am on it, Chief," his agent's voice came back.

Cars were honking around him, but there was not a taxi in sight. The sidewalks were mobbed, so Roarke kept to the street as he jogged back around the corner to Bryant Street, the front of the Hall, where there was always a line of black-and-white patrol cars at the curb.

He ran along the line of parked vehicles, suit coat flapping, until he spotted a uniform behind the wheel of a patrol car. He halted beside the car and slapped his open credentials wallet against the passenger window.

The startled officer lowered the window. Roarke shouted at him, "Assistant Special Agent in Charge Roarke. I'm in pursuit of a material witness to the hearing going on inside. Need assistance."

"Uh, yes sir."

Roarke pulled open the door and dropped into the seat just as his phone buzzed. Singh spoke into his ear. "Cab is headed to the bottom of Market. Number One Embarcadero."

Roarke's mind was racing. *The Ferry Building. So many stores. BART access. Ferry access. Christmas shoppers.*

"Ferry Building," he told the young officer beside him.

The uniform hit the lights and siren, but the street was so clogged there was no place for cars ahead of them to pull off.

Roarke sat in the stalled traffic in agonized frustration.

His phone buzzed again and he grabbed for it. Mills. "Where the fuck are you?" the detective demanded through the phone.

"I saw Jade."

"You're shitting me."

"I don't think so," Roarke answered, though he was beginning to wonder, himself.

"Why the . . ." Mills drifted off, clearly brooding on exactly what Roarke had been wondering since he saw her. *Why?* was the question. *What is she doing?*

The traffic ahead of them opened up, and the young uniform zoomed the patrol car forward.

"I'm in pursuit," Roarke told Mills. "Cab's dropping her at One Embarcadero. I'd appreciate some backup."

"I'll get cars on the way."

"She's in a motorcycle cap with her hair tucked up. Leather jacket, jeans. Alternating jacket on and off. White jersey underneath."

"Gotcha."

Market Street was decorated for Christmas: lights strung over the street; giant, glittery tinsel wreaths; extravagant window displays in the high-end retail stores. Roarke leaned forward in his seat, staring down the sidewalk through businesspeople rushing in and out of office buildings and tourists headed for the Ferry Building. Even on a good day nowhere near the holidays, the area was infamous for traffic jams. Two blocks from the bottom of the strip, Roarke was reaching for his door handle, unable to wait.

"I'll take it from here."

"Sir, can I assist?" the young uniform asked tensely.

Roarke took a millisecond to consider. *Tell the kid what Jade looks like? Have two pairs of eyes on the crowds?*

No time. And this was his. If anyone was going to spot her, it would be him.

"Thanks. I've got it," Roarke said, catapulting out of the cruiser.

But once on the street, he scanned the blocks ahead of him in despair. The bottom of Market Street hosted a street fair most days, tented stands where artists and artisans sold crafts, produce, jewelry, knockoff purses. At Christmas the fair was three times its normal size, swelled by seasonal craftspeople, street magicians and acrobats, carolers strolling, dressed in Dickensian finery, a steel pan band playing a Jamaican version of "Jingle Bells."

To top it off, the sky was starting to mist. Umbrellas popped up like mushrooms, making it even harder to see through the crowd.

Roarke turned on the pavement in the cold rain, taking in the aisles of stalls, scanning the shoppers. He figured there were two ways

Jade could have gone: to the Embarcadero BART station, which could take her to any one of four sides of the bay . . . or to the Ferry Building, with its artisanal shops and restaurants and the ferryboats that took commuters and tourists across to Oakland, Sausalito, and Vallejo.

Or she got out of the cab blocks ago and just took off anywhere in the city, he told himself. *Anywhere. Anywhere. What was I thinking, that I could find her?*

Except that he knew. He heard her voice in his head.

"Do you believe in destiny, Agent Roarke?"

Despite the odds, he found himself striding through the roughly parallel rows of tents in the fair, dodging singers and jugglers, winding past vendors minding their tables of embroidered bags, Christmas ornaments, fuzzy sweaters and ponchos, San Francisco memorabilia. And he felt a glimmer of hope.

It's like the Haight, the carnival atmosphere. Jade's kind of place.

He scanned everyone, everything around him for that hair. But more, for a *feeling.* A sense of her.

"Come on, Jade," he muttered. "I know you're here."

His pulse jumped as his phone buzzed in his coat pocket. He glanced at the screen before punching on to Mills' gruff voice.

"She's out."

Roarke stopped in the aisle of tables not following. "Out where? Jade?"

"Lindstrom. Lindstrom is out. Molina asked for bail and the judge agreed. They posted bond immediately."

Roarke turned in the crowded market, taking in the kaleidoscope of people around him. He was reeling.

"Where is she?"

"She and Molina never came out of the Hall."

Now Roarke felt a sick dread. "Call you back." He searched his contacts, punched Molina's number . . . strode past a cacophony of colors with the phone to his ear. Voice mail clicked on, then the lawyer's brusque voice.

He stood still, paralyzed. And in the end he disconnected without leaving a message, as there was nothing he could think of to say but "Where is she?"

And that point, he had a feeling, was already moot.

Chapter 19

She sits in the passenger seat of the Lexus as the lawyer inches through the downtown traffic, snarled in even more knots than usual because of the protesters. The car is a luxurious, soundproofed cocoon; she can barely hear the engine, much less any street noise. It intensifies the sounds going on inside her. Her whole body is humming; she feels as if her blood is too much for her veins, as if she will burst at any second.

She has been in a daze since the shadow appeared in the jail corridor, and in the moment that she fully expected to fight to the death, the second guard took her from Driscoll, out of the grasp of *It* . . . out of the jail to the courtroom.

Once again, against all rational odds, she has been spared, saved by whatever it is that guides her.

Now freedom is just outside the car door.

Beside her, at the wheel, the lawyer is jubilant. "I never had any doubt," she keeps saying. "It is simple justice."

Cara doesn't know about justice, but clearly it is meant. The instrument of her liberation at the courthouse is entirely unexpected, and unnerving. An image is clear in her mind: the flaming girl standing over another pimp, dead in a pool of his own blood. The implications are vast; the thought is vertiginous, the stuff of dreams or nightmares. But that she must consider later. Now she must be entirely in the moment. Nothing can distract her from the task at hand.

She looks out the window—right into the hollow eye sockets of a skull staring back at her. A figure in a long, white lace dress, with a skull mask, standing on the street corner as pedestrian traffic flows around her.

The car moves on, and the figure is gone. Cara sits back, holding herself very still.

The lawyer is asking her something, and she has to focus on the words. The lawyer repeats, "Where do you want to go?"

She has considered this, and she responds automatically. "The Hyatt. On Market Street." It is a huge hotel and the closest she can think of, just blocks away. And it has other advantages as well.

The lawyer glances at her, a quizzical look. "Are you sure . . ." She trails off, the question hanging in the air.

Cara waits. The lawyer finishes delicately. "Do you want to be so close by?"

To the jail, she means. To the courthouse. To Roarke.

"I need a shower," she answers. "And to sleep."

The lawyer looks at her, but whatever she is thinking, she merely nods.

Cara looks back toward the street corner, but there is no sign of the skull-masked figure.

Three blocks later the lawyer pulls the Lexus into the small drop-off area of the massive hotel and stops at the curb. She turns from the wheel to Cara in the seat, and Cara feels an emotion coming from the older woman that is hard to interpret. Ambivalence would not be surprising, nor would apprehension.

"We'll need to meet as soon as possible," Cara says, to circumvent the inevitable question.

"Of course." The lawyer sounds surprised. It was not what she expected, which is the point.

Cara continues, letting her voice be hesitant, as if she is thinking things through only now, in the moment. "Late tomorrow. I have to sleep. And if we could meet here, rather than your office . . . or someplace else you can arrange that is . . ." She trails off, letting the lawyer fill in the details in her mind. The reporters, the immense crowd at the courtroom—the shock of which is one of the things Cara herself must process, once she is out and alone. Her visitor has delivered on her promise. She may have gone much further than Cara ever expected.

"Somewhere private would be best, yes," the lawyer agrees. She does not, even obliquely, remind Cara of the penalties for disappearing. They understand each other. And as her client reaches for the door handle, the older woman says quickly, "I'm very glad for you, Cara."

She turns back. "Thank you," she says. "For everything." And she shuts the door, severing connection. She has no intention of seeing the lawyer ever again.

The Hyatt is a huge hotel, with plenty of foot traffic from local businesses, and something of a tourist attraction for its *Blade Runner*–style expanse of atrium, escalators, and terraces. People traversing the lobby tend to gape upward at the high-rise interior design with its dozens of ascending balconies and planters, or at the massive metal sculpture centerpiece, a circular whorl that could be anything from a giant pinwheel to an abstract flower or possibly even the sun. There is much ogling and photographing rather than paying attention to faces. And this distraction is useful to her. But the hotel's primary appeal at the moment is its location: just steps from the Embarcadero BART station.

The lawyer has given her cash, five thousand drawn from one of Cara's own accounts, and a prepaid credit card under the office name with two thousand more on it to cover hotels and other venues that require plastic. Far more than enough for now. No one has any idea of the rest of her resources; the numbers and locations are all in her head. There is nothing the jail took from her that she needs.

She looks around at the soaring space of the lobby and her eyes rest for a moment on the gleaming metal sculpture. She sees not a flower, or a pinwheel, or a sun. She sees a globe.

She can go anywhere from here.

Chapter 20

Molina returned Roarke's call as his taxi was fighting traffic on Market, heading back to the Bureau.

"Where is she?" he demanded.

The lawyer's voice was impeccable calm. "Agent Roarke, you know I'm not going to tell you that. After all she's been through, at the very least she deserves her privacy."

Roarke put his head back against the seat and closed his eyes and wondered how many ways what he was about to say would come back on him.

"Call her. Call her and tell her I want to see her."

There was a long silence on the phone.

"Incredible," Molina said softly. And then all Roarke could hear was the silence of her disconnect.

He put the phone on the seat beside him. Almost instantly it vibrated again and he grabbed for it.

Instead of Molina, he heard Singh's dark velvet voice. "Agent Epps phoned me that Lindstrom has been released."

There was a delicate pause, the meaning of which Roarke did not want to contemplate. *Is there anyone I'm fooling by now?* he asked himself bleakly. On the end of the line, Singh continued.

"I have been putting myself in her place, and I imagined that she would need not just immediate cash, but perhaps a credit card, which Molina may well have helped her with. An attorney of Molina's caliber is useful for so many incidental amenities."

Even through his distraction, Roarke was impressed by his agent's canny thinking.

"I did a search, and I have found a credit card issued to Molina's firm was used to charge a room at the Hyatt Regency on Market Street at 2:03 p.m."

Roarke felt an electric surge through his body. He was two blocks away. He reached for the door handle and his wallet simultaneously, pulling the door open even as he threw money at the cabbie, and then he was running down the sidewalk toward the hotel.

He barreled through the revolving door of the Hyatt, giving several startled guests a faster exit than they had expected.

The first sight of the lobby made him pause. He had been to the hotel for various functions but was always taken aback by the hugeness of the lobby, its expanse of high-rise terraces, the massive metallic sculpture.

He crossed to the reception desk, showed his credentials to get a key card for Cara's room, and rode the glass elevator up to the seventeenth floor in an agony of impatience.

There was a "Do Not Disturb" sign on the door of her room, and it slowed Roarke's approach as he realized the implications. What if she was inside? Could it be that simple, just to open the door and find her there, turning to him, or in bed, languid and vulnerable and . . .

Those thoughts came in a split second, before he had the presence of mind again to shut them down. He had another second's absurd contemplation about whether to knock, which would only be giving her time to prepare to kill, though in truth he knew she would not do him harm. Probably.

And then he used the key.

Chapter 21

He stepped into the darkened room.

The blackout curtains were drawn, and he experienced a simultaneous jolt of adrenaline . . . and a different kind of excitement. He fought down the immediate impulse to draw his weapon and let his eyes adjust to the light as he stared through the dark toward the bed.

The bedclothes were in disarray, which was a jolt of another kind. But as he focused through the dimness, he realized there was no one under the blankets.

He stood still in the room, absorbing it. There was no sense of any occupant.

He moved to the windows and pulled back the blinds. Light streamed in and he turned away from the brightness. His eyes moved over the disheveled bed, the clothes thrown on the armchair . . .

He strode to the bathroom door, pushed it open, hit the light—and saw towels on the floor, hotel bath products open on the sink. A honey fragrance lingered in the air.

Staged, his mind was telling him through the crush of disappointment and despair. *She was here for five minutes, if that.*

He could see it all.

After checking in, her next stop is the gift shop, where she uses cash to buy all new clothes in sizes too big for her, to conceal the real proportions of her body. She adds a bag, a winter hat, and sunglasses, which so many Californians wear even on winter days that she will not stand out.

Then she goes up to the room and in less than four minutes total she changes, tucks her hair entirely into the hat, tosses her court clothes on an armchair, pulls the bedclothes down on the bed and shakes them to create a slept-in effect. She stops for a moment, looking down at the bed, and imagines Roarke finding the room. What she is doing now may mislead local law enforcement into thinking she will be returning to the room, but it will not fool him. And she wonders. If it is only a game, why is she doing it? Yet it is what she has always done, and she continues.

In the bathroom she runs the shower for a few seconds and opens shampoo and conditioner and lotion, throws some towels on the bathroom floor, then hangs the "Do Not Disturb" placard on the outside doorknob and rides the glass elevator back downstairs.

She walks out onto the sidewalk into the gray mist and bustle of pedestrians and crosses the fifty yards to the BART station, where she uses a machine to buy a ticket with cash.

Then she rides the long, steep escalator down to the underground platform, feeling the rumble of the approaching train in the tunnel around her as a rush of exhilaration. Freedom . . . and anticipation.

There is much to do.

Chapter 22

He sat on the bed in the room that Cara had left, and his brain turned over possibilities.

She is so expert at this. It's been her whole life, on the road, in the wind. She could go literally anywhere. Anywhere in this country, anyway.

He doubted she would risk international borders. There was no need, and she hadn't shown any inclination to do it so far, though so much of her history was a blank to him that he couldn't completely rule it out.

She didn't seem to do planes, either. He had no doubt she had fake IDs, good ones, and credit cards, certainly. Pre-9/11 she might have traveled that way unimpeded. Now it was far too much of a risk. And she seemed to like the road. She was proficient at stealing cars, and perhaps she also made use of buses. Anyone with cash could buy a ticket. But he doubted she would easily stomach the loss of control that riding a bus would entail.

The Bay Area held its own particular challenges to tracking her, being that public transportation was so easy and accessible. The hotel was steps from the BART station—not merely a station but a transfer station, the hub of four different routes on both sides of the bay.

It was the same problem he had just faced with Jade, who very likely had disappeared that same afternoon from the exact same station.

The thought was so startling it brought him to his feet.

Did they meet?

Have they somehow been in contact?

Jade couldn't have visited her in the jail. Minors weren't allowed without an accompanying adult.

But if Jade has a fake ID of her own . . .

He forced himself to sit down, slow down, think. It was so very unlikely.

Is it?

He felt his thoughts veering wildly out of control. Paranoia, conspiracy.

No such thing as coincidence . . .

The jail had records of Cara's visitors. He was already digging in his coat pocket for his phone to call Singh when he realized he couldn't ask her to check into the visitor list. Because she would find his own name as perhaps Cara's most frequent visitor. It would have to wait until he could look into it himself.

But maybe, just maybe, finding Cara meant finding Jade, too.

So do that. Find her.

He walked the room, thinking.

She could have boarded to ride the train in any direction, gotten off anywhere to boost a car . . .

And then?

She would be far, far away. But beyond that, there was little he really knew about what drove her. Except that whatever she did next would be accelerated by the cycle of the moon.

And it would involve blood.

He reached for his phone again and called. "Lindstrom checked into a room at the Hyatt—"

Epps didn't wait for him to finish. "Singh filled me and Jones in. You there?"

"Yeah. She booked the room but was never really here. Maybe five minutes, if that."

There was a beat on the end of the line. "So start searching for stolen cars," Epps said wearily.

"Always," Roarke answered. "But the Hyatt has the BART station right here. She could be on any side of the bay by now." He paused and looked out the tall windows in front of him. The city lights floated eerily in the fog. "It's the BART station closest to where Jade's taxi dropped her off."

There was a silence at the other end of the phone. "What the fuck . . . ?" Epps said softly.

"I don't know," Roarke said. And there was more silence between them. Roarke finally broke it. "Look," he said. For a moment he had no idea what he was going to say after that. "Call Mills. Let him know. I'm going to Molina now. I doubt she'll tell me anything, but . . ."

"Right," Epps said heavily. "Right."

Chapter 23

On the opposite side of the bay, she walks along the chilly, Christmas-lit sidewalks of Shattuck Avenue near the BART station in downtown Berkeley, passing trendy restaurants and microbreweries, cinemas, small retailers.

She must be on the road again as soon as possible. She should be on it now. But there is work to be done before she leaves, and it is far too early in the evening yet for that, and she has preparation to do.

She has been on the road and under the radar for a long, long time. Certain behaviors are natural to her. There is always a contingency plan. When she followed Roarke to the mountains last month, she knew the risk of apprehension was great, and she'd stored her false identities, her cash, her cards, and her master keys—keys with teeth filed down to fit pretty much any car of a particular make—in a rented PO box in a nearby town. She has several such drop locations in various cities she finds herself returning to; there is one here in Berkeley, which she has just visited to pick up cards and papers.

For lodging she favors airport hotels, where clerks are accustomed to a high turnover and to travelers who stay for only half a night, even just a few hours, due to flight delays. Motels along major highways are also good. Sometimes she is guided to the seedier kind of inner-city motel that rents by the hour, where she can perform her own kind of cleanup. There are several of that sort on University Avenue, with an eclectic mix of patrons: students needing more privacy than their dorm rooms provide, misguided tourists on a budget, and, of course, dealers of all kinds.

She checks in to one of the motels after stopping at several of Berkeley's ubiquitous secondhand stores to buy some scruffy clothes—student attire—as well as travel disguises: several wigs, makeup . . . and other items she will be needing for what is to be done later in the night.

As she lies back on the creaky bed, the image she has been blocking all day comes into her mind again. The girl with the body art and the wild mane of hair, standing over the dead pimp, lying in his own blood.

But that she must hold for later.

Now, as she told the lawyer, she sleeps.

Chapter 24

The sky was growing dark, but it was not long past business hours, and Molina's office was in the Mission, walking distance from Roarke's apartment. It was not a walk that many people would want to take at night. The stroll led him past the BART station at Sixteenth and Mission, a drug hub, where the mist under the sodium vapor street lighting seemed actually green from the clouds of marijuana smoke. Dealers and other criminal elements scattered like cockroaches when they saw Roarke coming.

The shops he passed were heavy on the taquerias, bodegas, and botanicas, with their candles and herbs and charms. As he continued down the street, deeper into the heart of the Mission, he slowed, noticing that the iron grillwork set around the trees was decorated with cavorting *Dia de los Muertos* skeletons.

Everywhere, he thought. It was an uncanny manifestation of Bitch's mythmaking.

As he stood looking at the dancing skeletons, he recalled the Santa Muerte masks and costumes he had seen at the courthouse, and Singh's words came back to him in a rush.

"There is something larger at work . . . a force beyond the simply human. A female vengeance against outrages."

It occurred to him that in some way, the saint had saved Cara. A surreal and slightly insane thought.

He felt a cold touch, like eyes on the back of his neck, and turned sharply to survey the dark street. But nothing moved but a few shuffling shadows. Homeless, drunk, lost . . . all of the above.

His pulse spiked as his phone vibrated in his coat pocket. He picked up, bracing himself for whatever was coming.

"Nothing to report," Epps said into his ear. "Just thinkin' of Lindstrom being loose. Wanted to make sure you made it home okay."

Even though he understood that his agent was concerned for his safety, Roarke felt a rush of irritation at the question. *What does he think, that I'm with Cara?*

He forced himself to answer calmly. "Just walked in," he lied. "Get some rest. We'll regroup in the morning." He disconnected and walked on.

The building where Molina had her office was a former warehouse with a run-down brick facade, yet there was something about the structure that made it stand out: a certain elegance in the moldings and scrollwork. He found a side entrance and located her nameplate beside the steel door, in Spanish and English: "The Offices of Sra. Julia Molina, *Abogada*, Attorney-at-Law." He buzzed the intercom, and an accented voice answered only, "*Digame.*"

"Special Agent Roarke, to see Ms. Molina."

There was a long pause, then the door buzzed open with no further comment or instruction. He stepped into a hallway lined in Spanish tiles. The original elevator was nothing more than a freight lift, but the steel doors had been burnished to a dull gleam. He rode up to the third floor, where he rang and was buzzed through a second set of locked doors.

Inside, the offices were decorated in the weathered style of the Mission, but there was nothing cheap about anything here. He looked around at the hammered-metal sculptures, the murals, the crude folk art, the softly gurgling fountain that looked as if it had been excavated from some crumbling roadside church, and knew that some skilled decorator had achieved this weather-beaten, vaguely religious effect at no small expense.

A Latina receptionist regarded him impassively from her antique desk. Before Roarke could speak, a voice came from behind.

"Agent Roarke."

He turned to find the diminutive attorney studying him from the doorway to the inner office. She looked him up and down.

"I can't say this is a surprise, but I don't see what good you think it will do, coming here."

Roarke wasn't sure himself. "I'm just asking for a minute."

After a moment she moved back, offering him passage.

"*Pase.*"

He stepped into a long, high-ceilinged, rectangular loft with a desk area, a meeting space with sofa and chairs, and one entire wall of bookshelves. More folk art was scattered in the room, and the light was low, shining in mosaic patterns from cutout metal lanterns and candleholders.

The lawyer closed the heavy plank door behind them and walked to the sofa area without taking a seat. Instead she stood by a wide window, watching him.

Roarke was about to speak when his eyes rested on a familiar statue among the rest of the folk art in the office. At the statue's feet were a small pile of cigarettes, an airline-size bottle of tequila, flowers, perfume, bread, water, candles . . .

An altar to Santa Muerte. And the candles in front of the skeletal figure were lit. Looking at it, Roarke felt a disquieting sensation that he couldn't quite identify.

He turned to Molina. "I didn't realize you were a practitioner."

"A petitioner," she said, and Roarke sensed some secret amusement. "There are higher authorities than the law."

He stared at her, wondering if she could possibly be serious. "It was a smart play, that Santa Muerte stunt today. Very mediagenic."

The lawyer's face closed. "I assure you it was no stunt. No gringo can really understand about *La Santísima Muerte*. The men of the Church have tried to destroy her, but the people keep her alive in their prayers. Because Santa Muerte is a saint who *does* something. The other saints have failed us, Agent Roarke. Santa Muerte is the court of last resort. She does not fail. She does what must be done."

Everything in him was rebelling against her words. "Even if murder is what it takes? Is that what your saint is about?"

"To do whatever it takes to right wrongs. Sometimes death for one is salvation for another." The lawyer watched him through the haze of candlelight, her face as inscrutable as the saint's. "You tell me that your way is working, Agent Roarke, and I will call you the liar that you are."

For a moment Roarke was without words. He knew she was right. She was watching him, and she nodded.

"So ask what you know I cannot tell you."

Until this moment Roarke had had no idea what he was going to ask, or say.

"I get it. Lindstrom's gone."

The lawyer opened her mouth but Roarke continued. "Right. Until she's called back into court she's not a fugitive—yet. I have no legal jurisdiction. It doesn't matter. I'm not looking for her. I'm looking for Jade."

The lawyer was still. "How could I possibly know where the girl is?"

"I think she came to see—" He stopped himself just before he said *Cara*. "—your client. I think she visited her in jail." He'd called the jail's visitor desk, but it was too late in the day to get the information he needed.

"You're wrong," the lawyer said.

Roarke looked at her. She was impassive. He couldn't pretend to read her, though he sensed that she was telling the truth. But whether she was or not, he was sure he would get no more from her on that subject. No matter. He would find out.

"Then I'm looking for the blogger who calls herself Bitch."

Molina's eyes widened in what Roarke read as mock surprise. "And why would you ask me?"

He felt hot impatience. "I know you've been feeding information to her all along. So, fine, that's what your clients pay you for. But there's a sixteen-year-old girl at stake now. I want to find her before she does something that lands her in prison for the rest of her life."

Molina looked at him, a long, hard look, sparing him nothing. "You're an interesting case, Agent Roarke," she said softly. "But I'm not sure you know what you're dealing with. Have you ever asked yourself if you're the right man for this job?"

"Only every day since it started," he replied, and meant it.

"I would say you are not. I would say there is no man right for this job. I would say that men should have nothing to do with this. It is a problem of such proportions it can only be solved by women."

He glanced at the Santa Muerte altar, at the shadows dancing over the skeletal face. Then he looked back to Molina. "Or by a saint?" he asked her, with an edge.

She smiled thinly. "*Es tiempo para un nuevo camino.*"

Roarke struggled with the Spanish. He understood her to be saying, "It is the hour for a new road."

Molina watched him in the moving candlelight. "*Vete a casa*, Agent Roarke. Go home. Go home and save yourself."

Chapter 25

She wakes to the sound of screams echoing off the cold walls of the jail. She jerks upright, her eyes wide in the dark, her whole body tensed to fight.

But there is no looming cell, no presence, just the streaked walls of the motel on University Avenue. And her mind is clear.

She rises from the sagging bed and dresses for what she needs to do. Black jeans, boots, black T-shirt, black hoodie, and a bulky dark wool coat and cap that conceal her sex. Then she walks out into the night.

The seedy streets outside the motel are coming alive. Homeless people and drug addicts staggering through the cold fog, deals of all kinds taking place on side blocks and in deserted parking lots. Fog obscures the moon, but she can hear it whispering behind the clouds.

She walks along in her thrift store camouflage and is not bothered. If she were, there is the new razor in her pocket.

Her preparations go smoothly. Transportation is only slightly time-consuming without immediate access to her master keys: a pair of scissors, purchased earlier at a dollar store, is all she needs to boost an old Toyota Camry. Another purchase she is conveniently able to make on the street, from one of the number of peripatetic addicts in the neighborhood. And earlier that evening, the secondhand store had provided the last element needed to implement her plan.

She is tense as she drives over the pyramid lights of the Bay Bridge, back into the mist-shrouded city that was only that morning her captor. There is no official manhunt for her; she is legally free until the court calls her back in and it becomes evident that she has jumped bail. But at the moment, it is only Roarke who will be looking for her.

Roarke.

This time, she will not be caught.

She drives on, disappearing into the fog.

Chapter 26

The fog was so thick that the shapes of other pedestrians loomed up on the sidewalk in front of him like the walking dead in some third-rate horror movie. The adrenaline spikes rubbed his already frayed nerves raw. The skeletal face of Molina's Santa Muerte statue hovered in his mind, along with the echo of the lawyer's words: *"It is time for a new road."*

Eerily similar to what the blogger had said to him on the dark street outside his house.

But tonight as he mounted the steps to his front door, there was no sign of the young woman who called herself Bitch. He had a strong feeling she wouldn't be easy to find.

Upstairs, he stepped inside his flat and stood in his dim hall for a long moment without moving before he stripped off his suit coat and hung it in the closet, then unstrapped his shoulder holster and hung it on the hook to the side of the door.

He turned in the hall to put his weapon in the drawer, and it hit him. The sense of presence.

There was someone in the living room.

For a fleeting, disoriented moment, he thought, *Cara.*

Then he thought of the blogger, hovering outside his building in the dark. And then of Molina and that imperious Latin voice.

"Sometimes death for one is salvation for another."

His hand tightened around the Glock. He pressed his back against the wall and eased down the hall toward the open archway of the living room, stepping on the balls of his feet to avoid making any sound. At the frame of the door he paused, listening to the darkness inside . . .

A male voice spoke from within. "I'm here."

Calm, gruff, and familiar. Snyder.

Roarke felt lightheaded with relief. He set the gun on the hall table behind him and stepped into the room, switching on a lamp.

His old mentor was seated in an armchair in front of the window. He looked across the room at Roarke. "Sorry to startle you. I must have fallen asleep." He cut a striking profile, with his tall, lean body and Nordic looks, but these days he was showing his sixty-odd years.

Roarke came farther into the room. He'd been expecting Snyder later in the week, had sent him spare keys several days earlier. "For a minute there, I felt like I was in a training exercise."

The older man half-smiled. "I left a message that I was here. I did worry when you didn't answer your phone."

"You've heard, then," Roarke said.

"About Cara, yes." The older man looked at him from across the dark room. "I apologize for the intrusion, but I thought it was best that someone be here. It's not inconceivable that she would come straight to you. She undoubtedly has some kind of plan. It will undoubtedly involve you."

Since the night of the October full moon, the twenty-fifth anniversary of the massacre of Cara's family, Cara had sporadically reached out to Roarke. It was how Roarke and Epps had busted the trafficking ring in the desert. One of Snyder's theories was that consciously or subconsciously, Cara wanted to team with Roarke in her mission, to work with him in some way, enlist his help in the killing she was committed to carrying out.

Roarke was aware of wild and uninterpretable emotions churning inside him at the idea that Cara would come to him. "She's free," he said in the most neutral tone he could muster. "She's always been able to live under the radar. There's no earthly reason she would stick around."

Snyder looked at him and underscored that lie with his silence before he commented. "Except that Cara has her own reasons, and self-preservation is not high among them."

After a beat, Roarke said, "No. It's not."

"So it's a good idea to be ready for whatever is to come."

Roarke walked a circle around the room. In the alcove there were files spread out on the table that was never used for dining. For once the files were not his own; Snyder apparently had been working there. Roarke moved to the table and realized the files were on Cara: old medical records, court files, the diagnoses that various psychologists and psychiatrists had branded her with during her childhood and teenage years in the social services system. A whole smorgasbord of psychological hypotheses, many of them conflicting.

He looked up from the files. "Did you find anything new?"

Snyder lifted his shoulders. "The failing of psychology is that it rarely takes into account a philosophy of good and evil or a spiritual component to crime. Joan of Arc listened to God and Cara listens to the moon. Is that schizophrenia? Perhaps. But there is an element of moral conviction that implies choice, not just biological compulsion. She's delusional, certainly. But she's also accurate. Not many people would argue against the fact that her targets are loathsome examples of our species, fully deserving of punishment. And practically, it's not difficult to find perpetrators of the sort she targets."

No one had to tell Roarke. There were perpetrators enough to make anyone in law enforcement despair.

Snyder nodded. "So perhaps she's not insane at all. Perhaps she's on a mission fueled by a very particular worldview: that there is actual evil in the world and that the most valid response to it is to eliminate it whenever possible."

Roarke looked at the older man. "I can't believe I'm hearing that from you."

Snyder smiled bleakly. "I'm tired. But . . ." He stopped, and it was a long moment before he spoke again. "The man we are pursuing in Montana rapes and kills children. He literally tore his last victim limb from limb. The boy was five years old."

Roarke felt a dark hole open inside him. Snyder shook his head, and he looked old.

"I'm sorry that I was too late to visit with Cara before her . . . release. I would very much like for once to talk with someone who would simply call that what it is."

"*It?*" Roarke asked, ironically.

Snyder held his gaze and repeated, "Evil."

Chapter 27

The run-down house in Daly City, a bedroom suburb of San Francisco, is as despicable a dwelling as she would have expected, hunched in a dark neighborhood of blocky housing and unkempt yards. She cruises past in the stolen Toyota, taking it all in. The lights are off in the house, and there is no car in the drive.

Her eyes and ears had been open for the entire period of her confinement. It had not been difficult to learn the home location of the guard called Driscoll. She had picked up on the general neighborhood. A quick online search of tax records at an Internet café had yielded the address. It is frighteningly easy to find anyone online. It is always her own policy to avoid leaving any kind of trail: paper, biological, or cyber.

She parks down the street, then sits back in the car seat, contemplating. It is an old house. Access will be easy. And the method of dispatch presented itself the first time the man rubbed up against her, reeking of tobacco . . . and another scent beneath that smokescreen.

It will not be anywhere near what he deserves. But adequate to the bottom line.

She sits in the dark for an hour, watching the street and the houses nearby, assessing who is home and who is not, keeping a close eye on the cheap timepiece she bought at the secondhand store. Aside from a few furtive comings and goings, the block is quiet. She knows the guard's schedule. She has another hour at least. When she has determined the least visible route of approach, she leaves the car, with the items she has brought concealed under a bulky man's coat and her hair tucked tightly into her hat. She is gloved, of course. Always gloved.

She slips into the side yard of the darkened house next door and jumps the concrete-block fence from there, slipping over the top and dropping into Driscoll's yard. It is a ragged thing: dormant grass, a grill on a concrete slab, beer bottles overflowing the trash can, neglected landscaping. The tangled old-growth bushes have their use as concealment, enabling her to move unseen around the perimeter of the house, studying the windows. But it will be even easier than that. The back door has not been updated, or even insulated. There is no deadbolt, just the old metal latch.

She steps up to the door and runs her gloved fingers over the plate. The latch is curved away from the doorframe, which requires a bit more than a plastic card, but not much. She inserts a card and does some finessing with a bent paper clip. It takes barely a minute to pop it open.

She steps inside, carefully pulling the door closed behind her, then stands in the dark of the entry off the kitchen, listening. There is a sour smell: sweat and beer and the faint trace of pot smoke. The latter makes her smile, without amusement.

She moves into the kitchen slowly, holding herself still and contained, making barely a ripple in the atmosphere of the house. The room is full of greasy surfaces, with dishes piled in the sink and more beer cans and bottles overflowing the trash. All good signs for her purpose.

Easy prey, she thinks with contempt. Now that there are no bars between them.

She moves out of the kitchen into an ill-furnished and equally cluttered living room, paying particular attention to the sofa and the television there. The TV is an old one. No doubt there is another.

She eases into the hall and notes the four doors along it. Bathroom, closet, two bedrooms.

She steps to the open door first. Driscoll's bedroom; she can smell him before she even reaches the door. But at the moment, empty. The room is taken up by a stained king mattress with a basic metal bedframe, no headboard. The plasma TV she has been expecting is here above the battered dresser, facing the bed, and there are empty bottles and an overflowing ashtray on the night table, porn magazines loosely stacked by the bed.

So easy.

She checks the watch again. He will be getting off work just about now, which gives her half an hour before the first moment he could arrive back at the house. But there is no guarantee that he will come straight home, so she will need to find a place to wait.

She stays several more minutes in the bedroom, just standing, memorizing every detail of the room: the distance between door and bed, the number of steps to cross the room, the height of the bed. Rehearsing in her mind. The door has a slight squeak, and she greases the hinges with the Vaseline she has brought to eliminate the noise.

Then she backs out through the door and goes to the second bedroom. Though there has not been a human sound since she entered the house, she listens at the door before carefully turning the doorknob. She pushes the door open . . . into a room piled with odds and ends. The bedstead there is old-fashioned, with a wooden frame and headboard. Boxes, trash bags, broken appliances are stacked on top of it, and there is barely any room to walk across the floor.

The air is cold and stale. Unused except as a junk room.

Perfect.

Chapter 28

Snyder had produced a bottle of whisky, whether in celebration or mourning, Roarke wasn't sure. Now neat glasses sat on the coffee table in front of them. And finally he asked what he had been thinking since Snyder first spoke the idea.

"You do believe in evil, then."

"Of course I do," Snyder said calmly. "How can I not?"

"So what is it?"

"What is evil?" The profiler smiled ruefully. "You mean, is it a force beyond human?"

"I don't know what I mean."

The older man's face was reflective. "I've only ever seen human beings perpetrate it. But in some cases it does seem . . . cumulative. Another reason I regret not being able to speak to Cara myself. Perhaps it's a concept that is only done justice in metaphor."

Metaphors again, Roarke thought. He stepped to the window and looked out. "She told me . . . She said *It* can't be killed."

"But we know that. We can only kill its agents. *It* is always with us."

Roarke turned back to his mentor and stared at him. "You really sound like you believe."

"I understand *It*," Snyder corrected. "As a metaphor."

"The Reaper wasn't a metaphor."

"Hughes was not a metaphor, no."

Roarke noticed the ambiguity of Snyder's answer, and it only increased his agitation. "So what about him?" he demanded.

Snyder remained maddeningly calm. "You want to know if there was something about him in particular. Something beyond what we've seen before."

"Was there?"

"Your Agent Singh and I have been compiling his history. There's nothing new. There was violent pornography involving prepubescent boys. Pets missing in the neighborhood where he grew up. A teenage job at a stable where one horse was violently attacked. Nothing we haven't seen before." Snyder shook his head. "You know as well as I do. There's nothing artistic or poetic about this kind of killer. They are rapists who have escalated their sadism to murder. They torture and kill for their personal sexual satisfaction. That's all. They're not worth even a footnote in history."

Roarke circled the room in agitation. "Except that the Reaper—Hughes—was paroled and started killing again the *same week* that I . . ." He stopped, not knowing how to finish the sentence. *The same week that I met Cara? The same week I started hunting her? The same week that I got pulled into this vortex of a case that never seems to end?*

Snyder finished the sentence for him. "The same week that your path crossed with the Reaper's only surviving victim. The week that this case, which was so very much a part of your childhood and your subsequent career, resurfaced on your doorstep."

It was that, and so much more. There was so much that was inexplicable about this universe Cara had drawn him into that Roarke sometimes questioned his own grip on sanity.

Snyder was watching him. "It seems—for the want of a better word—supernatural."

Roarke's mouth was as dry as dust. "Yes."

The older man spread his hands. "You first encountered the Reaper when you were just a child. Of course the killer took on mythic proportions for you, just as he did for Cara. But I can't call that supernatural."

"Cara does."

"Cara does, within whatever world system she operates under." Snyder glanced toward the psychiatric files on the table.

Roarke couldn't seem to stop himself from talking. "I asked her why she does it, if she doesn't think *It* can be killed."

Snyder turned back to him. "And?"

"She asked me why *I* did."

Snyder nodded, seeming almost amused by the response. "And why do you?"

Roarke was angry now. "How can I not?"

"Exactly. How can we not? So why is all this so troubling to you now?"

Because I don't think our way is working, Roarke thought, but didn't say.

Snyder looked at him with a sudden laser scrutiny. "Matthew, clearly this case has been wearing on you since the start. I know that parts of it have been conflicting."

Roarke braced himself, sure that Snyder was about to cross into the forbidden territory of his feelings for Cara. But after a pause, all the profiler said was, "You need to find a way to keep some distance."

Roarke knew. He just didn't know how. It was under his skin. Cara was under his skin.

"How?" he snapped aloud, his voice raw with impatience.

"Focus on facts."

Roarke almost laughed. The facts were almost as strange as the idea of a supernatural entity.

"Right. Facts. You got my memo on the Tenderloin murder."

Snyder reached for his glass, sipped from it. "Yes, thank you. Very interesting."

"Cara's free now because our key witness very likely planted the evidence that set her free. If Jade did that, it means that she killed DeShawn Butler. She's sixteen years old."

"And?"

"And what do you think of that?"

"It's statistically unlikely."

"Like Cara is statistically unlikely."

"Yes. Like that."

Roarke was pacing again. "And there's a whole other factor. What happened at the courthouse today . . ." He paused, struggling to put the feeling into words. "I've never seen anything like it. Protests, yes. This was—there was something—it hooked into something . . ."

Again Singh's words came back to him. "*A force beyond the simply human.*"

Snyder watched him, waiting.

"What do you know about Bitch?" Roarke asked abruptly.

"Ah," Snyder said, turning his glass in his hands thoughtfully. "They've certainly been hard at work here. I've been reading the coverage."

Roarke thought of the dark young woman who had waited for him outside his flat. "There's one of the group in particular. A blogger who seems to be spearheading this . . ." He realized he didn't know the word for what he meant. *Cause? Movement? Quest?* He finally settled on "This action. But I don't know how to find her. I don't suppose you have an in."

Snyder shook his head. "The whole principle of the group is viral. If a protest catches fire, people show up. I see the calls to action on Facebook and Twitter just like everyone else. I can't argue with their causes. And I can't argue with their results. But no. I don't know anyone inside."

It wasn't surprising; Roarke wasn't even sure why he'd asked. He finally stopped his restless circling and stood in front of the window. "Then I don't know what to do next."

Snyder lifted his hands, and now his voice was grave. "I'm afraid you have very little choice. You wait for what she will do. The one thing that's certain is that she will kill until someone stops her."

Chapter 29

The guard returns a little over an hour later.

She presses herself against the cold hardwood floorboards and breathes slowly in and out, listening to the sound of an SUV engine in the driveway, then footsteps on concrete, then the front door scraping against the badly painted doorframe.

The space she has cleared for herself under the bed in the spare room is a cramped but effective hideout. Lying against the floor, she can hear everything that happens in the house. Heavy work boots clumping across the living room floor planks into the kitchen. The sound of the refrigerator door opening, the clink of bottles shoved onto a shelf to chill, the smell of greasy fried chicken from a fast-food stop.

The footsteps move into the living room, and the inevitable blast comes from the TV.

She waits through the sound of junk television, mindless channel surfing for an hour, and another hour, until finally the heavy tread moves toward the bedroom and a different programming starts, and a different smell wafts through the cracks in the floorboards. Her body tenses as she feels the time approaching.

And when it is time, she slides noiselessly out from under the bed. She stands and carefully flexes and loosens her muscles.

Then she eases into the dark hallway. The TV in the guard's bedroom spills a blue and flickering light from the doorway. The feigned animal sounds of porn from the speaker cover her approach, and by now he is both stoned and drunk and distracted by the antics on the screen. Accustomed to being the hunter, not the hunted, he is not expecting the ambush. The door is silent as it swings open . . .

It senses her before the man does. She can hear *Its* rasping breath, the quick, revulsive recoil . . .

She lunges at the bed and holds the guard's head down at the forehead, feeling the reptilian surge under her hands. But she is too quick for *It*, and she has the advantage of surprise and height. She slices the razor across the neck, not too deep, nowhere near bone or tendon, only the artery. The artery is enough. The man's *gaaah* of shock almost covers *Its* silent screaming. Immediately the carotid is gushing, draining life force, and it is no difficult matter to hold his shoulders down to the bed until he is too weak to fight.

When he loses consciousness, she puts the old foam cushion she bought at the thrift store under his head and lights it with a silver lighter, backing off instantly as the pillow goes up in a flash of flame. Polyurethane. Almost solid gasoline. These days such cushions are sold soaked with flame retardants, but the older, more lethal ones are still surprisingly findable at secondhand stores, if you know what you are looking for. She backs off and tosses the lighter on the bed, along with an onyx hash pipe well coated with the resin of many uses.

She retreats farther, watching the flames encompass the guard. The pain is probably short-lived. She has no feeling about that either way. His elimination is her only objective. He will no longer be able to torture anyone.

Death comes quickly now, along with the pugilistic stiffening of limbs that will indicate to the coroner that the fire began when he was still alive, lending credence to an initial assumption of accidental death.

She stands at the doorway, breathing shallowly against the smell of cooking flesh, lingering only to see that his head and neck are burned, melting the surface evidence of the slice to his throat.

Then before the fire can spread farther, before the neighbors can see the blaze behind the curtains, she leaves the house, pulling the back door locked behind her. She jumps the concrete-block wall into the next yard and heads for the car. She is already hearing sirens as she starts the engine and pulls away.

The pipe and the lighter will survive the fire in some condition, suggesting the scenario: another addict falling asleep or passing out with a pipe in bed. The tox screen will show THC in his system from his own use; tests can detect the chemical in the body for nearly two weeks, often longer for habitual users. The real cause of death may be revealed later in postmortem, but that could be days away.

Roarke will know, of course, and the fire will mean the body is discovered immediately. But it will be a difficult case to prove, and not particularly attributable to her.

She does not mind the quick discovery. The jailed women will hear, Kaz and Lin and the others, and know they are safer.

But now she must be gone from this place, get at least enough distance to think. She has been given her freedom. It is not accidental. She knows there is a plan. It remains for her to listen.

So she drives. Behind her, the house blazes into the sky, the flames sending Driscoll to hell.

DAY FIVE

Chapter 30

Roarke opened his eyes to morning, after maybe two hours of troubled sleep. He could feel the emptiness of the flat. Snyder was already gone, back to the serial case in Montana.

Cara was out there, somewhere. Free.

And the profiler's words of the previous evening were the first thing on his mind as he woke:

"The one thing that's certain is that she will kill until someone stops her."

Roarke threw back the bedcovers, dressed, and went straight to County #8.

Without the crowd of protesters, the sidewalks and streets outside the Hall of Justice seemed deserted by comparison. Roarke climbed the steps with the dreamlike feeling that none of it had ever happened.

The supervisor at the jail's visitor booth was a stern and efficient African American woman. Roarke had phoned ahead to Mills to grease the wheels. When he requested the visitor list for Cara Lindstrom, the CO checked his credentials and then provided him with a sheet of names, dates, and times.

Roarke stepped back from the counter to study it. His stomach started churning, and his head was buzzing.

Molina had visited Cara seven times.

His own name was listed four times.

Erin McNally had visited three times.

And there were two other names, one unfamiliar, the other too familiar.

Someone named Andrea Janovy had visited once, two days earlier, and had been scheduled to visit again that afternoon; the visit was notated *Cancelled*. The visitor information sheet she'd filled out listed a driver's license number, a Richmond address, a phone number, and a date of birth. Andrea Janovy was twenty-seven years old. A little old for Jade to get away with, but not outside the realm of possibility. The blogger would certainly fit the age range.

The other name on the visitor list was Special Agent Antara Singh.

She was down on the sheet as having had a scheduled appointment three days ago. That appointment was also notated *Cancelled.*

Roarke stood for a long moment. He didn't know what to make of it.

He'd checked his cell phone downstairs at security. So he went back to the visitor booth and asked for a phone line. He used it to dial the number listed for Andrea Janovy; he was not surprised to reach only an automated recording asking callers to leave a message.

Then he called Mills.

"I need you to run someone down."

After filling the detective in on the information about Janovy, Roarke returned the phone to the visitor booth. He had no idea what to do with the revelation about Singh. But checking the visitor list was not his only purpose at the jail. He signed in with the supervisor to see Kaz Spinoza.

Kaz was not as high on the security list as Cara had been, and he was allowed to see her in the general visitation room. The space was packed to overflowing with holiday visitors; two dozen inmates sat with lawyers and families. Roarke waited at a stained table, seated awkwardly in a cracked orange plastic bucket chair. He was too aware of an unnerving number of young children, sitting with tired, middle-aged women, old before their time. Grandmothers become mothers again as their daughters served their sentences. Children too young to know why their mothers had been taken from them, growing up with prison a regular landscape of their lives. An education in hopelessness.

But Cara's out, he thought again. *Escaped.* He felt a lightness almost like exhilaration surge through his body . . .

He was pulled back to reality as a corrections officer approached. Not Driscoll, the one Roarke had warned off Cara, but a Latino man. He led a solid and hard-edged woman with leathery skin and a buzz cut. She took a seat across from Roarke in a truculent pose, hands on knees, chin thrust out.

Lesbian, he thought, and wondered how she'd reacted to Cara.

Kaz's lip curled as if she had heard his thought. "You rang?" she asked sardonically.

Roarke ignored her tone. "I'm here to talk about your cellmate, Cara Lindstrom."

"No shit."

He suppressed a flare of impatience. "No shit, and I'd appreciate it if you'd cut yours. If you have information I can use, it could mean a reduction of sentence. If you're interested, we'll talk. Should I leave so you can think about it?" He pushed back his seat as if to stand. Around them, other inmates and visitors glanced over.

"You're here now," Kaz said quickly.

Roarke took a beat, then settled back into his chair.

"I'm looking for her. So I'm looking for anything she said that would point me in her direction."

"She wasn't a big chatter."

Roarke forced himself not to react. The woman couldn't help herself; she had a chip on her shoulder the size of the building.

He answered evenly. "You see, now, that's not information I can use. You're going to have to get specific."

There was a wary pause, in which Kaz might have been considering a real reply. But when she spoke, it was the same flip evasion. "We didn't talk about vacation hot spots."

"Again, not helpful. Any thoughts on what she would do next?"

Kaz smiled. It wasn't a joyous, happy kind of smile. "Seems like she's had the same plan for a while."

Roarke kept his face impassive. *So she does know about Cara's history. Now we might be getting somewhere.*

"Did she talk to you about it?" he asked, without changing his tone.

"Not really. That'd be why I said 'seems.'"

"All right. Then did you get the *sense* there was anyone in particular she might want to harm?"

Kaz stared at him. "I think we both know the answer to that. Way I see it, there's a whole shitload of people out there might want to start locking their doors."

True, but nothing Roarke didn't already know.

"I said, 'in particular,'" he repeated.

"I'd say *men* in particular," she shot back.

Roarke was tired of the sparring. He'd just about given up hope of getting anything useful out of her.

"What about *particular men?*"

That last prompt did something to her; he could see it in her stiffened posture, the sudden ambivalence in her eyes. He watched her face with interest. And for a moment he thought what he was seeing was fear.

But just as abruptly she shut down whatever was going on inside her. Her face was blank again. She had not said a word.

"No thoughts at all? Disappointing." He started to rise again.

"Driscoll," Kaz said suddenly, and so quietly he wasn't sure at first that he'd heard her. But he recognized the name of the guard he'd confronted. He felt a chill, and then a rush of anger so explosive he had to force himself to exhale, to feign calm. He sat back down carefully, spoke as softly as she had. "Did anything happen?"

Kaz's voice was so low he had to lean forward to hear. "She wouldn't be the first."

Roarke pressed his hands on the table, spoke slowly through the pounding in his head. "Has this been reported?"

She gave him a glacial look. "Not lately."

"I need to hear about it."

The cool vanished. He felt the quick, hot hatred coming off her. "You going to protect us in here, Secret Agent Man?"

"I will," he answered back, a reckless but automatic response.

"Sure you will." She shoved back her plastic chair and stood. "You get to walk out of here. We have to live with it. Fuck that. Fuck you."

She backed away from him, into the custody of a guard.

Roarke strode down the corridor, his head throbbing with rage. In the administration office he held out his credentials to the desk clerk. "I need to see your CO named Driscoll."

"Driscoll didn't come in for work today."

Roarke felt his fury dissolve into something less definable. It seemed to him that the air had gone very still. "Did he call in sick?"

The clerk shook his head. "Just didn't show up."

"You tried to call him?"

"Not answering."

Roarke spoke through a tight throat. "I need his phone number and home address."

The clerk checked the computer and wrote on a card, pushed it across the counter to him.

Roarke asked for the clerk's phone, but his call to Driscoll's cell number went straight to voice mail. His home number just rang and rang. Roarke listened to the ringing for longer than he had to, with a sick feeling in his gut, then headed for the elevator.

The address was in Daly City, a twenty-minute drive. Roarke knew he could have a patrol car there sooner, marginally sooner, than he could get there himself. But instead of calling it in, he left the jail and got into his fleet car.

Morning traffic added another twenty minutes to the trip, and that gave him plenty of time to envision scenarios, all of them involving blood and death. But he was not expecting the one he got. As he turned onto the run-down street, he spotted a crowd of neighbors, fire trucks, and an ambulance around a half-burned-out house. He didn't have to check the address to know it was Driscoll's. He didn't have to ask the uniforms stationed at the perimeter what had happened. And he knew Cara was nowhere near there anymore.

In the scraggly yard of the charred house, he showed his credentials to the uniform managing the scene and told her, "I may have some information for the investigators."

What he was going to say, he had no idea.

The blackened area of the house was in the back. A bedroom, no doubt. The fire department had caught it early; the damage was visible only from the side of the building.

The uniform who escorted Roarke into the still-smoking house had words with a detective who then stepped over to meet Roarke at the front door. He introduced himself as Vince Pinella. Daly City was in a different county from San Francisco, and Roarke had never met the wiry, middle-aged detective before.

"You've got a fatality here?" he asked.

Pinella looked Roarke over before he answered. "Adult male, burned to death in bed. You know something about it?"

Roarke glanced toward the inner hall. "Lawrence Driscoll, corrections officer at San Francisco County #8?"

"We don't have a positive ID yet, but that's the owner of the house."

Roarke nodded. "I was coming to question him on one of mine."

"As a wit or a suspect?"

"Nothing formal, but there have been allegations."

Pinella's eyes narrowed. "I'd like to hear."

Roarke thought of Kaz. "This was from a CI, but I'll help out where I can."

The detective nodded. "Fair enough. Want to take a look?"

"Want" didn't factor in to it. Roarke had seen far too many burned bodies. His suit would be a write-off; you could never get the smell out. The aversion went deeper than that, of course. Nothing made him feel his own mortality more than a body fried beyond recognition by merciless fire. But he couldn't help himself.

He nodded back to the detective while his body tensed with dread.

Pinella stepped through a doorway and Roarke followed, into the inner hall. The first half of it was a dirty white. The second half was black with fresh soot.

The bedroom doorway opened into a chasm of a room: blackened timbers, ceiling caved in from flashover.

The bed was a lump of charred mattress with a human figure cooked into it. The coroner's assistants circled, trying to figure out how they were going to get the whole ungodly mess into the van.

Roarke stayed in the doorway, which was not far enough away to spare himself the smell. His bile rose and he had to make his mind blank to keep from retching, or running. The corpse was unrecognizable, but he had no doubt he was looking at the remains of Driscoll. He noted the truculent stiffening of the deceased's arms and fists, an indicator the victim had burned while still alive.

He breathed in shallowly to counteract the lurching of his stomach, then turned away from the bed to find Pinella watching him. The detective spoke evenly. "No forced entry. We found this in the bed with him." He passed over an evidence bag with a blackened hash pipe, and another with a partially melted cigarette lighter. Roarke studied the contents while his mind played out the scenario. There had been drug paraphernalia found with another of Cara's suspected victims, one who on the surface seemed to have died of an overdose . . .

Pinella nodded his head at the bed, the corpse. "It all tells a story, but I'm guessing you could tell me another one."

Roarke thought of the look he'd seen in Kaz's eyes, her barely audible voice . . .

"She wouldn't be the first."

The detective's gaze was still on him. "You going to help me on this one?"

Roarke shook his head slowly. "Right now all I've got is a hunch. But I'm looking for a—witness. If I find her, I'll let you know." He realized only after he said it that he'd used the word *if*.

"So I should dig deeper," the detective said.

Roarke handed over his card. "Yeah. If you find evidence of foul play, I'd appreciate a call."

He turned back to look at the blackened bed, the fried corpse. The white skull grinned at him from the melted body.

He twisted around, strode through the blackened house past startled crime scene techs.

Outside the door he was pulling off his suit coat even before he reached the car, flinging it away from him, fumbling for his necktie and stripping it off. He stopped at the car, tearing his shirt open and off, trying to breathe through the overwhelming smell of flesh.

He closed his eyes and leaned against the hood of the car.

And saw the guard's skull, burned into his eyes.

Chapter 31

The team sat around the table in the conference room, looking up at images of the charred house that Roarke had taken with his phone, now displayed on the projection screen. Outside the windows, the sky was darkening into late afternoon. Roarke had stood in his shower for a full forty minutes, and he still had the stench of the guard's melted corpse in his nostrils. He willed his stomach to settle, and spoke.

"The deceased is Lawrence Miller Driscoll, corrections officer at County #8. He burned to death in the bedroom of his house last night, apparently while smoking a hash pipe in bed."

Epps was stiff with anger. "Last night. They kick her loose and eight hours later she's doing *this* . . ."

"More like twelve," Roarke said.

Epps turned on him. "Are you trying to be funny? Because dying by fire is no laugh riot."

Singh was speaking before Roarke could answer. "Do we know what he did?"

Epps exploded. "What *he* did—"

Singh's voice never lost that ineffable calm. "It is relevant to finding her."

Roarke glanced at Singh and was reminded that there was a whole other conversation he would need to have with her. But for the moment, he answered her question. "I think there was prisoner abuse. I'll be able to find out from her cellie. She was on the verge of telling me this morning."

"And that is how you knew to check on the guard?" Singh queried. "I did have bulletins out asking that all suspicious deaths be reported, but this did not come in this morning."

No, she didn't waste any time at all. She went straight to him.

Roarke banished the memory of cooked flesh and answered evenly. "Daly City is San Mateo County, and they weren't thinking foul play at first," he told the team. "I was at #8 questioning the cellmate, and she mentioned the guard but wasn't ready to give details. I think she might, now."

"Now, meaning . . . ?"

It was Jones asking the question, but Roarke glanced at Epps as he answered. "Now that there's no danger of retribution by Driscoll." Roarke had to brace himself again to deflect the memory of the corpse.

Epps moved angrily in his seat, but Singh spoke first. "So we have Lindstrom leaving the courthouse at approximately thirteen hundred hours. Molina dropped her off at the Hyatt Regency on Market Street. She checked in, but . . ." She looked at Roarke. "You arrived there within the hour, and she was already gone. Last night it appears she went to Daly City and killed Driscoll."

Jones was studying the city maps posted on the whiteboard. "The Hyatt's right next to the Embarcadero BART station, and Daly City is on the BART route. But Driscoll's house is a good two miles from the BART station. Which means she probably boosted a car. We could question Driscoll's neighbors to see if anyone spotted an unknown car—but chances are she's already dumped it."

"Perhaps at the Daly City station," Singh said. She typed into her tablet. Then she looked up at Roarke questioningly, and he realized he hadn't spoken for some time. Talking seemed a great effort.

He cleared his throat against the taste of the dead guard. "We need to be anticipating her next moves, not trying to play catch-up. I think Driscoll was a one-off. Unfinished business. Now that he's out of the way, I doubt she'll be sticking around. I think we can safely say that she's jumped bail."

Epps made a contemptuous sound in his throat. Roarke ignored it and continued evenly. "But it's not going to be official until she misses her next court appearance, and we have no idea when that's going to happen. Stanton is going to have to go back to the judge with more evidence. We can't even put out an APB. As far as the law is concerned, she's no longer a fugitive. For the time being, anyway."

"So what now?" Jones asked.

"Mills is running down another lead," Roarke said obliquely, avoiding mention of the visitor list.

Singh spoke, her face distant with concentration. "If I were trying to evade capture, I would go out of state. I would also avoid any state that *you* know her to have been in." She said this looking directly at Roarke, and he felt his stomach flip with discomfort. "You know the most about her. You have anticipated her moves before. So if I were she, I would drive at least halfway across the country, to someplace you, personally, do not associate with me."

There were many nuances in her last few sentences that disturbed Roarke. He focused on the most troubling.

"*If* you were trying to evade capture," he repeated, as neutrally as he could manage.

"I do not know her motives," Singh answered slowly. "But she did not have to follow you to the mountains last month. She could have gone far out of state after surviving her injury in the desert, and she did not. She did not leave San Francisco the instant she was released but remained very close. So no, I do not think that evading capture is her primary goal."

The same thing Snyder had said.

The team sat with that for a moment. Then something flashed in Roarke's mind, a moment of clarity through his detached state. A mental image of crimson on white. Blood streaming from cuts on pale flesh. And he remembered the one person who might keep Cara in the city. Or who might know where she had gone.

"Her cousin is in town," he said aloud. "She may try to contact her."

"Erin McNally," Singh said thoughtfully.

"Lindstrom was very concerned about her." He'd almost said *Cara*. "I haven't been able to reach her." He had tried several times, by phone and email. "There's a slight possibility she'll know where Lindstrom might have gone." Even as he said it he knew Erin would never disclose where Cara was, but he continued, "I'll try going by her hotel tonight."

"Is that likely to get us anywhere?" Jones asked, voicing Roarke's own doubt.

"Probably not," Roarke admitted.

Singh was watching him, a frown in her eyes. "So for the time being, we focus on finding Jade?"

"As what, though?" Jones asked. "As a witness against Lindstrom? Or as a murder suspect? Are we looking to deal with Jade on the pimp murder, to testify against Lindstrom in exchange for a reduced sentence?"

It was a good question, but Roarke found himself lost for an answer. He had no idea what the plan was. He had no idea what he wanted. He had no idea at all.

"Maybe what we do is stop."

It was Epps speaking, after several minutes of complete silence from his corner. The thought was so startling that Roarke and the rest of the team turned in shock to stare at him.

Epps looked back at them. "Serious. The judge let Lindstrom out. She could be in any state, or another country by now. So could Jade. It's out of our division. We could let it go. Get back to our own damn business."

The possibility had never occurred to Roarke.

They had not been on the case for long. No more than two months. Compared with the length of other cases they'd worked, it was a fraction. A drop in the bucket.

And yet it was different from any other case. At every turn, Cara had slipped through their hands like water, like the wind.

There was a strange urgency in Epps' voice now. "A pimp's dead? Fuck him. Let San Mateo County handle the guard. Let someone else make the case. Go on with our real jobs. Last time I looked, my business card still said 'Organized Crime.'"

Across the conference table, Jones shifted uncomfortably. As agents, giving up was not what they did.

"That is unacceptable," Singh said.

The team turned toward her. She was sitting straight up in her chair, and her face was flushed. "That is not what we do. That is not how we function. That is not how we live."

It was the most emotional reaction Roarke had ever seen from her, and it threw him. Looking across the table at her and Epps, their defensive postures, the slight trembling in their hands, he was aware that for the first time in his memory, his two exceptional agents were about to fight. Epps had a temper, no doubt, but Roarke had never before heard Singh even raise her voice. The whole case was affecting his team as well as himself. Even Jones looked startled at the escalating friction.

Is this what it's come to? What's happening to us?

It was enough to pull Roarke out of his trance, at least for the moment. "We sleep on it. We reassess in the morning."

There was a numb silence around the table.

"I'm down with that," Epps said stiffly.

Roarke waited for the other agents to leave the room, then stopped Singh on her way out.

"Your name was on Lindstrom's visitor list."

He watched her face. Her eyes flickered, but her expression remained neutral.

"Yes. I had hoped to speak with her."

"Why?"

She held his gaze. "I suppose I have become equally fascinated by her."

Roarke had to fight to keep from reacting. Was she really saying what he thought she was saying?

"Fascinated how?" he managed brusquely, although he knew. Of all people, he knew.

"As an agent, I find her psychology riveting. As a woman—" She stopped. "I want to know why."

"But you cancelled."

"I reconsidered."

Roarke lifted his eyebrows, waiting.

Now she avoided his eyes. "I felt I was . . . overstepping my professional bounds."

"So you never saw her." He stared at her until she looked at him. She didn't blink.

"No."

They remained looking at each other, at an impasse.

"All right, Singh."

He watched her as she left the conference room, elegant and unfathomable as ever.

In his own office he slumped back in his chair. Immediately his cell phone buzzed, and he flinched at the sound before he glanced at the screen. Mills. Roarke picked up and the detective spoke without preamble.

"So you're right. There's something hinky with this 'Andrea Janovy.'"

"It's a fake ID?" *Meaning Jade?*

"Nope, it's a valid driver's license, passed through the background check just fine. But the actual owner of the driver's license wasn't the one who visited. The real Andrea Janovy hasn't used the license in two years, being that she was injured in an accident back then and lost the use of her legs. Which yes, is true, I checked."

Roarke sat still at his desk.

"The Richmond address on the license is four years old. The real Janovy currently resides down south in Goleta. And no, she says she has no idea who would be using her ID to get into a jail."

Roarke was thinking fast. "So someone who knows about her injury either stole her license or claimed it was lost to get a replacement. That's a pretty sophisticated setup."

And it sounded more like something Bitch would be able to do than Jade.

"Can you send me through the license photo?" he asked.

He waited until his email pinged, then clicked into the mail to see a scan of the driver's license.

The photo was of a serious young woman with gray eyes and auburn hair. She wasn't a match for the blogger, but with hair dye and colored contacts, some makeup, the blogger might have passed. Or not.

"So what are you thinking?" the detective demanded in his ear.

"Doesn't look like Jade."

"Yeah, I'd worked that out for myself. But the CO on duty that day didn't get much of a gander at her. It's the holidays; there's been a shit ton of visitors this week. You think it could be your blogger?"

"Possible."

"Then rustle yourself up a sketch artist and get us a composite. I want a look at this Bitch."

• • • • •

The sitting with the sketch artist took an hour, and mercifully, it concentrated Roarke's mind away from everything else. In the end they had a reasonable approximation of the young blogger.

Roarke scanned the drawing through to Mills, then left the building in a fog.

Moving on autopilot, he drove his fleet car out of the Civic Center garage and turned on Mission. He stopped at a traffic light . . . and realized he had no idea where he was headed. He could go to the Haight, to the hotel to see Erin. He could go home.

Thoughts swirled in his head. The mystery visitor and the new questions that discovery opened up. Singh's sudden interest in Cara and his own close call there; Singh clearly knew about his visits to Cara and was not going to say anything about them.

They were all too involved, dangerously involved.

And for what?

As he looked out the windshield at the darkening sky, the drifting fog lit by city lights, he allowed himself to consider Epps' idea.

I could drop it.

The force that seemed to guide Cara now also seemed to have freed her to continue her business.

So what if we did just let it be? Let her go on with what she does?

His inner turmoil was extreme. There was a whole other dimension to the possibility. He thought, had often thought, he might be the only one who could catch Cara. So if he were not to chase her, would she go free? Would that be the best outcome? Was it actually what he wanted? To be relieved of the responsibility of catching her, jailing her again?

So. Let the case go . . . and never see her again?

He felt a sudden lightness. Everything in him was leaning toward the possibility.

Salvation . . .

It was almost within grasp.

And then the light changed, and he made the turn toward the Haight.

Chapter 32

Golden Gate Park was shrouded in mist, black shapes of cypress looming in the haze. In the drifting gray tendrils, the Stanyan Park Hotel looked like something out of a Victorian novel.

Roarke took the inside stairs two at a time and then had to force himself to slow down, just to be capable of knocking at Erin's door in a way that wouldn't alarm her. Even before he got to the door, he noticed the "Do Not Disturb" placard hung on the doorknob. A bad sign.

Again he listened first. This time he heard nothing . . . no sign of movement. He knocked, called softly, "Erin? It's Agent Roarke."

Again, listening. Nothing.

"Are you there?"

Silence.

Roarke had a memory flash of the blood, the word she had cut into her flesh:

D I E.

He felt a dread that he couldn't ignore. He turned sharply and headed back downstairs.

At the desk he held his credentials out to the gangly and pleasant young clerk to save time. "Erin McNally, room 204. Is she in?"

The young man looked Roarke over, then took an appropriately serious and concerned tone. "I haven't seen her today."

"I need to get in there. She may be in danger."

Upstairs the desk clerk opened the door into the dim cave of Erin's room. Roarke had to keep himself from pushing past him to get inside. The feeling of dread was extreme.

He took in the room at a glance. There was no one in it. The bedspread had been drawn up, but not to any hotel housekeeping standard. He could see no suitcase; the bureau drawers were closed.

The clerk hovered anxiously in the doorway.

Roarke stepped quickly to the bathroom door and pushed it open, half-expecting the worst. But there was no body in the bathtub, no crimson water against white porcelain. The bath and the room were empty, and devoid of personal toiletries.

He turned and crossed to the antique wardrobe that served as a closet. He pulled open the door . . . to find his own image looking back at him in a mirror. Empty hangers dangled from the clothes rod.

The bureau drawers were likewise empty. She was gone.

Downstairs, he paced in the office while the manager, an older, more expensively groomed version of the young clerk, typed into the office computer, then looked up. "She hasn't checked out, no. She booked two more nights last night."

She added nights and then cleared out without checking out—and leaving a "Do Not Disturb" sign on the door?

It was a kind of misdirection that was ominous.

"She booked the extra nights with you?" Roarke asked.

"That's right."

"On the phone or at the desk?"

"On the phone," the manager answered.

"You didn't see her?"

"No."

So she may have been gone already, just calling in, Roarke thought. It was exactly the kind of thing that Cara did. *And why would Erin suddenly start acting like Cara?* he wondered uneasily.

"What time was that?" he asked aloud.

"Around five o'clock," the manager said. Then he glanced down at the computer screen. "5:04."

"Anyone visit her? Any calls in or out?"

The manager used the mouse to click through the record.

"No calls on record."

Of course, that meant nothing in this age of cell phones. No one called out from a hotel phone anymore.

He handed the manager his card. "I need to know immediately if she comes back in, or checks out, or contacts the hotel in any way. Please let the rest of your staff know."

"Of course, Agent Roarke," the manager said with a dutiful smile.

Roarke stepped out of the hotel and stood on the stairs, looking out over the park. It was dusk, the fog turning to purple in the gloomy twilight. Just beyond the trees was the tunnel where Cara had slit Danny Ramirez's throat.

His feet were moving down the sidewalk toward his car, but the thought of going home, of being confined within walls with no plan, was intolerable. He passed his vehicle where it was parked on the street, turned the corner onto Haight, and kept walking, past the mega record store and its sidewalk constituency of skate punks and dreadlocked junkies, who ducked their heads down as they saw him coming.

Erin's disappearance made him uneasy in a way he hadn't quite wrapped his mind around.

Cara, Jade, Erin . . . they were all out there on the street now. And the timing of it. All of them disappearing at roughly the same time.

Not to mention Molina and the mysterious Bitch. And now another mystery woman, whose name wasn't Andrea Janovy.

And Singh. What is she up to?

What is going on with these women?

Across the street, the sidewalk in front of the free clinic was already lined with homeless encampments: sleeping bags and cardboard shelters, like a three-dimensional extension of the sprawling mural painted on the clinic's front wall. Roarke stopped in his tracks, staring up at the mural.

In the background, a skeleton wearing a wreath of roses grinned out of the painted faces of the crowd.

A chill started from the base of his spine.

Santa Muerte. She's everywhere.

And then he realized the image was the iconic band logo of the Grateful Dead. He shook his head, berating himself.

Seeing phantoms now. What are you even doing here?

But he knew the answer to that. He could tell himself he was working the case, looking for Erin, looking for Jade, looking for Bitch. But the truth was, he was looking for her. For Cara. After everything.

The image of the guard, cooked into his bed, floated in his mind. And out of nowhere, a cold, hard voice spoke in his head.

Let's face facts, brother. How do you really think this is going to end? What kind of death wish do you have?

A feeling of doom washed over him, so powerful that his legs were shaking. He wasn't sure he could stand.

At that moment, a female voice spoke behind him, so familiar: "Roarke."

His heart leaped, and he turned . . .

Rachel Elliott stood on the sidewalk in the shadows and spill of Christmas lights.

As she looked at him, the quizzical expression on her face turned to alarm. She stepped forward and took his arm, and he realized she was half-holding him up. She spoke urgently.

"Are you all right?"

"Fine," he said thickly.

"Have you eaten anything?"

He could suddenly smell roasted flesh. He turned away from her, seconds from retching. She hovered as he swallowed back bile.

"Come on," she said. She took his arm again and steered him across the sidewalk and through a red leather door.

Music and darkness surrounded them. Through the buzzing in his head, Roarke recognized the dim cavern of the Zam Zam, a semilegendary dive that had been around since the seventies. It was approximately the size of a postage stamp, with a Persian theme: Byzantine arches, dark red lighting, brass smoking pipes on a shelf above the door, and a mural of some kind of Ottoman pastoral scene on the wall. The space was taken up mostly by a large semicircle of bar.

"I'm all right," he said to Rachel.

"No you're not." He was about to contradict her when she said, "Just sit. For a minute. Please." She looked past the bar at an archway leading to a dark back area. After a moment, he nodded, followed her. She stopped at a table in the corner, put her coat on a chair. "I'll be right back."

Roarke sat, and once he was down, he recognized the signs. It was not just his stomach roiling. His pulse was jumping, his vision blurred. *No food all day. No sleep.* He realized Rachel had called it: he was nowhere near all right.

He took a slow breath and looked around the space, illuminated by Arabian lanterns that cast chips of light on the red walls. Ella Fitzgerald sang from a red jukebox set into a glass case in the wall. Seated around Roarke were some aged hippies reeking of pot and two tables full of hipsters: boys with porkpie hats and girls with Betty Page haircuts, a veritable gallery of tattoos among them.

Rachel stepped back to the table and set down two glasses. Roarke recognized straight whisky. He looked up at her and she smiled wryly.

"Food would be better, but I thought I'd have more chance of getting you to drink that. Medicinally."

He picked up the glass and downed it. The whisky burned his throat, stung his eyes, and for the first time that day he did not taste the guard in his mouth.

He set the glass on the table and felt his stomach settle.

Rachel was watching him. "What happened?" she asked softly.

He looked into her worried gray eyes and almost told her. The burned house. The sickening sight of the guard's blistered body. His deep, panicked dread, as if he had caught a glimpse of his own fate . . .

Almost.

Instead he shook his head. After a moment, she tried again. "I know she's out . . ."

"Free on bail," Roarke said, looking away.

"Which means . . ." She hesitated. "It means she's gone, doesn't it?"

"We won't know for sure until she's called back into court."

Rachel's jaw tightened. She sipped from her drink. "So . . . what's next?" She glanced at him.

He had no answers, only a million questions. Was it the start of another bloody rampage? Would it ever end? Could he let it go? Let *her* go? For Rachel? For himself? For anyone?

"Are you safe?" she asked bluntly.

He looked at her, startled. She'd put her finger right on what he was feeling.

"I don't know."

Her eyes widened slightly and she bit her lip, but said nothing. He tried to focus, to make the conversation about the job.

"Did Jade ever talk about her?" he asked.

"Cara?" She said the name now, deliberately, watching his face. "Not really. Only what she said to you and Mills the other day."

"Do you think she might have visited her? In jail?" Now Rachel gave him a startled look. "I know she's a minor, but surely she has a fake ID—"

Rachel cut him off. "I'm sure she wouldn't have."

Roarke frowned. Rachel herself had told him that the first thing pimps did was get the girls fake IDs. Not just as a precaution to avoid stiffer criminal charges for any offense involving a minor. Changing the girls' identities was also a crucial step in the indoctrination process, and it made them harder to find if someone who loved them was looking for them.

"I thought fake IDs were standard operating procedure," he said, and waited.

Rachel hesitated for just a moment. "Yes, of course. I meant she wouldn't have used it for that. The girls are so terrified of prison. Not that it's worse than the street. But walking straight inside a jail?" She shook her head. "I can't see it."

"Jade was at the courthouse yesterday. I saw her."

Rachel did another double take. "That can't be . . ."

He looked at her, even more perplexed. She shook her head. "I mean, if she killed DeShawn, wouldn't she be gone? I just don't understand why she would . . ." She stopped. "I don't understand much about it." She looked down, then back at him. "Any of it."

Roarke knew the subtext had moved from Jade back to Cara. "I don't understand much, either," he said, and reached for his glass. But of course it was empty.

Rachel stood. "Hold on." She threaded her way through the tables.

Roarke looked up through the red haze of the club to the mural, a tapestry-like rendering of a forest with a young Persian woman washing at a stream. A turbaned prince watched her from horseback, concealed in the trees.

Rachel returned with two more whiskies. She avoided Roarke's eyes as she set them down.

Why not? This is what normal is. This is what normal people do.

He reached for the glass of amber liquid. Rachel took a swallow from hers, looking at him. He glanced away. "Has Erin McNally contacted you?" he asked.

Rachel gave him a cynical look, her pause emphasizing the subtext that he was avoiding. "I haven't seen her since—that night."

Just two nights ago, now, but it felt like an eternity.

"And she hasn't called."

"No." She looked at him. "Why?"

He drank, tasted the amber burn. When he set the glass down he said flatly, "She's gone. She just left the hotel, without checking out."

Rachel frowned. "Do you think something happened?" Her eyes narrowed. "Or do you think it's something to do with the case? With Cara?"

He flinched inside as she spoke Cara's name again. Too real, and too strange.

"I don't know. I hope she's all right. I hope . . ." He didn't know how to finish the sentence, and he didn't even know who he was talking about. He suddenly felt drunk.

She's gone. She's gone, and I may never see her again. The thought was a wave of anxiety, or maybe it was fear. *I should pray I never see her again.*

He reached for his glass, and drank.

Another drink later, or maybe two, they were standing under the red lights on the sidewalk outside the bar. They turned to each other and spoke at once.

"Are you going home . . . ?"

"Are you working tonight . . . ?"

They both stopped at once, too.

"Just going back to the House," Rachel answered, avoiding his eyes.

"I'll walk you," he said.

"It's two blocks—" she started.

"Don't," he said. "Don't walk around alone at night."

She hesitated, nodded.

They fell into step, a fraction unsteadily, and the air was thick between them, the chemistry palpable, a tantalizing pull. He was painfully aware this was the way they had ended up in bed together the first time.

And what's the alternative?
Save yourself. Something normal. Something sane . . .

At the foot of the halfway house steps, she turned and swayed into him, and he had no time to wonder if it was accidental or on purpose, because they were kissing, his tongue deep in her mouth, his hands holding her slim, taut waist, and he could remember the feeling of being inside her, surrounded by that lush heat . . .

Her fingers were stroking the front of his pants, and through the rush in his head he felt—

Watched.

He pulled away.

He looked down at Rachel in the dark, and their eyes were locked through their rapid breathing. He saw hurt and accusation in hers.

"Right," she said. "Right."

"Rachel—"

"You don't have to say it. I know. We'll be good friends, all that. Of course."

His heart sank at the bitterness in her voice. "It's not you—" he started.

Now anger flashed on her face. "You assume a lot."

"I don't mean to—"

"You're so irresistible, aren't you? Fuck you, Roarke. Just fuck you." She backed away from him. "Don't come here again. Don't call me again." She turned and fled up the steps of the House, slamming the security gate behind her.

It was a long time before he turned back for home. And when he got there, it was a long time before he slept.

Instead, he lay awake thinking of Cara.

Pale in the moonlight, as he always saw her in his mind. Free now. Under the growing moon.

But when he dreamed, it was of a skull screaming out of burning flesh.

Chapter 33

The shadow moves across the darkened streets, surveying its domain. The fog is like a living thing. It seems especially so tonight. It swirls in the alleys of the Tenderloin as the tricks creep in the dirty back passageways like roaches.

They are scum. They are legion. Crawling on the streets in the fog, cruising in their metal traps. Greedy, slathering. Hunting.

So many to choose from. So many who deserve what is coming.

The shadow pauses, listening, looking, sensing . . . and then it comes. The smell. It is unmistakable, the stink of rutting.

And the shadow moves forward.

In an alley behind a Dumpster, a man stands against a brick wall, his pants down around his knees. Thrusting his cock into the mouth of a fourteen-year-old girl.

He doesn't think about her age. There are any number of useful phrases that cover that inconvenience. *"She looked older." "She came on to me." "It wasn't her first time."*

And after all, he's paying, isn't he? Isn't that all there is to it?

The girl keeps her head down, focused on the task. He grabs her hair, forces himself deeper into her mouth. "Suck it, bitch. Take it all. Now. *Now.*"

He thrusts, spasming and grunting . . . and when he is finished, he shoves her away. She falls on the dirty asphalt, scraping her palms. He adjusts his clothes and leaves her on her hands and knees, gagging behind him as he walks along the side of the warehouse, out toward the street. Truth be told, a little unsteadily; he has a buzz on from his climax and is feeling no pain.

And as he rounds the edge of the Dumpster, something grabs him from behind. He knows immediately this is not a joke. The hold is inexorable, the purpose unmistakable. He feels primal terror, a surge of adrenaline meant to help him fight for his life . . .

But he is spent, weak, off-guard, and finds himself off-balance, falling heavily to his knees.

There are hands in his hair now, jerking his head backward, and the blade slices deep: cold metal across his throat, then hot blood spurting from his veins.

His last thoughts are vague, helpless outrage at the unfairness. He has done nothing.

Nothing at all.

DAY SIX

Chapter 34

The city wept.

Roarke, Epps, and Mills stood in the gray dawn and pouring rain, watching it wash the blood from the asphalt of the alley. Red rivulets ran into the gutters, diluting to a watery pink.

Another alley in the Tenderloin. Another corpse in a bloody pool.

And all the forensic evidence washing away with the rain, while SFPD crime scene techs struggled to put up a protective tent.

At the end of the short block the shadowy shapes of uniforms moved in the gray downpour. A line of yellow tape stretched from building to building, sealing the alley. They were just two blocks from where DeShawn Butler had died, in a tableau just like this one.

Mills had to shout through the rush of water and wind. "Andrew Goldman, lately of Millbrae. Razor-fine slash to the throat. Fresh come on him. Or there was before . . ." The detective looked up into the sky, and the rain ran down his face.

Roarke looked down at the clothes on the man: a medium-priced business suit, Florsheim shoes. "A trick," he said, just to have it out.

There was a certain kind of man who enjoyed the thrill and the danger of cruising the street and the hunting of girls in these dirty alleys.

As Roarke had walked the Haight, and drunk with Rachel, and dreamed of a burning skull, someone else had been stalking these streets. Hunting the hunters.

"We have got a major fucking problem," Mills said. He looked strange. Roarke had to rouse himself from his own distraction and study Mills a moment to get a handle on what he was seeing in the veteran detective's face. Consternation. Confusion. And—*fear?*

"This is Jade again, right?" the detective finally asked.

For a moment there was no sound but the hammering drive of the rain. They were all envisioning the scenario. Jade could approach a john without triggering the slightest hesitation on the man's part.

"Or Lindstrom," Epps said, but there was doubt in his voice.

Roarke couldn't get his mind around it. *Cara back in the city, killing this one so soon after the guard?*

And then there was the other thought, even stranger than the first two possibilities. *Or was it Erin? Or Bitch?*

He felt lightheaded, and he didn't know if it was lack of sleep or a hangover or the complete sense of unreality they were facing in this scene in the storm.

Last night he'd been on the brink of . . . he didn't even want to name it. Some kind of breakdown. He knew he had to get a grip. And then a thought came through clearly.

This is not Cara.

The guard, oh yes, that one was hers. Danny Ramirez, certainly. But this one was not. He could feel that. And yet . . .

"A pimp and a john," he said aloud. In her brief time in the Haight, within the space of two days, Cara had beaten a john in an alley and killed Jade's pimp. And now they were dealing with the same configuration, within two days.

A pattern, then?

Jade surely knew from Shauna about Cara's assault on the john. And Jade had directly witnessed the killing of her pimp. So is this Jade emulating Cara exactly?

"Jade knew DeShawn Butler and had motive to kill him," Roarke continued. He looked back toward the corpse. "Maybe she knew this one, too. A sick trick."

Mills nodded. "We need to find out. I'll get on his phone and email records."

"What's scarier is if she didn't know him," Epps said.

They all stood contemplating what that would mean. Mills finally spoke. "So to state the complete fucking obvious: Have we got a teenage serial killer here?"

Roarke felt the tug of his old training. "Not a serial killer."

There was a flash of anger on the detective's face. "Get technical if you want. You know what I'm askin'. She did DeShawn, got a taste for it, whatever the fuck. Decided she'd do it again."

Roarke stared out through the curtain of rain. Whoever it was, there was no longer any question of letting the case go. There was a killer loose literally in their backyard, almost in the shadow of the Federal Building.

As he thought it, he looked automatically down the block, toward the Civic Center.

At the end of the alley, a crowd had gathered outside the crime scene tape, standing around despite the downpour, trying to get a glimpse of someone else's tragedy. And suddenly Roarke was jolted by the sight of a figure that shouldn't be there, that *couldn't* be there: a grinning skull among the other faces, staring out from the hood of a raincoat.

Roarke stood in shock—and then ran for the barrier, leaving Mills and Epps shouting after him.

He barreled down the alley with rain battering his face, his shoes splashing through puddles. He halted at the crime scene barriers and scanned the onlookers, who moved slightly backward, looked back at him warily. A crowd of startled and very human faces.

He stood on the street, staring into the rain, and felt colder than ice.

But the masked figure was gone.

Chapter 35

Back at Bureau headquarters Roarke went in to Reynolds' office with a hard knot in his stomach. Standing in front of his SAC's desk, he started, "This isn't what any one of us was expecting—"

Reynolds lifted a hand, dismissing the apology. "We're beyond that."

As Roarke looked down at his superior officer, he got a glimpse of the computer screen in front of him. The text was a blog article. The byline was, simply, Bitch.

Reynolds turned the screen toward Roarke so he could read.

Lady Death Strikes Again

San Francisco's Tenderloin has long been synonymous with sex for sale: brothels, escorts, streetwalkers, massage parlors. For most of the women euphemistically called sex workers, it is a life of constant exploitation, degradation, and abuse.

Many of these "women" aren't women at all. They are children. The average age of entry into prostitution is twelve years old.

There are few laws protecting victims of the sex trafficking trade, at least few that are enforced. Pimps and johns abuse these teenagers, and children younger than teenagers, with impunity. Until now. Now vengeance stalks the alleys of the Tenderloin. For the second time in three days, a man has died in a pool of his own blood.

Someone is saying, "Enough."

Roarke had time to think, *This is so out of control*, before Reynolds was speaking again.

"No way to muzzle the media, obviously. That's going to get hot."

Hotter, Roarke answered in his head. *Infernal to nuclear.*

"Is it the same doer?"

Roarke tried to focus. "This new one could have been Jade Lauren. It could have been Lindstrom. Either way, finding Jade is imperative, and at this point I think my team might have the most knowledge about her to find her. I know it doesn't seem like we've been that successful—"

Reynolds cut him off. "You brought Lindstrom in. You can't be blamed for what the court does or doesn't do after that."

Roarke would have appreciated the vote of confidence, if he hadn't been fully aware how undeserved it was. *If only you knew*, he thought.

The SAC shook his head. "Bottom line is, the office can't back off of it now."

He gazed into his computer screen. Roarke wasn't sure if he was reading the article or simply lost in thought. Finally Reynolds spoke again. "Whatever this is, there's no getting around it's yours."

Roarke recalled that Snyder had said something similar to him. It was his, and it was totally beyond him.

"Singh is coordinating a task force with Inspector Mills on the SFPD," he said.

Reynolds nodded.

"We'll get it done," Roarke finished, and felt it might prove to be the biggest lie of his life.

• • • • •

"Teenage serial killers are a fact," Snyder said from the videoconferencing screen.

The team looked up from the conference table at the profiler's craggy face. Singh had patched him in from Montana.

Roarke knew that for the veteran agent it was irresistible: the possibility of a sixteen-year-old girl on a murder spree. In all the years of every form of human lunacy he had witnessed, it was unprecedented.

Snyder had laid the groundwork for this kind of investigation thousands of times before, and his summation was unrushed. "The deviant behavior of serial killers tends to start early, surfacing in young adolescent males and even younger boys. The operative word is *male*. Serial killing is a behavior closely aligned with rape: the object is sexual gratification through sadism and violence. In fact, most serial rapists, if uncaught, will graduate to serial murder. It is a pattern we see over and over again."

Roarke sat impatiently through this introduction; he knew the speech word for word. It had been his own job for six years.

"Female mass killers are very rare and overwhelmingly fall into two types: the Black Widow, who kills husbands, lovers, or relatives for money; and the Angel of Death, a medical professional who kills patients either in a desire for control, or a twisted sense of euthanasia, or a form of Munchausen syndrome by proxy. None of these models apply here. For profiling purposes, our one point of reference for both Lindstrom and Jade, if Jade is indeed our second killer, is Aileen Wuornos, a spree killer who demonstrated neither the cooling-off period between kills nor the sexual motivation that is typical of serial killers. Also with Wuornos there was a strong element of retribution: one could take the point of view that every single victim was a sexual abuser."

Just as we seem to be looking at now, Roarke thought. *Only the kills are happening more quickly, and we have no idea if it's just one killer.*

The older man looked out from the screen. "So the parallels here are obvious. Your killer might be writing the next chapter of a new book, joining Wuornos and Cara Lindstrom to define the pattern of a new kind of killer: the female vigilante."

Beside Roarke, Singh shifted in her seat. He glanced at her, but before she could speak, Snyder continued from the screen.

"However, we may be getting ahead of ourselves. Before I go any further, my question to you is this: Are we reasonably certain Jade did both killings?"

A thick silence fell over the team. *That is the sixty-four-thousand-dollar question, isn't it?*

Finally Roarke began. "Both new victims died by slashes to the throat. Not the same weapon, obviously, since the first weapon, a razor, was left at the first scene. It's Lindstrom's preferred MO, but we know she couldn't have killed Butler, and—" He shook his head. "I don't see her as the doer for Goldman, either. I think she's long gone."

She must be, he thought silently. And forced himself to refocus.

"Jade had motive to kill the first—" he corrected himself, "—the second pimp, DeShawn Butler. According to one of Ramirez's other girls, Butler raped her as part of her initiation into the life. Obviously Jade would also have had easy opportunity to approach Goldman, the john. She may have had motive there as well. Inspector Mills is following up to see if she knew him. I can question Ramirez's girls, the ones staying at the Belvedere House, to see if they know anything about Goldman, or any connection he had to Jade. But . . ."

He stopped, not at all sure what he was about to say.

But there's something else going on here, was his thought. *And I don't know what it is.*

He spoke slowly. "Lindstrom's cousin Erin McNally is also missing. She disappeared from her hotel room without checking out. No one's seen her since the night of DeShawn Butler's murder. I've been trying to reach her, but she's not answering her phone or email. Her roommate in San Diego hasn't seen her, either, and she hasn't posted on Facebook for a week."

"What the hell?" Jones muttered.

"You think Lindstrom and the cousin might have teamed up?" Epps asked, startled.

All eyes turned to Snyder on the screen. His eyes were clouded. "There have been several instances of women killing multiple victims in tandem with a male partner. I've never come across a pair of women—or girls—killing more than one victim together or killing in more than one incident." He looked to Roarke. "What do you think?"

"I don't see it," Roarke started. Cara was such a loner that he was finding it hard to believe she'd recruit other people for her bloody work.

Except for me, he admitted to himself.

He also knew he might not want to believe Cara would use Erin that way.

"But?" Epps prodded.

"But I could see Erin emulating Cara." He'd used her name without thinking, and there was no taking it back. "When I last saw Erin, she was experiencing some kind of breakdown. And there is a good bit of hero worship going on there."

"Heroine worship," Singh murmured beside him.

Roarke glanced at her. She seemed tense. They all were, but he was uncomfortably aware that he had been watching Singh throughout the briefing. He didn't know what was going on in her head anymore.

He refocused and continued. "Also, Erin is a med student. She'd be more likely than Jade to be able to cut a throat, both in terms of accuracy and the nerve it would take to do it."

Epps leaned forward intently. "Erin McNally also visited Lindstrom in jail. Lindstrom could have kept the razor from the Ramirez killing, hidden it, then told the cousin where it was so she could plant it at the scene of the second pimp killing. To exonerate Lindstrom."

Roarke looked at his agent. It was the same thought he'd had himself.

Snyder spoke from the screen on the wall.

"Or the cousin is emulating Lindstrom of her own accord."

The team turned to the conference screen. "Without Lindstrom's knowledge?" Roarke asked, startled.

Snyder tipped his head. "Lindstrom's killings are so unique, statistically speaking, and the victim profile in these latest kills is so similar, that it's fairly clear that you have a copycat vigilante on your hands."

Singh spoke abruptly. "Female vigilantism is *not* unique to Lindstrom."

The men turned to her. Her normally serene face was flushed. "In the fall of 2013, an unknown woman boarded buses in Ciudad Juarez, Mexico, and shot two bus drivers point-blank. She sent emails to the authorities calling herself Diana, the Hunter of Drivers, and claimed that the men she'd killed had been raping women who rode the buses from work. In India, in Uttar Pradesh, there is the Gulabi Gang, the Pink Gang, a group of women who arm themselves with *lathis* and use force and intimidation to threaten men accused of abusing women. The gang now numbers in the thousands. There is also an all-female armed squad of vigilantes in Mexico, in the state of Michoacán, which is fighting back against the drug cartels. One might even say that the phenomenon is on the rise."

On the screen, Snyder looked down at Singh with an expression Roarke recognized as admiration. "You're quite right, of course. I hadn't been thinking globally."

A vigilante gang? That's sounding more like Bitch, Roarke thought, remembering the figure in the skull mask in the alley, in the rain . . .

"But our prime suspect is Jade," Epps said. There was an edge in his voice. "She has motive. She's had opportunity. And there's the timing of her taking off the night of Butler's murder. Interesting as all the rest of this is, we need to be focusing on Jade's psychology here."

Roarke realized he was right. After a moment, Singh nodded and sat back.

Snyder looked down from the screen. "I can tell you: viral murder is not an uncommon phenomenon among teenagers. We see it in mass shootings especially. School shootings very frequently inspire other massacres or attempts, frequently among teens."

Roarke felt warm and cold at once. It was a feeling he was familiar with. A feeling of significance, a hot trail.

Snyder continued. "Cara Lindstrom's murders have become an Internet phenomenon, and in these days of Internet vigilantism it's not so surprising that a teenager would pick up on that energy. What's unusual of course is for a young girl to kill like this."

Epps looked up toward the screen. "You used the word *spree*. But is it really likely that Jade would kill again so soon?"

Snyder lifted his hands. "We're in uncharted territory. Teenage mass killers usually plan one grand, extravagant gesture and often end the killing binge with their own suicide. Obviously Jade differs from this kind of killer in many respects. She's female. She doesn't use guns or explosives. If she *has* killed both men, then already it's not an isolated event. There's no place, like a school, that she's targeting, unless she's thinking of the streets metaphorically as a place. We do have the case of spree killer Joanna Dennehy, a thirty-year-old British woman with both sadistic and masochistic tendencies who killed three men and attempted to kill two others in a two-week spree in early 2013. She shares characteristics with Wuornos, and perhaps with Jade—before her arrest she was a violent drifter living on the outskirts of society, an alcoholic and addict with severe antisocial tendencies, whose sense of empathy and reality had been further blurred by her various addictions. Her victims were not strangers, but men known to her: two short-term sexual partners and a flatmate. She claims to have killed these men for 'fun.'"

Fun is not what this is, Roarke thought. *Not by a long shot.*

Snyder paused. "But your killer differs substantially from the Dennehy case in that—whoever she is—she's very clearly taking a page from Cara Lindstrom: using the exact weapon and MO and victim pool. She may have a list of her own, however, and subsequent killings could be men who are personally known to her. Which would reduce the pool of potential victims."

A pimp and a john. A pattern? Roarke wondered again. He said it aloud. "Or she could be making a point. Deliberately targeting abusers from both ends."

Which also sounded more like the blogger than Jade.

The team all sat, thinking. Epps spoke first.

"Okay, thing is, is she on a rampage *here*, in the city? Whoever this is, she knows these streets. Are there going to be others?"

"We are of course monitoring all killings of adult males in California," Singh said. They had been since Cara came on their radar.

Snyder answered. "If it's Jade, the likelihood is that if she kills again it'll be here, simply because teenagers are less mobile than adults."

"So we get out on the street," Epps said flatly. He turned to Roarke. "*You* can't. Jade knows you. But she never met me. Me, Jones." He looked at the younger agent. "We get in civilian cars and go out cruisin'. We don't know for sure who we're hunting. But we damn well know *where* she's hunting."

Roarke felt a tremor of apprehension. And it was not for Jade. It was for his agents. He hated the idea. But it was proactive, it was protective, it was a clear strategy.

"Yeah," he agreed reluctantly. "Okay."

"We start tonight," Epps said. "Go out cruising the Tenderloin and the Haight."

Jones was frowning, thinking. "Hold up. If it was me, I'd be figuring the TL is too hot now. I'd want to mix it up."

Roarke knew he had a point. Jade wasn't stupid.

"So what about Inty?" Jones continued. "There's more street action there, anyway."

He was talking about International Boulevard in Oakland, otherwise known as "the Track"—a major prostitute stroll. These days a lot of the street action had moved across the Bay to Oakland. And the Track was infamous for its large selection of underage girls.

But Epps was already shaking his head. "Uh-uh. White girl on the Track? She'd stand out too much."

Roarke knew Epps was not simply speaking professionally. The agent had grown up on the streets of Oakland.

"I agree," Singh said. "She has not been seen on the Track." The men turned to her. "I have been monitoring the online sex forums: Backpage, Yelp, Redlight. Inspector Mills and I thought there might be talk from the men who post on those forums, the tricks—things they have seen that could be useful to our investigation."

She stepped to the podium to connect her laptop to the overhead projection. An online web forum came up on the screen.

"There are several quite active forums dedicated only to Street Action. The men who frequent those forums act somewhat as reporters for the other men: they routinely post what they call 'intel' or 'recon'—camera phone shots they take of the streetwalkers while they are cruising, and descriptions of the women they see out working. The posters are very explicit," she said, and neither her tone nor her face changed, but Roarke could feel her cold disgust. She scrolled through the threads so the other agents could see.

Users with screen names like Justanotherdick, MrDiscreet, and Beaverstretcher had posted camera phone photos of girls walking particular streets, often with links to classified ads that listed a sex worker's prices, dimensions, and specialties. Some threads were individual reviews or queries asking details from anyone in the forum who had "done" a particular sex worker.

Roarke caught glimpses of some of the comments. *Some dick-sucking lips on that one. Love to get a girl like that to gobble my load . . .*

Singh continued clicking through the threads. "I have been thinking that a girl of Jade's looks would draw comment, if she had been seen. Inspector Mills and I have created several online accounts of our own so that we can interact with other posters. Under these aliases we can post as sex workers as well as 'mongers.' For the last two days we have been establishing a presence so that our queries will not come out of thin air. The men who post in these forums tend to be suspicious of newcomers." She clicked on a thread to open it. "Here Inspector Mills has posted directly asking if anyone has seen a sex worker of Jade's description, under the pretext of wanting a second 'date.' We have received no useful answers. But this afternoon I found this separate query, from a poster who uses a photo of his infant son as an avatar."

Roarke was startled at the loathing in her voice. Not that it wasn't entirely justified, but he had never seen her react so strongly in a professional setting. Or anyplace else.

"There is no overt description of her, but see here." She clicked on a thread. "This was posted last night."

The agents looked up at the screen.

HUNGMAN: Need intel on young wsw spotted near bakery on Polk. Smoking little body, tight hot ass, black short hair, silver tube top, black mini, freaky all-over tats.

"Hungman," Epps said, his voice dripping contempt. "I just bet."

"Doesn't sound like Jade to me. He says 'black short hair,'" Jones pointed out.

"Hair is the easiest and most dramatic identifying characteristic to change," Singh answered. "It is likely the first thing Jade would do to disguise herself. The post specifies 'wsw': a white sex worker, which are more prevalent in the Tenderloin than on the Track, but still in the minority. And this is what particularly caught my attention." She used the mouse to highlight a phrase: *freaky all-over tats.*

"Admittedly a long shot, but there is a chance this Hungman was a witness to Jade's presence and activities in the Tenderloin last night. Perhaps he even got the 'intel' he was asking for and actually found her."

"Which means he might already be dead," Jones said. There was a sudden chill in the room as the rest of the team realized he was right.

"Shit," Epps said softly.

Roarke turned to Singh. "How do we find him?"

She frowned. "Unfortunately, there is not enough in the posting for us to get a warrant to compel the website to give up names and addresses. Also the site makes it quite easy for users to register by money order, so there is no paper trail to most of the accounts. But—I have searched all posts by Hungman. I found this photo he took from inside his car as he was cruising."

Roarke tensed and stared up at the projected image of a girl in high heels and miniskirt, walking along a neon-lit sidewalk. The photo was shot through the windshield; the figure was grainy, barely visible, but he was almost certain the girl was Latina.

"That's not Jade," he said.

"No," Singh answered. "But look there, at the dashboard of the car. Hungman drives a MINI Cooper. Black, or perhaps dark blue."

The dashboard instrumentation was visible in the photo, and Roarke realized she was right.

Epps leaned forward with a surge of excitement. "So we're on the lookout for a dark MINI during the stakeout tonight."

"Just so," Singh answered. "And as we monitor the boards for real-time street activity, we will have a bigger picture of the action going on and can respond to any potential sightings."

Snyder spoke from the conference screen. "I think you have your plan. And I'm being paged, so this is where I wish you luck and sign off. Be safe." His screen went dark.

Roarke sat back. He wasn't happy with the plan for his own reasons, but he couldn't deny it was solid.

"Finally, there is this." Singh clicked on a thread and scrolled down through camera phone photos of various sex workers. She stopped on one photo of three girls in short skirts and tube tops walking on the sidewalk, and moved the cursor to highlight a shape in the background. "There," she said.

"Whoa," said Jones.

There was a blob of white where the face should be. Roarke was startled to make out the fuzzy shape of a human skull.

"A Santa Muerte mask," he said.

"Yes," said Singh. "That is how I saw it, too."

Roarke finally brought himself to say it. "I think this person was at the crime scene this morning. There was someone standing at the barrier. Wearing a skull mask."

Epps and Jones turned to him in disbelief. Singh did not look surprised. "So. There is someone else we must be on the lookout for. What that means, I do not know."

Roarke couldn't believe it was Cara. It wasn't her style at all. She wore disguises, but her purpose was *not* to be noticed. And Jade's particular advantage over these men would be to approach them as herself.

So who's out there in the mask? Erin? The blogger? Or— He didn't even want to think it.

"It means this killer may not be anyone we're looking at," he said. "It could be someone else entirely."

Chapter 36

Singh was very quiet in her chair as Roarke filled the team in on the mystery woman who had used Andrea Janovy's identification to visit Cara in jail.

"I don't know who this visitor was. But the blogger who writes under the name Bitch is one possibility." He distributed the composite sketch of the blogger to the team, and they all looked down at the young, intent face as Roarke continued.

"When I saw that onlooker in the skull mask at the crime scene, that was my first thought. That it was her."

Epps was shaking his head. Roarke held up a hand.

"We focus on Jade. But tonight we need to be on alert for Bitch, too."

The team spent the next hour laying the groundwork for the stakeout. Roarke agreed with Epps and Singh that Jade would most likely avoid International Boulevard and stick to San Francisco. The Tenderloin wasn't huge, which would make patrolling it manageable. And it was the most likely place to find Jade if she was out there hunting.

Hunting. It was a surreal thought.

But action in the Tenderloin didn't start until late at night, so Roarke dismissed Epps and Jones to get some sleep before zero hour.

"I want you sharp, and rested."

As he left the room, he stopped beside Singh. "That was interesting thinking, about female vigilantes."

She nodded without smiling. He paused, then added, "We need to find that blogger."

Singh was immediately focused. "I have begun to search for her through the IP numbers and accounts—Redlight, the blog. Of course she is using encryption, proxies, and rerouting methods to conceal herself. It is standard operating procedure for these cyberorganizations. They are very expert at it. But I have just begun."

As usual Singh was a step ahead of him.

"Good. I'd also like you to monitor any online activity by Bitch—not just the blogger but the whole organization. Any calls to action. Any chatter between Twitter accounts."

"I see," Singh said.

"Now that they're involved they may attempt to reach out to Lindstrom somehow. Or Jade. Both. They may have already."

"Yes," she said. "You are right."

"And Singh . . ."

She looked at him.

"I know it's a lot right now, but we're going to need to look into Kaz Spinoza's suggestion that there was or is prisoner abuse going on at County #8."

"Of course," she said softly. "I will begin that process."

Back in his office, Roarke sat down behind his desk and fished out his cell phone, punched up a contact. When Snyder answered, Roarke started in.

"I wanted to thank you for your input today—"

"You're welcome. And?" Snyder's tone was amused.

"And we really could use your help down here," Roarke admitted.

There was a pause on the phone. When the profiler spoke, his voice was grave. "You know I would be there if I could. But this case takes priority."

"I understand. Just know that I can requisition your full fee at any time—"

"That has nothing to do with anything," Snyder said sharply. "The man we're looking for up here is hunting children. If I'm correct about previous victims, his cooling-off period has become shorter and shorter. We're running out of time."

"I'm sorry," Roarke said.

When Snyder spoke again, his voice had softened slightly. "Your killer, whoever she is, will almost certainly kill first, I fully understand that. But in the grand scheme of things, I can't say I consider her victims a priority."

"Right," Roarke said. It was a feeling he knew too well, and the stark truth of it. Who could?

He wished Snyder luck and disconnected, then sat back in his chair and let his mind go to the one thing he'd been wondering about all day.

Cara.

Where was she?

Chapter 37

Fire is all around her.

She stands in the middle of the burning street, the heart of the Haight lit up in the bright glow of flames. Inside the fiery circle, the street is alive with music and hilarity, guitar riffs and the thump of bass. The music overlaps, reggae, nouveau punk . . . the sidewalks pulse with it, while people dance in the street between the food carts and craft tables of jewelry and art and batik T-shirts and blown-glass drug paraphernalia.

All of them completely oblivious to the flames around them, even though those on the periphery catch fire and flare up like paper.

The walls of the shops are covered in a mural, a sprawling painted street scene that mirrors the live scene in front of it. A skeletal figure crowned in roses grins down from the mural, larger than life.

As she looks up toward it, the painted figure raises a bony arm and points.

Cara turns slowly to look.

In the midst of the revelers is the girl with the flaming, flowering tattoos, dancing by herself in the crowded street, the tattoos on her back coming alive, a tree dropping blossoms of flame that fall from the girl's skin and explode in sparks on the street.

She watches as the girl twirls in a circle, laughing, shrieking. Suddenly the girl catches sight of her and stops her spinning. She smiles, a strange, high smile in the midst of that pounding street music . . .

Then the street is gone, the fair is gone. There is just them, her and the girl and the flames, dancing higher and higher. They are in a cave . . . no, a tunnel . . . with the pimp's body lying between them, facedown in his own blood, and flames crawling up the wall.

Her heart is pounding in her chest, echoing in her ears. She stands in the darkness above the body, feet planted to hold herself up. The girl watches her with cat's eyes.

Behind her falls the towering shadow of a robed figure. Robed, with a crown of roses and a grinning skull of a face . . .

She jerks awake, her heart still hammering.

As she lies still, breathing shallowly, the smell of blood and death and fire fades.

The bedclothes are drenched underneath her, but her cheeks are cool. The fever has broken. She remembers the jail cell, Kaz's hacking cough—and understands she has been ill.

She sits up slowly. The walls around her are gleaming oak panel and there is a fireplace, and heavy drapes at a recessed window with a window seat. Outside, the wind pushes at the panes of glass; she can hear it slipping like silk through trees.

She cannot remember getting here, but it is too well appointed to be a motel. The pillows and mattress are high-quality, and the air has a subtle ginger and orange fragrance.

Now she stands. Every inch of her body is aching, as if she has been beaten, and she has to be still for a long moment, bracing her legs to stop the room from spinning.

Fever. No food for . . . how long?

There is no stench, though. She is not reeking of smoke or burned flesh. She is wearing only a T-shirt, and her hair smells of the ginger-orange fragrance. There has been a bath, a shower . . .

She does not remember washing. But she remembers the street fair, and the girl dancing, and the cave and the ominous shadow of a robed figure. A dream . . . but that does not make it any less significant.

She crosses shakily to the window, pulls open the drapes, and looks out on daylight. The hotel is perched high on a cliff. There are trees above, Monterey pine, and below, a crescent of ocean bay. North of San Francisco, she thinks. But not a place she immediately recognizes.

She turns from the window, fighting a wave of nausea. She crosses to the writing desk and finds stationery from the hotel. Bodega Bay Inn.

She does not know the inn, but she knows the place. She has gone north, then. She has no idea of the time frame. *Last night? Days ago?*

The clothes she finds on the armchair are not the ones she wore to take care of the guard. There are jeans, a sweater, some low-heeled boots from the Berkeley thrift store where she found the lethal pillow. Obviously she changed sometime during the day and night she cannot remember.

Except for the dream. The dream she remembers. It cannot be ignored.

Dressed now, and adequately disguised in a wig and makeup, she makes her way downstairs, uses her room card to let herself into the empty business center, and logs on to one of the computers. She rarely uses computers, and only public machines. But at the moment she feels safe enough. If she had no idea where she was, then the chances are slim that anyone else knows.

The first thing she notes is the date. A full day and a half after the burning of the guard. What else she has done in the interim is a complete mystery to her.

She pulls up a search engine. It takes her only seconds to find the pertinent news. This blogger, one of the ones who call themselves Bitch, has found details that would not ordinarily be released. Another man has been killed in an alley, throat slashed, his own semen fresh on him. A trick. A monger, as they call themselves.

The news brings a rush of sensations through her. Heat and cold, startlement and confusion, curiosity and anger. And fear.

She breathes slowly and tries to focus as she reads carefully through the article, her pulse rising as she reads the references to the dark saint. When her visitor offered help, she'd had no idea how far it would be taken. Someone is invoking. Deliberately. Rashly.

When she has finished reading, she knows that something has begun that will not end on its own. And not without far more blood.

She clears the history from the computer and stands.

Outside the hotel she finds a sandy path on the cliff, and a trailhead leading down to the beach. The day is windy. Strong gusts whip her hair and push her against the rock wall as she winds her way toward the muffled roar of the ocean. She has no thoughts, only a mass of feelings rising up from her gut, threatening to choke her, and a single, stark word.

Trap.

She reaches the sand and runs across it toward the water, pushing against the wind and the downward pull of the sand. At the water's edge she halts and paces along the tide line, feeling the waves rumble like a train in the earth beneath her feet. The wind beats against her face, lashes her clothes.

The urge to flee is overwhelming. Staying anywhere near here is madness, a sure road to imprisonment, with no possibility of a second reprieve. She must not get caught up in this new game.

Go. Now. Run.

But the girl.

The girl is both the instrument of her liberation . . . and her biggest obstacle to freedom and life. She is dangerous. She cannot be left out there alone.

The girl. The girl. The girl.

She holds her head and screams into the surf.

Chapter 38

Roarke sat in his office for some time, clicking through the links Singh had sent him to get to the Street Action forums. He was shocked at how many threads were virtual real-time records of the cruising on the stroll. It was a gold mine. There were threads for the Tenderloin, and even more for International Boulevard in Oakland, as well as pinned threads with useful tips for "hobbyists": *Keep a cleanup kit in the car so that a spouse or significant other doesn't catch on to the "hobby." Keep a dedicated cell phone for the "hobby," with bills mailed to a PO box under a different name.*

There were camera phone photos, links to classified ads showing sex workers with availability "right now," and warnings of law enforcement sightings and transvestites.

It would be like having dozens of eyes on the street with them, unknowingly reporting in.

Reading through individual posts, he experienced much the same kind of disgust he had felt emanating from Singh. But he also noted an interesting groundswell of panic among the regulars on the board. In the middle of the usual threads warning about law enforcement sightings, there was one thread titled:

SW Gone Wack?

Roarke clicked on it to read the posts.

MRDISCREET: Heard a monger got offed the other night by some loca SW.

MONGER83: On Inty?

MRDISCREET: No dude, in the TL.

BONEDADDY: I heard the same. Got hisself robbed and knifed after a BJ.

Roarke scrolled through useless speculation and conflicting reports . . . then stopped on a response by a poster with the screen name *Ballsout*.

BALLSOUT: Maybe he deserved it. Maybe the great goddess karma is walking the streets.

Naturally the responses that followed were violent reactions to the suggestion: profanity-laced, misspelled invectives against the poster.

There was one last chilling post:

BALLSOUT: There will be more. It's time for a reckoning.

And then the thread had been closed by the moderator to further comment.

Roarke reached for the police sketch in his in-box and studied the image of the young blogger: that cool, assessing gaze . . .

He started as someone stepped into the office doorway. He looked up to see Singh. She held her tablet in her hand. "Your theory that Goldman was a sick trick seems to have been corroborated."

He tensed up. "Mills found something?"

"Not Mills. Your blogger." She passed him her tablet. He looked down at another article.

The Secret Life of an Ordinary Citizen

Meet Andrew Goldman. By day he sells high-end office equip-ment. He has a wife, two children, a mortgage on a house in Millbrae.

By night he downloads rape porn and trolls the streets of San Francisco looking for underage prostitutes.

That is, he did. Until this week. When his hobby got him killed.

Something is happening in San Francisco. Someone has said, "Enough." And said it in a way that sex offenders can't mistake.

Roarke read on.

The blogger had hacked into Goldman's porn accounts, including links to videos in categories like "Schoolgirl Rape." She had reprinted some of his posts from the Redlight forums, where apparently his handle had been Beaverstretcher.

Roarke pulled himself away from the article as Singh spoke. "She is a very skilled hacker," the agent said. She was looking down at the sketch on his desk, and Roarke heard admiration in her voice. "I would like to talk with her about her methods."

Roarke dropped his gaze back to the article.

The blogger had also interviewed sex workers about Goldman.

Girls on the street were familiar with "Beaverstretcher." The more experienced knew to avoid him. "Bad news" was the general consensus. "He raped a girlfriend of mine," said one sex worker, who asked to remain anonymous.

Goldman may have believed, as many men do, that there's no such thing as raping a prostitute. Or, being a rapist, he may not have cared one way or another. But whatever he believed, he won't be raping any more prostitutes, or schoolgirls, or anyone else. Because Goldman was killed on Thursday, his throat cut from ear to ear in an alley off the Tenderloin stroll known to "mongers" as a safe spot for a quick blowjob. Just two days ago a pimp was killed two blocks away, in exactly the same manner.

There is a killer out there who gets it.

Singh spoke from the other side of the desk. "I find it interesting that she has not written about the murder of the guard, Driscoll."

Roarke looked up sharply. Singh was right. He didn't know what it meant, though. *She doesn't know? She's not in touch with Cara? Or she knows and is protecting her?*

The article went on.

> *Some people reading this may not believe Goldman's crime was as great as that of the pimp DeShawn Butler. Men like Andrew Goldman tell themselves that they're paying for a service. But a "sex worker" under the control of a pimp is not working for herself. Five prostituted girls can earn $1,500 a night for a pimp, and the women see almost none of that money themselves. In exchange for servicing ten or more men a night, these women get nothing but clothes, fast food, and the drugs that keep them enslaved to their exploiters.*
>
> *Mongers like Andrew Goldman perpetuate that hell.*
>
> *Let's be clear about the men who have died. They are sex traffickers. Rapists. Child predators. Abusers of every ilk.*
>
> *Pimp or john, they're finally getting what they deserve.*
>
> *This is a call to arms. This is a war against rape culture.*

Roarke looked up from the tablet with a knot in his stomach. The words *arms* and *war* echoed in his head.

Hyperbole? To an extent. But how many people were reading this? And how seriously might some of them take this "call to arms"?

Singh was watching him. He spoke slowly.

"I think the blogger is on the forums. This poster seems to have her phrasing, and she used a sentence . . ." He turned to his own computer and clicked on a few threads, located the poster with the screen name Ballsout.

Singh leaned forward to scan the thread, then looked up. "Agreed. The diction is similar."

"The question is, is she instigating, or is she more physically involved?"

Singh thought on it. "Obviously she has been in contact with other girls on the street and has gleaned what we suspected: that Goldman was an abusive trick."

"Which means that Jade might have been after Goldman specifically, not just randomly hunting . . ." Then something inside him went still. "Has Bitch been talking to girls? Or has she been talking to Jade?"

Jade had been at the courthouse during the demonstration. Certainly the blogger would not have stayed away.

And what am I thinking now? That they're all in it together? Madness.

He looked up at Singh. Her gaze was far away.

"I think we must find this blogger."

When she had gone, Roarke swiveled his chair to look out at the city. The Tenderloin was literally at his feet, fifteen stories below.

The feeling of dread was back, in full force.

What am I sending my people into tonight?

Chapter 39

She has been driving for some time. South on the 101, then east through the vineyards of the Sonoma Valley.

Driving to be on the move, driving to calm her agitation, driving to pass the day until the dark, when the moon will talk to her.

The safe thing would be to go north, into Oregon, Washington— to cross as many state lines as she can, put distance between herself and San Francisco, get lost in the endless miles of forest in the states between California and the Canadian border. The fewer people the better. Always.

But that is no longer possible. There will need to be a plan, a lure. She must set her own trap now, and not become tangled in the other's web.

She concentrates on the road, on the bleak winter light over the pale grass on gently rolling hills. As she nears San Francisco, she can feel Roarke focusing his thoughts on where she might be. Tracking her. He has his job, just as she has hers.

So she veers off the main highway onto the 116 toward Napa, taking different small highways, the 29, the 12, wending her way east in the largest circle she can make around the San Francisco Bay Area, before heading south again.

Near Lodi, the road signs give her the choice of continuing east, and her hands tighten on the wheel. The pull is strong to make the turn, to drive far out of reach. She can be in the Sierras by nightfall, and she has a cabin there, bought for cash years ago, completely off the grid. She could hole up, recover from the disorientation and displacement of jail, sleep for a month in the peace of the wilderness . . .

Impossible.

There is no such thing as safety with the girl out there, loose. She cannot leave this unfinished. And she cannot do what she needs to do without Roarke out of the way.

So when she sees the turnoff to the I-5, she takes it south, watching the road and waiting for a sign.

There are vast stretches of California with no houses, no businesses . . . where the blank canvas of the white-gold hills and fields makes certain configurations stand out and assume meaning. Trees and animals grouped into signs that can be read. Streams of slanting light through holes in the clouds. Dust spiraling up from a field like smoke from a witch's cauldron. An inexplicable field of uprooted trees, all laid out like corpses in their rows, bare roots obscenely exposed.

The clouds move quickly, casting looming dark shadows over the hills. She thinks of the shadow in the cave and is reminded that there is something else at work now, beyond the blogger, even beyond the girl, a wild card she cannot begin to interpret. The thought starts a coldness deep inside her.

She grips the steering wheel and drives on, asking for a sign.

Chapter 40

Roarke exited the BART station at Twenty-Fourth and Mission and walked blankly toward home. In his mind he saw Jade sitting in the dark of the Belvedere House lounge, covered in her defiant body art, small and still.

A sixteen-year-old girl out there in the night. Planning . . . *hunting*.

Is it Jade, though?

Who are we setting this trap for?

Multiple killers. Viral murder. Santa Muerte.

And what had Singh said, after the first blog article?

A living myth. A force beyond the merely human.

As if it all hadn't been strange enough to begin with . . .

His steps slowed as he became aware that something about his surroundings seemed off. He stood still, disoriented . . . and realized he'd made the first turn off Mission and strayed from his usual route. He was now on a darker side street.

The facade of a building ahead blazed with a mural, the wildly colorful Mexican artwork so typical of the Mission District. The painting adorned a basement-level shop with stairs descending from the sidewalk to a low door. A botanica, a Mexican occult shop. They were so common in the neighborhood, these tiny shops squeezed between the liquor stores and groceries and bars, that Roarke barely noticed them anymore. But now he moved toward it and stopped on the sidewalk, staring into the lower window of the building. The feeling of unreality hit like a slow-breaking wave.

A life-size skeleton figure stared out on him, dressed in a white gown, globe in one hand, scythe in the other. An owl was nestled in her robes, and candles of all colors burned at her feet, along with the now-familiar offerings: candies, tequila, cigarettes. The entire window was an altar to Santa Muerte.

How often have I passed it? he wondered as he looked into the saint's bony face. *A hundred times? A thousand?*

He moved down the stairs with a sense of sleepwalking.

The doorway was low and he had to duck his head to enter. Inside, the shop had the low ceiling of a converted basement. The air was thick with incense and candle smoke, and the shop was crammed with a maze of shelves that reached all the way to the ceiling, holding prayer books, candles of all colors, glass candleholders decorated with pictures of saints. Cellophane packs of herbs hung from clotheslines stretched above counters full of more esoteric items. Roarke scanned the shelves, taking in brown bags labeled in Spanish and sometimes in English, leaving no doubt as to their contents' purpose: *Attract Love. Big Money. Protect the Traveler. Take Away Evil.* Underneath the scent of incense he could smell garlic, peppermint, chamomile, tobacco, and any number of familiar and unfamiliar herbs.

A hushed conversation in Spanish came from deeper in the shop. He stepped to the end of an aisle to look down and caught a glimpse of a tiny woman garbed all in white. She stood behind a long glass counter, engaged in intent conversation with a middle-aged female customer. Roarke recalled that many of the Mission's Latino immigrants had no health insurance, and the *curanderas* of the botanicas provided herbal cures, as well as spells for less tangible troubles.

He turned away, giving the women their privacy. Against the next wall were four altars with near-life-size statues: the Virgin Mary, a dark male figure Roarke was unfamiliar with, yet another Santa Muerte, and some Egyptian animal god. Each altar had numerous lit candles and offerings of all types: money, roses, food, alcohol, dishes of what looked like honey. The Santa Muerte altar was the most eclectic and startling: smoke curled from a lit cigarette stuck in the skeletal mouth, and a wad of dollar bills was tucked into the crook of her arm.

Roarke moved into the next aisle . . . and was unnerved to find himself facing a whole row of the saint figures, three feet tall, grinning bonily down from the top shelf. Lower shelves held smaller figurines dressed in robes of different colors. Hundreds of them.

A line from Bitch's blog ran through his head. *"Numerous shops report half or more of their profits are earned from Santa Muerte paraphernalia."*

An underground he'd had no idea existed. Now it seemed vast, and ominous.

A voice spoke behind him, so close he twisted around in the narrow, crowded aisle.

"La Santísima . . . Santísima Muerte."

The white-garbed *curandera* stood directly behind him. She was as tiny as her shop; the top of her head didn't reach Roarke's chin. But there was a presence about her that commanded attention.

Her eyes flicked to the rows of saints. *"Usted la conoce."* You know her.

She spoke Spanish as if she were certain he would understand, and to a point, he did. He had a grasp of the basics of the language—part of the job, part of being a native Californian.

"No mucho . . ." he responded. *Not much.*

The tiny woman nodded emphatically. *"Sí. Está muy cerca de usted."* Yes. She is very close to you.

Roarke looked at her, wondering. She dropped her voice and spoke rapidly. *"Está de su parte. Pero debe tener cuidado. Mucho cuidado. Hay enemigos."*

He was struggling to follow, but he thought he understood most of it. *You have her favor. But you must be careful. Very careful. There are enemies.*

He found the whole conversation unsettling. Of course, he'd been looking at the Santa Muerte figurines. It didn't take a detective to glean that he had some interest, and these native healers were expert at sussing out physical cues. She'd said nothing that wasn't general, standard fortune-teller patter.

She fixed him with a hard look, as if she'd heard his thought. *"Alguien que tiene cerca, miente."*

Roarke felt a prickle of unease at that last.

Someone close to you is lying.

The *curandera* reached inside a bag tied on the belt around her waist and drew out something small that he couldn't see. She held it up: a small metal charm, a tiny Santa Muerte figure.

"Para que le proteja. Tome." For protection. Take it.

Roarke reached for his wallet, out of obligation and a growing desire to be out of the claustrophobic little shop, the strange conversation. But the *curandera* shook her head adamantly and spoke for the first time in English. "Is for you. You keep."

She took his hand and pressed the amulet into it. *"Para que le proteja."*

He let her close his fingers close around the piece, and nodded. *"Gracias."*

He left the shop feeling distinctly odd. The darkness felt close around him and the aura of the shop was still with him; it was a few moments before he could hear the normal sounds of the street. And the *curandera's* words echoed in his mind.

Someone close to you is lying.

Chapter 41

Night now, and in the darkness, after the commuters are safely back in their homes, the trucks come out. She watches the far lane, the slow crawl of ghost rigs in her night mirror. The moon whispers below the horizon line, nothing clear yet. But she can feel something coming.

She pulls off at the convenience store just after moonrise. As she gets out of the car the wind pushes at her, strong and cold. She looks up at the sky and shivers.

Inside the garishly lit shop she uses the restroom, then buys raw nuts, raisins, and water, three of the largest bottles. She still feels the prickling of fever and could easily drink an entire case . . . but a purchase like that would make her stand out from the endless stream of road-weary patrons, so she refrains. She is dressed in worn jeans and an oversize sweat jacket zipped up to her neck, her hair pulled back in a ponytail, a fake pair of glasses concealing her eyes; there is nothing to distinguish her from other travelers, and the young Latina clerk barely glances at her as she counts out cash. The clerk hands her the bag of purchases and she turns away from the counter.

She reaches to push through the glass doors to the parking lot . . . and finds herself face-to-face with a photocopied flyer. She stops, fixed on the photographic image, and feels familiar rage surging through her veins.

It is the sign she has been looking for.

She rips the flyer from the glass and pushes through the doors. Her mission for the night is clear.

Two birds with one stone.

Chapter 42

Upstairs in his flat, Roarke stopped in the hall and stripped off his shoulder holster, the evening ritual.

He walked into the living room . . . and the full force of his exhaustion hit him. He stopped and leaned against the archway, closing his eyes. The stakeout wouldn't start for hours, and he knew some sleep would be saving . . .

A rattle came from the corner of the room.

The spike of adrenaline had him reaching in vain for the weapon he had just discarded; then he realized the rattling was the fax machine in the dining alcove kicking to life. In these days of scanning and email, it had been so long since he'd gotten a fax that he'd forgotten the sound.

"What the hell . . ." he muttered, half-aloud. Who would be sending him a fax?

He stepped over to watch it printing out and saw the word at the top of the page: MISSING.

He felt the hair rise on the back of his neck as he had two simultaneous jolts of certainty: that the fax was from Cara, and that he was about to solve the mystery of Jade's real identity.

As he stood in the dark he could sense Cara standing on the other end of the line, looking down at whatever machine was transmitting whatever it was that was appearing before him. He could feel her intention, the urgency of her message, the force of her focus on him, toward him. His heart was beating out of control; the overwhelming, primal response he always had to her . . .

He wrenched himself out of that feeling as he realized what he had to do. His eyes shifted to the control panel of the fax machine, and he stared down at the phone number illuminated there, burning it into his memory before he turned and ran into the hall for the phone he had left on the accessory table.

He grabbed the phone and speed-dialed Singh. "I'm getting a fax transmission from Lindstrom. I need the location of the transmission and officers dispatched from the nearest police department. Immediately." He recited the fax number.

Singh's voice came through instantly. "On it, Chief."

An electronic beeping sounded from the dark of the living room, signaling the completion of the fax.

He strode back into the room. A single sheet of paper lay on the floor, a stark white rectangle in the middle of the hardwood. He walked toward it, stopped in front of it, stooped to pick it up.

A teenage girl smiled up at him in black and white. Dark hair and dark eyes, a candid photo that captured the heartbreaking natural beauty of that age. He had seen thousands of photos like this one, a moment in time captured before the child was struck down, seized by evil. Before the rape, the mutilation, the torture, the agonized death. He felt his gorge rise in outrage and what some might call his soul cry out . . . in the split second before the protective shield slammed down and he could do his job again.

And a new confusion hit him as he realized that the photo was not of Jade.

The phone buzzed in his hand, startling him. He lifted it to hear Singh's voice.

"I have Agent Epps on the line as well."

Roarke read the text of the flyer into the phone for them: a call for help from a traumatized family.

"'Sarah Jane Jennings, age fifteen, missing since 12/7 from Abilene, Texas, feared abducted into sex trafficking. Five foot three inches, last seen Bakersfield, California, wearing gray hoodie and blue jeans, Converse high-tops.'"

There was a pause, then Epps spoke into the phone. "You think Lindstrom sent it."

I know it, Roarke thought. Aloud he answered, "Who else?"

Singh added, "The fax came from an OfficeMax in Salinas—"

Roarke was already interrupting her. "Did anyone there see her?"

"It was a self-service fax machine."

And Cara was inevitably long gone.

Singh continued. "I have been in touch with the Abilene police department. The girl's brother has been all over central California posting those flyers. The facts listed are correct. Jennings was walking home from school and never made it home. A witness saw her being grabbed and pulled into a late model SUV by two Latino men. There has been a rash of similar abductions in surrounding towns in Texas and Oklahoma."

Roarke thought of Rachel's outburst about DeShawn. A "guerilla pimp," she'd called him. And Shauna's haunting words, *"I hear them say, 'Get that girl.'"*

"One of the other girls similarly taken was recovered at a truck stop on the West Coast prostitution circuit. Some local law enforcement suspect gangs affiliated with the *Sureños* are abducting girls from border states and bringing them into the Central Valley to pimp on the circuit. Although it must be said that this practice is not limited to gangs. Some girls have also been rescued from men with no gang affiliation who have decided to go into the pimping business."

Because dealing girls gets you less prison time than dealing drugs, Roarke thought. *Here we are again. This same sickness.*

The agents were all silent on their respective phones. "What are we supposed to do with this?" Epps asked, finally. "What does she want?"

"I don't know," Roarke said. There would be a purpose to all of it, but they were on Cara's time now. He felt the crush of frustration at the new mystery, even as he knew all they could do was wait.

"So now?"

Roarke looked into the dark outside his window. "We go out in the Tenderloin as planned. What else can we do?"

But that thought was a whole new level of worry.

Chapter 43

Neon burned through the drifting fog, garish reds, greens, blues, and ambers in the mist.

The surveillance van painted as a twenty-four-hour locksmith was parked on Jones Street, between O'Farrell and Geary. Inside the dark of the van, Roarke and Mills sat hunched over the rectangular gray lights of several video monitors.

One screen showed the street view outside their own van: the X-Press Market, a pizza joint, a narrow building with a sign advertising the Garland Hotel. Roarke watched the shady street denizens moving through the fog outside: addicts, dealers, homeless, criminals, the mentally ill, all of the above, drifted across the monitor, pushing shopping carts, getting into fights, cruising aimlessly or with nefarious purpose.

The other two screens showed the street views from the video cameras mounted in Epps' and Jones' cars. Jones was at the moment driving past a neon-lit strip club where two nearly nude women posed in the doorway. A hulking bouncer loomed between them with arms folded across his chest. On another screen Epps' car motored on a

darker street past bundles of the homeless camped in warehouse doorways, using their shopping carts and belongings as makeshift privacy
barriers.

On another computer, Mills was logged into the Street Action
forum boards, monitoring posts as they appeared.

Roarke shifted his gaze among screens. He knew it was critical to
focus on the sting, but he couldn't get the girl from the flyer out of his
head.

*"Sarah Jane Jennings, age fifteen . . . feared abducted into sex
trafficking."*

Like Shauna. Like Jade. Like how many other lost girls?

He had filled Mills in, showed him the fax.

"The fuck does it have to do with ours? Is it about Jade?" The detective's voice had been frustrated, raw with impatience.

It was all Roarke had been able to think about. It was a message
from Cara, clearly, and possibly it was a call for help, or reinforce-
ments, as Snyder had posited before. Was it about Jade? Maybe.

"No way of knowing. Yet," he'd told Mills.

They would find out. Inevitably. But for now, all they could do was
focus on the task at hand. Roarke knew he *had* to focus. His agents
were out there on the street with a killer. Maybe more than one.

He reached into his coat pocket and fingered the charm the *curandera* had given him—and had a sudden, uneasy wish that he'd given it
to Epps.

And that's just crazy.

But everything about this case had him spooked.

So he gritted his teeth and breathed the trapped air that smelled
of stale fries and greasy burgers and read the mongers' posts as they
appeared. Tedious interplay, ranging from depressing to enraging.

*HOBBYHUMPS: Hot little bsw, corner Sutter and Van Ness. Like to
stick that one on my dick and spin her.*

*PPP: Nice selection out on the Track 2nite. Had about seven bitches
come up to my window asking me if I wanted to date.*

TALLDUDE: Drove the Mish, 18th from Mission to Harrison. DEAD.

BIGBOPPER: Lushus spinner out on Bush and Larkin. Pink streaked hair, pink jeans, black top, huge tits. Would love to tap.

2COOL: Stay away, bro. No BBBJ, no GFE, problems with sucking on her titties, too. Hot eye candy but only with clothes on.

HOBBYHUMPS: Second dat. Bitch had the nerve to smoke a cigarette while I was pounding her.

LONGDONG: Shouda stuck a blunt in her ass and tol her you weren't finnished yet.

Mills looked up from the screen, shifted in his seat, twisting his back to crack it. "I ever get this pathetic, just shoot me."

"You got it," Roarke muttered.

Camera phone photos were going up, too, shots taken from the windows of passing cars. Roarke stared down at grainy images of girls standing on street corners or walking the sidewalks in micro skirts and high-heeled boots. Some shivered in bare arms; some of the more confident wore short coats over their tube skirts.

On the screen in front of Mills, a new photo of a sex worker popped up with the caption: *TL Hottie.* Roarke glanced at the image. Not Jade.

COOCHRAIDER: Found this girl by the O'Farrell Theater, went to her room on Sutter, paid 80 and left satisfied.

Other posters started in with the comments.

NINJA: Man, she look hott.

2COOL: Nice catch

FCKINBERG: You have a much better snatch-dar than I do.

Another photo went up. Not Jade. But Roarke felt his stomach go to bile as he read the accompanying post.

GIRLLUVER: Just turned this bitch loose on Hyde and Sutter. She is cheap but needed coaching. Didn't want to take it in her mouth but I held her head down and she swallowed. Then I fucked her in the back seat she was so tight I was a minute man and didn't need her to change positions.

The image of the girl on the MISSING flyer drifted in Roarke's mind.

Sarah Jane Jennings. Pulled off the street and forced into this hell . . .

"Check this," Mills said, his voice suddenly tense and focused. Roarke swiveled to read the post the detective was pointing to. "It's our boy."

HUNGMAN: Couple bitches hanging out on Polk and Sutter, and I do mean hanging out!! Wowzers!! Goin back around for a second look.

Roarke felt his pulse jump at the name. Hungman. The poster who might have seen Jade the previous night. Mills leaned forward and typed a response:

BONEDONOR: Yum. Pics pls.

Roarke grabbed for his phone to call Epps. "We've got a post from Hungman. He's cruising Polk, just posted from Polk and Sutter."

"On my way," the other agent replied.

Roarke leaned over to read the action on the screen. Mills had switched over to a different account to try to grab the monger's attention, make a date. Roarke watched intently as Mills typed out:

NIKKIFOXXX: Im the one your lookin for, hun. Got a room here on Polk. Message me.

"Nice," Roarke commented. "Just that right touch of illiteracy."

"Eat me," Mills suggested, and hit refresh. "Uh-oh, we got competition." Another sex worker had posted:

BLONDE4U: Me and my gf are out on Polk. We can show u a good time.

Mills typed again:

NIKKIFOXXX: Where u at, hun? Will cum to u.

They waited in silence, tense. Mills hit refresh again. Nothing. And again. This time there was a new post, with a selfie.

AMBER69: You know Im the one yr looking for, baby. Message me.

Roarke jerked forward, fixed on the grainy photo. It was shadowy, but the girl was Jade's body type, and her short, black hair was an obvious wig. Intricate tattoos covered the exposed skin of her neck and shoulders.

"Jade?" Mills asked.

"Not sure . . ." Roarke muttered. The two men stared at the screen, waiting for a response from Hungman.

"Shit. He's not posting. Could be messaging her right now."

Another post appeared.

BALLSOUT: *She looks like a kid. You do know what's happening to fucks like you who troll for underage girls? You're taking your life into your hands.*

Roarke tensed, starting at the poster's name. "This could be trouble," he told Mills. In the thread on the screen, the responses started in immediately.

COOCHRAIDER: *Not gonna let some freak chick cut down on my hobbying.*

FKINGBERG: *Some hoe tries to stick me I'm gonna stick her good.*

"Come on, Hungman," Mills muttered. "Post, you motherfucker."

The invective continued from the online mongers, but there were no further posts from Hungman. More worrisome, there were no more forthcoming from Ballsout.

"This isn't good," Roarke said.

He jumped as the radio crackled to life. A deep voice filled the van: Epps, reporting in. "I got a visual on a dark blue MINI parked on Hemlock off Polk."

Roarke and Mills exchanged a glance in the dark. Hemlock was one of several parallel two-block streets sandwiched between Larkin and Van Ness, and prime parking for car sex, being just off Van Ness' main thoroughfare. It was three blocks from where DeShawn Butler was killed.

"Copy that," Mills said, and he and Roarke focused on the screen that showed the camera view from Epps' vehicle as he slowly cruised by the dark parked car.

"Don't see a driver," the agent's voice muttered.

In the van, Roarke and Mills stared into the monitor at the car. No driver in it. No passenger.

"Unless they're in the backseat."

"Or he's on foot."

"I'm getting out," Epps said from the monitor. The view from the car showed the vehicle slowing to the curb as he parked. There was the sound of the car door opening and shutting. Then the camera stared implacably forward at the street, lit by hazy streetlights.

Roarke watched the screen, scanning the shadows. Empty sidewalks . . . dark doors . . .

Then he caught a glimpse of a white blob hovering in the blackness of a doorway. He felt a violent, full-body chill.

"I just saw something," he muttered, his eyes fixed on the screen. *A skull?*

Mills looked over at him. "What?"

As Roarke stared into the screen, the shadows shifted. A figure in dark pants and a black hoodie moved out from the doorway, headed in the direction Epps had taken.

Adrenaline shot through Roarke's body. "Drive," he yelled to Mills. "*Now.* Polk and Hemlock."

Mills heaved his bulk into the front seat of the van and twisted the key in the ignition. The engine roared to life. Roarke stared into the monitor, searching the shadows as he half-shouted into the phone.

"Epps. There's someone in a mask, following you. Dark pants, dark hoodie. Use extreme caution."

"Copy that," Epps' voice came back.

Polk and Hemlock was maybe three minutes away as the crow flies, but the narrow, one-way streets of downtown San Francisco were a logistical nightmare. Mills drove like a madman, one hairpin turn after another. As the van swerved, Roarke held on to the sides of his seat to stay upright and glanced into the monitor at the static street scene, snapping into the phone, "Epps, where are you?"

Silence from Epps' end.

"Epps," Roarke repeated sharply. And felt his heart drop . . . as the phone disconnected.

He reached for his weapon, twisted around in the dark, and was pushing open the back door of the van before Mills had come to a full stop. Roarke was out in an instant, hitting the sidewalk and sprinting toward Hemlock.

It was a short block, just four large buildings long, but felt like the longest run of his life as he pounded the pavement. He whipped around a corner . . . and pulled up short as he nearly ran into three startled streetwalkers. Two of them screamed, sending his pulse sky-rocketing. He held up his Glock in a flat palm.

"You're all right. Looking for a tall African American man. Jeans, dark hoodie. Have you seen him?" he demanded.

The girls shook their heads, wide-eyed.

His eyes swept the hazily lit street behind them. A few scattered transients drinking. Nothing like a sexual transaction going on . . .

Then he spotted the opening of an alley between two warehouse structures and bolted toward it, Glock at the ready again . . .

He rounded the corner and saw two silhouettes moving ahead of him in the mist: a portly man with his arm around a much slighter figure in a tube skirt, wobbling on high heels.

As Roarke barreled toward them, the man whipped around to face him.

"FBI," Roarke shouted. "Don't move."

Both the man and the girl froze. Roarke looked the young woman over quickly. Black hair . . . older and thinner than Jade.

He walked up to them, his weapon in one hand and his credentials in the other. He focused on the man, a pasty-faced, pudgy man in his late forties. "Are you Hungman?" he demanded.

"What? Who? No," the man said. The look on his face said otherwise.

A shadow suddenly loomed up behind the couple.

"Freeze!" Roarke shouted, aiming the Glock in the dark . . .

And recognized Epps. They locked eyes; then his agent lowered his own weapon, looked from the young woman to the man. "Looks like we caught ourselves a monger."

Roarke glanced toward the young woman. "You can go."

She needed no persuasion but teetered away as fast as she could move on too-high heels. Roarke turned back to the man, who shifted on his feet, looking trapped and defensive. "You—are taking a ride."

Hungman sat hunched into himself on the bench seat in the van, glaring at Roarke and Mills and Epps, reeking of pot and sweat.

On the computer screen, the bust was already being documented on the Redlight forums.

BIGBOPPER: *Hey bros watch out! LE just dragged a monger into a locksmith van at Polk and Hemlock.*

NINJA: *Game ovah 2night.*

"Well now, look at that," Epps told their collar. "You're famous."

Mills was already on the guy. "This you?" He pointed to the screen, showing him the post by Hungman.

The man glared and said nothing.

Mills looked him over. "Hungman. You're a man of subtlety, aren't you? Here's the deal, Hungman. At the moment you are under arrest for soliciting. You have the right to remain silent. If you give up that right, anything you say can and will be used against you in a court of law. On the other hand, we could have a conversation. And at the end of this convo we turn you loose . . . *if* you talk about this girl you posted about last night. No booking, no record, no hard feelings."

The pudgy monger looked from Mills to Roarke sullenly. "Or?"

"Or we take you in right now. Booking, charges, plenty of hard feelings, not the good kind."

The man settled back on the bench of the van and waited truculently. Mills put his beefy hands on his knees.

"Alrighty then. Let's get this party started. Name?"

"Frank Wilson."

"Address?"

The man looked trapped.

Mills shrugged. "Hey, the wife never has to know. Long as you cooperate."

Wilson answered reluctantly. "453 Green. Hayward."

"So you were out cruising last night and you saw this sex worker you describe here?" Mills turned the computer screen toward Wilson so he could read the post:

HUNGMAN: Need intel on young wsw spotted near bakery on Polk. Smoking little body, tight hot ass, black short hair, silver tube top, black mini, freaky all-over tats.

Wilson glanced at it, glowered. "That's what it says."

"Yeah. It also says 'Hungman.' This is why I don't believe everything I read."

Before Wilson could protest, Mills put the mug shot of Jade down on the makeshift table between them. "This the girl?"

Roarke felt himself tensing as the john looked it over. "Hair's different. But it looks like her."

Roarke and Epps exchanged a quick glance.

"You ever get with her before?" Mills asked.

"No."

"Now, hold up. I want you to think about it. Consider your response. Remember the nice, cushy cell we got waiting for you."

"I never went with her," Wilson said, sounding injured. "Not last night, not ever."

"You saw her, you were askin' for intel on her, but you didn't go with her," Epps said flatly. "I don't guess it was a flash of conscience, so what happened?"

A rush of expressions moved across the man's face: anger, resentment, embarrassment.

"The truth," Epps warned.

"She just left, okay?" Wilson snapped. "She looked me over and said, 'Move along, asshole. Not your night.'"

Roarke and Mills exchanged a glance.

Jade. It sounded just like her.

"Were you posting in real time, soon as you saw her?" Roarke asked.

"Pretty close."

"So this was just before midnight last night, 11:40 or so?"

"If that's what it says."

"What about the tats?"

"What about them?"

"A description."

The john shrugged. "She had on a tube top. There was art all over her back. Like, fire. Winding up her neck into her hair."

Roarke felt a twinge of excitement. Lots of sex workers were tattooed, but Jade's were heavy on the fire imagery and she definitely had them running up into her hair. It was a dangerous and painful procedure, not as often seen. He was both glad for the ID and sick over it. Jade had been cruising the Tenderloin the night of Andrew Goldman's murder. Not good news.

"About how old was she?"

The man started to respond and then stopped himself. "Eighteen," he finally said sullenly. "Nineteen. How do I know?"

"Try sixteen," Epps said.

"Don't know anything about that."

Mills shook his head. "Now, see, we thought that your use of the word *young* in your postings might indicate otherwise."

The john sat in silence.

Mills sighed, leaned forward, and slapped a photo of the dead john, Goldman, in front of Wilson. "'Kay, let's try this. You see this guy while you were out last night?"

"No."

"Do you know him?"

"No."

Mills replaced the photo of Goldman with the composite sketch of the blogger. "How about this woman? Ever seen her before?"

Wilson barely glanced at the sketch. "Not my type."

Mills looked two seconds away from murder. "You think I give a shit? Take a good look and tell us if you've seen her before."

Wilson dropped his gaze to the sketch, studied it. "I don't know."

Roarke reached for his own iPad and pulled up a photo. "You see anyone dressed like this out there?" He passed the tablet over to Wilson, who looked down at the skull head, the shadowy shot from online. He startled back in his seat.

"Jesus. No."

Mills and Roarke exchanged a glance.

"Sure about that?" Mills demanded.

"You think I wouldn't remember?"

"You got lucky," Roarke said. The john looked stupidly blank. "Guys like you are getting killed for mongering."

For the first time, Wilson looked genuinely shaken. "Thought that was just some bitch trying to stir things up on the boards."

"Oh no," Mills said. "It's for real. Body count's rising."

"So why don't you catch this cunt?" Wilson asked petulantly.

Roarke had to keep his arm pinned to his side to keep from hitting him. Instead he spoke tightly. "You really don't get it, do you? How close you came?"

"Not doin' anything wrong," the john said.

There was no point in staying out. The takedown had been broadcast on the forums; streetwalkers and johns alike had scattered. The streets were deserted. The agents got Wilson's details, then turned him loose. The three of them sat in the dark back of the van, just the light of the computer screens on their faces.

"It was Jade, right?" Epps said. "She was right there with him."

Mills nodded slowly. He looked to Roarke to confirm. "But she didn't kill him. Why?"

Roarke was thinking on it. "Maybe they're not random kills. According to Wilson, he didn't know her. She came up to his car but didn't go with him. Maybe she mistook the car for someone she did know and backed off when she saw Wilson instead of Goldman."

"Goldman didn't drive a MINI," Epps pointed out.

Roarke realized it was true. "Maybe Goldman wasn't the only one she was looking for," he replied. Then he felt cold at the implication. *Does she have a list?*

"You mean, it's personal," Epps said.

Chapter 44

The moon is waxing. December moon. Cold Moon.

Through the windshield, she watches it rise in the sky, bathing the hills in icy light, illuminating the long, slow serpent crawl of trucks in the far lane.

So clear, what it is saying to her now, and it is not hard to find what she needs.

She has circled the freeways and highways around Salinas for several hours, but there is one stop in particular that draws her. Off the 101, and large enough: the exit ramp is crowded with several gas stations and a couple of motels, and there is a constant flow of travelers off and onto the freeway, stopping to use the facilities and moving on.

And there is the truck stop, a good-size one, with a gas station, convenience store, and diner. Restrooms with shower stalls. A weigh station. A truck wash.

She parks the Toyota among two dozen other cars on the window-less side of the diner and convenience store, across from the truck lot with its rows of eighteen-wheelers. She turns off the engine and kills the lights, pulls the hood of her sweatshirt up over her head, then sits in the dark and watches the aisles of trucks.

The grounds are flat, and it is easy to survey the lot: a full ten long rows of enormous rigs with their big, dark windows and different colors of shiny hoods nosing out from the aisles. Mist drifts from the surrounding farmland and snakes through the corridors of looming vehicles, illuminated by the lights on top of the truck cabs: blue, white, pink, yellow, like a bedraggled, oversize string of Christmas lights.

She ignores the first nine rows. There is only one to watch: the last one, farthest away from the diner and closest to the field. The darkest row, in more ways than one.

All over the country, at stops just like this, that last line of trucks is known as Party Row. The women who service the truckers are called "commercial ladies" by the more polite. The rest of the men call them lot lizards. An ugly phrase for an uglier reality.

She sits, and she waits, watching the corridor of trucks. It does not take long. She sits forward as a shadow emerges from between two trucks. Immediately several headlights flash on, a universal signal, beckoning the shadow.

She watches intently as the shadow of another woman emerges from a different aisle.

The women stop briefly to talk to each other, with the tall walls of the truck sides towering above them. One is heavyset, a roll of fat visible between her cut-off blouse and her tight jeans. The other is thin and jittery. The heavier one turns to indicate a truck parked in the aisle. The thin woman listens, nods. A truck turns into the aisle, and the women are lit up in the blinding headlights. Both move quickly back into the shadows, toward the truck the first woman indicated.

But Cara has seen their faces and the way they move. They are not why she is here.

She sits back again and waits, and she watches as the moon creeps slowly higher in the sky. It is not yet full enough to obscure the stars. She can see the constellation Orion, the Hunter, at the far edges of the horizon—and she thinks of Roarke. He will have received her message by now. He will be wondering, and looking out for the next sign. When he gets it, he will come.

At the far end of the row, a truck flashes its lights.

It is a matter of seconds before she sees two more shadows emerge: a wiry man in boots, jeans, and a denim jacket, propelling a girl by the arm toward the truck that has flashed. The girl staggers on wedge heels, her slender legs and arms bare in cutoff shorts and a pale halter top even in this cold. Their bodies in the headlights throw huge, grotesque shadows.

The pimps usually drop the girls off, then stay out of view in nearby motels while the girls earn money for the night. Which means this girl is new and needs watching to prevent her from running. She appears so stoned she likely could not walk without the pimp's assistance.

As the man strong-arms the girl down the aisle, Cara opens the car door silently, slips out, and walks, following them through the maze of trucks. Not too quickly, not too purposefully, with a bit of a drift to her step. There is only one reason for anyone female to be walking here, and she is flashed by several trucks, but she ignores the lights.

Her hand is in the pocket of her hoodie, fingers loose around the razor. She can hear the night breathing around her. The night breathing . . . and the restless coiling of *It*.

She waits as the pimp steers the girl to the driver's side of the first truck that flashed. She watches as the trucker pulls the girl up and inside the cab. The pimp hovers in the shadows, keeping his eyes on the cab's door as he steps to the side of the truck to fire up a joint. The pungent smoke drifts in the misty air.

She circles the truck, skirting the huge wheels, moving without sound, and is there to meet the pimp on the rear side. A kick to the knee to stagger him, a quick jerk forward on his jacket to land him on his knees, then she is grasping his hair and slicing his neck. His shout is lost in a gurgle of blood. It spills warm and wet on her gloved hands. She tightens her fingers in his hair and holds him just long enough for him to drain out, jerking and shitting himself. Then she drops him to the dirt and turns toward the truck. In one quick move she is up on the runner of the truck, pulling open the door.

Behind the front swivel seats, the girl kneels on the floor of the cab between the trucker's legs as he sits back on the narrow bed. Even drugged as she is, the girl is alert enough to sense the new danger. She scrabbles backward on the small floor space, away from the trucker and out of Cara's way. The trucker has no hair to grab. Cara lunges forward, seizes his balding head with both hands, and slams it against the back wall of the cab, once, twice, three times. Bone crunches against metal, pulping flesh. As the trucker's body jerks and slumps, she presses his skull against the back wall with one hand and cuts his throat with the other. The blood sprays, an arterial surge.

She steps to the side and watches the body spasm as he bleeds out on the pallet of the bed.

When he is dead, she turns away, taking in long breaths to slow the wild racing of her heart.

The girl huddles on the floor of the cab, staring up at her, eyes wide and glistening in the dark. The copper smell is thick in the air.

"Don't scream," Cara tells her.

The girl shakes her head. She doesn't move as Cara stands in the dark, her hands at her side, regaining her balance.

"Where are you from?" she asks, finally.

The girl seems to have to search far back in her memory. Her voice is slurred as she answers in a broad accent, "Tulsa."

"Do you want to go home?"

"*No*," the girl says savagely. "No no no no no."

Cara hears it in her voice and doesn't have to hear any more. *Scratched.* She nods. "Then listen."

She speaks, and the girl listens.

DAY SEVEN

Chapter 45

Buzzing. Rattling.

Fire alarm? Burning?

Finally consciousness penetrated enough for Roarke to identify and reach for his phone, by now jumping and clattering at full strength on the bed table. He picked up to Singh's urgent voice. He was still asleep for the first three seconds of the conversation, but then two words jarred him awake.

" . . .double murder."

A sick taste roiled up into Roarke's mouth. *We left too soon. Chased a shadow and missed the action . . .*

"In the Tenderloin?" he asked aloud. His own voice grated in his ears.

"A truck stop."

As Singh started recounting the details, Roarke shook his head, thinking he must not be following. "A pimp *and* a trucker?"

"A pimp and a trick at once," she confirmed. "Both with slashed throats. The truck stop is outside Salinas, on the same stretch of the 101." Roarke knew without asking for clarification that she meant the same stretch of central California highway where Cara had killed a predatory trucker at a deserted rest stop. *Only two months ago.*

Singh continued. "The trucker in the cab of his rig, the pimp just outside. The trucker was killed on his bed and had his pants around his ankles."

A pimp and a trick. The same configuration as the San Francisco murders. In Salinas.

It had to be Cara. And it was deliberate. She was saying something. And he knew it had to do with the girl on the MISSING flyer. The flyer sent from a Salinas office store. Sarah Jane Jennings.

But how? What?

No time to think of that for now. Singh had just said something else that instantly electrified him: "There is a witness."

Roarke shook his head to clear it. "Call Epps. I'll pick him up."

"Will do, Chief. I have sent the initial report to your email, and I have informed the Salinas detectives that you will be there."

As Roarke dressed, the phone buzzed again. This time he picked up to Epps' voice. "Singh just called. I'll come get you."

"I can drive—" Roarke started.

"Been up for an hour," Epps said. "Let's beat it before traffic."

Roarke had just closed his front door behind him when he heard an engine through the dense, early-morning fog, and Epps pulled up at the curb in a fleet car.

He had two large takeout coffees in the console and looked considerably more polished than Roarke felt.

As Roarke dropped into the passenger seat, Epps nodded briefly and set off down the street, concentrating on negotiating the car through the gray wall of fog until they were on the freeway going south.

Salinas was a two-hour drive from the city on the 101, an agricultural town ringed by low hills and surrounded by the fertile farmland that had earned it the nickname "the Salad Bowl." It was famous as the home of John Steinbeck and as the focal point of the Delano grape strikes led by Cesar Chavez. More recently it was notorious for leading the state in gang-related homicides: turf wars between the *Sureños* and *Norteños* Mexican gangs.

Despite their grim mission, Roarke felt a kind of relief being out on the road, with unpopulated miles going by outside, away from the tangled mess of the crimes in the city. As he stared out the passenger window at the fog blanketing the hills, it occurred to him that this case had started on the road and kept moving back onto the road. It was Cara's nature: she was a traveler.

But the tension in the car grew thick and thicker, as morbidly gray as the fog around them, relentless tendrils snaking across the freeway lanes, while Epps drove in silence. Roarke could feel the agitation coming off his agent.

And finally he allowed himself to feel what he hadn't been acknowledging.

Loss. Even—grief. Epps was not just one of the finest agents, but one of the finest men he knew. The chasm that had opened between them since Cara had come into their lives was one of Roarke's biggest regrets. And last night, for a few seconds in that alley, he'd been afraid that he'd lost this man for good . . .

Is it worth it?

Without turning to look at Roarke, Epps spoke for the first time. "Salinas."

Roarke glanced at him.

"The fax from Salinas. The girl on the flyer. The murders at the truck stop. This is Cara."

Roarke looked out the window beside him. "Yeah."

"She's up to something."

Roarke didn't answer.

"Is it connected at all? To the Tenderloin kills? Or is it just Cara doing what she does?"

Roarke hadn't had much time to think about it. It had occurred to him that Cara was deliberately drawing them down to Salinas, out of

San Francisco. *But why?* To speak to him, perhaps? His pulse started to race just at the thought, and he forced himself to breathe deliberately to slow it.

Epps was speaking again. "And another trucker . . . She did that trucker in Atascadero. Is she targeting truckers now?"

Roarke didn't think so. Her hunting had always seemed more random than that, driven by a purpose known only to her, a purpose he may have been as close as he would ever get to understanding when he was visiting her in the jail.

And yet . . .

These new pimp and john killings at the truck stop . . . after the pimp and john killings in San Francisco. There was something deliberate about that, the double pairing.

He finally said it aloud. "A pimp and a john."

"Yeah," Epps answered. "I know. 'Pimp or john, they're finally getting what they deserve.'"

Roarke looked at him, startled—then realized he was quoting Bitch's article.

"Right. But we know that Lindstrom didn't kill DeShawn Butler. This pair happened in the same night, almost simultaneously, and the first pair were killed several days apart. Even so . . ."

He thought of the last words of the blog, *"This is a call to arms,"* and felt a cold touch of foreboding.

He finished reluctantly. "I'm thinking there may be others. Singh should be looking."

"She already is," Epps said. Roarke glanced at him. "She said so when she called this morning. I'm pretty sure she's looking at everything."

Roarke had no doubt.

Epps shifted his large frame in the seat. "You and Lindstrom . . ."

Roarke could feel the change in the air, and his stomach plummeted. It was the moment he'd always known was coming.

He knows I've been going to see Cara. Singh told him.

At the same time, Roarke was sure that Singh would never do it. Whatever she thought, whatever she had to say about it, she would say directly to him.

Then Epps said stiffly, "I don't know what you two got between you. But I know it's there, and I know you better start using it. We're talkin' about a sixteen-year-old girl out there now, getting into all kinds of shit. It has got to stop. You need to use what you *know*, however you can. And you get no more grief from me about how you do that."

Roarke was startled, and grateful. He nodded, looked out the window into the fog.

If only I did know.

It was nearly eight a.m. as they motored down Salinas' historic Main Street, with its Gold Rush–style buildings interspersed with cheap, bland modern structures.

The truck stop was outside the town, a little south of it: a triangle-roofed mini-mart stuccoed in desert colors, set in the middle of a bleak, sandy expanse, with wide, flat farm fields stretching for miles around it.

There was a diner and a comfort center with men's and women's showers, a large drive-through truck wash, and a parking lot with spaces for about seventy-five rigs. A neon sign advertised FUEL–WEIGH–WASH. The only other décor was telephone poles, spiky round cactus clusters, and oversize sandstone boulders, all of it shrouded in slowly rolling coastal fog.

The Monterey County detectives, Escobar and Morales, met the agents inside the diner.

Roarke looked past a chalkboard menu advertising tri-tip steak sandwiches and burrito combos, to survey a room full of truckers hunched at tables and pacing at the windows. Several uniformed cops circulated in the room, talking to the truckers, scribbling notes on spiral pads. Workers hustled behind steam tables to keep the steel trays heaped with scrambled eggs, bacon, sausage, refried beans.

Escobar saw Roarke watching the assembled men and smiled bleakly. "We detained 'em as witnesses. They're all eating for free, but they're not too happy about it. Your Agent Singh filled us in on the trucker in Atascadero. You thinking someone's targeting truckers?"

The agents exchanged a glance.

"You said there was a pimp dead, too," Roarke said.

Morales answered, "Guy had a drug record for sale and possession. But yeah. He brought a girl to the stop last night."

"Is that the witness?" Epps asked, and Escobar nodded to him.

"She's down at the station. She's pretty strung out—haven't got much out of her yet."

"We'd like to see the scene first," Roarke said. "If you don't mind."

Outside in the parking lot, the detectives walked them between trucks toward, inevitably, the last aisle. Party Row.

Along with showers and large, hot meals, truck stops all over the US provided easy access to sex and drugs for drivers who wanted to partake. Meth and other forms of amphetamine were popular, of course: something to keep the drivers awake on the long hauls. But a whole smorgasbord of illegal substances was on offer.

There was less variety in the women. Hooking at truck stops was the lowest of the low, the women generally hard-core addicts. Survival prostitution, it was called.

Roarke looked ahead to where one eighteen-wheeler had its passenger door standing open. A uniform hovered, on watch.

"Found the one guy on the ground, there." Escobar motioned to the evidence flags, an unnecessary gesture: the body had been taken away, but most of the blood was still clotting the dust beside the rig. "Leon Jonas. Not a trucker, and not a local—his license shows him living in Chico. Motel owner down the road says he checked in last night. His car was in the motel lot. We found cash and bags of crystal on him. Meth is what his record's for."

"Until he decided to branch out," Epps said.

Morales nodded. "The gangs do a lot of the pimping around here but mostly in town. The truck stops, though—we get a fair amount of pimps bringing in girls from all over the state. Most nights this place is crawling with . . . commercial ladies."

Roarke knew he'd been about to say something harsher. "And last night?" he asked.

"Unidentified male phoned 911 around one a.m., reported that a guy had collapsed outside his truck. Makes sense it looked like that from a distance: the open truck door, the guy on the ground. Ambo gets here 1:19, paramedics see the DB, call it in. First officer on scene investigates the truck, finds the second body in there. Pants down, throat cut. Driver of record, William Michael Nesbitt." The detective gestured up to the cab of the truck. "Cab's a mess. Stay to the left of the runner."

Roarke stepped up on the runner and balanced there, holding on to the doorframe to get a look inside. A mess was what it was. Drying arterial blood spray curtained the inside of the cab. So familiar to him now, the crimson trail Cara left in her wake.

Why here, though? Why does she want me here? What is she up to?

He looked back out the door over the lot, the scattered trucks. Not the usual configuration of neat, closely parked rows; instead a seemingly random scattering. "Not a lot of vehicles," he said to Escobar. The detective nodded.

"According to the diner manager, this place was packed last night. Lot of the rigs disappeared 'tween the time we got the call and the time we got to the stop. News must of been all over the CB waves. It's the ones who slept through it we got corralled in the diner."

Epps spoke tensely. "And the girl?"

"When the uniforms searched the scene they found her passed out in the field." Escobar turned and pointed out into the fog beyond the last row of trucks. "She's got blood on her but nowhere near what it would have to be for her to make sense as the doer. Plus she's pretty young, looks to me like. Can't see it."

Roarke and Epps exchanged a glance. *The girl on the flyer? Could it really be?*

Epps opened the binder he was carrying, passed the flyer over to the detectives. "This her?"

The detectives studied the photo of Sarah Jane Jennings, looked at each other. "No," Morales said. Escobar shook his head.

Roarke saw his own confusion mirrored on Epps' face.

Escobar handed the flyer back to Epps. "We got this as a BOLO. There are a bunch of them circulating."

"A bunch of these flyers?" Roarke asked, although he knew the answer before the detective said it.

"A bunch of BOLOs on missing girls."

Epps shook his head, tight-lipped. Roarke could feel the anger coming off the other agent. It was a struggle to keep his own voice even.

"So who is this girl? The wit?"

Escobar shook his head. "No idea. No ID on her of course, can't get a name out of her, but I can tell you she hasn't been arrested here before. We got a desk clerk pouring coffee down her. Like I said, she's pretty strung out."

Morales spoke up. "But she saw the kill—one of them, anyway. She said, 'She came in the truck and killed him.' *She* killed him," the detective repeated, in case the agents hadn't heard. "When we talked to your Agent Singh, she said you'd seen this before?"

"It sounds like ours, yeah," Epps answered, since Roarke was silent.

"The killer's a lot lizard?" Morales asked in disbelief.

"No," Roarke said. "Where's the girl?"

The police station was a long, low, blue-and-white box in downtown Salinas.

The girl was in the station office, seated on a sprung couch, wrapped in a blanket and clutching a mug of coffee. Roarke's immediate, visceral impression was that he was looking at a child. She was red-haired and freckled and seemed a bit older than Shauna, probably not as old as Jade.

"That's a kid," Epps muttered. Roarke turned to Escobar.

"Have you called Social Services?"

Escobar's face tightened. "This isn't San Francisco, Agent Roarke. Social Services doesn't have enough workers for the kids they take away from their parents, let alone . . ." He gave the girl a glance.

Roarke's face tightened at the unspoken word. Far too many law enforcement officials still thought of prostitution as voluntary. Many agencies still focused on arresting the girls rather than the men who trafficked them.

"We'd like to have a few minutes," he told the detectives. Escobar didn't look pleased, but he nodded to Morales and they stepped out.

Epps stayed near the door and did his best impression of being invisible, which was surprisingly good, while Roarke took a chair and placed it not too near the girl, then sat facing her and cleared his throat. "I'd like to talk to you about last night, if that's okay."

She didn't look at him but stared at the floor, glassy-eyed. Her blanket had slipped off one shoulder, and he could see her neck and chest were still dotted with dried blood, presumably from the arterial spray when Cara cut the trucker's throat.

"I'm Agent Roarke," he told her.

The girl glanced up, a quick, wary look.

"You're not in any trouble," he assured her. "No one's bringing charges."

She was silent, fixed on the floor again.

"I know you've had a rough night," he told her, he hoped gently. It was probably the understatement of the year, and he found himself wishing Rachel were with him. "We just want to find out what happened."

There was no response from the girl.

"Can you tell me your name?"

She didn't look up, didn't look at him.

"Or where you're from?"

Silence.

"Everyone's from somewhere," he suggested. There was no response.

"How old are you?"

A dozen answers flickered on her face, clearly too many for her to choose from in her state.

"If you're going to make me guess, I'm going to say fifteen."

She looked startled, then nodded warily.

"How'd you get here?"

Her face tremored. She looked down and shrugged. "Leon brung me," she finally said, in a voice that was rough as sandpaper and barely above a whisper.

"Leon's your pimp?"

"My boyfriend," she said dully.

Typically what prostitutes called their pimps. Voluntarily or otherwise. Roarke saw the tightness on Epps' face as he shook his head, the barest of movements.

"Your boyfriend?" Roarke repeated. "For how long?"

There was a brief, haunted look on her face. "Couple weeks, I guess."

"Where were you before then?"

She cleared her throat but didn't speak.

"Are you here willingly?"

She was silent.

"If you tell me your name, we can get you some help. Help you get home—"

The girl jerked her head up. "*No.*"

Both agents flinched, and Roarke felt a flash of tired anger. "Or help you get someplace new as a home," he finished. "Whatever you want."

She didn't look at him, and her voice was barely audible. "He said he'd find me."

"Leon said that?"

She nodded, her hair falling over her face.

"Leon is dead," Epps said, his voice hard. "Leon won't be finding anyone anywhere."

She started to cry then, silent tears running down her cheeks. And the story began to come out, one halting sentence at a time.

She'd fought with her mother a month or so earlier and had been staying at a friend's house. The only other thing she would say about it was that she didn't like her mother's new boyfriend.

She'd met Leon at a party. He was older and very attentive. He bought her dinners and clothes. There was drinking. There were drugs. There were photo sessions, because, of course, Leon was a "professional photographer." After a few days he said he was going back to California "to shoot a commercial" and suggested she come with him.

So often it was the same story, the same lies: *You're so beautiful, you could be a model." "I bet you're a great actress." "You could make a lot of money with that face."*

Roarke sat, and listened, and tried to contain his fury.

The first night, she and Leon stopped at a motel. There was more drinking, and more drugs. When she woke up she found another man in the room with her, who raped her. For three days Leon brought men back to the motel to have sex with her.

The next night he took her out to a truck stop. He told her no one would care if she tried to tell tales on him. She was committing a crime herself, so she could be arrested. If she tried to run he would find her and kill her.

She tried to run. He caught her and "trunked" her: locked her in his car trunk without food, without water, for two days. After that he kept her drugged. By then the drugs were all she wanted.

She was on the road with Leon approximately three weeks; she wasn't sure, because they moved on to another stop every few days.

They had arrived at the Salinas stop in the early evening. She had just gotten into the cab with the trucker when someone else entered the cab. Her first thought was that it was Leon. Instead the curtains separating the driver's area from the bed were pulled back and a blond woman was standing there with what the girl called a knife.

And then there was a lot of blood.

Roarke took a long moment before he spoke, trying to manage his fury and despair. "Did she talk to you?"

"She said 'Don't scream . . .'" And then the girl hesitated. Roarke sat forward, on alert.

"What else?"

"She said, 'Agent Roarke will be here soon. He'll help you.'"

Roarke stared at the girl. Epps stared at Roarke.

Roarke reached for Epps' folder and showed the girl the MISSING flyer, with the picture of Sarah Jane Jennings. "Have you ever seen this girl?"

She looked down. Her face was blank as she examined the photo-copied plea. "Uh-uh."

"What's your name?" he asked, again, gently.

The girl didn't speak for a long time. And then she said, "Becca."

The two agents stepped outside the office. Roarke closed the door on Becca before he turned to the two Monterey County detectives. "Where does she go now?"

Escobar shrugged. "Juvie's the best we can do. At least she won't be out on the street tonight."

Epps shook his head, his jaw tight. No one said anything.

The agents walked out into the parking lot. They stopped beside their car and looked out on the acres of farmland beyond the police station, cultivated green fields alternating with brown, dormant ones.

Epps spoke without looking at him. "She wanted you here. She knew you'd come."

Roarke said nothing.

Epps put a big hand on the back of his own neck, massaging it. "What's your feeling? Stay or go?"

At the edge of the parking lot, a tumbleweed rolled in the wind. Roarke watched it, wondering. *Is it a setup? How can we know?*

He couldn't see any way around it. "Probably she's long gone, but—"

"Before she wasn't," Epps finished. When Cara killed the other trucker at the rest stop, just a hundred miles from where they were now, they had assumed she would move on immediately, when in reality she had taken refuge in a town less than half an hour away.

"Right," Roarke said heavily. "So we stay overnight. Just in case. Maybe something will happen—"

"Oh, something's going to happen," Epps said. Roarke looked at him. "This is the third month we've been doing this. Chasing this woman. First month, she tries to take out the trafficking gang at the concrete plant."

Tried and succeeded, Roarke thought. *With a little help from us.*

Epps continued. "Last month it was the Reaper. The Reaper's killing families, watching his next targets. And Lindstrom's right on the scene. Again. Takes him out. And both times, it's on the night of the full moon."

Roarke felt a chill of understanding.

Epps nodded at him. "The real shit always goes down on the full moon. So it looks to me like we got just two nights left to figure out what's going down this time, what kind of big thing she's got planned."

Roarke was blown away. It was the kind of thinking that he should have been doing himself, and hadn't been. What *was* the plan for this moon? Though he had his doubts that even Cara herself could tell them what she intended, Epps was right. There was a path she would be following.

"You're right," he admitted aloud.

"I know I'm right. I just don't know what the fuck that means."

The fax. The pimp/john pairing. She wants us here. But for what?

"It means we stay," Roarke said. He hoped to God he was right.

Chapter 46

She is nowhere near Salinas.

She walks along Telegraph Avenue in Berkeley, past the street vendors behind their folding tables and makeshift tents lining the sidewalk, hawking their Christmas wares. The store windows on either side of the street are lit up with nontraditional holiday decorations, and music overlaps from street musicians on every other corner.

She is still buzzing from the events of the night before, and nervous about being around so many people. The newspapers and blogs have been carrying her photo. Her past has been connected to her present, and entirely against her will, she is famous again. But it cannot be helped. The streets here are crowded with shoppers, and students finished with exams but not yet returned home for the holidays, and she is relatively safe, camouflaged in worn jeans and hoodie and bulky thrift store coat. She has bought herself some time with her lures: the flyer from the convenience store, and last night's blood. With Roarke and the agent called Epps out of the way in Salinas, she can search for the girl Jade without having to worry about crossing paths with her hunters.

She meanders past stalls of pottery and crystal jewelry and feath-ered dream catchers, past tarot readers and palm readers, and she considers the girl. Her instinct is that the girl will be close; she will not move far out of her comfort zone, but she will vary her hunting ground. Surely she is canny enough to avoid places she knows will be heavily patrolled now that the murders are under investigation.

And Telegraph Avenue is the East Bay version of the Haight.

These streets, the carnival atmosphere, are the girl's milieu. She is a night creature and will probably not show her face this early, but her taste for the psychedelic is obvious. So Cara keeps alert, keeps her eyes peeled for a sign of the girl, or just a sign.

Her mind drifts to her dream and the real-life scenes it reflected. The girl at the fair, on a street not unlike this one . . . the girl in the cave, locking eyes with her over the dead body of the pimp . . .

And the other presence. The bony shadow on the cave wall. That ancient, implacable force, creaking to life at the scent of blood.

Unfamiliar, yet inevitable. A wild card if ever there was one.

The girl . . . and the crone. A collision of destiny.

As she walks past tables full of jewelry and metalwork, brooding on it, one of the numerous fortune-tellers catches her eye. A small Mexican woman, seated at a folding card table draped with a silk shawl. The little woman looks up without speaking a word, and holding Cara's eyes, she turns over a card.

Cara steps to the table and looks down on a skeleton figure astride a horse, wielding a curved sword, as human figures fall prone in its path.

Death.

She pulls out the rickety folding chair opposite the fortune-teller and sits.

"*Donde?*" she asks.

Where?

Chapter 47

Roarke and Epps found a rig through the police station. There were several in impound. So they picked an SNC Century and drove the massive vehicle out to the truck stop and they parked in the last row, Party Row, and turned off the lights, and they ate pizza and waited in the encroaching twilight.

Epps settled his long and elegant frame in the back of the cab on the bed, while Roarke sat in the passenger seat, which swiveled to the rear to create something of a living room setup. First he called in to the office to brief Singh on their stakeout, putting her on speaker. As they talked, he could picture her in the office, the gold bands on her wrists, her dark fall of hair.

"The Monterey County detectives were talking about a series of BOLOs. You mentioned that there were other missing girls who might have been trafficked to the Central Valley—"

"I have identified eleven similar cases reported in the last six months," Singh answered. "Suspected abductions in Arizona, Texas, and Oklahoma. All teenage girls, pulled off the street."

Roarke and Epps looked at each other in the dim light of the cab. The number was chilling, particularly given that this kind of crime was like any infestation of vermin: one sighting was inevitably only the tip of the iceberg.

Singh continued. "Inspector Mills and Agent Jones are in position in the Tenderloin. We are monitoring the Street Action boards. Three SFPD undercovers are out on the street as well."

Roarke felt an acid rush in the pit of his stomach. "Keep us posted."

"Will do, Chief."

After disconnecting with Singh, he turned the swivel chair away from Epps and called Rachel. And got voice mail. He stumbled through a message, leaving the basic details of Becca's situation and a contact number for the juvenile hall in Salinas, all the while knowing that his last encounter with Rachel did not bode well for her ever speaking to him again, much less doing him another massive favor.

He turned back in the chair . . . to find Epps shaking his head. "You ain't treating that woman right."

There was nothing Roarke could say to that.

Epps reached for another slice of pizza. "That shit always comes back on you." He passed Roarke the pizza box and for a while they ate in silence, looking out the wide windshield of the truck at the bleak sunset over the fields.

Chapter 48

*I*t is cold . . . and the moon is angry.

The ancient light shines down on the girls bunched on the street corners. Long colt legs in platform heels. Glassy-eyed with drugs. Lost children, coerced and sold by men who do not even think of them as human.

On the street, the cars slow, drivers eyeing the merchandise. Product. Cattle. Slaves.

But tonight another hunter is cruising.

Tonight there will be a price to pay.

Tonight the moon will have her vengeance.

Chapter 49

The agents had been sitting in the dark rig for what felt like a lifetime, gazing through the drifting fog and watching the shadows of four women as they worked the truck stop, responding to the flashing of lights. Stick figures in short skirts, backpacks slung over their shoulders, slumped with the weariness of abuse: drug abuse, physical abuse, sexual abuse, life abuse.

Roarke felt ill, soul-sick. Whatever the scene said about the essence of humanity, it wasn't good.

But so far none of the women appeared to be under the obvious coercion of a pimp. So far none of them looked underage. So the agents watched, and they waited, as the swelling moon rose above the drifting fog and the occasional flash of lights.

After a while Epps spoke again.

"Does that girl Becca have something to do with Jade?" he asked, his voice sounding raw. "Is all of this tied in together, somehow? Was Jade abducted, like Sarah Jane?"

Or like Shauna? So many girls . . .

Roarke half-shook his head. "I don't know."

"But Lindstrom told Becca to wait for you."

"Yeah."

"It's the cement plant again, isn't it? She's bringing us into it, bringing *you* into it, just like before."

It was what Snyder had said. That Cara had some kind of plan, some form of the bust of the cement plant in the desert, the victims rescued there. Once again, she wanted them, or him, involved. The fact that local law enforcement was obviously not making a dent in the trafficking problem made it even more likely that she would apply her own solution.

Epps was watching Roarke. "You thinking another trafficking ring? That Cara wants us to bust?"

Is that it? Is that the whole plan? Is there a ring she saw while on the road and meant to get around to, before she was distracted by the Reaper and held up for a time in jail?

"Maybe," he said aloud. "It is our job."

"And I'm just so happy that Cara Lindstrom is being so helpful," Epps said bitterly.

But Roarke was thinking on it. The light penalties for trafficking were a major reason the sex trade was burgeoning.

He spoke into the dark. "Every time the Bureau takes on one of these trafficking situations and makes a case for Federal prosecution, it puts the traffickers away for longer." In the case of the cement plant, instead of six-year sentences in the state system, the men Roarke and Epps had arrested were looking at fifty-year prison terms. And every case that ended in a stiffer sentence made it less appealing for gangs and rogue criminals to get into the business.

Epps was shaking his head in the dark. "You really think her head is any way straight enough to plan like that?"

He had a point. Cara didn't think like a lawyer. But she always had a purpose. They had been brought here, lured, even, and Roarke was increasingly unsettled about it.

"I don't know," he said. He looked out the truck window, out at the rising moon.

Becca's story. Shauna's story. Jade's story. Sarah Jane's story. They all ran together in his head, a vast, polluted river.

He swiveled in the chair to look at the lot outside. He watched through the windshield of the rig as another truck flashed lights and one of the prostitutes teetered through the fog toward the cab.

"Do you know how many active serial killers there are out there in the US at any given time?" he asked.

Epps looked at him, frowned. "No idea."

"When I was in the BAU, the number we estimated was between thirty-five and a hundred."

"In the whole US?" Epps said.

"Right." Roarke looked out at the rows of trucks. "How many of *these* guys do you think there are out there right now? Leon Jonas? DeShawn Butler? Danny Ramirez? Not to mention whole gangs? Selling kids like that?"

A wary look crossed Epps' face. "I don't know. Thousands. Tens of thousands. A shitload."

"Right," Roarke said.

Epps leaned forward urgently. "But we get them the only way we can get them. With the law."

"Tens of thousands," Roarke said flatly. "Hundreds of thousands."

"And every *one* we get counts," Epps said.

Roarke didn't answer. Couldn't. Epps studied him, and his expression was worried. "Why don't you take the bed? Get a few z's. I'll watch."

Roarke shook his head and stood, felt the numbness in his legs. "What I need is some air." Before Epps could protest, he added, "Just across the lot to the diner."

Epps started to say something, then shook his head. "Watch yourself."

"Want anything?"

"Vodka," Epps said.

"Yeah," Roarke said. "I'll work on that."

He didn't go toward the diner. He circled the truck, to the back of it where Epps couldn't watch him, and walked out into the field where Becca had run to hide after Cara cut the trucker's throat.

Moonlight spilled over low, leafy rows of some vegetable that looked a lot bigger actually growing out of the ground than it did in a supermarket. Artichoke, maybe. It had a rich, loamy smell. Above him, the moon was icy and very white. He'd Googled the name for the December full moon.

Cold Moon.

And it was.

What are we doing here?

But he knew, had known all along. If this was where Cara was, then that was where he had to be.

Beautiful, deadly Cara.

He looked up at the cold moon and felt the same dread and longing he always felt, imagining her. Without thinking, he spoke to her in his mind.

Just come. Make it now. Let's end this, one way or another.

"I'm so tired," he said aloud into the moonlit dark.

He felt a presence behind him and closed his eyes briefly, then opened them.

He turned . . . and saw a female shadow. His heart stopped.

"Lookin' for a party?" the shadow asked. Her words were slurred, and Roarke took her in quickly. Halter top, a pale roll of belly fat spilling over too-tight jeans, wedge heels. A commercial lady. Not a minor. But he thought she might do anyway.

"Sure," he said, through the sudden race of his pulse. "Rig's right over there."

She took his arm and leaned against him coyly, wobbling from the heels and the drugs, as he walked her through the leafy ground crop, over uneven dirt toward the truck.

They stopped beside the metal wall of the rig, and he opened the passenger door and climbed up on the runner to help her. She swayed as she mounted the step, and he reached out to take her arm.

He caught the metallic smell of meth as she stumbled past him into the cab—and then she stopped still, seeing Epps sitting on the bed. "Uh-uh. No way," she muttered, and started to scramble back out of the truck. Roarke didn't know if she was objecting to two on one, or to Epps' race, but he blocked the door, trapping her.

"Take it easy. We're FBI." Before she could freak out more, he added quickly, "You're not under arrest. We just want to talk. You get full price."

He showed his credentials, which had no apparent effect on her, then he pulled out his wallet and showed her a hundred-dollar bill, far more than full price. Now she nodded warily.

"Have a seat."

She dropped heavily into the passenger seat, which swiveled under the sudden weight. She had to dig her heels into the floor of the cab to steady herself.

Roarke leaned against the cab wall and studied her in the dim light from outside. She was both twitchy and spacy, stoned on probably a mix of chemicals, and definitely not a kid, a worn woman of probably thirty who looked much closer to fifty.

"Where are you from?" he asked her.

She shrugged. "Here."

"Salinas?"

"Yeah. *Here.*"

"Been working this stop long?"

She gave him a flat stare. "Long enough."

"What about last night? Were you here?"

"My kid was sick."

Roarke and Epps exchanged a quick glance.

"I'm sorry to hear that," Roarke said, not entirely meaning the illness. "Would you say you know the regular girls here?"

"I guess."

"You seen any new ones recently? Young ones?"

She gave him a narrowed look but said nothing. Roarke tried for a neutral tone. "I'm talking about girls who aren't working on their own. Brought here by pimps."

"Yeah . . ."

"'Yeah' as in you *have* seen some young new girls?"

She looked out the window beside her. "You see a young one for a few days, then they're gone and there's another one. Been happening for a while now."

Roarke felt the pull of significance. "How many have you seen?"

She shifted in her seat. "I don't get you."

"In the last month, how many young ones have you seen?"

She looked momentarily . . . *angry*? Roarke wasn't sure. Then she shrugged. "Five, six."

Epps leaned forward and showed her a mug shot of Leon Jonas. "Have you seen this man before?"

She struggled to focus through her drug haze as she looked down at the photo. Then shook her head. "Don't think so."

Epps sat back. "So the pimping out of these younger girls: Is it a gang thing?"

"The gangs do it." She nodded to the mug shot of Leon Jonas in his hand. "Guys like that do it. Who doesn't do it? What's your point?"

Roarke looked at her and had no answer. "Have you ever seen this girl?" He showed her the MISSING flyer, shone his camera phone flashlight on it so she could see the photo of Sarah Jane. The woman looked down at the photo, glanced back up at Roarke, then looked back down at the photo, nodding slowly.

"Yeah. Yeah, I think I seen her."

Roarke's pulse spiked. "Where?"

"The Stop Inn. Motel 'crost the freeway. I stay there sometimes. When I got enough together."

Epps reached over and took the flyer, held it up in front of her again. "*This* girl. This is the one you saw."

"I don't know. I think." She glanced at Roarke again. "A young one looked like that."

Roarke looked at Epps. "How do we hook up?" he asked the woman.

"Backdoor," she said. It was the name of an "adult classifieds" website. The woman caught the glance between the two agents. "You guys never hooked up before?" she asked cynically. "Go to the Salinas page. Any action at the motel gets listed under Ninety-Ninth and California."

Roarke handed over the hundred. She looked down at the bill, then at him. "Right," she said, and he had no idea what she meant. She stood abruptly and brushed past him as she exited the truck, dropping from the runner. Her feet hit the ground heavily, and she staggered off.

When she was gone, the agents looked at each other in the dark cab. Epps was already shaking his head. "You know she just made the ID to get the money."

Part of Roarke knew it was true. Probably.

"Straight up—what do we think's going to happen?" Epps asked. "We show up to the no-tell and we're just going to find the girl on the flyer? Does any of this have a snowball's chance of being Cara's doing? And what about Jade?"

Roarke didn't answer, just looked down at the MISSING flyer on the console, at Sarah Jane Jennings' smiling face . . .

Epps sighed. "Right." He reached for the iPad and typed in Backdoor.com.

Chapter 50

She cruises the long blocks of International Boulevard in the stolen Toyota, past liquor stores and run-down motels, auto repair shops, Latin grocery stores and Mexican food dives, and of course the taco trucks, the gleaming aluminum trailers parked in almost every street-corner parking lot, and every one with a group of men congregated in front, starkly lit by the sodium lights. Bleak scenes in the black-and-white of night.

The towering shadows of palm fronds loom above the street. There are large crepe-paper flowers tied to the tree trunks and streetlamps, possibly left over from a *Dia de los Muertos* celebration, a forlorn attempt at festivity in the stark surroundings. Clumps of young men in baggy pants with baseball caps turned backward hang on every other corner.

And the girls walk the streets. Some in jeans and backpacks, as camouflage, looking marginally like students—though what kind of student would be walking this strip at night is another story. Other girls are unmistakable: long and leggy in fetish shoes and micro skirts, with fake eyelashes thick enough that she can see them from the car.

The ones on the corners stare straight into her windshield, a practiced laser come-on.

They are young. There has been not one she has seen who looks over twenty. Many are much younger. They stagger on their four-inch platforms; their developing bodies have nothing like the strength required to make that walk look effortless.

The presence of *It* is overpowering in this cesspool. She can barely breathe from the rankness. It slithers between the cars, lurks around every corner, crouches in the Escalades and SUVs where the pimps watch the girls on the corners from their tinted windows. Her body stiffens in revulsion as she passes them. The moon is high and the urge is strong to stop, to put an end to their business on the spot.

So many. It should be torched. Razed. Destroyed for all time.

Every girl she has seen so far is Latina or African American or some mix of the two. The flaming girl will be easy to spot. It is a good reason for the girl not to be here at all, and she knows the girl is not stupid.

For the same reason it is dangerous for Cara to be here herself. She has done her best: dressed in layers, with the top layer an anonymous hoodie and loose sweatpants; darkened her skin tone with makeup; lined her eyes; concealed her blond hair under a brown wig tucked into a hat. Even so, she stands out on this street, and while Roarke is for the moment safely out of the way, if any of his people are on stakeout, she will be easily recognized, out in the night.

But this is where she must be. It was clear in the cards. So she drives on.

Chapter 51

The lights of their iPads glowed on the agents' faces as they navigated the Backdoor website. The home portal had links for all fifty states, with cities listed under each state. Clicking on SALINAS brought up a simple list of categories of items for sale, including an ADULT section. One click on ESCORTS, then one click to agree to the Adult Terms of Service got them to a list of links:

```
*DISCOVER JUICY. Love me all over* - 19

21 in Salinas

Young and sweet, new girl in town - 19

Get ready for love in 10 min! - 23

I am a Married Mans Best Kept Secret - 19

DON'T YOU WANT THIS!!! - 19

Big BOOTY on Duty - 23

Hey boyz, Im Stormy Im waiting to meet you
right now - 21
```

"Amazing how many of these girls are nineteen," Roarke said. His stomach was roiling. "Nineteen" seemed to be the universal code for "underage."

"Ain't it just." Epps' face was stony in the dark of the cab.

A click on a link led to the come-on, complete with seminude photos and a phone number:

```
Hey gents if your looking for something beau-
tiful young and hot look now further Im your
newbie dream Im open minded flexible and boy
do I get juicy I cant sleep and I wanna have
a good time with someone for the right dona-
tion Im posted in Salinas with an incall on
California Text or call me.
```

Semiliterate male fantasies, composed by pimps. About girls like Becca. Like Shauna. Like Sarah Jane. Teenagers. Abducted, trunked, raped, drugged . . . and sold online, with one click of a mouse.

"Just like ordering a pizza," Epps said, his voice tired. It was that easy.

Roarke skimmed the links, looking for keywords. *Young and hot. Sweet. Bubbly. Newbie. Shy yet freaky.* There were too many to count.

He forced himself to focus and look for the specific address, Ninety-Ninth and California, code for the motel. He stopped on a link . . . and stared down at his iPad screen at the words:

```
New girl in town 2nite only - 19
99th/California
```

"New girl in town," he said aloud. "New, meaning like Becca?"

Abducted, terrified, traumatized . . .

Epps shook his head. "Not sayin' you're wrong. Just wondering what we're doin' it for."

Roarke was silent.

"You can't save everyone. That kind of thinking'll drive you insane."

Roarke knew it. They all knew it. There was no way to live that way. The web page he was looking at now was one of hundreds of thousands across the country. How many were minors? How many were minors when they started? How could they even begin to make a dent?

And yet . . .

He looked at Epps without speaking. Epps ran a hand over his head, and his face was tense. "A'ight. If we call or text and make a date, chances are there's going to be screening. We'll need a private line, a false ID. We don't have that kind of time."

Roarke was about to argue, but his agent continued. "If she's really a 'new girl in town,' she's not going to be on her own. The mack's most likely screening johns in the lot. So we go over and watch. We got witness testimony that a minor reported abducted is being held at this motel. We go, see what's going down. If we need to go in, we claim exigent circumstances. Probably we lose out on convicting the pimp, but we might get the girl out."

"Yeah," Roarke said, gratefully. "That's a plan."

Epps muttered something he couldn't hear and climbed into the driver's seat to start the engine.

Chapter 52

She drives a good sixty blocks on each of her first few passes. International Boulevard stretches for forty more. But she has gone far enough, enough times, to see that, aptly, the bulk of the street action is in the teens: Thirteenth Avenue to Nineteenth, with another spate of activity in the forties and fifties. She spends a little time cruising the higher blocks, on the lookout, without seeing anyone who looks remotely like the girl Jade. Then she heads back for the lower-numbered blocks.

There are more girls out now. Men slow their cars by the curb, pale men in shiny cars who have no other possible business in this neighborhood but to buy these children. The girls stroll or stagger up to the windows to negotiate.

She does not slow the car. She tries to control her trembling, and stares out at the sidewalks, searching.

She is cruising that long loop for the fourth time when she sees a flash of white in one of the dark doorways. She turns her head to look out the side window as she passes . . . and feels a spike of shock.

A skull glares out at her from the blackness.

She slows the car and looks back over her shoulder . . . but the face has disappeared.

There is another car behind her and she must keep driving. She breathes in to slow her racing heart . . . and focuses on the street ahead of her.

But all of her skin is prickling. As soon as she can she makes a U-turn to head back toward the block where she saw the skull face, then makes a sharp right at the street corner nearest the storefront.

The side street is dark. She drives slowly, past empty cars parked at the curb in front of run-down clapboard houses . . . cracked sidewalks devoid of people. There is no sign of the figure she saw.

She parks her car halfway down the street, kills the headlights and engine, and sits, thinking.

Not the girl. The Other.

Her pulse is racing.

Get out. Leave now.

She reaches for the key to start the engine again, but hesitates. She was directed here. She needs to know.

She strips off the hoodie and sweatpants she is wearing.

She exits the car in a completely different street garb: a tube skirt and skintight mesh shirt, fishnet stockings. She shuts the car door and locks it, then strides on high-heeled vinyl boots past the dark houses.

The night outside is cold on her exposed skin, but the chill she feels is more anticipation than temperature. She breathes in the dark and follows the moon.

There is the opening of an alley ahead, access to the backs of the shops on Inty. She slows as she approaches, her skin prickling again. She keeps close to the filthy stucco wall and glances down the dark passageway.

An SUV is stopped in the alley, with lights off . . . and the driver's door open.

She takes a step into the alley. The moon is straight up in the black dome of sky, and her shadow is long and stark in the spill of moonlight.

She approaches warily, staying well away from the side of the car as she moves forward to get a look inside. She can smell it first, blood and shit, the unmistakable stink of death.

She stops before the open door to look in.

The man in the driver's seat is deader than dead. A gunshot has exploded half his head; blood and brains drip from the windshield.

She is very still as she notes the clothes: the turned-to-the-side ball cap, the baggy pants and oversize T-shirt. Pimp garb.

She is not the only one hunting tonight.

She pulls back from the carnage and backs away from the driver's door, her heart beating fast as she scans the dark around her . . . but there is no sign of anyone living.

As she turns from the car, her gaze falls on a pale arrangement of objects beside the wall of the building. She walks a few steps toward it, staring down. A candle, with white flowers laid in front of it. A fifth of some liquor. Cigarettes in a small, neat pile.

The night is cold on her skin, and her thoughts are racing.

Offerings. Someone is invoking the Bony One. Playing with fire.

She wants no part of it. And yet . . . there is opportunity here.

Above her, a shadow passes across the moon.

A sign.

She stoops quickly to the pile of offerings, then stands again. Now she does not linger but walks toward the street at the other end of the alley.

She steps out of the alley and turns right to move toward the corner of the boulevard. She slows her walk to a languid stride on the four-inch heels. She lets her hips roll and feels the taut muscles of her legs in perfect balance on the boots, and her breath catches in anticipation . . .

Then she steps out onto the street and looks toward the cars, a blatant laser come-on.

The first one who approaches will do. The act of choosing her is enough.

A lesson to anyone who chooses her.

Chapter 53

Roarke phoned in to Detective Escobar as Epps drove the rig across the freeway to the motel. A small blessing: the detective was out, and Roarke could simply leave a message through the office manager. "We've got a sex worker at the truck stop telling us a minor reported as abducted is being held at the Stop Inn on 99. Going over there to eyeball it."

There was a back section of the parking lot for the bigger trucks. Epps parked alongside two other huge rigs. On this side of the freeway there was a high wind up, blowing debris across the lot and shaking the cab of the truck. The moon was nearly blinding in the clear sky, and its light plus the height of the cab gave them a good outlook on the lot surrounding the motel. It didn't take long to spot the pimp. He hovered in the dark beside the building's short outside corridor that housed an elevator, ice and vending machines, and a stairwell.

The agents stared out the cab windows at the shadow figure: a Latino man in his thirties who moved with a prison swagger, tattoos visible on his chest and neck above the wife-beater tank he wore under a satin athletic jacket. He watched the lot like a hawk as he spoke on his phone.

A battered Bronco pulled into the lot. Both agents leaned forward as the truck cruised past the empty spaces in front of the motel office. "Here we go," Epps said under his breath.

The Bronco drove all the way past the cars parked in front of the downstairs rooms and stopped at the end of the building, near the elevator. The headlights blinked off.

A man squeezed himself out of the truck. He was overweight and sloppy. Roarke caught the gleam of thick glasses on his doughy face. Nobody's idea of Prince Charming.

He waddled on the sidewalk in front of the lower row of rooms toward the outside corridor, then stood in front of the vending machine without buying anything.

"Wait for it . . ." Epps muttered, watching.

After a pause, the pimp moved out of the shadows and up to the fat man. They spoke briefly, then the pimp handed the man something. The fat man turned and crossed to the elevator. The pimp disappeared back into the corridor.

"He's got the room key now," Roarke said under his breath.

"Mack's got another one on him, I bet," Epps answered. And the agents looked at each other.

An impromptu sting like this was a majorly bad idea; they both knew it. They had no idea how many accomplices the pimp might have. Whoever they were, they might be selling drugs or arms. The level of weaponry thugs had with them these days was sometimes like a small arsenal.

All Roarke could think of was Becca. Fifteen years old. Shauna. Thirteen years old. Sarah Jane Jennings. Fifteen years old. And whatever girl of whatever age was up there in that room right now.

But it was Epps who said, "Hell, let's do it."

Roarke left the cab of the truck and walked through the wind, across the parking lot, up onto the sidewalk, into the open corridor that housed the elevator as if he were a motel guest, while Epps waited a few moments before he exited the cab himself and circled around toward the back of the motel.

When Roarke moved past the elevator and out the end of the corridor to the back side of the motel, the pimp was still on his phone . . . and a beat too late understanding he was surrounded.

Just as he was turning to deal with Roarke, Epps had his Glock to the guy's head, ordering, "FBI, don't move."

The pimp froze . . . then sprinted. Epps sprang, did a full-on tackle, and both men hit the ground, Epps on top. There was a satisfying crunch of bone as Epps ground the guy into the asphalt, and Roarke was over him in the next second, grabbing his arms, locking them behind his back, securing the plastic cuffs. The man spat a curse in Spanish, but ceased struggling.

Epps held his head to the concrete as Roarke searched him, pulling a Ruger from his waistband, a cellophane bag of powder from a pocket, and a plastic key card from another. The key was still in its cardboard sheath, with the room number in blue ballpoint: 212.

Epps reached for his service belt, handed his own set of cuffs to Roarke. "Be my guest," Epps said. "I'll keep our friend company."

Roarke climbed the stairs, his adrenaline climbing even higher. The last time he'd been on a takedown like this, just over a month ago now, he'd shot a man point-blank in a filthy brothel, a virtual prison of enslaved women and girls.

At the top of the stairs he looked out the doorway into a stuffy, filthy hallway. A twenty-year-old carpet. Smears of substances he didn't even want to know about on the walls.

He moved silently to room 212, used the key card, and pushed open the door, leading with his Glock.

"FBI, don't move!"

The fat man sat on the bed with his pants around his ankles, oversized gut mercifully shielding his nakedness. The girl stood above him in a tank top and panties. The john froze in place on the bed, looking dully alarmed. The girl backed up toward the wall, slid down it to sit heavily on the floor, arms crossed protectively over her head as if to ward off blows.

There was another woman in the room, sitting frozen in an armchair in the corner, a bleary-eyed, mixed-race, fleshy woman in her late twenties or early thirties, dressed in a robe. The "bottom girl," there to keep the new one in line, keep her from running.

"You," Roarke ordered her. "Get down on the floor. Facedown, hands behind your head."

He watched her lower herself to the floor while he kept the john at gunpoint.

When the woman was stretched out flat, he motioned to the john. "Now you. On the floor. Hands behind your back."

The fat man dropped awkwardly to his knees, then onto the stained carpet. Roarke kept the Glock trained on the woman while securing the cuffs on the man.

Then he shut the door behind him and stood in front of it, barring it. The room was small and rank. Rubber curtains, a garish bedspread, toiletries and clothes strewn on the floor. The surface of the dresser was cluttered with liquor bottles and fast-food wrappers. There were pill bottles and scattered powder on the desk. The smell of spunk and stale alcohol was heavy in the air.

With both adults now immobile, Roarke turned toward the girl and tried to speak gently.

"What's your name?"

She glanced up, and he got his first good look at her. She had caramel-colored skin, with brown hair and brown freckles, and her face was plump with baby fat. He felt a crush of disappointment.

Not Sarah Jane.

He fought that initial feeling down and willed himself to be there for the girl in front of him. He kept the Glock trained on the john as he asked her, "How old are you?"

The girl mumbled, "N-nineteen."

"How old are you really?" Roarke said without missing a beat.

"Fifteen," the girl answered automatically, and then looked frightened. She shot a glance at the woman on the floor.

Roarke turned his eyes to the john. His face behind the glasses was shiny with sweat. "Fifteen. That would make you engaged in a felony."

"I didn't know," the john muttered.

Roarke strode forward. The fat man flinched, anticipating a kick. Instead Roarke stood above him and demanded, "Look at her."

"Then she shouldn't be on the website," the john said petulantly.

"We just here partying," the older woman complained from the floor.

"You ask for two?" Roarke asked the john.

"Bitch was here when I got here."

"Making sure no one runs?" Roarke said to the woman. "Kidnapping. False imprisonment."

He stared down at his captives, bile rising in his throat. He wanted to say something, anything, to name the extent of their depravity, to reach anything that was still human in them.

Instead he reached for his phone and called Escobar.

Chapter 54

Down at the station, the girl gave up her story to the female detective Escobar had brought in to question her. Her name was Carmen. She was fifteen and she was far from home.

Unlike Becca, she had a home to go back to. Her aunt had reported her missing from Phoenix two weeks ago. The pimp from the motel was not her abductor; apparently she'd been sold to him upon arrival in California and was being held in the motel and "seasoned": one of the pimp's prostitutes was with her twenty-four hours a day, including while johns came in to have sex with her.

When Escobar had shown up at the motel, he'd looked at Roarke and Epps through narrowed eyes, but he'd made the arrests and taken the pimp and the john and the older woman away.

Another three down.

But in this case they had no idea if anyone would be prosecuted. It was up to Monterey County now.

The agents drove the rig back to the impound lot and picked up their fleet car. Roarke took the first shift driving and headed for the 101 North.

They were both silent, dazed by the roller coaster, the adrenaline rush of a bust, combined with the downer feeling that they'd been had, lured away from the real action into a dead end.

At least Carmen was going home. If she wanted to go.

Roarke knew he should be glad for it. Instead he had a crushing feeling of failure.

Molina's voice suddenly spoke in his head. *"You tell me your way is working, Agent Roarke, and I will call you the liar you are."*

He had the overpowering sense she was right.

He stared out the windshield at the road, the slash of headlights through the fog, and more questions swirled through his head.

Was all that what Cara had wanted them here for?

The chances of finding the sex worker who would point them to the motel, where they would see the john transacting business with the pimp . . . no one could have set that up. It felt too random.

"It's good," Epps said abruptly from the seat beside him, as if sensing his thought.

Roarke looked at him.

"S'all that counts. She's out. Becca's out, too. It got done."

"Yeah," Roarke said, and all he felt was despair. Epps studied him in the dark of the car.

"Is this because of Cara? You feel like you didn't get it right?"

That's exactly what it is. Nothing was solved. It's a drop in the bucket. Not even a drop.

He gripped the steering wheel, struggling with his feelings, and finally spoke. "I feel like we could've gone into just about any motel along I-5 and had a good chance of finding the same thing. I think I could throw a rock right now and just about hit someone up to the same damn thing. I think that's where we're at."

"Maybe that *is* the message," Epps said.

Roarke looked at him . . . then flinched as his phone buzzed on his hip. He picked up to Singh's voice, taut with tension.

"Chief, there is some kind of event in progress."

Roarke handed Epps the phone and repeated, "Action going down," and pulled the car over to park on the shoulder.

Epps hit the speaker button on the phone so they both could hear and asked Singh, "This in the Tenderloin?" Roarke held his breath, thinking of Mills and Jones.

Singh's voice answered. "Not the Tenderloin. International Boulevard. I have been monitoring the Redlight forums. I am copying some posts to your emails."

Epps grabbed for his iPad and a moment later passed the tablet to Roarke.

The top subject thread on the forum was:

Weird shit going down Inty/19th

"Nineteenth. That's the peak of the stroll," Epps muttered.

The first post read:

TRACKSTER: Some bsw is freaking the fuck out on Inty and 19th. Hoe just ran out on the corner screaming her brains out.

"Are Mills and Jones over there?" Roarke demanded.

"On their way. I am on dispatch with Oakland PD—" Singh said something he couldn't hear, and then came back on the line. "Dead body found in the driver's seat of a late-model Lexus SUV, in an alley just below International and Nineteenth Avenue . . ." Her voice cut out again.

Epps hit the dashboard with his fist. "Fuck, it's Cara. She brought us down here so she could hit up there. Goddamn it." His face was stormy in the dark.

Singh's voice came back on the line. "Male, early thirties, gunshot to head . . . Wait."

Gunshot to the head? Not Cara, then?

Now Epps looked as confused as Roarke felt.

Singh returned to the call. "I have just heard again from Oakland PD. There is a second dead body in a Mazda CX5 parked off International on Twenty-Third Street. Male, thirties, passenger door open, condoms on passenger seat."

Four blocks from the first.

"Cause of death?" Roarke asked tightly.

"His throat is cut."

Roarke and Epps turned to each other in the dark of the car.

"Another pair," Roarke muttered. The one in the Mazda with the condoms, obviously cruising; the other in a luxury SUV, favorite of pimps.

"A pimp and a john," Epps said.

"But the pimp . . . Gunshot to the head?"

The agents stared at each other as the fog from the fields rolled around the car, nearly drowning the headlights.

And Epps finally said it. "Who the hell are we dealing with now?"

DAY EIGHT

DAY EIGHT

Chapter 55

Roarke jarred awake to find himself in a postapocalyptic landscape of barred-up liquor stores and run-down motels, auto repair shops, Latin grocery stores and Mexican food dives. And botanicas. Every few blocks, another botanica.

In the driver's seat beside him, Epps cruised the dismal track of International Boulevard, gravel-eyed from the long night and the two-hour drive from Salinas through mind-numbing fog. Roarke had taken the wheel the first hour so Epps could grab a nap, then they'd switched.

Roarke looked out the passenger window. Shiny aluminum trailers were parked in almost every street-corner parking lot, with groups of workingmen lined up to get breakfast. In one lot, a news van was parked beside a taco truck. A blond reporter in a tailored crimson suit interviewed the men huddled at the counter, a splash of bloodred in all the grayness. The vultures descending, now that the action was over.

Another pimp and john dead.

And no worries about whether those two will ever be prosecuted. They're out of commission for good. Done.

There was an appeal to that idea that suddenly terrified Roarke.

He turned sharply to face forward again and looked out the windshield at the strip. While the Tenderloin was a grid of short blocks built on hills, the gray blocks of International seemed to go on forever in one endless line. "How long is this thing?" he said aloud.

"A hundred blocks straight just from Oaktown to San Leandro," said Epps. "That's what makes it so damn hard to patrol. You stake out twenty blocks and the pimps just move the girls forty blocks down."

In his half-conscious state, Roarke heard Molina's voice again. *"You tell me your way is working, Agent Roarke, and I will call you the liar you are."*

He closed his eyes and tried not to think.

By the time they arrived at the alley off Nineteenth Street, they were too late to see the bodies in situ. The coroner's van had already taken them away. But the crime scenes remained, taped off in the gray dawn. Both men killed in their cars. Two new wrinkles: the little piles of offerings left beside each car . . .

And the incontrovertible fact that one of their killers was now using a gun.

• • • • •

"Two men are dead after a bloody rampage last night on Oakland's infamous International Boulevard."

In the conference room, Roarke, Epps, Jones, and Mills watched the screen as the blond reporter Roarke had seen beside the taco truck spoke into the camera, her blue eyes wide and dramatically serious.

Singh stood at the podium, playing the news broadcast on the TV monitor suspended from the conference room wall. The remains of an enormous breakfast lay on a side table: Mexican pastries and carne asada and breakfast tamales.

On the screen, the camera panned across the grim block behind the reporter.

"International is known as a prostitute stroll, glamorized in rap songs like 'Pimp of the Year,' 'Rules of the Game,' and 'Pimpology.' The reality is much bleaker. On Inty, pimps routinely sell girls as young as twelve years old, dooming these children to a life of violence, exploitation, and abuse. Oakland police declined to speculate who is responsible for the murders. But residents of the neighborhood have their own theories."

The camera focused on a makeshift shrine on a street corner. Roarke stared up at a three-foot-tall idol positioned on the sidewalk, the familiar skeletal figure, with offerings piled up at its feet, spreading out on the sidewalk in a ten-foot radius: flowers, candles, cigarettes, candy, bottles of tequila.

The reporter continued in voice-over. "The statue you are looking at is known as Santa Muerte: Lady Death. These shrines are appearing on street corners up and down the five mile 'Track' of International Boulevard. Shrines to an unconsecrated saint that the Catholic Church has refused to acknowledge. The people you are about to hear from would not show themselves on camera for fear of retaliation by the pimps and gangs who control this strip of Oakland. But these residents are speaking out nonetheless."

The camera cut to the silhouette of a hefty woman who spoke from the shadows in a thick Hispanic accent. "For years our children are living with these criminals selling their drugs and these young girls. The police do nothing. Now we ask the saint's help."

Next was a man in shadow, speaking in low Spanish, with voice-over translation creating an eerie bilingual echo to his words. "They are offerings of thanks to the saint, *la Santa Muerte*. The police have tried, but the gangs are too powerful. *La Santísima* guards the neighborhood now. The people give prayers for her continued protection."

The reporter came back on screen. "We'll have more on the Santa Muerte Murders after the break."

Roarke felt a chill at the phrase. He had always disliked the media's habit of nicknaming notorious killers, but this was more than simple irritation. This was a whole different kind of trouble.

Singh paused the news video. "These interviews continue in the same vein."

Epps was on his feet, shaking his head in disbelief. "Two murders in their 'hood and they're offering 'prayers for continued *protection*'?"

Mills tossed a half-eaten samosa onto his plate and shoved it away. "The 'Santa Muerte Murders.' So now we got some specter to deal with, too? Tell me this is a bad dream."

Roarke knew exactly what he meant.

Singh turned to the two new whiteboards standing in front of the previous ones. "I have compiled photos of the scene. The crime scene videos are loaded for display on the monitor, as well."

The agents moved over to stand in front of the boards, studying the shots, fixated on the one glaring addition to the mix: the corpse slumped in the front seat of the SUV with the remains of his head splattered on the windshield.

Jones said it first. "So who's using a gun now, Lindstrom or Jade?"

They all felt the dissonance of it.

"These killings are different from the previous ones in several aspects," Singh said. "Before we make assumptions, I must also submit this." She stepped back to the computer control and hit a button. A website appeared on the screen. "This blog post went up online at five a.m."

And the War Begins

Roarke looked up at the screen as Singh scrolled through the article. "The article is the first instance I have been able to pinpoint of calling the killings the Santa Muerte Murders. That is how the news stations picked up the phrase. And the blog author has been constantly updating the blog with links to other news articles and broadcasts about the Santa Muerte connection: the shrines on Inty, the interviews with residents."

She scrolled to the bottom of the blog article and highlighted the last sentence.

Santa Muerte is out there. And she is pissed.

"Fanning the flames," Epps said.

Singh nodded to him. "The blog author has written about both the Salinas murders and the Inty murders and is making an issue of the paired kills, linking them to the murders in the Tenderloin. Again, the article specifically points out that the killer is striking at abusers from both sides, pimps and mongers. No one guilty is safe."

"So she's spelled out a blueprint for further killing," Roarke said. Then he thought of the arrests at the motel the previous night. *A pimp and a john. Probably back out on the street already.*

"Not she. *They,*" Singh said. The team looked at her. "This is a different blogger."

Roarke's mouth was suddenly dry. "I thought you said she was using different IP numbers and rerouting—"

"She is. And this blog author also calls herself Bitch. But the styling of this article is different. I ran it through a text analysis program to compare with the other blogs. It is a different writer entirely."

Roarke felt a shock as he tried to process it. Singh added, "Also this blog was originally posted less than a half hour after the Inty kills were called in. She is getting insider information."

Mills moved agitatedly. "Or she did it, you mean."

"She, or another of the group," Singh answered.

Epps looked ready to explode. "Hold up. These cybergroups. They break laws, they go beyond the pale, but there's no record of anyone doing any killing."

"We also know she's been monitoring the Street Action forums. She could've found out that way," Mills pointed out.

"All of these things are true," Singh acknowledged. "But I have been monitoring the number of shares and retweets of Santa Muerte images. Hundreds of thousands. That number is growing every hour."

Roarke stared at her. "You're saying our suspect pool just got bigger."

"I am saying our suspect pool is enormous," Singh answered gravely. "It is safe to say that millions of people are now aware of this 'call to action.'"

Viral murder, Snyder had called it.

Roarke was feeling the raggedness of no sleep and no discernible progress. He could sense that his agent was trying to express something more than the charts would indicate, but he was too near exhaustion to follow. "What are you getting at, Singh?"

She actually avoided his eyes. "There is a purpose to this. I think we have underestimated the scope . . ." She paused, considering her words. "These articles are raising the circumstances to a meta level. Metaphors are powerful. There is a manifestation going on. It is taking on an energy of its own."

Epps looked agitated, and there was a warning note in his voice. "We don't need to go mystical on this. We need to focus on facts. The blog articles started *after* the first kill, DeShawn Butler. And the real anomaly is that someone used a gun on that pimp on Inty. And left the offerings." His eyes were fixed on the photo of the second scene. "A lot of Inty is Hispanic neighborhoods. Whoever did it, it was smart business, planting that stuff."

Singh was silent for the slightest moment, then spoke. "Agreed," she said. Roarke was aware that he had been on edge waiting for her response. "The offerings both activate superstition and make a larger political point."

"Doesn't sound like Jade to me," Epps said, looking to Roarke.

Roarke knew his agent was waiting for a sign from him. He nodded. "I'd like to get a closer look at those offerings." He felt the room relax around him. They were back on track, on the same page.

"They are upstairs in the lab," Singh told them. "Lam and Stotlemyre are processing them."

Chapter 56

In the crime lab, the team found places between the gleaming metal lab tables and refrigerators and scopes to face Lam and Stotlemyre.

Roarke summoned himself and got straight to the point. "We now have six murders in the last four days." He stopped as the word *executions* hovered in his mind. "Two in the Tenderloin. Two in Salinas. Two on International Boulevard last night. And each pair consists of a pimp and a john. We need to know how many killers we're dealing with."

The two criminalists exchanged a look.

"Officially, we have no opinion," Stotlemyre said.

"Understood," Roarke said.

Lam nodded. "Okay then. Unofficially, the two in Salinas are absolutely Cara Lindstrom. They're just like her. But you knew that."

Stotlemyre continued. "Inty of course gives us more evidence left at the scenes. The offerings are a new element." He stepped to a long lab table where the left objects were laid out in evidence bags, arranged to duplicate the crime scene photos of the original piles, which were propped up on the table.

The tech gestured to the first pile. "These offerings were found in the alleyway, beside the pimp's SUV. The candle was almost certainly brought to the scene. It's been ritualistically prepped—that is, it was anointed with oil, and there's carving in the wax." He showed them the candle. Gouged into the wax was a crude skull. "I've called several botanicas to confirm the meaning: it's a candle dedicated to Santa Muerte."

"Can we trace the candle to a specific shop?" Roarke asked.

"The candle comes from a manufacturer who supplies esoteric shops all over the Southwest. They produce ten million per year."

The agents stared at him, all staggered by the number . . . except for Roarke. He'd seen the entire aisle of Santa Muerte idols in the botanica.

Stotlemyre gestured to the table. "As for the other offerings at this first shrine: the tequila bottle is nearly full, although it was opened and some of the alcohol was spilled on the ground at the scene. The flowers are fairly fresh. The cigarettes are new. All of them were lit but burned out almost immediately. Apparently live fire is an important part of the saint's worship."

Lam took over, stepping down the table to the next pile. "Now, in the second pile, we have a different set of objects: cigarette butts, a beer can, sequins, and flowers. Our feeling is these are improvised offerings. It's all stuff anyone could have picked up on the street."

"Is that allowed?" Epps was being ironic, but Lam answered matter-of-factly.

"The mother goddesses aren't very picky about their votive offerings. Cigarettes, candy, soda cans, they'll take any of it. It's the thought that counts."

The rest of the team looked at him. He was speaking as clinically as he would about any forensic evidence, as if "mother goddesses" were an actual fact of life.

The tech continued. "I think the sequins are an especially nice touch. I'm thinking this killer pulled the sequins off whatever she—or he—was wearing. There are broken threads still attached."

"*This* killer," Roarke repeated. "As opposed to—"

"The shooter," Lam answered instantly. "Different doers for sure. Of course, that's unofficial."

"But here's what's interesting," Stotlemyre said. "The flowers are the same as from the first shrine. Carnations. Available at any street corner flower vendor."

Roarke looked at him, putting it together. "So the killer was in the alley and took flowers from the first shrine to leave at the second scene."

"Very possibly. Also, the slash to the neck of the second victim from Inty, the john, was a clean slice, like what we've been seeing all along from Lindstrom. The shooter's weapon was a compact semiautomatic Smith and Wesson .45."

Roarke stood still, thinking. *So was the second kill Cara? Leaving offerings to tie the scenes together? Trying to confuse things? Why?*

Mills suddenly spoke up. "'Kay, I'm just a lowly visitor to the Death Star, but here's how I see it. We got maybe three killers, maybe even more, but so far it's only Lindstrom who's hit outside of the Bay Area. Our other two or however the fuck many are operating in our general area. Since we don't know who we're looking for, we're going to have to find her, or them, on the street. So we're going to have to stake out both sides of the Bay now. The TL and Inty."

He eyed Roarke and Epps.

"And it's not my call, but I would highly suggest the two of you go home and get some shut-eye before then. The kid and I can coordinate the stakeout and update you." He nodded to Jones, who looked unperturbed at the diminutive. Roarke had been impressed with how well the junior agent had been getting along with the notoriously abrasive detective. Jones was coming into his own as a lawman, and Roarke felt a pang of regret that he had not been there to foster it himself.

Then he realized Mills was right, on all counts.

He nodded, slowly. "That's the plan, then."

Chapter 57

Roarke rode the escalator up from the BART tunnel to exit the station at Twenty-Fourth and Mission . . . and stepped into a swirling vortex of fog. He started toward home, more sleepwalking than walking. The pinprick drops of mist on his face were all that was keeping him upright. Despite his best intentions to follow Mills' advice, he'd ended up wading through four hours of paperwork on the Salinas scene.

Now that he was alone, he had to face the fact that he was vastly uncomfortable with the plan. Another stakeout, this time for three killers, or more, if someone out there was taking it viral?

Multiple killers. Viral murder. Santa Muerte. If this genie is that far out of the bottle, what the hell are we doing?

He turned abruptly down the shadowy side street, heading toward the botanica. The mural of Mexican artwork blazed on the building ahead. The shop was dark, and he briefly wondered what he would have done if it were open.

Ask for a reading? Is that where I am?

He moved up to it and stopped on the sidewalk, looking into the window at the skeletal figure of the saint: white-gowned, globe in one hand, scythe in the other, candles at her feet along with the now-familiar offerings.

The offerings with the latest two murders. The deliberate association with Santa Muerte. Someone came to one of these shops, bought a candle, went through the ritual of anointing it.

Would Jade do it? Would Cara?

He didn't believe it. It seemed more calculated than either of them. Someone was politicizing the case, grabbing for publicity.

It's official, then. A third killer, at least.

As he turned away from the window, he suddenly recalled the words of the *curandera: "Alguien cerca de usted le miente."*

Someone close to you is lying.

He walked the remaining three blocks to his street in a fog of his own. He trudged up the steps of his building and was reaching to unlock the front door when he felt movement behind and below him.

He twisted around, reaching for his weapon—

And saw a feminine figure in a tailored winter coat on the sidewalk. Rachel.

She looked up at him through the drifting fog, focused on his hand, half-inside his suit coat, fingers on the holster.

"I'm sorry. The office said you'd just left, so I took a chance you were coming straight home . . ."

Roarke stared down at her, thrown. She had never been to his place. He hadn't known she even knew where he lived. He hadn't heard from her since the night in the Haight, when she'd told him to stay away from her.

He withdrew his hand from his coat, walked down the few steps to the sidewalk. "I was pretty sure you never wanted to see me again."

She lifted her shoulders. Her face was blank, unreadable. "I came to tell you that I've got Becca."

He was so tired he didn't understand what she was saying. "Got her?"

"I drove down to Salinas this afternoon. She's at the Belvedere House."

And finally it clicked. Rachel had gotten his message. And she'd taken Becca in, as he'd requested. He felt a rush of gratitude and some immense relief.

She was watching him. "Have you noticed you call me every time you have a lost child?"

It could have been accusatory, but instead her tone was ironic, almost teasing. He shook his head. "I'm sorry. If there were any other place I could take her—"

She cut him off. "You don't have to tell me about it." The anger was back in her voice. But Rachel was Rachel. No matter how she felt about him, no matter how angry she was, he knew she wouldn't let a child down.

One of them is safe, then. At least there's that. One. Out of how many?

She was studying him. "You really look terrible."

He felt in his pocket and pulled out the MISSING flyer, extended it to her. She looked down at the photo and the text, then looked back up at him. He saw his own rage and hopelessness reflected in her face.

"How . . ." he said, and didn't know what he was going to say next. "How do you do it? There are so many. How do you not go crazy?"

She smiled, but it was nothing but haunted. "What makes you think I haven't?"

She looked down at the flyer again. "Does this have to do with your case?"

He didn't know how to answer that. *It's so much bigger. It's so beyond me by now.*

"I don't know what the case is anymore."

She watched his face. "Then why don't you let it go?"

Let it go.

He pressed his hands into his eyes. "That's not up to me. Even if I could—"

"But it doesn't have to be you, does it? *You* could let it go."

He looked out on the hazy night lights of the city and shook his head, not only in denial, but because he couldn't talk to her about it, much as he wanted to.

"I can't."

She lifted her shoulders in what looked like resignation, and turned to go.

"Rachel."

She turned back to him.

"Thank you. For taking Becca, for—"

"Shut up," she said.

He put his hand on her arm . . . then pulled her close.

Across the street, sitting in the dark car, Cara watches as Roarke and the woman embrace.

She is shaky from her long night, not yet recovered from the bloodshed. But she cannot sleep. Not now. The moon is large and very present, two days to fullness, and its light will reveal all, as it has just done at this moment.

Roarke does not see it. But it is there, plain in the social worker's body language. She is hunting.

So Cara sits until Roarke has turned back toward his house, then starts the car and follows the social worker's Prius through the dark streets, heading uptown toward the Haight.

Chapter 58

Roarke watched Rachel's Prius drive off. He turned toward his building, then paused on the steps, feeling a strange reluctance to go inside. He knew Mills was right; he needed sleep before the night's stakeout, needed it desperately. It had been nearly thirty-six hours, approaching the danger zone. But he stayed on the steps and turned from the building to look into the dark.

Something's not right.

He stared out into the night, and he could almost feel the moon growing, somewhere beneath the fog. Full in less than forty-eight hours now. He felt a black hole of dread.

There was no time to sleep.

It wasn't just the Santa Muerte element. It was Cara's *It*, and the meta of it too, all of it. He couldn't get his mind off what Singh had said.

"There is a manifestation going on."

He didn't know if he had metaphysical questions or purely forensic ones. He only knew that he felt out of his depth, and that lately Singh seemed to have a better grasp on the case than any of them. She *knew* something. He was suddenly desperate to talk to her.

Instead of going upstairs, he went into the garage for his car.

Chapter 59

Cara follows the Prius on Haight, cruising past the clusters of teens on the corners. The social worker turns on Belvedere and stops the Prius outside the house where she works . . . but she parks illegally. It will be brief.

Cara waits, watching from the street outside.

The social worker comes out of the house within minutes, carrying an oversize tote bag, which she puts into the trunk of her car. Then she drives toward the park, drives the forested avenue that cuts through to the 101, which she takes south.

Cara follows.

The night and the fog are excellent cover; no one could know she is on the Prius' tail. She sits forward behind the wheel of the Toyota, watching out the windshield through the thick mist floating between towering pine trees on either side of the twisting road. Every so often she glimpses the red taillights of the social worker's car.

They drive the 101 South, out of San Francisco and skirting the west side of the Bay. Daly City, Millbrae, North Fair Oaks. The social worker has been nearly an hour on the road with no sign of stopping.

The 101 extends all the way to Mexico; Cara has driven the entire length of it often. It may be a long night. But after Mountain View, the Prius takes the 85 west, then turns off a few miles later onto CA-17 toward the coast. And as Cara reads the road signs, she suspects where they are going.

She focuses through the mist on the taillights in front of her and drives on.

Chapter 60

South of Market was a trendy, gentrified area of warehouses, condos, art spaces, and nightclubs. Roarke had been to Singh's SoMa loft only a few times, just brief stops to drop her off or pick up a file that couldn't be scanned. There was no parking to be found, of course. He used his official placard to park illegally on the street.

He buzzed at the building entry, and when Singh's dark velvet voice answered, he told the intercom, "Singh, it's Roarke."

There was a silence. "One moment." He waited, a long minute, and then was buzzed in.

He rode up in a gleaming and modern elevator.

In an upstairs hall, his agent opened a blue-painted door. She was dressed in a tunic of deep purple with a design of embroidered gold, and matching trousers, traditional Indian garb that perfectly complemented her dark beauty. Roarke had never seen her wearing anything other than a formal suit, and seeing her this way he had the instant and overwhelming sensation that he had done the wrong thing by coming by, after hours and unannounced. It was too personal, too many boundaries crossed. He stood on her doorstep in a sudden uncertainty, fumbling for words.

"I'm sorry to drop in like this. It's an intrusion—"

"Of course it is not," she said serenely, and opened the door wide. "Please come in."

Roarke stepped into a long, high hallway with theatrical lighting. Singh took his overcoat to hang in the closet; then he followed her past what he was vaguely aware was interesting abstract art hung on the soaring walls.

She stepped through into the main living area, a sweeping two-story loft space, and turned to him. "May I get you coffee?"

"Coffee would be great," he admitted.

"If you will excuse me," she said. She moved through a door into what he assumed was the kitchen; he had never been farther inside than the entry hall before.

He walked around the room. It seemed vast, clean, like a particularly well-laid-out gallery or museum. There were clusters of furniture creating living and conversation spaces, but most notably there was art: huge canvases and sculptures of both abstract and classic themes; medieval iconography, aboriginal art, strange surrealistic installations. There was one work in the corner that drew him, a statue in an alcove cut into the wall. He moved toward it, and an odd feeling was building in his gut even before he reached the wall.

Inside the oval space was an altar, with lit votive candles in front of an idol: a black-skinned, four-armed figure with facial features contorted into a fearsome grimace. Her foot was planted on the body of a headless man lying naked and prone on the ground. She brandished a bloody, curved sword in one hand while raising the severed head in another, and a necklace of skulls hung around her neck.

Roarke felt his stomach flip. Not quite Santa Muerte, but familiar, and just as menacing. He stared down in confusion, fixed on the candles surrounding the sculpture. They were burned down to a quarter of their original length. Not new.

His eyes moved again to the statue's curved sword . . .

The bright-burning candles flickered, and a voice spoke from behind. "Kali Ma."

Roarke turned his head to see Singh in the doorway, watching him from the shadows.

She looked behind him to the idol. "She is called the Destroyer. But she is also known as the Redeemer. I have been meditating on her. To better understand the force that is Santa Muerte. They are the same, in essence. Kali's earliest incarnation was as an annihilator of evil forces."

The atmosphere was so charged that Roarke felt a prickling of alarm. Singh moved farther into the room, and there was an agitation in her that he had never seen before.

"I believe in the existence of evil, of course. It is manifest in every aspect of our work. I would like to believe there is also some counterforce to the dark."

"Isn't that supposed to be God?" he asked, partly to break the hypnotic flow of her words. His own voice sounded hollow in the industrial space.

She looked ironic. "The Christian god, you mean? A single, male deity?" She turned toward the altar, and the shadows from the flames played across her face. "Most of the rest of the world finds that metaphor . . . limiting."

"I get that," Roarke said. He did. At the same time, he felt cold. He wasn't sure how much of the conversation was real.

"There have been a dozen blogs from Bitch today. By my analysis, they come from at least seven different authors." Roarke stared at her. She lifted her shoulders. "There is a new metaphor now."

A new metaphor. A new road.

Roarke looked away from Singh, at the savage face of the idol, and the chill deepened in him.

Behind him, in the hall, he heard the sound of a key turning and the door opening. He twisted toward Singh. The look on her face was something uninterpretable. And his pulse was suddenly pounding, his breath short.

Someone close to you is lying.

Footsteps moved in the hall, approaching. Roarke automatically, instinctively, reached for the weapon in his shoulder holster . . .

Epps walked through the doorway. He carried a bag of groceries in the crook of his arm. A bouquet of flowers stuck out of the brown paper, and he held a bottle of wine in his other hand.

The candles flickered in the altar as Roarke looked from one agent to the other in complete disbelief.

And then he understood.

Epps nodded to Singh, the briefest of gestures, and without a word Singh took the grocery bag from him and disappeared into the kitchen.

Then he turned. Before Roarke could ask, "How long—" Epps said, "August."

Roarke stared at him, stupefied. *Four months. Five. They've been together all this time . . .*

His agent shook his head. "You—are a damn fool. I am not."

Through the shock of it, Roarke realized Epps was right. It all made perfect sense, and it had all been going on under his nose, and he hadn't seen a thing. He grasped for balance, for the right thing to say.

"I should have known. I can't believe I didn't know. I'm happy for you. I just worry that—"

Epps held up a hand. His face was ominous. "If you say one word about this affecting the quality of our work, you're a bigger hypocrite than I thought."

Roarke felt himself bristling, but there was no way Epps wasn't right. He nodded.

Epps lifted the bottle. "Now I'm going to open this wine. We've got shit to do."

Chapter 61

Santa Cruz: one of the last true counterculture bastions. A crescent of glimmering bay with its famous boardwalk and amusement park, a coastal town that since the sixties has happily drawn more than its share of freaks, hippies, surf rats, cultists, druggies, punks, environmental hard-liners, and other elements of the extreme left.

The social worker called Rachel walks under the holiday lights strung across Pacific Avenue, the city's central strip. And Cara follows her at a discreet distance.

Now that they are here, the setting seems inevitable. There is a Main Street sense to this drag, with its brick sidewalks, antique streetlamps, and plate-glass windows decorated for the holidays in twinkle lights and fiberglass snow and mechanized toys and dreamy angels. But the psychedelia of the Haight is also here, reflected in the more outré window decorations, and there is a similar war between upscale boutiques and funky dives: the head shops and record stores and used clothing stores fighting to hold their ground against the Gap and Urban Outfitters and Starbucks.

Cara is cautious, but efficiently disguised in her bulky wool sweater and wool hat, and so far the social worker is completely unaware of her, caught up in her own mission. After all, there are many strollers doing their Christmas shopping along the avenue, and other camouflaging distractions: musicians, jugglers, the ever-present panhandlers, the endlessly pacing schizophrenics—the street is a haven for the mentally ill as well.

And there are the street children. Ragged, dreadlocked teenagers in big thrift store coats. Runaways and addicts, drawn by the magic of the town, the hippie dream. So many of them. So seemingly invisible to the affluent Christmas shoppers.

It is these waifs that occupy the social worker's attention.

She has a photo she is showing to the huddled groups of teens on the street. Cara must give her credit: the street kids show very little wariness at her approach. The woman knows how to talk to them: she maintains an intent focus on their responses, is easily able to solicit information with a few words. A natural in this environment. Comfortable on the street. She can move here almost without notice.

And she is closing in on her prey.

Cara watches and follows, feeling a convergence of destiny.

For the first time, she sees the glimmer of a way out.

Chapter 62

The three agents sat in one of the conversation clusters, glasses of wine on the geometric curve of table in front of them. But the wine had gone untouched.

Instead, the agents were fixed on the television screen, watching news images of reporters standing on street corners, beside statues of saints surrounded by offerings.

Different reporters. Different cities. And the same shrines, over and over again. Appeals to Santa Muerte.

"That's it," Roarke said. His voice seemed to come from a great distance. "It's gone viral."

But for the first time in days, he also felt the stirrings of purpose. He rose and walked the room, too tired to sit, too wired to stand still. "We have to regroup. Right here, right now. We can't solve it all. It's too much."

His agents looked at him, shocked—and wary. He'd probably never said anything like it, officially, in his life. But given what Singh had outlined about the various new blogs trumpeting the "call to arms," given what they were seeing on television, he knew it was true.

"It's too many jurisdictions already. We can only focus on what *we* can control." He spread his hands. "So what can *we* do? What's the most important thing?"

In his own mind he saw Rachel's wall of lost girls. And across from him Singh and Epps looked at each other and spoke in one voice, without hesitation. "Jade."

"Exactly," Roarke said. "Jade."

Everyone in her life had failed her. All of society had failed her. But against all odds, this lost girl had decided to strike back.

"We have to . . ."

Stop her wasn't what he was thinking at all. What he wanted to say was: *Save her. Pull her back from the brink.* He didn't know if it was possible. Maybe they were past the brink already.

But he looked across the room at his agents, and he knew from their faces he didn't have to say it.

"Do right by her," Epps said softly, and Singh looked at him, without moving, but Roarke had the impression she had just reached over and touched his hand.

"Right," Roarke said. "So from here on in, that's what we're doing."

They ordered dinner in from a Thai restaurant, with Roarke and Epps watching the clock; Mills had called the stakeout for ten thirty that evening. Mills and Jones would be working Inty; the detective had given Roarke and Epps the Tenderloin beat to give the agents more time off before they had to report.

Singh was curled on a sofa with her long black hair down and her legs tucked up under her. Epps sat back in an armchair next to her. The two of them did not touch, but there was no way for Roarke not to notice the way they looked at each other in the low light.

It's not some office thing. This is the way it's supposed to be. And what he felt was pure envy.

But also, he was experiencing a welcome sense of relief. The air had cleared between the three of them. The interpersonal tension was gone, and they finally had a laser focus: *Find Jade.*

The question was, how?

"If we can separate out which killings are hers . . ." Singh suggested.

"We don't even know that she's done *any* of them, let alone all of them," Epps pointed out.

The three of them sat in silence, looking at one another.

Dead end? Roarke fought a sick feeling of despair. Was there really no place for them to go?

Epps spoke suddenly. "Here it is. Let's place our bets."

Singh tilted her head to look at him. "You mean, guess?"

"Educated guesses," he told her.

She considered, and nodded. "Yes. I see." Roarke did, too. They needed a breakthrough, and they needed a plan. Sometimes you just had to roll the dice.

Epps started. "The Salinas kills are Cara's. We can take those off the table, at least."

Roarke said slowly, "Jade killed DeShawn Butler. She had motive. And the timing—she disappeared that night and he ends up dead. It's too precise."

"Agreed," Epps said tensely.

Singh spoke next. "Goldman, the john in the Tenderloin, was a rapist. And Hungman—Wilson places Jade there on the street cruising the night of his death. I believe that killing was Jade as well."

Roarke nodded, but he had a sick feeling. Two men that she had killed, almost certainly. How they were going to keep her out of prison for life was a question he didn't want to contemplate.

"Agreed," Epps said. "Those two."

"And the pimp shot in his car last night?"

"Not Jade," Singh said, and Roarke saw her look toward her altar with the statue of Kali. "The gun and the offerings are completely different in those killings."

Roarke spoke slowly. "Wait a minute. Let's think this through. We know Cara did the Salinas kills, at the truck stop. And I think that was partly because of Jade. She was covering for her. Getting us away from the city and away from Jade; confusing the investigation by adding similar murders to the mix. And the second Inty kill, the john, is also classic Cara. She killed Danny Ramirez because of Jade. Now she's covering for her."

Epps looked at him. "You're saying last night Jade shot the pimp, and then Cara killed the monger and left the offerings to confuse the issue."

Roarke paused. The gun was the one thing he wasn't sure about.

"Jade could get a gun," he argued. "Anyone can get anything on these streets. It's a hell of a lot easier to kill someone with a gun than with a straight razor. And why would Cara leave the offerings if not to cover for Jade?"

"Perhaps to confuse things in general," Singh said. She turned away from the statue to face the men. "So let us not allow ourselves to be confused. We have multiple killers. I believe there is a mature woman—or women—with a political purpose, who could be Erin McNally, or the blogger, or someone else entirely."

"And she's the shooter, you mean," Epps said, and Singh nodded toward him.

"Yes. She, or possibly they, shot the pimp in the alley and left the offerings to tie that killing to Santa Muerte. Then there is Cara, with her own motivations. And there is Jade. A young girl who has been wronged in the extreme and is fighting back. We must focus on Jade only."

Roarke realized she was right.

Singh continued. "DeShawn Butler. The Tenderloin trick, Goldman. They are men Jade knew, men who had abused her. Those two are not random targets. They are personal."

Roarke looked to Epps, who nodded tensely. "Agreed."

"Which means if she kills again, it is likely to be someone she knows," Singh summed up.

Suddenly Roarke remembered. "Rachel said something about teachers. That Jade is good at math, and a teacher would remember a girl with her looks and math skills."

Epps shook his head. "And how many teachers are there in the California school system? How many kids?" The same question Mills had asked. "It's a needle in a haystack."

"Perhaps not so difficult," Singh said. "There are teacher forums online. Listservs as well, where we could post queries to teachers and librarians."

Roarke sensed Singh was right, and it was a shortcut to what Mills had been unable to find out. At the same time, he had a sinking feeling. "We don't have that kind of time."

The agents looked at one other, at a loss.

So what now? Roarke thought. *What the hell do we do now?*

Chapter 63

The fog drifts sluggishly between the gleaming vehicles. The air reeks of exhaust and the stench of malevolence.

He stands in the shadows, smoking, waiting.

Another bus will be here soon, and he is on the lookout for flesh.

They flock to this town, the young ones with their backpacks and their hope and their desperation. So easy. Easy to spot, with the marks on their bodies and on their souls. With their tentative steps when they stagger on travel-numb legs toward the street.

Easy pickings.

He waits and he watches.

He does not know he is being watched, too.

Tonight, the moon sees him.

He never sees it coming.

Chapter 64

Roarke stood in Singh's granite-tiled shower letting water pour over him, as hot as he could get it. A desperate attempt to freshen up—to wake up—before the stakeout. For better or worse, they had not come up with an alternate plan.

By the time he had dressed and walked back into the living room, Singh was on the phone, while Epps paced tensely.

She listened to whoever it was on the phone, and her eyes were darker than night. She spoke into the phone, "Thank you. I will call back." She disconnected and looked to the men.

"It is the Santa Cruz police department. A man has been discovered dead at the bus station downtown. His throat was slashed."

The three looked at one another.

"It is two hours out of town. Cara?" Singh asked.

Is it? Roarke wondered.

"Or—" Epps started, then stopped. None of the three agents wanted to say it.

Or are the Santa Muerte murders spreading?

Roarke had a sudden, awful vision of copycat killings popping up in multiple states.

And yet . . .

"Santa Cruz," Roarke said aloud. "It's a magnet for runaways. Homeless kids. Kids like Jade."

And where there were homeless teens, there was prostitution; there was rarely any other way for runaway kids to make a living.

"Guy was killed at the bus station," Roarke added. He didn't have to explain what he meant. Bus stations were classic trolling grounds, a preferred pickup spot for pimps everywhere. They cruised the stations, grabbed runaways right off the bus.

"So this could be Jade." Singh's face was tense.

"Or Cara could be trying to draw us away from the stakeout again." Roarke looked at Epps, knew the other agent was considering the same thing.

"I say we go," Epps said suddenly.

Roarke turned to Singh. "You'll have to explain to Mills."

"Done," Singh responded.

She jumped back on the phone to the Santa Cruz PD to coordinate while Roarke and Epps headed for the door. But as Roarke reached for his coat in the entry hall, Epps hung back, mumbling, "Be right there."

It was the first time Roarke had ever seen his agent flustered, and he knew why. He felt it again, a stab of envy.

"Yeah," he said, and busied himself with his coat.

DAY NINE

Chapter 65

Navigating the winding road on CA-17 to Santa Cruz was a dream in itself, like driving through low-lying clouds: the thick, gray-white fog often obscured the road entirely. This time Roarke slept for the first hour and then switched places with Epps to drive so the other agent could catch a nap. At times his sleepless state seemed to merge with the fog outside. But their new, clear focus kept him going.

Find Jade.

He felt a chill: half excitement that they might finally be getting somewhere, and half dread of what "somewhere" might mean.

The bus station was off Pacific Avenue, the main commercial street of the city, a kind of hipster drag. Mist blanketed the whole downtown; the agents peered through the windshield at the hazy glow of security lights of businesses, strings of Christmas lights left lit and twinkling in the shop windows. And the bleak contrast of piles of sleeping homeless lumped together for warmth in the doorways of shops.

The bus station was as fogged over as the rest of the town, with several long, pewter buses lined up, waiting for departure time. Even the low roar of idling engines was stifled by the fog.

The crime scene tape blocked off a narrow alley; the murder had been shockingly close to the boarding areas. Roarke's heart sank as he took in the scene, feeling the familiar jolt of déjà vu. A short set of steps leading up to the door of a corrugated metal storage facility, a pool of blood at the bottom of the steps, and red arterial spray spattering the side of the building.

Epps took in the scene and silently met Roarke's gaze.

The steps. The pool of blood. It's Jade.

Jim Williams was the detective in charge, a veteran lawman with a counterculture edge: thick-framed, black Buddy Holly glasses and long, graying hair. He looked right at home in this hippie bastion. The agents introduced themselves; then Williams got straight to the point.

"You fellas think this one's related to yours?"

Roarke and Epps looked at each other. "Were there objects left at the scene?" Roarke asked.

The detective gave them a look. "Like?"

"Candles, cigarettes, flowers, bread . . ."

Epps added, "Candy, liquor, jewelry. Anything that seemed ritualistic."

Williams nodded slowly. "There was a beer can, cigarettes, and Milk Duds in a little pile. Didn't seem random. We got the stuff bagged."

Roarke glanced at Epps. "It's ours." He figured even if it wasn't Jade or Cara at all, it still was theirs. His. The whole thing. "Take us through it," he said to Williams, hoping it didn't sound like a demand, but not really caring if it did.

Williams didn't seem to mind. "Body was discovered by the station security guard during a routine sweep of the depot at twenty-one hundred hours. We know there was no body in this alley at twenty hundred, 'cause security did a sweep of the yard then, too. Bus from Phoenix got in thirty-seven minutes later. We're running down the passengers from credit cards, questioning everyone we can find to see if anyone saw anything. And to develop a passenger list—descriptions of everyone on that bus."

Roarke nodded. It was solid work, but probably useless in the long run. "Everyone we can find" was the operative phrase. The convenient thing about buses, in a criminal sense, was that anyone could pay cash and not leave a record of travel.

"You've ID'd the guy?"

"Clyde Lester Cranston. Got a sheet for narcotics trafficking, assorted minor drug offenses, weapons, gang-related stuff."

"He's local?" Roarke asked.

"Sacramento."

"So what's he doing here?" Epps asked.

Williams looked weary. "The usual. Selling, buying."

Roarke glanced back at the buses. "Or picking up kids to pimp in Sacramento?"

The detective gave him a level look. "Been known to happen. That what you're saying was happening?"

"It wouldn't be a total surprise in this case," Epps said dryly.

"So who're we looking for?"

Epps removed mug shots of Jade and Cara from a binder. "Have you ever seen either of these women?"

The detective immediately zeroed in on the photo of Cara. "That's the Lindstrom girl, right? The one that got away from the Reaper."

Roarke felt the familiar tightening in his gut at any mention of the old case. "Right."

"So she *is* doing these kills?" Williams whistled softly. "That's quite a woman."

Roarke answered too quickly. "We have several suspects at this time."

Epps gave him a sideways look. "But we are actively looking for her," he told the detective.

"No reports of any activity involving anyone of her description. But there're no witnesses to this so far." Williams looked down at the photo of Jade. "Who's this one?"

The agents already knew Jade had never been arrested in Santa Cruz. Singh had sent her mug shot to the Santa Cruz office, and no matching record had come up.

"She goes by the name Jade Lauren, but it's an alias. You've never seen her before?" Roarke asked. "On the street, maybe?"

"Working it?" Williams asked shrewdly.

"Or living on it."

The detective studied the photo, shook his head. "Not me. We can distribute the photo, though. What is she, a witness?"

Roarke and Epps exchanged a glance. Epps answered, "She's missing. Possibly related."

Williams took a longer look. Finally he looked up. "Sorry. But we get a huge turnover of kids. Place attracts them. The boardwalk, the beach, the counterculture thing. You know."

Roarke did. *And it's just like Jade*, he thought. *I can see her here.* "Is the city still having a problem with youth prostitution?" he asked. He saw a conflicted look on the detective's face, quickly neutralized.

"Well, Santa Cruz. The town's always had a decriminalization policy toward prostitution. Sex workers' rights and all that. But there's been a surge in activity because of the gangs. Big spike in Central Valley and Sacramento gangs selling minors."

Roarke and Epps exchanged another glance, recognizing the common thread.

"Pacific Avenue isn't the main stroll, though, is it?" Roarke asked.

The detective shook his head. "Lower Ocean. Around Broadway is the hub."

Roarke was loath to say it; it was hard enough to work up sympathy for the men who were being killed. But prevention had to be the first priority. "These killings we've seen so far . . . they're coming in pairs. You probably want to have extra officers on the street."

Williams looked startled, then grim. "Gotcha."

There were any number of cafés to choose from on Pacific Avenue. Roarke and Epps grabbed extra-large coffees at the Verve Café and sat at a tall window with a sweeping view of the street.

They drank coffee and warmed their hands on the mugs, watching the cocoons of homeless stirring in their doorway shelters, waking up in the mist, slowly gathering their belongings to move on before the shopkeepers arrived.

Epps started in, summing it up.

"So the bus pulls in from Phoenix, and Mr. Clyde Scumbag Cranston is waiting for it, looking for kids. And Jade is standing there in that alley, waiting."

It was too easy to picture.

Epps was moody, frowning. "One thing bothers me. The offerings. Unless Jade did the Inty kills, which we're thinking she didn't, she hasn't left offerings before. So why would she do it here?"

Roarke stared at him, realizing he was right. He looked out at the street. The lights were going on in a few of the shops. In windows up and down the block he could see Tibetan idols, psychedelic clothing, rock and grunge and hip-hop posters.

He'd always found the place eerily similar to the Haight, Jade's recent stomping ground. The psychedelia, the incense and sitar music drifting from head shops and ethnic boutiques, the clouds of pot smoke emanating from the bedraggled clusters of homeless teens on the street, with their matching dreadlocks and dogs that all looked to be from the same litter. And the tattoo parlors. The tattoo parlors . . .

"I don't know," he answered slowly. "Maybe she's reading the blogs, too. But this place has Jade all over it. I can *see* her here. And the killing taking place on the steps. It's just like DeShawn."

"So we're thinking she knew Cranston, too. Maybe worked here?"

The pimps moved the girls from city to city, and often; it was how they kept them isolated and in line. But then Roarke thought of Jade's lazy drawl, her sun-bleached hair. Was she a beach girl? It wasn't hard to imagine. "Or maybe—"

Epps was watching him. "She *lived* here?" he guessed.

Roarke felt a spike of urgency. "Let's hope we're that lucky."

Epps looked out on the street at a wandering pack of teenagers. "The cops don't know Jade, so . . . we ask the kids, right?"

Roarke finished his coffee and stood. "Let's do it."

The main drag of Pacific was only six or seven blocks long. The agents split up so they could work their way down both sides of the street, showing the photos of Jade and Cara to the street kids and the few shopkeepers who were open early for business.

It was heartbreaking work. There was a hauntedness about the kids, especially the girls, but a fair number of the boys, too. They all had a similar reaction to Roarke: a deer-in-the-headlights kind of stillness, a wary pulling back as he approached.

The problem with this plan quickly became obvious. When he asked the teens how long they'd been in Santa Cruz, most of them said it had been only weeks, or just days. Not anywhere near long enough to be acquainted with Jade, who, according to Rachel, had been living in San Francisco for the last several months at least.

The agents met at the bottom of the drag to report: no luck. Then they started again, working from the bottom to the top of the avenue, as many more street people had surfaced since the beginning of their troll.

Roarke had been on the second pass of the street for an hour when he struck gold. A boy of maybe sixteen with a round face and straw-colored hair sat against a tree with a guitar in his lap, a tambourine with scattered change in front of him, and one of the generic dogs beside him. The boy was hazy-eyed, but when Roarke put a ten into the tambourine, he glanced at the proffered photo of Jade and answered, "That lady was asking the same thing last night."

Roarke tensed. "What lady was that?" he asked softly. He reached for the other mug shot that he kept with him at all times. Cara's. He extended the laminated image to the boy. "Was it her?"

The boy stared down at the photo, looking as if he was having trouble focusing. "Uh-uh. She had this really curly hair. Kinda red."

Roarke stared at him.

Rachel? Here?

Looking for Jade, obviously. What else would it be?

There was a sick taste in his mouth.

But why here specifically? Why wouldn't she have told me?

"Last night when?" he asked the boy.

The kid shrugged. "Eight. Eight thirty."

Which means that she came here after she talked to me at the house. Which means she knew something then that she wasn't telling me . . .

"What did she say to you?"

"She was looking for that girl in the picture and she wanted to know if anyone'd seen her."

"And then what?"

The boy looked down at his dog. "We hadn't." The dog lifted its head and thumped its tail.

"And what did she do then?"

"She went on down the street."

"Which direction?"

The boy looked around tentatively, then pointed. "That way."

Roarke turned with him and looked . . . toward the bus station. "Thanks," he muttered.

He stepped away from the boy and the dog, moved down the street, then dialed Rachel's number. His anxiety spiked as he got voice mail. He spoke through a dry mouth. "Rachel. I need to talk to you right away. Please call as soon as you get this."

He disconnected and immediately called the Belvedere House. A counselor he'd met only in passing answered. Janet.

"This is Agent Roarke. I need to speak with Rachel."

"You'll have to try her cell. She took the day off."

He stood still on the sidewalk. "Do you know where she is?"

He heard the sound of papers rustling in the background under Janet's voice. "She just said she needed a personal day."

"When did you speak with her?" he asked sharply.

"I didn't. She emailed last night."

"Saying what?"

"Saying she needed to take a personal day," Janet said, with a cold edge in her voice now.

The sick feeling intensified. "Would you please give me a call if you hear anything from her? Text, email, anything."

There was a pause at the other end of the connection. "Is something wrong?"

For a moment he couldn't answer. "I don't know. Just . . . have her call me, please."

He disconnected blankly and started back past the shops in search of Epps, reviewing the time frame in his head.

She must have left immediately after talking to me. It's the only way she could get down here by the time that street kid said he saw her. And then Cranston was killed within an hour of that.

"Rachel, what are you up to?" he said aloud.

Now he couldn't stop the thoughts.

She was here in Santa Cruz last night when Cranston was killed. She was out all night the night DeShawn Butler was killed. And . . . He was jolted by the next thought. *Jade was at the Belvedere House with her for two weeks. Jade could have given her the razor that Cara used to kill Danny Ramirez.*

Could she kill though? Rachel?

The thought was nearly overwhelming. But then that train of thought derailed as his phone buzzed.

Not Rachel. Detective Williams. There was a lilt of excitement in the lawman's voice.

"Think I found your girl."

Chapter 66

The Santa Cruz police department had ninety-four sworn officers, but the station on Center Street looked more like an industrial garage than a police headquarters.

Williams met Roarke and Epps in his cubicle. After all they'd tried, the detective had found Jade with one phone call.

"I have a teacher friend at Santa Cruz High. Emailed her a scan of your girl. She remembers Susannah Collins. A sophomore, smart kid, but wild."

Roarke and Epps locked eyes. *Jade all over. Finally. A break.*

"She stopped going to class back in May, 'fore the end of the school term," Williams continued. "School hasn't seen her since."

But the detective was able to fill them in on Jade's mother. He handed over a file. "Alison Collins. Couple busts over the years for possession, growing 'shrooms." The agents looked down at a mug shot of a petulantly attractive woman in her thirties with Jade's wild hair.

"Collins was brought in for questioning six months ago about a real bad guy she was hooked up with. Darrell Sawyer. Ran a biker gang. Rap sheet out the door. Drugs, guns, all kinds of bad news."

Drugs, guns, and people, Roarke thought. *It's always the same.* He stared down at Sawyer's mug shot: a rail-thin man in his thirties, thickly tattooed, a face hardened by drugs, alcohol, and vice.

"Can we get that sheet from you?"

The detective pulled up the record on his computer and printed it out for them. Roarke scanned it quickly, glanced up at Epps.

"Sawyer was living with Alison."

"With Jade—Susannah—in the house," Epps finished.

The agents stared at each other with the same thought. *Runaway kids are always running away* from *something.*

And if Jade has a list . . .

Roarke looked at Williams. "You have an address on this guy?"

The detective shook his head. "Nothing. He vamoosed 'fore we could bring him in. Alison claimed no knowledge of his whereabouts."

He knew Alison's, though.

Jade's mother lived in a rustic bungalow—little more than a shack—in the woods a bit outside town. Monterey pines surrounded the structure, shielding it from any neighboring houses, and the windows were covered, swaths of fabric completely obscuring the glass. Never a good sign.

Roarke and Epps stood beside the car, looking at the house, then at each other. Epps shook his head in resignation, and without speaking, the men unbuttoned their suit coats and unsnapped their shoulder holsters. Against whom was another question. But they were after a killer, and there was no telling what was waiting for them inside the decrepit little house.

The steps and porch were buckled with age. The warped boards creaked under their weight as they mounted the steps.

Epps moved to the side of the door, a hand on his weapon, as Roarke stood in front of the door and knocked.

The door swung open to reveal a woman with a wild mane of blond hair. Roarke knew from her file that Alison Collins was not much past thirty, but drugs had taken a toll. Her too-thin body was wrapped in a silk kimono, and she had a languid detachment—which disappeared as soon as she got a glimpse of Roarke. Dismay flashed across her face, then anger, as if she'd been expecting someone else and felt tricked.

She tried to shove the door closed but Roarke got a foot in and held it open with his left hand.

"FBI, Ms. Collins. Special Agent Roarke, Special Agent Epps. We'd like to talk to you about your daughter, Susannah."

"Let's see the warrant," she snapped.

"We're just here for a friendly chat."

She snorted. "Friendly. The Feds. That's a new one."

She tried again to shove the door closed and Roarke stopped it with the flat of his hand. "We're here to talk about your daughter. Now be a good mother and give us a few minutes."

Her eyes flashed fire, but then she lifted her shoulders with exaggerated nonchalance and stepped back. "Of course. Anything for my government."

She was unmistakably related to Jade; there were hints of the girl in her bone structure, in her easy sensuality, and of course in her wild, thick hair. No doubt where Jade had gotten her *fuck you* brashness, either.

Roarke and Epps moved through the doorway and inside, hands hovering beside their weapons, eyes scanning the premises.

Inside was hippie décor, shabby chic, emphasis on shabby. Velvet pillows and zebra-patterned throws, everything tattered. No Christmas decorations here, or even much attempt at basic hygiene. There seemed to be a layer of dust on everything.

Alison stepped to a table that had the remains of several drinks on it and picked out a pack of Camels. The bravado was largely put on; Roarke could see she was nervous. Whether those nerves were about Jade or about the drugs that he would have bet money were in the house, he couldn't be sure. She tapped out a cigarette, lit up, exhaled.

"Look, I don't know what kind of trouble Suze is in, but it's got nothing to do with me. I haven't seen her for six, seven months."

Wonderful, Roarke thought bleakly. *A sixteen-year-old kid on the street and all her mother cares about is keeping herself out of trouble.*

"So you haven't seen her since she was, what, fifteen?"

Alison's eyes narrowed. "Something like that."

While Roarke spoke, Epps was casually circling the room, glancing into doors, taking note of everything that could be seen. She watched both men at once, like a cat watching birds.

"Do you know where she lives?" Roarke queried.

She took a drag of smoke before she answered. "We don't talk."

Roarke felt a quick anger. He could see Alison caught it. She stroked a hand through her hair, and even through the obvious hostility he could feel the come-on underneath the gesture. "Suze made her own choices. You can't stop a girl who wants to go."

"When was the last time you heard from her?"

"I can't remember."

Roarke kept his face impassive. "So she was fifteen when she made this 'choice'? Kind of young to be out there on her own, isn't it?"

Alison gave him a slow, cold smile. "As old as I was when I left home. So?"

"How long have you lived here?"

"Five years."

"And Jade . . . Susannah was with you for four of those years."

Alison looked offended. "Of course she was with me. Where else would she be?"

"Was anyone else living with you at the time?"

The woman's gaze narrowed. "In four years? Sometimes there was, sometimes there wasn't."

Classic evasion.

Roarke recalled his conversation with Shauna. "We heard something about a stepfather."

Alison gave him a lofty look. "You heard wrong."

"A boyfriend, though, surely," Roarke said, making it a compliment. He saw a flash of a preening smile, quickly suppressed.

"What, I'm supposed to be celibate?"

"We'd never expect that," Epps said dryly.

She shot a sharp look at him, smoothed her hair back. "I like to keep it simple. I don't need a man to be happy."

"What about Darrell Sawyer?"

An angry, furtive look crossed her face. "Who?"

Roarke shook his head. "Come on, Ms. Collins, it's all there in your record. The SCPD questioned you about Mr. Sawyer."

"So?" she challenged him.

"So we'd like to talk to him. Do you have a phone number? An address?"

She flipped her hair back. "Like I told the cops. I don't have a fuckin' clue. It's ancient history now."

"It was six months ago," Roarke pointed out. "That's when you talked to the police. Not long after you say Susannah left home. Sawyer was living with you while she was still here. So what I want to know is, what made her leave?" He caught the fleeting, guilty look in her eyes and felt anger flare again. "Did Sawyer ever touch your daughter? Did she ever ask you for help?"

Alison turned on him. "Is that what she told you? It's a lie. You don't know what it's like, having a girl like that little—"

Before he could even process what he was doing, Roarke was stepping forward, backing Alison against the wall. Just as instantly, Epps had a hand on his arm, holding him back.

Roarke spoke into Alison's face. "Here's how I think it went, Ms. Collins. Your scumbag boyfriend raped your daughter, and you didn't want to lose the gravy train, so you kicked her out of the house. That sound about right?"

She snarled back at him. "You don't have a clue, you Federal motherfuckers—"

"All right, now. All right." Epps' hand was on Roarke's shoulder, pulling him away from the woman.

"Coming into *my* house and accusing *me* . . ." Alison raged.

Roarke fought down his fury and allowed Epps to hustle him out the door, while Alison screamed behind them. "You *better* get him out of here. I'll sue. I have rights. I'll sue—"

Her voice was cut off by the slamming of the front door.

On the porch, Epps turned Roarke loose. Roarke walked in a circle on the worn boards to control himself. "Sorry," he managed.

Epps stood on the sagging steps below him, waiting. "No worries."

"I could have killed her," Roarke said through a sinking feeling.

"I doubt it," Epps said.

"I wanted to," Roarke said.

"Well now. You're not exactly alone with that."

Roarke nodded, and they moved down the steps, both dropping it. When they were out of earshot, Epps looked back at the front door. "So, we bring her in? Try to sweat her?"

Roarke had already been thinking on it. "To find Jade? I don't think she knows."

"Or find Sawyer," Epps said tightly. "I know what you're thinking. If Jade's got a list, sounds like Sawyer's on it."

"If she even knows how to find him." It was a big *If*. He glanced back at the house himself. "But I can't see her going to that one for anything."

Epps shook his head. "No. No help there." He looked at Roarke. "You do think it was Jade's kill last night?"

Roarke felt an acid rush to his stomach. He'd been so focused on the trail to Jade he'd been able to block out the other glaring revelation of the day. He answered evasively, to buy himself time to think.

"I think we're here for the night. These kills have been in pairs all along. Chances are if there's a second, it's going to be close. And soon."

The sun managed to burn through the fog as Epps drove them to a hotel he'd spotted on Beach Street, the road running parallel to the boardwalk. The Moroccan-style building wasn't exactly four-star, but it clung to the side of a small, steep cliff right across from the wharf, overlooking the bay.

After checking in and settling themselves, the agents met in Roarke's third-floor room and sat on the couch and armchair beside the wide window as sunset streaked the sky outside.

Roarke had made all the calls he could. No word from Rachel. So he looked across at Epps, and finally said what he had been avoiding.

"Jade isn't the only problem we have, now. We don't know that she was here last night. But Rachel was."

Epps stared at him.

"One of the street kids described her. She was asking around about Jade. She was on Pacific an hour before Cranston was killed."

Epps stood, ran a hand over his head. "What the fuck, now . . . ?"

Roarke looked automatically down at his phone, as if a text or call would suddenly appear. "I've left messages. No response. She didn't go in to work today, either. Took a personal day."

"I don't get it."

"I don't get it, either. But I don't like it. She's been strange."

"Strange how?"

Roarke had a sudden, clear memory of Rachel's outburst about DeShawn Butler. *"Someone should just take a blowtorch to all of them. Pimps, johns, the whole fucking lot of them."*

"This thing is getting to her," he said aloud.

"Getting to her *how bad*?" Epps demanded. Roarke looked at him. He didn't have to break down the implications; Epps was already there. Rachel was political. She was angry. In her own way she was as angry as Cara about the same kinds of abuse.

"Jesus Christ," Epps said, walking the room. "Jesus Christ."

Roarke took a breath and tried to think. "We grab some sleep and hit the streets tonight. This isn't that big a town. If the local cops are out on Ocean, we can cover Pacific Avenue, and maybe the boardwalk."

Epps stopped and looked across the room at Roarke. "Looking for what?"

"Looking for Jade . . . and Rachel."

"And Cara?"

Roarke looked out the wide window into the twilight. The moon was rising from the water, leaving a shimmering trail of white across the bay.

One night from full.
Cold Moon.
"And Cara," he said.

Chapter 67

Santa Cruz's hundred-plus-year-old boardwalk was a tourist attraction, with a Victorian arcade and an extensive amusement park: a beach strip of roller coasters, haunted houses, Tilt-a-Whirls, and the original 1911 carousel with its hand-carved horses.

At night it became a pulsing fantasy of wheels and lights, a giant child's glowing toy set lit up on the sand. Organ music from the antique carousel and eerie calls and creaks from the haunted houses wrestled with the strains of Abba, Def Leppard, and Beyoncé coming from more modern rides: Whirlwind, Crazy Surf, Tsunami, Cliffhanger, Fireball. Screams of exhilarated terror echoed over the shimmering water of Monterey Bay.

Roarke stood in the midst of the brightly lit cacophony.

Detective Williams had the Santa Cruz police out in force tonight: on the Ocean Avenue stroll, on Pacific Avenue, patrolling the bus station.

But this carnival was Jade's kind of place. If she was still in town, it wasn't beyond reason that she might be here. So while Epps walked Pacific Avenue, Roarke was taking a chance on the boardwalk. He braced himself and plunged into the crowd.

He wove his way through the food trucks and game booths and the shops selling sparkly souvenirs, fast food, and saltwater taffy, eyeing every cluster of teens he passed, on the lookout for Jade's wild mane of hair.

Like her mother's, he thought, though he was using the term *mother* loosely. His rage at Alison Collins seared through him again. He'd texted Singh, updating her on the interview—or whatever you could call it—with Alison. Recounting it had only made him more angry, had chased away any chance he'd had at sleep.

How did it go with Jade? Did she run from her mother's piece of shit boyfriend? How long was she on the street here before Ramirez snatched her up?

What chance do they have, these kids? Against men who think nothing of abusing them for fun and profit . . . so-called mothers who facilitate the abuse . . .

And now there was Rachel to think about.

He felt an acid rush of fear.

Could she be responsible for the Tenderloin killings? Or the Inty ones? This latest one?

She had been living on the front lines of hell for so long. Would it be any surprise if she finally snapped?

Snyder's voice suddenly spoke in his head. *"I've never understood why we don't see more women acting out in a similar way. God knows, enough of them have reason."*

Roarke breathed in against the uncertainty and moved on toward the lights of the Casino Arcade.

The old casino was now called Smuggler's Arcade: a huge wedding cake of a building at the end of the boardwalk, just before the stairs that led down to the ocean. In the old days, the likes of Artie Shaw and Benny Goodman had played there while the California elite danced in silk tuxedos and glittery gowns. Now the halls were crowded with teenagers. The décor was pirate-themed, clashing with the modern booths housing video games with names like *Crimson Skies* and *Lord of Vermilion* and *Terminator Salvation*. And the noise was deafening: the pings and revving engines and gunshots and tinny music of the vintage machines and modern video games, the pops and explosions of the shooting gallery, the shrieking dance machine where lithe Japanese girls quickstepped to a rapid pattern of lights on a screen.

Roarke stared around him at the kaleidoscope of noise and lights and felt exhaustion and despair.

What was I thinking? What are the chances that Jade will show up here?

But he held on to one slim hope: that she might return simply because she had grown up here. In years, at least, she was little more than a child, and children were drawn to their childhood places.

Maybe especially someone like Jade, who had had her childhood ripped away from her.

So he moved farther inside, bracing himself against the din as he walked through the dark, tiered space, surrounded by flashing lights and video screens.

And kids. So many kids.

Kids like Jade. Like Shauna. Like Becca. Every one of them just a heartbeat away from capture by predators like Ramirez. Butler. Cranston. Sawyer. Predators who were undoubtedly out on the boardwalk right now, even trolling this arcade at this moment.

Roarke's head was pounding, and not just from the overlapping music. The screams of kids surrounded him, and for a moment what he heard was no longer the excitement and adrenaline of an amusement park, but the agony of unimaginable pain.

Whose pain? Rachel's? Cara's? Jade's? Every kid out there on the street?

He stopped in the middle of the pulsing lights, his heart suddenly racing out of control.

What am I doing? Taking down one pimp at a time? One john? How can it ever be enough?

Rachel's voice was in his head now.

"Someone should just take a blowtorch to all of them."

And Molina's.

"You tell me your way is working, Agent Roarke, and I will call you the liar you are."

And Cara's.

"It *never dies. You can kill* It *over and over and* It *only comes back."*

Their voices overlapped in his head, crying, accusing, begging. Gunshots, shrieks, screams. For the second time in days, he felt himself close to the abyss, to some complete breakdown. He bent over, put his hands on his knees, and gulped back bile.

Out. Get out.

He straightened and shouldered his way through the crowd.

He shoved through the doors of the arcade and strode outside, out onto the promenade, with its elegant arches looking out on the beach and the moon, almost full now over the bay, casting a cold white trail on the blue night water.

In the sudden silence, he took slow breaths and tried to calm his pulse, to think through the black and deafening rush in his head.

He stepped to the arches of the balustrade and leaned on the concrete railing, staring out at the sea. The salt air was cold on his skin.

You haven't slept in days. You're not yourself. Go back to the hotel before you do some serious damage.

But there was more to it than that.

"I'm done," he said aloud. "Enough."

He felt a strange elation, an immense weight falling away from him.

"I'm done," he said again, testing it.

No more of it. He had no idea what he would do for the rest of his life, but it didn't matter. Life and death would no longer be in his hands. No one's life or death but his own, to do with as he pleased.

He held on to the concrete railing and breathed in the night.

And his heart constricted.

There was someone below on the sand, looking up at him. The pale, sculptured face, blond hair almost white in the moonlight. Still as a statue, watching him.

Cara.

Chapter 68

She turns, and she does not run—she walks across the sand.

He walks, then runs along the concrete balustrade, heading for the steps down to the beach.

He clatters down the steps, grinding concrete under his shoes. And then he is on the sand, sinking into its soft weight as he struggles to follow her into the dark.

Icy moonlight spills over the strip of beach. It is cold, so cold.

He plunges across the sand, as if in a dream. Away from the carnival lights and the raucous music, until there is nothing but the sound of surf churning and waves crashing on the shore and the lonely cry of some gull.

And the moon.

She walks in the stark spill of light toward the black and looming pier and disappears into its forest of pylons below.

He steps into the darkness beneath and stands, listening. The surf rumbles through the drifts below his feet. He can barely breathe as he looks around him at the tall, dark shapes of posts, straight, diagonal, fallen . . .

There is presence behind him, more felt than heard, and he turns. She steps out from behind one wooden trunk and looks at him.

He does not know who moves first, only that she is against him, her body in his arms, icy hot and fiery cold, liquid as moonlight. His mouth is on hers and her hands are inside his clothes, moving on his skin, a maddening, delirious touch. He shuts his eyes against the light of the moon and feels soft darkness closing around them and heat racing through them as they meld, her mouth opening to his, kissing, clinging . . . his body is alive, aching with want . . .

And then something else. Something black and terrifying, rising up from the core of him. Beneath her soft and yielding flesh he can feel the bones in the slender body he holds in his arms, an ancient skeleton, unrelenting death.

And in the dark behind his eyes he sees the white mask and empty eyes of a skull.

The fear is instantaneous, paralyzing. And he is staggering backward, away from her. Through the roaring in his head he cannot tell if he has moved or if she has pushed him away, reading his thoughts.

She is striped with moonlight, breathing shallowly, her glistening eyes locked on his, and her face is glass.

"Cara . . ." he says.

Suddenly she is twisting from him, running in slow motion through the pilings toward the beach.

His legs are like lead, the sand beneath him like concrete, holding him. But deep in the back of his mind, some sense of duty stirs. His hand reaches for the Glock in the holster at his side . . . he can feel the metal against his fingertips as he draws, aiming after her into the dark . . .

And then he drops his arm.

Chapter 69

The dark shapes of the posts towered around him, the crashing of waves echoed off the plank walk above. His chest felt as if something had been ripped from inside him.

He didn't know how long he'd stood there, but when finally he moved, his head was pounding, a headache so blinding he could barely hold himself upright. He smelled salt and surf, and a spicy scent that he knew was hers. His head still swam from desire and fear. And at the same time, he wasn't sure that any of it had happened at all.

He forced himself to walk, weaving mindlessly through the shadows of posts, stepping out onto the dark sand. The crashing of waves was deafening in his ears.

And it was only then that he felt his suit coat pockets were light. Too light.

He shoved both hands into the fabric, searching. His gun was there, and his wallet. It was his phone that was gone.

My phone? What would she want with it?

He stood under the moon, surrounded by the rolling thunder of the surf.

Then it hit him. His texts to Singh. All the updates on the interview with Jade's mother.

A wave of sick guilt crashed over him as he recalled his own rage. *If she's going after Alison . . . Oh, Jesus.*

He forced himself to slow down, to think rationally. Of course the phone was fingerprint- and password-protected, data-encrypted. It was next to impossible that Cara, or anyone, would be able to access anything on it at all.

But if she had been following him, he might have led her straight to Alison anyway.

And if he had been half a second from killing Alison . . . what would Cara do to her?

He stared up at the cold moon, just a sliver from full. Then he lurched forward, running on the sand for the stairs to the boardwalk.

In the arcade, he slammed coins into a pay phone, dialed Epps, and shouted over the roar of motors and gunshots and music. "She's going after Alison."

"Jade?"

Roarke closed his eyes. "Cara."

He left the phone, burst through the doors of the arcade, ran down the stairs to the sidewalk. Providentially, there was a taxi just letting a couple out at the hotel across the street.

He pounded down the arcade steps and dodged traffic. In front of the hotel he jerked open the cab door, dropped into the back seat and flipped his credentials wallet at the cabbie as he snapped out Alison's address. "As fast as you can."

It was a living nightmare of a drive. He fought visions of the house burned down, leaving nothing but a torched husk of a human being, a skull grinning out of the ashes, like the guard in Daly City.

It was on him. It was all on him.

The cabin was intact, the first relief.

He ran from the cab, plunging into the scent of pine needles, taking the sagging steps of the cabin in two strides, and pounded on the door. "Ms. Collins."

No response. No sound within.

He stood back, raised his thigh, and kicked in the door.

The house was dark, and the smell of incense and scented candle-wax was thick in the air. He felt along the wall for a light switch and couldn't find one, but strong moonlight streamed through the window, and as his eyes focused he saw her . . .

Sprawled on the couch and so still . . .

"Ms. Collins," he said, his heart in his throat. She didn't move.

He strode toward the couch, his eyes taking in the drug parapher-nalia scattered on the coffee table. Cara had killed at least one man by overdose in the same scenario.

"Ms. Collins. *Alison.*" He rolled her over and felt for a pulse. Her face was pale and clammy, her mouth slack. But her blood fluttered under the pressure of his fingers, and she was breathing, slow and shallow.

He was relieved . . . and then livid. He pinched her earlobe hard and was rewarded with an angry groan.

"What did you take?"

He pinched her again, under the arm this time. She flung a limp hand at him, trying to bat him away. "Whafuck . . ."

He strode to an upright lamp in the corner to switch it on, then back to the couch, where he pulled her up to sitting and stared into her eyes, now half-open. Her pupils were pinpricks. Downers, then. He scanned the selection of chemicals on the coffee table. There was no heroin rig, just scattered pills that he didn't immediately recognize. "What did you take?" he demanded. "Valium? Oxy?" He hoisted her to standing and held her, doll-like and limp, against his hip, forcing her to walk around the living room.

She mumbled, slurred. "Sh's here."

"She's here?" He swiveled around, looking toward the bedrooms.

"*Was* here. Was here."

"Susannah?"

"Yr fuckin' agent."

Roarke fought confusion. *Singh? Impossible. But . . .*

"Dark hair?" he demanded. "Or blond?"

Alison's head lolled. Roarke held her upright. "The blonde. Your fuckin' agent."

Cara, then.

"She drugged you?"

She started to twist in his grip, trying to push him away. "I'm fine. Lemme go."

"She *didn't* drug you."

"I'm *fine.*"

Roarke sat her down on the couch, hard. She let out a howl. "Fuckin' Feds . . . gonna sue . . ."

He tried to maintain some level of calm. "This agent. What did she say to you?"

Alison wasn't that out of it. For a moment she looked as sullen as a teenager. "Bitch said she would cut my face."

Roarke felt the words as a punch to the gut as he envisioned the scene. He'd gotten nothing out of Alison. But Cara, with her unerring radar, had looked at this vain, pathetic woman and had known exactly what button to push for results.

"What did she want you to tell her?"

She glared at him, truculently silent.

"Do *I* need to cut your face?"

Her eyes blazed fire, and for a moment he saw Jade in her again. "Where Darrell is," she said sullenly.

Roarke had a sudden flicker of understanding.

"And? Where?"

She stared at him. "Don't know."

He took a step forward and she flinched back. "He had a place outside Napa, okay? On Valley of the Moon. That's what I told that crazy woman."

"You're going to write down directions."

Epps arrived ten minutes later, just after the ambulance. By then Roarke was fairly convinced Alison had passed out rather than been given an overdose, but he wasn't taking any chances. The woman was loathsome, but he was beyond grateful he hadn't inadvertently killed her.

There was one more thing he'd asked her before they took her away.

As he walked with Epps out of the house into the night, preparing to fill his agent in, he had to fight a crush of emotions. Relief that Alison was alive. Guilt over his unforgivable lapse. And most shameful of all, the fierce joy of abandon, the overwhelming sensation of Cara under the moonlight . . . regret and loss and desire . . .

He pushed those thoughts away. He knew his career as an agent was over. But there was something yet to be done.

So the story he told Epps as they sat in the fleet car under the moon was not the whole story.

"I was on the boardwalk, and I kept going back to this in my head," he lied. "We know Jade grew up here. We think she was here last night. We think she might be going after people who have wronged her. So . . . wouldn't she come after her mother? I couldn't get it out of my mind, so I came back. Jade wasn't in the house, tonight, but she *was* here sometime today. I pressed Alison on it just before you got here, and she said that money was gone from her secret stash. She says only Jade would have known where it was."

Epps, of course, wasn't buying it. His eyes were hard. "Alison just gives that up to you. Just like that." He fixed Roarke with his level stare, and Roarke gave him the truth. Some of it.

"She was scared. Cara got to her first."

He could feel the nuclear reaction building in his agent. "Lindstrom was here."

"Yeah."

"Doing what?"

"Same thing we are, I think. She's looking for Jade."

Epps gripped the steering wheel. "Looking for her? Or is she *after* her?"

That, Roarke didn't know. He was afraid to think about it. He shook his head. "But this is what Cara threatened Alison to find out." He passed Sawyer's address to Epps.

Epps was still for a moment, processing this.

"Cara's thinking Jade is going for Sawyer."

Roarke didn't know for sure, but he was willing to bet Cara understood Jade's state of mind better than they did. "If Jade was here looking for money, maybe she got hold of Sawyer's address, too. And now Cara has it . . ."

It was his best guess. There was a miniscule chance that they could find Cara's whereabouts by tracking his phone, but he was certain she would be aware of that, that she might even plant the phone somewhere to fake her location.

And his gut said it was all about Sawyer now.

The agents sat in the fleet car, looking out on the road. Epps finally spoke. "So we're goin' up there. Napa."

"I think it should be me—" Roarke started.

"What kind of bullshit is that?" his agent said.

They sat in silence. Roarke could feel Epps raging internally in the seat beside him. After a moment, the other agent spoke. "We could call the locals. Jade's got . . . how much of a head start on us? Sawyer's a meth dealer. We want this sixteen-year-old kid going in to confront that waste of skin on his own turf?"

Roarke shook his head. "She could be armed. Local cops not knowing even what we know . . . how are they going to react?"

Epps was silent.

"Napa's two hours and change from here," Roarke added quietly. The address Alison had given him was on the outskirts.

Epps shook his head. And shook it. And then reached for the ignition key and started the engine.

DAY TEN

Chapter 70

They drove into a thin dawn, on CA-17 out of Santa Cruz, winding through the misty, forested hills to I-880 and past the suburban malls between San Jose and Oakland. While Epps drove, Roarke reached into the back seat for his iPad and under the pretext of checking email, he used his phone tracking app to try tracing his phone. It was offline, of course. He initiated a remote wipe and lock of the device, then shut off the tablet and stared out the window.

Jade. Focus on Jade, he told himself.

The two agents were silent for a long, long time, watching the towns go by. The silence was dangerous . . . it allowed Roarke to slip into a half-trance state that was filled with sense memories. The roar of the ocean in his ears. The feel of Cara's skin under his hands, ice cold and shivering at his touch. The fire of her mouth . . .

He was jarred out of his near-sleep as out of nowhere Epps said tensely, "Valley of the Moon."

Roarke didn't answer. He didn't have to.

Valley of the Moon. Of all the places Sawyer could live. And the full moon coming up tonight.

It was inexplicable . . . and inevitable. And ominous.

After quite a few more miles, Epps spoke again. "We even got a plan here?"

"Try to get Jade before she does this."

This, meaning killing her mother's ex-boyfriend. Her fourth kill? Fifth kill? Sixth? Unless Sawyer killed her first . . .

Epps' next question was inevitable, too, and heartbreaking. "Get her—and then what? What the fuck do we do with her?"

Roarke gave the only answer he could. "Get her Molina as an attorney."

The agents shared the silence, knowing it wasn't enough. Epps shook his head bitterly.

"She never had a chance, did she?"

Roarke saw Jade's face in his mind: that beautiful, wild, doomed girl. He couldn't answer through the pain in his chest. He stared out the window, and Epps drove.

Epps merged onto I-680 toward Sacramento to skirt the Bay Area traffic, and they headed north and east around Oakland to Benecia and Vallejo. Then over the bridge spanning the Carquinez Strait into the Napa Valley. And suddenly the suburban sprawl was gone. On the left, bare hills rolled away from the highway, nearly white with winter grass, with pockets of sage-green trees, fronds of willows and bare-trunked birch. On the right was swampy marshland dotted with pale, fuzzy pampas grass. White mist rose from the water in the freezing air.

In the sudden isolation, Epps spoke again.

"Why didn't Cara kill the Collins woman?"

Roarke had been wondering that himself, and he didn't know that he had an answer. *Because she doesn't kill women? Because of something in Alison's past that we can only guess at?*

He heard Alison's voice in his head.

"Fifteen—same age I left home. So?"

And then Rachel's voice, the thing she had said to him once, that never left him.

"Runaway *is a literal word. They run* away." And nearly always from the same thing.

Alison had left home at fifteen. And maybe whatever had happened to her then had earned her some reprieve now.

But there was another thought, both troubling and insanely hopeful.

Or maybe Cara didn't kill her because she knows I couldn't have lived with the guilt of it?

He stared out the window. "Who knows?" he said aloud.

The clouds in the sky were gray and white and dense. *Heavy*, Roarke thought. *Pregnant.* When the agents stopped for gas and coffee and the restroom, their breath showed in the air outside. Roarke looked up at frost sparkling on the rooftops, the tree branches and telephone poles adorned in ice.

"They're predicting snow," Epps said as he got back into the car, looking bemused. Of course snow happened in places all over in California, but living in a city like San Francisco, snow was something one chose to go to, not something that came uninvited.

They continued the drive on into Napa, a town that had been fighting its outlaw reputation for years, lately fairly successfully. The new Riverwalk with its artisanal food shops, luxe restaurants and boutiques, galleries, and tasting rooms had brought a new class of tourist to the wine country's poor cousin.

But the motorcycle shops and bail bond agencies were still there in abundance. Darrell Sawyer wasn't the only drug dealer to have found refuge for his illegal enterprises in the undeveloped acreage of the Napa Valley. Not by a long shot.

Outside of the town, two-lane roads wound through vast stretches of hills covered with patchworks of vine fields. Roarke had been to the wine country many times, but never in the winter. He was startled at the severity of the landscape. So lushly golden in the summer and autumn, the cut-back vines were now just gray sticks sparkling with frost, the fields between them dusted with snow.

The agents motored past the castlelike estates of the wineries, with their wild variety of architecture: replicas of Mexican haciendas, French estates, Belgian monasteries, surrounded by more of the severely trimmed grapevines, more bare trees in a thick, low-lying mist. The sky grew darker and darker above them, black clouds heavy with snow.

In between the opulence of the wineries there were stretches of road with strange, run-down dwellings: dingy horse barns and sagging silos and hop barns, and farmhouse after farmhouse set far back from the road in fields, each one approachable only by a dirt road through the field, each house with a thicket of old-growth trees clustered around it, shielding it from view.

Perfect hideouts for just about any illicit activity imaginable.

"You can just smell it," Epps said.

Roarke looked at him.

"Trouble," his agent finished grimly.

Following the directions Jade's mother had given them, the agents turned off the highway and onto an untraveled parallel road. The clouds were thicker, darker, here, the fields devoid of human or animal life.

"That's it," Roarke said from the passenger seat, staring through the windshield toward one of those isolated farmhouses, set far off in a field.

And outside the car, it started to snow.

Chapter 71

Epps stopped the car beside a cluster of oak trees at the side of the road so the agents could survey the farmhouse from behind cover.

The fields surrounding the house had recently burned. The whiteness of the softly falling snow was a stark contrast to the blackened vines in the field. Roarke scanned the side of the house and saw several burned trees on one side of the thicket. He had seen this kind of damage often. A meth fire.

Beside him, Epps echoed his thoughts. "Meth blowout. Not good."

They were silent, both thinking of Sawyer's record for dealing.

After a time, Epps spoke again, his voice tight with agitation. "Guy could have any number of soldiers in there. We can't see for shit. And do we think he's armed? Only to the teeth."

Roarke nodded, without speaking. Armed would be the best-case scenario. Meth lab busts often turned up stashes of weapons that ranged from submachine guns to military-grade rocket-propelled grenades.

And that was only the start. The labs were highly combustible locations. The cooking process involved extremely flammable chemicals: ether, lithium, lantern fuel, anhydrous ammonia, sodium hydroxide, pseudoephedrine—any combination of which could be lethally explosive. The toxic gases produced in the cooking process were rendered more lethal by meth cookers' tendency to seal the windows and doors of their makeshift labs. It was not a matter of *if* they'd blow up, but *when*.

Roarke stared out at the frost gleaming on dead grass, the dormant vines, the blackened, twisting trees, while Epps continued his assessment in a low, tense voice. "I don't see a car, either. How do we think Jade even got up here?"

The bus system in Napa and Sonoma was extensive, though, catering to the multimillion-dollar wine-tasting industry. The wine country was spread out, and transportation was readily available.

"Bus," Roarke said aloud. The last one he'd seen was at the turnout they'd taken from the highway, less than a mile away. Easily walkable.

"Not good," Epps repeated. "We wait."

"Wait for what? What if Jade's already in there?" *What if Cara is?* he added, but silently, in his own head.

It wasn't as simple as calling for backup. Federal law expressly prohibited law enforcement officers from entering a structure known to contain a meth lab. Only "clandestine lab certified" officers were allowed to do so. It could easily be a day or more before they could get a team lined up. If Jade was in there, they couldn't risk waiting.

Epps hit the steering wheel with the flat of his hand. "Fuck. Fuck." He took a deep breath, controlling himself, and then spoke tightly. "Going in is crazy. We have no idea what's going down."

"What else can we do?" Roarke asked quietly. Unnecessarily, as it turned out, since Epps already had the car in gear.

They drove the car off the road, into the concealing shelter of the oak trees.

As the agents got out of the car, Roarke noticed with total disorientation that it was already getting dark.

Of course. The solstice. It was the shortest day of the year.

And the full moon would be rising. *Cold Moon.*

The agents moved slowly through the grove to the outer trees and looked across the snowfield toward the house.

Snow fell around them in thick flakes, so softly it seemed like slow motion. Roarke felt a dreamy detachment as he watched the thicket, waiting for some kind of sign.

Then a car engine started somewhere inside the trees. The muffled roar carried across the snowy field. Both agents took cover behind tree trunks, pressed themselves against rough bark, and squinted across the whiteness toward the farmhouse, watching.

A 4Runner SUV emerged from the thicket, motoring down the dirt driveway toward the access road.

Roarke stared hard at the truck windows, counting heads inside.

"Two men," Epps said from beside him. "No. Three."

The truck made a left at the end of the drive, onto the road, and sped off in the direction of the highway.

The agents watched, waiting in silence . . . but no more vehicles emerged from the thicket.

When Epps finally spoke, the words seemed brittle in the cold. "Okay. Okay. What now?"

"That's three less men inside," Roarke said.

"Three out of how many?" Epps shot back.

Roarke had no idea.

Epps shook his head violently. "Go in someplace we have no idea what's inside. That could explode any second. We don't even *know* Jade is there."

He was right. Roarke knew he was right. It was madness, against all rational training and protocol. At the same time he knew, with or without Epps, he was going in.

And then they saw it: a wraith moving in the snowfield. A small, white shadow, bundled up in thick clothing of white and gray, heading into the thicket.

Chapter 72

The agents stared through the trees, watching the ghost figure as it slipped into the thicket and disappeared. They both knew they were not looking at a man.

"Is it Jade?" Epps asked, his voice brittle with tension.

Roarke was relatively sure it wasn't Cara. For a moment he felt her body under his hands, the lithe length of her. He banished the thought and forced himself to focus. The figure they had seen was shorter, less in control of her body.

"I think it's her," he answered.

Epps shook his head. "All right, goddamn it."

The agents took the car and backtracked several hundred yards down the road, so they could cross the field under cover of another thicket and approach Sawyer's farmhouse from the rear. Epps motored up the drive of the next farmhouse and stopped the car inside another cluster of oaks. The house looked deserted: no cars in what passed for the yard, dark windows, leaves piled up on the porch. A perfect place to stash their vehicle.

Outside the car, the men stripped off their jackets and suited up in Kevlar vests and loaded their pockets with tools from the kit in the trunk. Wire cutters. Maglites. Neither of them spoke about what they would actually do with their weapons once they reached the house, but using them was out of the question. It would be suicide.

Then they headed in a line horizontal to the road, crossing the barren grape field toward the back of Sawyer's property. As they walked, snowflakes sifted down, slowly covering their tracks, and the sky darkened and the storm clouds moved fast, clumping and dispersing.

The thicket surrounding Sawyer's farmhouse was a tangle of old-growth trees. Roarke was sure some of them were over a hundred years old. The farmhouse was close to that age as well: decaying clapboard that had been well built in its time, before decades of neglect.

They were in luck: there was no surrounding fence to cut.

The agents' breath showed in the air as they moved into the scraggly bushes of the undergrowth.

They were silent, scanning the ground in front of them as well as the trees around them. Meth labs were often booby-trapped, with trip wires, grenades, even land mines. The snow had stopped and Roarke's adrenaline was sky high; the dim woods seemed hyper-clear. Or maybe that was the light of the rising moon.

Both men froze at the sound of a sudden, slight movement . . . a crackling of leaves, a crunching of snow . . .

In total silence, Epps pointed ahead, toward the clump of trees where the sound had come from, and then indicated right. Roarke nodded and moved toward the left, the two moving in tandem, circling the trees . . .

Roarke heard a rustle behind him and spun, his weapon trained in front of him—

He faced a woman aiming a handgun. Her face was heartbreakingly familiar. He stared at her—at the weapon in her hand. "Rachel?" he said, through a dry mouth.

A shadow leaped from behind . . . and Rachel staggered as Epps grabbed her waist and her wrist, forcing her gun hand high above her. She didn't struggle as he shoved her face-first against a tree, applied pressure to her wrist. "Drop it. Now," he said, his voice rough and low.

She gasped and released her grip. The gun fell to the ground.

Epps twisted her around to face them, keeping a strong arm locked around her neck. "What is this?" he growled. "You come for Sawyer?"

She shook her head violently, spoke in a shaky whisper. "Jade. I thought if I could find her first . . ."

Roarke's mind was racing, trying to put it together. *Was it the truth?* Or had she been deceiving him all along?

"How did you find her?" he demanded.

She hesitated—only a moment, but his heart sank during the pause. "I've been putting out queries in high school teacher forums. I tracked her to Santa Cruz High. She dropped out months ago but I knew where to start . . ."

And then you talked to the street kids, he realized. But that could wait. There was a far more pressing matter. "She's inside?" he asked.

Rachel nodded, her eyes wide and glistening in the dim light. "I saw her go in."

"Anyone else?"

Another pause. *Rachel, you're a terrible liar*, he thought. *How blind must I have been not to notice?*

"I saw three men get into a truck earlier. About twenty minutes ago. Then Jade went in the house—"

She fell silent at the sound of an engine. With a hand on her shoulder, Epps forced her down to sit on the ground beside the tree trunk, and the three of them looked at one another in the gloom of trees, listening.

"Same engine," Epps said under his breath. *Three men*, Roarke thought, and knew his partner was thinking the same thing.

He looked toward the house. Jade inside, with God only knew what and who . . .

"Go," Epps said. "Get her out. I'll make sure they don't get here."

"Be safe," Roarke said. Way too late for that, of course. And it was a toss-up who would be headed into the most danger.

"*You* watch yourself," Epps retorted. "Just get Jade." And he slipped away, off through the trees.

Rachel rose to her feet and faced Roarke, her eyes huge and dark in the pale moon of her face. "I can help. Let me help."

He reached for her arm, then turned her around, reached into his service belt, and cuffed her. "You'll want to stay put," he said roughly. "If you move, you'll probably be shot."

He left her beside a tree and went up the rickety back steps, cringing at every creak. To his surprise, the back door was cracked open. *Jade must have used it.*

He pushed it open and slipped through. His breath came hard and fast as he scanned the dark around him, willing his eyes to adapt . . .

He was in a mud room. Coats hung haphazardly on hooks on the wall. The inner door was cracked as well, and he eased it farther open, wincing at the creak of it. His eyes focused and adjusted to the dark, and he stared down the long hall before him and strained his ears to listen . . .

The house was silent, but the silence felt heavy, loaded. *Inhabited.*

He had to fight the urge to reach for his weapon. Firing it in a chemically laced situation like this could easily be the death of him and anyone else in the vicinity.

He had his Maglite, heavy enough to use as a club. It would have to do. He moved forward toward the inner door . . . but felt a prickling of memory from previous busts. He turned and stared down at the detritus piled next to the back door, then nudged junk aside with his foot . . . and spotted what he'd hoped would be there.

A hatchet. Redneck home-defense system.

He stooped and picked it up.

His breath frosted the air, white puffs in the dark, as he moved forward, wielding the hatchet.

The farmhouse was a wreck. It was dark and dank inside, but razor-thin slants of moonlight cut in through cracks in the boarded-over windows, allowing a dim view. He glanced around him at wallpaper hanging off the walls, exposing slatted boards, furniture covered with dust, holes in the ceiling.

Uninhabitable. But then, it wasn't being used for living.

The farmhouse kitchen had all the familiar accoutrements: camp stoves, pressure cookers, stacks of kitty litter tubs, cans of lantern fluid, propane tanks. The pantry door was open, and the wooden shelving held sloppy rows of canning jars and glass jugs with sediments inside, a clutter of plastic tubing, funnels, coffee filters, aluminum foil. The air was saturated with a smell of acetone and cat piss . . . that didn't come from cats.

Anything could catch fire. Anything. Just the debris that made up this kind of cooking could spontaneously combust.

An unwanted vision of the guard, roasted alive, was suddenly clear in his head.

He clenched his fingers to dismiss the image, then eased through the clutter, careful not to touch anything. The wind had picked up outside; he could hear it moaning under the eaves, whistling along the boarded windows. He stepped through the next open doorway into the hall . . .

There were bedrooms lining one wall, and the wide arch of what he presumed was the living room at the end of the other wall.

Someone was walking around in that room.

And then Roarke's pulse shot up. From farther inside the house, there was a violent scrabbling and a man's shout. "What the *fuck*—" And then "Fucking *bitch*—"

But anything further was cut off by a yelp of pain.

And then silence.

Roarke breathed in, moved into the inner hall, leading with the hatchet . . .

The hall was a tunnel of near dark. A long passage ahead of him, with moonlight filtering in from cracks in a few panels of the front door.

The sounds had come from the living room, or main room, or whatever you called it in a farmhouse.

He stood still to listen through the sound of the wind. Nothing.

He eased his way past the open door of a bedroom . . . glanced in to see cracked boards over the windows, a sagging iron-frame bed with a filthy mattress. He could smell piss and vomit, and another smell, troubling but elusive. He swallowed through the rush of bile and moved on past another, similarly wrecked room, stopping before the archway of the living room. He pressed himself against the doorframe and listened. A man's voice rasped, "I'll kill you . . ."

The voice he heard next was low, light, and feminine, slightly hoarse, and achingly familiar. "For real, Darrell? Who's gonna kill who?"

Jade.

Roarke raised his voice, calling out, "Jade. It's Special Agent Roarke."

There was a silence, then a low laugh. "Agent Roarke. What brings you to hell?"

He didn't know what she meant, but whatever was on the other side of the wall, he doubted it was good.

"I'm coming in, all right?"

"Why the fuck not?" The girl's voice was almost cheerful. "The more the merrier."

He stood for a moment, paralyzed with indecision. He couldn't fire his weapon in this chemically volatile atmosphere. But he couldn't step into the unknown without it. He would have to hold it and not fire under any circumstances, and hope that its mere presence helped.

He drew, then stepped into the archway and stared through the dark.

In the filthy, freezing room, a man sat in an armchair. Rail-thin with ropy muscles, thickly tattooed, slicked-down hair, flint-hard face. Roarke recognized him from his mug shot. Sawyer.

Jade stood behind him, with one hand laced in his greasy hair and something small and silver gleaming in the other.

She looked across the room at Roarke. "Special Agent Roarke. We meet again." Her breath misted white in the freezing air.

"Jade," he said, as calmly as he could manage. She wore jeans and boots and a white down parka with a fur hood. The bulk of the jacket made her look younger, like a bundled-up child. Her eyes seemed enormous. Dilated.

High on something. Not good.

She looked down at the man seated below her. "This is Darrell. Darrell, say hey to Agent Roarke." She pulled his hair back, jerking his head up to face Roarke.

The man in the chair glowered at him. Roarke saw hope and hatred in his face. "For Christ's sake. Do something—"

"Shut up," Jade snarled.

There was something so strange about the situation. Sawyer was still as death, but Roarke couldn't see any ropes or cuffs holding him to the chair. *So why is he not struggling?*

Then Roarke caught the smell in the chill of the air and finally recognized it. *Lantern fluid.*

Sawyer's hair wasn't greasy. It was wet. His clothes were soaked.

And what Jade held in her hand was not a knife but a lighter.

Roarke's stomach dropped. The image flashed in his mind again: Driscoll's charred body, the skull grinning out of his blackened remains. He banished the vision and spoke carefully. "Susannah—"

Jade jerked her head up. Her eyes blazed in the gloom. "*No.* Susannah died. Darrell killed her. Didn't you, Daddy D?" She dug her fingernails into the back of Sawyer's skull.

Roarke spoke quickly. "Talk to me, Jade. I'm listening."

The girl eyed the Glock in his grip. "I talk better not at gunpoint."

Roarke opened his palm, displaying the weapon. *Epps, where the hell are you?* he wondered, through the hammering of his heart. He hoped to God his agent was circling around to the hallway on the opposite side of the room.

And in the same instant he hoped to God Epps was nowhere near the house. Because the chances were good that everyone inside the house would die at any second.

Jade was fixed on the Glock in Roarke's hand. "You don't want to have one of those in a place like this anyway. Do you, Darrell? Whole place could go up like a torch."

"You're right," Roarke said quickly. "I'll put it away."

Then slowly, so slowly, he opened his suit coat to reveal his empty shoulder holster. Jade nodded warily, and he holstered the weapon.

In the chair, Sawyer let out a groan. Jade shoved the side of his face. "One more sound out of you, asshole, and I flick this Bic." Sawyer froze, silent again.

"Okay, Jade," Roarke said. "No gun. Let's talk."

She shook her head. "It's way past talk. But I like you, Agent Roarke. So I want you to take a walk. Walk yourself out of here. Darrell and me, we're gonna stay here and burn."

Roarke's heart plummeted. "I can't let you do that," he said softly.

Her eyes were on his. "You need to get out. That's what these places do. Cook the cooks."

Roarke kept his voice steady. "I'm not going anywhere without you, Jade."

The girl gave him a tolerant and crazy smile. "But I'm not going anywhere. Not to prison. Nowhere. It all ends here." And then she cocked her head. "You never answered me. Do you believe in destiny?"

Roarke was paralyzed, silent, knowing his answer could mean all of their lives.

The girl was watching him. "How about karma, then? You know, karma? What goes around, comes around?" She waved the open, unlit lighter in front of Darrell's face. "What d'you think, Darrell? I remember coming 'round here with you and Mommy Dearest. Three, four years ago . . . I couldn't remember exactly where, but Alison helped out with that." Her voice got harder. "And I remember exactly *what* happened here. *All* of it. Don't you?"

She jerked his hair, yanking his head back as he yelped. Her eyes were gleaming, almost feral in the slanting rays of moonlight.

"Tell Agent Roarke what you did," the girl said, thumbing the lighter tauntingly.

Sawyer was stiff and still in the chair, his eyes hooded, his mouth open as he took shallow, uneven gasps. Roarke could almost smell his rage and terror.

"I understand, Jade," Roarke said. His mouth was as dry as dust. "Vermin like this. I know what he did."

"You *don't* know." She tightened her fingers in Sawyer's hair. "He *sold* me. To his poker buddies. Didn't you, Darrell? Right here."

Roarke felt a wave of nausea. It was too clear a picture. The filthy farmhouse. The men around the poker table. The drinking. The drugs. And the twelve-year-old girl on the sagging bed.

He struggled to speak evenly. "You don't have to do this, Jade. Let me take him. I can put him in prison for a long, long time."

Jade's eyes widened. "You can promise that? For real?" Her voice was like a child's, naive . . . and completely mocking.

No one had to tell him she was right. He knew.

"No. I can't promise. But I'll do everything I can. I'll . . . I'll do everything I can."

Jade shook her head. "That's not good enough. Whatever it is, it's never gonna be long enough. So this time, we're gonna do it my way."

"Jade . . ."

She held the lighter up, and the moonlight made the silver gleam.

And then, in the hall behind him, Roarke heard something. Someone. A presence. Barely moving, barely breathing . . .

Epps? Jesus, let it be.

He spoke slowly. "Okay, Jade. I know I can't stop you. I don't even think I want to."

Sawyer stiffened in the chair. "Wait. You can't fucking leave me," he said in a panic.

Roarke stared at him through the cold dark of the room. "I just wish I could see you burn."

"Fuck you," the man raged. "You can't do this."

Roarke ignored him and looked at Jade, her round, child's face in the dim light. Heartbreaking.

"I'm sorry," he told her. "You deserved much better."

She looked at him with those extraordinary eyes, inscrutable. He nodded and stepped back out into the hall. And in the dark corridor, he froze, as he felt the cold metal barrel of a gun against his face.

Chapter 73

H e knew from the touch.

"Cara," he said.

He could smell her, the spicy heat of her skin and the faint salt tang of the ocean. He felt her hand on him, skimming his chest as she reached from behind him into his jacket, taking his Glock from the holster and pocketing it, then stepping around him and reaching into his clothes, deftly searching him.

Her face was pale in the dank cold, and he was very aware of the gun at his cheek. He had a quick, sick rush of fear. *Epps—did she take him down?*

She pulled something from a pocket and he heard the muffled jingle of handcuff keys. Then his pulse rate shot up as someone stepped up right behind her in the dark hallway.

He stared into the blackness . . . and saw Rachel. Her hands still cuffed behind her. Her eyes wide and terrified.

Roarke stared at her.

They're together? What the hell is going on? Through his shock, his dread was nearly overpowering. *Where the hell is Epps?*

"Rachel," he whispered, and felt cold steel jab against his face. He turned his eyes to meet Cara's gaze. "Unlock her," she ordered, barely audible. Never taking the gun muzzle from his cheekbone, she pressed the handcuff keys into his hand.

Outside, the wind pushed at the house. He could hear the wild scrabbling of snow blowing against the windows.

Cara moved with him as he reached out to Rachel, and she turned in the dark so he could unlock the cuffs. And when they popped open, he caught them in his hands so they would not hit the ground and betray their presence. He turned his head slowly toward Cara, and felt the muscles of his jaw against the gun. "You can't fire that," he said, barely audible. "The whole house could blow."

She said nothing. Her eyes were cold and shining in the dark.

"Is Jade in there?" Rachel asked in the barest of whispers, but Roarke could still hear her voice shake.

He nodded slowly, feeling gun metal against his skin. "She's got Darrell Sawyer. She says she's going to burn it all. Him, her. The house . . ."

"No," Cara said. And she lowered the gun she held at Roarke's head and walked down the hall, as deliberately and silently as a cat.

Roarke turned on Rachel. "Get out of here. For God's sake . . ."

She shook her head hard. "We just want Jade out of here. That's all we want."

He was just able to register the "*We.*" Then he grabbed her arm and pulled her down the hall, toward the archway of the living room. As they reached it, everyone inside twisted to face them: Jade, Sawyer . . . and Cara.

"Oh, hell," Sawyer moaned from the chair. "Who are these bitches?"

Jade looked from one woman to the other. "*Now* it's a party," she said, but Roarke heard the sudden uncertainty under the brashness of her voice. She tightened her fingers in Darrell's hair again and turned his head hard toward Cara and Rachel. "Look at all these nice people come to watch you die."

"I'll handle him," Cara told Jade quietly.

Jade looked at her, and Roarke didn't know what to make of what he saw in the girl's face. *Fear? Fascination?*

Whatever it was, she shook her head. "He's *mine.*" She held the lighter up and ran her thumb over it. All their lives in her hands . . .

"I know," Cara said. "And you got him. It's over." She looked toward Rachel. "Tell her."

"Jade." Rachel's voice trembled, but she looked the teenager in the eyes. "He's not worth throwing your life away. Don't do that for this piece of shit."

"He has to die!" the girl wailed.

"He's dead," Cara said. She aimed Roarke's Glock squarely at Sawyer's chest. "I promise you." She and the girl looked at each other from across the freezing room. "I want you to go with Rachel now."

Roarke stiffened. Cara shot a look at the social worker, and Rachel looked back . . . and he could not have voiced what passed between the two of them in that moment. Not if his life depended on it.

Jade seemed mesmerized. She took a faltering step back, and Cara moved swiftly to take her place behind Sawyer, pressing the muzzle of Roarke's weapon into his cheek.

Then she looked at Rachel. "*I* killed those men. *I* did. Do you understand?"

Roarke saw tears on Rachel's face. "I understand."

"Then take her."

When Rachel didn't move, Cara raised her voice. "*Take her.*"

Rachel grabbed Jade's arm and pulled her toward the front door. The girl went with her without resistance, without protest.

And Cara and Roarke were left alone. Cara holding Darrell, the Glock against his head.

"Please, oh sweet Jesus . . ." Darrell babbled.

"Shut up," Roarke shouted at him. Darrell dropped the noise to a whimper. "Cara," Roarke said, looking at her, remembering the feel of her skin against his. "Don't."

She shook her head.

"Cara."

She looked into his eyes . . . and unbelievably, miraculously, he saw her lower the gun.

He gasped from the full body rush of relief . . .

. . . and suddenly there was a flash of silver, in her other hand, and a spurt of crimson as she sliced a razor across Sawyer's throat. She held his head as his body jerked and blood sprayed, then pumped from his severed carotid, and her eyes never left Roarke's.

Then she pushed the body forward, and Sawyer's corpse slid off the chair to thud onto the floorboards.

Roarke looked into her face, and she held his own gun on him.

Blood dripped from her hands and their breath clouded white in the air . . .

And then she slipped backward, through the doorway behind her, and was gone.

JANUARY

Chapter 74

Epps was unharmed. He had rounded up the three members of Darrell Sawyer's posse they'd seen leaving the house. They would be indicted for meth trafficking and arms dealing and were expected to face long prison terms.

Sawyer was dead, and that was some justice. Some. No one would ever be prosecuted for what was done to Jade. But of course, it was much easier to prosecute a man for selling drugs than for destroying a child.

Rachel was gone. Cara was gone. Jade was gone.

And Roarke was gone.

A voluntary, indefinite leave of absence.

He took a place at Pismo Beach. In January the town was nearly deserted and the cost of renting a beach house not out of reach.

Epps and Singh called his new cell phone every day. Separately and together. He had not told them where he was going, and he never answered their calls, though sometimes he kept their messages for days before deleting them.

He took long walks on the sand, beside the surf. Sometimes he lingered in the forest of posts under the pier and listened to the crashing of the surf, and tried to breathe through the memories.

He didn't miss her. He craved her. It was a constant ache.

He replayed their night on the sand, searching for nuance. He didn't know if she'd only used him that night to get his phone. He didn't think so. But he imagined Mark Sebastian probably thought she hadn't used him, either. Roarke's regret was not that he had been used. He only regretted that he'd pulled back.

He had no idea where she might be, only knew that it would be far. He was almost certain she had left California. It was too dangerous for her there, not just because of her fugitive status. There was too much attention in the news: her photo, her background, all the old stories resurfacing about the Reaper and the Miracle Girl, the madman's only surviving victim.

She would be far. But in what direction, Roarke couldn't guess. It was a big country.

So he walked on the beach, and he waited for a sign.

Once he was out on Main Street and he saw the boy, Jason Sebastian, shopping with his father. Jason saw him, too, but the five-year-old didn't wave and didn't turn to speak to his father to point Roarke out. He just looked, and nodded. And somehow Roarke was comforted.

Sometimes he dreamed of fire, the derelict farmhouse going up in a ball of flames in the dark, snowy night. Often he needed only to close his eyes to see the fireball, feel it scorching his face; to hear the yawning booms of the explosions . . . a roaring like the world cracking open in slow motion.

Because the last thing he had done, on his way out of the house, was to fire backward into it, with the backup piece from his ankle holster.

Darrell Sawyer's body had been consumed in the resulting inferno. As far as Roarke could tell, no one would ever be able to say exactly how he died. And the idea of trace evidence, anything that could shed light on who had been at the scene, was absurd. It was a meth lab. It had combusted like an accident in a small nuclear power plant.

Destruction of evidence. Tampering with a crime scene.

The list of his offenses went on and on.

It was ten days into his self-imposed isolation that she called.

Not Cara.

Rachel.

"Where are you?" he managed, through a suddenly constricted throat. Outside the windows of the beach house, the surf rumbled and rolled.

She half-laughed, and he thought she sounded . . . different. "Somewhere else."

There was a silence between them before he could finally speak. "You don't have to do this—"

"I know what you want," she said, before he could finish. "I'm not bringing her back."

So she still had Jade. He spoke his next words carefully.

"We'll get her the best attorney. Molina will take the case—"

"*No.* No one helped her. No one has the right to judge her."

"You can't throw your own life away—"

She interrupted savagely. "It's my fault. I left her that night and went with you because I wanted you." There was a catch in her voice, and he knew she was crying. "I failed her."

Roarke felt his heart was about to burst. All those tangled emotions. She was a rescuer; she couldn't help her nature. He took a breath and prayed she would listen.

"Rachel. If it's anyone's fault, it's mine."

Silence.

He spoke so softly. "Don't do this. Talk to me."

There was nothing but dead air.

Erin had not resurfaced. She had not returned to medical school, she had not notified the school of her absence, she had not posted to her

Facebook page. The blogger Bitch had not been found; or rather she had morphed into a legion. Eleven anonymous bloggers calling themselves Bitch had claimed credit for the Bay Area killings, starting with Danny Ramirez, plus the Salinas murders, plus the bus station murder in Santa Cruz.

Roarke knew most of that was smoke. The shooting of the pimp in his car on International Boulevard remained unsolved, but Roarke was sure in his own mind that Jade had killed DeShawn Butler, the "guerilla pimp"; and Andrew Goldman, the "sick trick"; and the pimp Clyde Lester Cranston at the bus station. There would be no reason for Cara and Rachel to go to such lengths to hide Jade away if she had not killed the men. He was also convinced that Jade had planted the murder weapon that bought Cara bail and freedom, and that Cara had started copycatting the paired kills to cover for Jade.

In his secret heart, he was glad.

Sometimes he imagined them together. Erin, Cara, Rachel, Jade, the blogger, the mystery woman who was not Andrea Janovy. *Doing what? Planning what?*

Even Molina—who claimed to know nothing of Cara's whereabouts. Roarke didn't believe her, of course. He didn't believe anything anymore.

He scoured the Internet for every post and tweet by Bitch. They reported on another two kills in Tucson, a pimp and a john. Another two in Dallas. All of which they attributed to Santa Muerte:

> *She is out there. But she's not the only one.*
> *This is a call to arms. This is a war on rape culture.*

He read the blogs. And he thought of saints, and goddesses, and myths, as he walked on the beach and listened to the surf.

Under the growing Wolf Moon.

Acknowledgments

I have so many people to thank for this series, I could write a book. I am eternally grateful to:

My most awesome editors, Anh Schluep and Charlotte Hersher. Anh, you've been a lifesaver!

My superstar agents, Scott Miller and Frank Wuliger.

The Thomas & Mercer team: Alan Turkus, Jacque Ben-Zekry, Grace Doyle, and Tiffany Pokorny. There are not enough superlatives!

The Amazon KDP, ACX, and CreateSpace talents of Lael Telles, Nicole Op Den Bosch, and Lauren McCullough, through various versions of these books.

My priceless early readers: Diane Coates Peoples, Joan Tregarthen Huston, Joseph Wrin, Jim Williams, Sharon Berge, and Rebecca Wink.

Timoney Korbar, Amanda Wilson, and Adam Cruz for brilliant publicity support.

Visionary original cover designers Robert Gregory Browne and Brandi Doane.

The initial inspiration for the Huntress from Val McDermid, Denise Mina, and Lee Child, at the San Francisco Bouchercon.

My mega-talented critique partners, Zoë Sharp and JD Rhoades.

My incomparable writing group, the Weymouth Seven: Margaret Maron, Mary Kay Andrews, Diane Chamberlain, Sarah Shaber, Brenda Witchger, and Katy Munger.

Lee Lofland and his amazing Writers Police Academy trainers/instructors: Dave Pauly, Katherine Ramsland, Corporal Dee Jackson, Andy Russell, Marco Conelli, Lieutenant Randy Shepard, and Robert Skiff.

The learned Dr. Doug Lyle, for forensics help.

RC Bray for his terrific narrative interpretations of the books.

Joe Konrath, Blake Crouch, Scott Nicholson, Elle Lothlorien, CJ Lyons, LJ Sellers, Ann Voss Peterson, Robert Gregory Browne, Brett Battles, and JD Rhoades, who showed me the indie publishing ropes.

Siegrid Rickenbach, Captain John Rickenbach, and Alison Davis, experts in all things California.

Leslie Goldenberg, Jennifer Nickerson, Patti Frick, and Elaine Sokoloff, who inspire me to hold up my half of the sky.

Madeira James, for her visual inspiration.

And Craig Robertson, for a million things, but especially for always being willing to boldly go just about anywhere for the sake of research.

About the Author

Photo © 2009 Lawrence Smith

Alexandra Sokoloff is the Thriller Award–winning and Bram Stoker, Anthony, and Black Quill Award–nominated author of the supernatural thrillers *The Harrowing, The Price, The Unseen, Book of Shadows, The Shifters,* and *The Space Between,* and the Thriller Award–nominated Huntress/FBI crime series (*Huntress Moon, Blood Moon, Cold Moon*). The *New York Times Book Review* has called her a "daughter of Mary Shelley," and her books "some of the most original and freshly unnerving work in the genre."

As a screenwriter she has sold original horror and thriller scripts and adapted novels for numerous Hollywood studios. She has also written two nonfiction workbooks: *Screenwriting Tricks for Authors* and *Writing Love,* based on her internationally acclaimed workshops and blog (www.ScreenwritingTricks.com). She writes erotic paranormal on the side, including *The Shifters,* Book 2 of *The Keepers* trilogy, and *Keeper of the Shadows,* from *The Keepers L.A.*

She lives in Los Angeles and in Scotland with the crime author Craig Robertson.